WARPED ALLEGIANCE

A JO RISKIN MYSTERY

DEBBIE S. TENBRINK

Warped Allegiance
Red Adept Publishing, LLC
104 Bugenfield Court
Garner, NC 27529
https://RedAdeptPublishing.com/

This is a work of fiction. Names, characters, places, and incidents either are the product of the author's imagination or are used fictitiously, and any resemblance to locales, events, business establishments, or actual persons—living or dead—is entirely coincidental.

For Mojo—my writing buddy, my constant companion, and my confidant. I miss you every single day. I'll see you on the other side, my friend.

Chapter 1

"So, what's the latest debauchery in Grand Rapids, Jo?" Christine's eyes twinkled. She was always ready for a good story.

"I hate to disappoint, but it's been pretty normal for the last few weeks." Not one for superstition but no dummy either, Jo rapped her knuckles on the heavy wooden tabletop.

Christine's face fell as she dramatically flopped back in her seat. The metal legs of the chair scraped the old wooden floor as she pushed it back. "So disappointing," she moaned.

Sherri stirred her RumChata and root beer, studying the creamy mixture as the color lightened and the ice clinked in the stout glass. "What exactly does a homicide lieutenant do without any murders?"

"I didn't say there weren't any. But they've been pretty typical."

"Oh, *typical* murder. I see," Sherri retorted.

"You know, easily solved, no real exciting depravity or degeneracy." Jo took a swig of her Corona. She enjoyed the relative quiet of the Grand Rapids streets that winter weather brought. Having fewer people out and about typically meant a slowdown for her job and a chance to catch up on the unsolved cases. It also gave her more time to spend at the schools, where she could at least attempt to get to the younger kids before the streets did.

"Well, that's no fun."

"You want debauchery? I've got a good one!" Diane chimed in from the other end of the long table.

Becky held both hands above her head. "Wait. We need another round first!" She waved her arm at the bartender then made a circular motion.

Jo contemplated her almost-empty beer then checked the time, always conscious of alcohol consumption when she was driving. The last thing the Grand Rapids Police Department would tolerate was a drunk-driving offense from an officer. She could swing one more drink if she stayed another hour. The bring-the-house-down noise and raucous laughter coming from their table told Jo her friends weren't thinking about going home anytime soon.

The bartender set a drink in front of each of them. Jo looked over her shoulder at the pretty redhead as she set down the Corona. "Hey, Kim. Have a seat. Diane's about to tell us a story of debauchery and depravity."

Kim scanned the almost-empty pub. The Conklin bar, with its old-school curved half-top bar and walls cluttered with wood-framed beer signs and Irish quotes, was a hot spot for snowmobilers. But the ones who had been there when Jo arrived had kids in tow. They had donned their heavy snowmobile gear and braved the below-freezing temperatures to enjoy Taco Tuesday, but they were long gone. One man sat alone on a maroon-topped bar stool, nursing a draft beer and staring at the small television hanging over the rack of bottles lined along the back wall.

Kim's face broke into her signature bright smile. "It looks like you ladies are going to close me down, so why not? I hate to miss a good story." She snatched a chair from another table and nestled between Jo and Lynae.

Jo crossed her legs and propped her drink on her knee, settling back into her chair as Diane launched into a hilariously raunchy story plucked straight from her work in the county jail system. Though Jo didn't recognize the case, she could envision the scene and all the players from Diane's animated play-by-play to her captivated audience. She nursed her beer while joining her friends in peppering Diane with questions and side-splitting commentary on her story. Diane fielded the questions and shot back equally uproarious answers.

With a few drinks in them, the group could make a go of it on *Whose Line is it Anyway?*

When Jo's phone rang, she reached around to the back of her chair to pull it out of her coat pocket. At the same time, Lynae's head snapped to her phone, which was lying on the table. Jo gave her a knowing glance. Both of their phones ringing at the same time could only mean one thing—they weren't heading home anytime soon.

Resigning herself to a ruined night out, Jo extracted her phone from her coat and thumbed the talk button. "Riskin."

Christine put on a severe expression, mimed answering her phone, and deadpanned, "Suddenly serious badass cops. What crime can we solve today?"

After throwing her an exasperated look, Jo turned her head and covered her free ear as boisterous laughter rose from the others at the table. Lynae pushed her chair back and stepped away.

"Lieutenant, this is Heather in dispatch. We have a body at—"

"Detective Parker and I aren't on call this evening, Heather. You should contact Breuker and Lainard."

"I understand, Lieutenant, but Breuker and Lainard caught a call two hours ago."

Jo rolled her shoulders. "Since when do we have two suspicious deaths in Grand Rapids in one night?" She glanced over her shoulder to see Lynae sliding her phone back into her pocket and yanking her coat from her chair.

"Sorry. I don't commit 'em. I just report 'em."

Jo snorted. "Glad to hear it, Heather." She scrounged in her purse and found a pen. "All right, what's the address?"

The dispatcher rattled off a street address, which Jo wrote on the damp napkin that held her beer.

"Is that a private residence?"

"Yes, it is."

"Victim's name?" Jo asked as she lifted her scarf from the back of the chair and wrapped it around her neck.

"Victor Manton. The call came in from his wife."

Jo cringed and hoped for the wife's sake that the scene wasn't too bloody. "Who's on scene?"

"Ryan and Hubert."

Solid cops. She swung her coat on, expertly maneuvering the phone from ear to ear. "Okay." She glanced at her watch. "I'm a good thirty minutes out, possibly more, depending on the roads."

"I'll let them know."

Jo hung up then sent a text to Myla, her always-reliable dog sitter, and received an immediate reply that Mojo was in good hands for the night.

Diane stared her down from the end of the table. In an instant, her eyes went from those of an entertaining storyteller to those of an experienced cop. "What's going on?"

"Two damn homicides in one night is what's going on."

A chorus of groans and shocked sentiments rose from the table.

"So much for things being quiet," Christine said, giving Jo a sympathetic look.

Jo puffed out a loud sigh. "Why didn't I keep my big mouth shut?"

She pulled her purse from the back of her chair and reached inside for her wallet.

Kim laid a hand over Jo's and shook her head. "I've got this, hon."

Jo raised an eyebrow, drew out more than enough cash to cover her tab plus a healthy tip, then slapped it into her friend's hand. "I don't think so. You're going to *generous* yourself right out of business."

Tammy raised her glass. "Don't worry. We'll keep her in business."

Everyone raised their bottles and glasses in a cheer of support.

Jo snapped off a quick salute. "Carry on, my friends."

She shoved her wallet back into her purse and grabbed her gloves from the table. Lynae waited with her keys in hand. "Right behind you, boss."

Wagging her finger at her friends, Jo used her most stern cop voice. "But don't carry on too much. Get home safely, and take care of one another."

She snorted at the chorus of "Yes, Mom," "Of course, Officer Boring," and "Can we stay out past curfew?" that followed them to the exit.

When Jo pushed open the heavy wooden door, she was assaulted by blustering wind and blowing snow. "Shit, when did this start?" Flipping up the hood of her coat, she trotted to her truck. She reached in and started the engine then got the snow brush from the floor and worked on the windows while Lynae did the same.

"You okay to drive?" Jo yelled over the vehicle that separated her truck from Lynae's car.

Lynae tapped her snow brush on the clean windshield then threw it into the back seat. "Oh yeah. I've been nursing that last drink forever."

Jo tossed her brush into the Ranger and hopped in. "All right, then stay behind me. I'll blaze a trail and be there to pull you out when that little car of yours hits the ditch."

Lynae rolled her eyes as she got into her Mazda.

Jo drove away from the little bar and headed toward the northeast side of Grand Rapids, where someone's mayhem waited. She white-knuckled the steering wheel as she maneuvered her truck over snow-covered back roads, checking the rearview mirror every couple of minutes for Lynae's car. To her credit, Lynae kept her little car right on Jo's tail. When the country roads finally wound to the highway on-ramp, Jo glanced one last time in her rearview then sped up on the much-clearer road.

When she left the highway, she snaked through the streets of the northeast side of Grand Rapids before turning into a quiet subdivision of older, well-kept homes. Following the directions of the calm male voice she had chosen for her GPS companion, she turned right at the third street. Blue and red lights strobed rhythmically at the fourth house on the left, illuminating the barren trees and throwing macabre shadows across the snow-covered lawns. Two black-and-whites, an ambulance, a fire truck, and a county van vied for position along the street. People milled about outside their homes, winter coats and boots thrown on in a rush over pajamas and sweatpants.

Jo parked along the side of the road, as close as she could get to the light-brick ranch house that bore the address she had been given. Her breath caught as her gaze settled on a Christmas wreath sparkling on the bold blue front door. The remnant of the holiday, forgotten in the bustle of life, was a sad reminder of a happier day.

When Lynae tapped on Jo's window, she jolted, then she grabbed her bag and stepped out of the truck. Hunched against the cold, Lynae had her hands jammed into her coat pockets and her hood hiding her face.

Jo tapped on the window of the idling ambulance. The paramedic inside hastily brushed crumbs off his uniform shirt and stowed the chip bag at his feet.

When he rolled the window down, Jo asked, "Did you call it?"

Missed crumbs sprinkled his bushy mustache. "Yes, ma'am. He's very much dead." He pointed a stubby finger. "County's here now, so we're gonna take off."

"Appreciate it."

Jo waved in the direction of the county van, even though she couldn't see who was in it. She flicked her flashlight on then aimed it at the sidewalk and moved slowly toward the house.

As she skimmed the light over the small cement porch that led to the front door, she found shattered glass, a sparkling mosaic in the fresh white powder that covered everything. Plenty of snow had fallen since the glass was broken, and it was still coming down hard. The wind whipping from the west had blown drifts across the lawn, which had peaked at the porch. Jo snapped a couple of pictures and made a note to have the official photographer shoot some for the file.

Jo continued her scan of the driveway, Lynae's flashlight bobbing beside her and scanning the opposite direction.

"They're covered in the new snow, but there are tracks coming and going all over the place here," Jo said. Different sizes, they trampled over one another in the normal, everyday comings and goings of a busy house. "I bet there are kids."

Aiming her flashlight at the driveway, Lynae said, "Multiple vehicle tracks coming in, two going all the way to the garage."

Jo took gloves from her bag and snapped them on then went to the garage service door, where a brass lantern-style light lit up the entrance. After tapping her boots on the lip of the doorframe to knock off the snow, she stepped into the two-stall garage. Shelves lined one wall, piled with tools, paint cans, bags of bird seed, and large clear Rubbermaid tubs overflowing with sporting equipment. A Toro push mower and a gas can sat in the corner next to a chest freezer. A snow shovel and large boots waited next to the inside entrance.

"Nothing seems out of place," Jo said.

Lynae's eyebrows shot up as she surveyed the area. "How would you ever know?"

Jo shrugged. "Nothing obvious anyway." She shined her light on the tub of sports equipment. "Kids. Typical garage for a family."

A dog barked frantically inside as Jo opened the door and stepped into the entryway. Boots sat on a rubber mat under cubbies lined with heavy coats. Scarves, gloves, and hats spilled out of the small shelves above each space. A backpack-style baseball bag hung on a hook in its own cubby. A pocket on each side held a bat. White letters stood out against the red-and-black canvas: *Gilly*.

Jo rounded the corner to the next room and spotted a middle-aged woman sitting at the dining room table, staring blankly, a glass of water clutched between her hands. A box of tissues sat beside her, with several wadded in a pile. The German shepherd, growling menacingly, pushed against the metal kennel he was locked in.

A lanky officer sitting with the woman pushed his chair back and approached Jo.

"What can you tell me, Nate?" Jo asked.

He glanced over his shoulder at the woman. "Victim's wife," he said under his breath.

"Why is she still here alone?"

Nate crossed his arms. "She called a friend, who's coming, but it's taking her a while."

Jo did a quick scan of the area. Spotless kitchen counters in a deep green were surrounded by light oak cabinets and stainless-steel appliances devoid of fingerprints. Someone in the household was an immaculate housekeeper. "Where's the victim?"

"In the bedroom," he said, jerking his head toward an open staircase to Jo's left.

"Alone?" Jo asked.

The officer cocked his head. "Hubert's outside the door."

Jo shook her head and positioned herself so that her back was to the woman. "No, I mean was he alone when he died. Is he the only victim?"

"Oh, yeah, it was only him."

"Good. What's the wife's name?"

"Lisa. Last name is Manton."

Jo turned to Lynae. "Let's talk with the wife for a minute before we go in there."

Lynae sat on one side of the woman, and Jo pulled out the chair on the other side.

"Mrs. Manton, my name is Lieutenant Riskin." She gestured to Lynae. "And this is Detective Parker."

The woman slowly turned her head to Jo. "Lisa," she whispered.

"Lisa, we're so sorry for your loss."

Her brown eyes were glazed and swollen, her face unnaturally pale against the red splotches staining her cheeks. She pressed her quivering lips together and shook her head, blinking rapidly. Her shoulders shook as a sob shuddered through her. Jo scooted her chair closer and put her arm around the woman's shoulders. Words were futile, so Jo simply rubbed her back while she cried.

After a few minutes, Jo asked, "Were you home when this happened?"

Lisa shook her head.

"Do you have any idea who would hurt your husband?"

"No. Everybody loved Vic."

The woman suddenly jolted and jumped to her feet. "The kids..."

Jo glanced around the small dining room. "Where are they?"

"My daughters are at friends' houses for the night, but Ethan—I don't want him to come home." She patted her pockets then whipped around and searched the kitchen counter and finally gripped her cell phone. She stared at the screen for a second before her shoulders relaxed. "He's staying at his friend's house."

Jo waited for the distraught woman to sit back down then leaned forward, resting her arms on the table. "We'll have to get in touch with them. They can't hear this from anyone else."

Lisa closed her eyes and bit her lip. "I know. But not until..." She glanced over her shoulder then dropped her head. "I can't go in there."

"Of course not," Lynae said quickly. "Officer Ryan said you have a friend coming."

Lisa stared longingly at the entrance door. "She had to get someone to stay with her kids. She should be here soon."

Jo decided she wasn't going to get much out of Lisa. She was too traumatized to communicate. It would have to wait. "We'll sit with you until she gets here."

Lisa pushed her fingers against her mouth while fresh tears clung to her eyelashes then spilled down her cheeks.

They sat quietly while they waited. Jo tried to stay focused, but her brain insisted on flashing back to the night her husband had been killed, and her life came crashing to a halt. The phone call, the frantic rush to the hospital, the agonizing reality that she was too late—she knew Lisa's pain and what it meant to know the man you loved would never come home again. Mike had been shot in the line of duty, a drug stakeout gone intentionally bad. Someone's greed had taken everything from her. She wondered why someone had done the same to her victim.

Finally, headlights flashed through the picture window that faced the driveway. Lisa's head shot up from where it rested in her hands. The entrance from the garage flew open, and a stunning brunette rushed into the kitchen, frantically searching.

Samantha? Her impossibly high cheekbones had softened slightly, but the shock of dark hair that had made her the envy of their sorority sisters still fell in perfect waves over her shoulders.

Lisa's face crumpled as a sob ripped from her throat. She stood and stumbled away from the table. The other woman bolted forward and caught her as she collapsed into her arms.

"Oh God, Samantha. Vic. He was in the bathroom, and I..."

Samantha wrapped her arms around her friend and held on while gut-wrenching sobs shook her body. "I'm so sorry," she said soothingly through her own tears.

Lisa drew in a hiccupping breath. "What am I going to do?"

Samantha stepped back, laid her hands on her friend's shoulders, and looked her in the eyes. "We'll get through this. I promise. I'll be with you every step of the way."

Lisa dropped her head back to her friend's shoulder.

Samantha caught Jo's eye. Her brow knitted as she blinked a few times. "Jo?"

Jo forced the corners of her mouth up in an imitation of a smile. "It's been a long time, Samantha."

Lisa's head popped up. "You two know each other?"

Samantha's eyes softened. "We did a lifetime ago."

"We'll catch up later." Jo motioned toward the hallway leading to the bedrooms. "Right now, I have to do my job."

"And you'll find who did this," Samantha said.

Jo raised an eyebrow. "Yes, I will." She laid a hand on Lisa's arm. "We're going to be going through your home... your things. It's going to feel like an invasion of privacy, but it's necessary."

Lisa nodded, scanning the room. "Okay."

"And we'll have to ask you some questions," Jo continued gently.

Lisa jerked. "What?"

Samantha scowled. "Why?"

Jo eyeballed her old friend then returned her attention to Lisa. "It's standard procedure. We have to eliminate you from the suspect list."

Samantha inhaled deeply then blew the breath out slowly through her nose. "I'm sorry. You have to do what you do."

Jo cocked her head. "No need to apologize. No one can prepare for this or know how to handle it."

She motioned toward the front of the house. "With all of the vehicles out front, word is going to spread quickly. Your kids should hear this from you. This will be the hardest thing you'll ever have to do." She glanced up at Samantha. "I'm glad you have a friend to go with you, but I'm also going to send an officer with you."

"No, I—"

Jo held up a hand. "Neither of you should be driving. The roads are slick, and you're not in any condition to deal with them. The officer will stay in the car and bring you wherever you have to go."

Samantha wrapped an arm around Lisa's shoulders. "That makes sense. He can bring you all back to my house. You'll stay with me."

Jo looked gratefully at Samantha. "Thank you."

Lynae pushed away from the table and reached for her bag while Jo did the same.

Jo straightened her shoulders and lifted her chin at the officer standing in the doorway. "Officer Ryan, can you take care of that for us?"

The officer shifted his weight, his thumbs hooked in the wide belt that hung askew on his angular frame. "I sure can, Lieutenant."

Samantha's eyebrows almost disappeared into her wavy hair. "Lieutenant?"

Jo half smiled. "Like I said, it's been a long time."

Chapter 2

Jo and Lynae strode out of the room and up the stairs.

Nudging Jo with her elbow, Lynae asked, "Who's Samantha?"

"An old friend."

"Am I sensing some tension between you and your old friend?"

Jo ran her tongue over her teeth. "I don't know what you mean."

Lynae stopped dead in her tracks.

Jo huffed. "Later, okay?"

At the top of the landing, an officer was propped against the wall outside an open door to their right. The three doors to their left and one at the end of the hall remained closed.

The officer straightened. "Lieutenant."

"Officer Hubert." Jo acknowledged him with a curt nod. "I assume those rooms have been cleared?"

"Yes, ma'am, Lieutenant. We cleared and closed immediately." The young officer looked at Lynae, his expression visibly softening. "How's it going, Lynae?"

"It's all good, Trevor." Lynae grinned and held up her hand for a high five.

Jo sighed as she removed gloves from her bag. "Do you know everyone, Nae?"

Lynae snapped on a nitrile glove and winked at the officer towering over her. "Only the handsome ones."

Jo rolled her eyes as the officer blushed and ducked his head. She eyed Lynae pointedly. "How's Doug these days?"

"My *friend* Doug is just fine, thank you." Lynae glared at her.

Jo suppressed a smirk as she lifted her chin at the officer. "Anyone been in or out?"

Officer Hubert shook his head. "Not since the first responders. Nate and I were the first people here. We cleared the rooms then waited for the ambulance. Once they declared him, we told them to wait for you."

"Good work. Officer Ryan is taking the wife to talk to the kids."

Trevor gulped, appearing nauseated. "Sucks to be him."

Jo fought with the sticky fingers of the glove. "Because our job is so much better."

"I didn't mean—"

The glove yielded with a snap. "Relax. I'm just messing with you. Notifications are the worst. Why don't you go ahead and call in the forensics crew?"

The officer nodded then stepped away, pulling his communicator from his belt.

"Ready?" Jo asked, eyeballing Lynae as she pulled on her second glove.

Lynae swept her hand over the door. "Lead the way."

As Jo stepped into the bedroom, she was assaulted by the overwhelming smell of blood. The tangy copper taste that settled into the back of her throat brought her back to her childhood, when she and her brother tested nine-volt batteries on their tongues.

She tuned out the devastated wife and the memories of her old friend that tried to push to the surface. The fun she'd been having with her friends only an hour earlier seemed to exist in another life. Instead, she isolated her focus on the scene in front of her while the cop she was born to be forced everything else to the back of her mind, to be visited another time.

The master suite of the Manton household was dominated by a king-sized bed that sat slightly to the left of the doorway. A mauve bedspread covered the cherrywood four-poster, and a flat-screen television hung on the opposite wall.

Jo stepped farther into the room, scanning for her victim.

Lynae scanned a massive walk-in closet then raised her eyebrows at Jo. "Nope."

Jo pointed at where a light glowed from an open door to their right. "That must be the bathroom. Bet he's in there."

"Seems like they could have told us that," Lynae grumbled.

Jo shrugged. "Well, we *are* the detectives. It seems like this room may be part of our crime scene anyway. Since the bed is neatly made, and every room I saw downstairs was clean and tidy, I'm going to assume that the rest of this mess isn't normal." She eyeballed the turned-out dressers, which had clothing hanging from the open drawers. Other articles were strewn across the room.

After opening two jewelry boxes filled with beautiful pieces, Lynae said, "If this was a robbery, they left some pretty valuable stuff."

"And things that are easy to pawn," Jo replied, pointing at a watch on the nightstand. Squatting, she looked at a picture that lay on the floor. A family of five dressed in white shirts and blue jeans beamed for the camera. A boy and two girls, who all appeared to be in their teens or close to it, flashed bright smiles. Both girls, who were either twins or very close in age, wore braces with red and black bands—the same school colors as the baseball bag that hung in the entryway. Lisa Manton's eyes radiated fierce pride.

Jo focused on the man, who stood a full head above his teenage son, who already dwarfed his mother. Victor Manton was a handsome, athletic-appearing man with a beard so tightly trimmed that it bordered on five-o'clock shadow. His receding hairline was the only thing that gave away his middle age. They were a better-looking-than-average middle-class family.

"If a struggle happened in here, there would be more than a picture on the floor." Jo lifted one hand, palm up, toward the nightstand. "There are pens and a lamp there."

"Any real struggle, and those would be on the floor, or the whole stand would be knocked over."

Jo pointed at the bed. "He hadn't made it to the bed yet, apparently."

She stepped into the master bath. A man, naked but for Detroit Tigers slippers, lay sprawled facedown on the floor. Blood pooled around his head and crept along the grouted edges of the white tile floor.

Lynae whistled softly. "Not a dignified way to go."

"No, this would not be my preferred way to be found murdered," Jo said.

Lynae raised an eyebrow. "You have a preferred way?"

"Well, I know for sure I want to have all my clothes on. And I want to have been seriously kicking someone's ass." She squinted, imagining the fight. "Kicking three people's asses, and the fourth one does me in. But only because he has a gun and shoots me in the back while I'm kicking the third person's ass. So in my perfect scenario, they'll find me next to at least three other bodies."

"You've given this way too much thought."

Jo shrugged. "Give it time, and you will too. It goes with the job."

"Something to look forward to."

After setting down her bag inside the door, Jo crouched beside their victim.

Lynae hunkered down next to her. "Bruising on his shoulders and back." She pointed at the obviously fresh welts. "Blunt force trauma, definitely a weapon and not hands."

Jo gestured at his right hand. Drying blood, changing from deep red to black, streaked the inside of his forearm, where dark bruises formed. Two fingers were splayed in unnatural directions. "Defensive wounds."

Tacky blood caked his thinning hair. She ran a hand over his head, pushing his hair back. Above his right ear was a ridge, and a bump ran along the entire side of his skull. "Nailed him solid right here. If I were a betting woman, I would lay money on that being the fatal blow."

She stood and stepped away from the body. "We can't move him until we have pictures."

"Forensics should be here soon." Lynae glanced at the doorway.

Jo stepped carefully around the prone body and moved to the glass shower door, which hung open. A gray towel lay on the floor next to a silver towel rack that had been yanked loose from the wall. Chunks of drywall and white powder littered the floor. Standing with her back to the door, facing the towel rack, she said, "He was getting ready to get in the shower, back to the door, and bam, someone surprises him from behind. Hits him with something hard enough to leave a solid ridge on his head."

"Surprises and hurts him but doesn't knock him out," Lynae added.

"That probably shocks the attacker a little. You think a blow like that is going to lay somebody out flat."

"Well, that's how it would happen in the movies." Lynae shrugged. "And that's where most people become experts on this stuff."

"But it doesn't work, and the victim turns around." Jo spun and studied the toned body crumpled on the floor. "He's a big guy, and he's fit. Why doesn't he grab the weapon?"

"Attacker is bigger? He has the upper hand by coming at him from behind and surprising him."

Jo pursed her lips. "You don't have to be that big to take someone down, if you have the element of surprise, I suppose. But adrenaline should have made this big guy go after his attacker. Unless that first blow to the head had him reeling. Imagine how disoriented you would be if you took a blow to the head that hard."

"And a blow like that would drop you. If he was on the floor when he tried to defend himself, maybe he couldn't grab the weapon."

Nodding, Jo circled the body. "The first blow knocks him to his knees. He grabs for the towel bar, trying to pull himself to his feet, rips it off the wall in the process, and is dealt another blow or two for his effort."

"He probably never even saw who hit him."

Jo shook her head. "At one point, he faced his killer."

"How do you know?

"The bruises are on his left shoulder, his back, and the back of that arm. Those blows came from behind. The blow to the head is on the right side. Unless we have a switch-hitter on our hands, that blow came while they faced each other."

"And our killer is left-handed."

"It would appear so," Jo replied.

"Kent will be so proud."

"He's not super fond of other people doing his job, but I think he'll be okay with us determining that much."

"What have we already determined?" someone with a husky voice asked.

Jo turned to the middle-aged blond woman standing in the doorway, a black bag slung over her shoulder. The woman stepped forward and pointed at the ID lanyard hanging from her neck. "I'm Dorothy Zahm with the coroner's office."

"Lieutenant Riskin and Detective Parker. It's nice to meet you, Dorothy." Jo held her gloved hands up at her shoulders, palms out. "As you can see, we've done a preliminary."

The woman's face scrunched, her full cheeks pushing up until her eyes became slits barely visible under heavy eyeliner and blue eye shadow. "Yeah, probably not. I'll stick to taking pictures."

"I figured we'd see Mallory tonight," Jo said.

"Nope, not tonight. She's pretty busy these days, with the county lab expanding and such. She just hired me on a couple weeks ago."

"Welcome to the team," Lynae said.

"Thanks. I'm happy to be here. I think it will be a nice change from Chicago." She nodded at the body sprawled across the floor. "Although people do terrible things to one another everywhere, don't they?"

"I'm afraid so," Jo said. "This guy took quite a beating."

"Is that the position you found him in?"

"Yes, but I didn't ask the wife if she moved him at all. Blood pool suggests he's where he fell, so I guess she didn't move him." Jo waved a hand in a circular motion over the area next to the body. "The smears here suggest someone kneeling, and the footprints leading away are barefoot."

Lynae pointed at smears in the blood pool. "There's a bit of a mess here."

"Best guess is the wife dropped to her knees, could see he was dead, freaked out, then ran out of the room to call 911," Jo said.

Dorothy unzipped her black bag and selected a camera then added an additional long lens. "I'll start and get all that before you move him."

"Can you get some snaps in the bedroom first?" Jo asked. "Then Lynae and I can work that room while you finish up in here."

"Of course," she said and led the way out of the bathroom, a significant limp causing her to waddle. Her confidence in her stride indicated she had dragged her right foot long enough that she no longer thought about the extra labor it required for her to walk.

Jo stepped back and watched as she expertly took dozens of pictures, the shutter the lone sound filling the room.

After a full scan of the space, Dorothy said, "I think I have everything. I'll head to the other room to photo our victim, unless you have anything else in here."

"No, please do so that we can be ready to move the body when the techs get here." Jo walked with her to the bathroom, pulling off her bloody gloves. She picked up her bag from the floor, pulled out a plastic bag, shoved the dirty gloves into it, then took out a clean pair.

A door closed, and muffled voices floated from another room.

"I bet that's Forensics," Lynae said.

Jo held up the bag in her hand. "Good timing."

The bedroom door opened, and Officer Hubert poked his head in. "They're in here."

Two men clad in blue county forensic jackets pushed through the door. "Thanks, man," the younger one said, nodding to the officer.

Jo lifted her chin. "'Sup, Hammy."

Paul Hammond's face lit up, laugh lines crinkling the corners of his dark eyes. "JoEllen! I thought I might see you here."

Jo pointed up at him. "Call me JoEllen again, and all you'll be seeing is the unemployment line."

Paul threw his head back and laughed. He parked the shiny case he'd dragged in next to the door then wrapped an arm around Jo's shoulders and squeezed. "It never fails."

"It never gets old for you, does it?" Jo chuckled, giving him an elbow to the ribs.

Paul wiggled his eyebrows. "Nope. But if you'd ditch that boyfriend and go out with me, I'd stop."

Lynae snorted and attempted to cover it with a cough.

Jo crossed her arms and cocked a hip. "You realize I could get you on sexual harassment."

Paul yanked off his jacket and opened his case. "Nah, I've been asking you out for years, and you keep knocking me down."

Jo chuckled. "No one was more entertained by that than Mike."

Paul's face grew serious. "Yeah, he was a good sport." He winked at Jo. "He won't mind that I keep asking."

Jo rolled her eyes and sighed. "You're impossible."

She swept her hands toward the bathroom. "Our victim is in there. Dorothy is currently taking evidence photos, so why don't you start in here?"

Paul glanced at the younger tech, who had stood quietly, taking in the scene. He leaned in conspiratorially. "This is Brad's first case," he said quietly.

Jo grimaced. "It's pretty ugly in there."

Paul shrugged. "It's pretty much always trial by fire in this job." He straightened and raised his voice. "All right, kid, let's get to it."

The young tech gulped then gripped the handle of his case and trailed it behind him across the room, gawking like a country kid on his first visit to New York.

Lynae held up her hands, fingers splayed. Jo knew what she meant: *Ten bucks says the kid goes down when he sees the body.* Jo shook her head. The kid was green. She wasn't taking that losing bet.

Paul ran a UV light over the bedspread while the other tech watched intently. He motioned at his young protégé to get closer. "We've got a hair here." Paul pointed with a gloved hand. "Grab your tweezers and an evidence bag."

Brad fumbled with unsteady hands at the clasps on his kit. He finally freed them and extracted blue-handled tweezers and a plastic bag from his immaculately organized case then held them out to Paul.

Paul shook his head and pointed. "It's all yours."

Brad used tweezers to pick the hair from the bedspread and drop it carefully into the bag. "There are two of them," he said, indicating the other one.

"Grab them both. We don't have to worry about transfer with hair, so they can be in the same bag."

Brad confidently plucked the second hair from the bedspread and added it to the bag.

Paul took a broad-tip pen from the pocket of his suit and handed it to him. "Date, contents, and your initials."

Brad complied then reached into his pocket, pulled out his phone, and held the bag up next to his face.

Jo's shock had barely registered when Paul flung his hand in front of the phone. "What the hell are you doing?"

The young tech jolted. "It's my first evidence. I was just—"

"This is a crime scene. You can't take a fucking selfie!" Paul bellowed. "Don't they teach you anything in school anymore?"

"I w-wasn't—"

"What did you think you were going to do? Post it on Instagram? This isn't a damn joke."

"No, sir. Of course it isn't. I wasn't going to do anything with it."

Paul pointed at the bathroom. "There's a dead man in that room and a grieving widow somewhere." He indicated the family photo on the nightstand. "And three kids who will grow up without their dad. And you're going to snap a goddamn picture to commemorate your big day?"

Jo ground her foot into the carpeting and studied the pattern it made in the thick pile. She felt bad for the kid and wouldn't add to his embarrassment by gawking at the scene. Lynae shifted beside her, clearly feeling the same discomfort.

"I'm sorry. I didn't mean to be disrespectful. I wasn't thinking," the young tech mumbled.

"We don't get to *not think* in this job." Paul heaved a heavy breath. "Don't let it happen again."

Brad shook his head rapidly. "It won't. I'm sorry."

Jo glanced up from her carpet study in time to see Paul gently bop the kid on the back of the head. "Already forgotten. Let's get back to work."

Brad shoved his phone back into his pocket then secured the evidence bag in his case, his hands shaking.

Jo caught Paul's eye and pushed down a chuckle when he rolled his eyes and mouthed, "What the hell?"

When Brad closed his case and turned to the bed, Paul straightened and went back to the job at hand, as if nothing had happened. The two techs tugged down the blankets and top sheet from the pristinely made bed then ran the light over the remaining sheet and pillowcases.

"These look freshly washed. Not even a hair or skin shed," Paul muttered.

Jo leaned against the five-drawer dresser and surveyed the room. "I'm not surprised. The rest of this mess came from the perp, guaranteed. Hell, I can see the vacuum lines in the carpeting, so there's no way this mess is normal."

Lynae shoved her hands into her pockets. "I'm going to be a lot better about keeping my bedroom clean. It would be pretty embarrassing to have people taking pictures of it the way it usually is."

Jo shoulder-bumped her partner. "See, now you're starting to think about how you want—or don't want—to be found."

Lynae squeezed her eyes shut and rubbed her forehead. "Crap, I'm starting to think like you."

"Sorry. It's a little scary to be in my head, but you get used to it."

Chapter 3

Dorothy emerged from the bathroom, the enormous camera hanging from her neck. "I have what I need until you move him, Lieutenant."

Jo nudged Lynae. "We're up."

"Let's do it," Lynae said, pushing away from the wall.

Back in the bathroom, they rolled the body over, carefully avoiding stepping in the pool of coagulating blood. The cheekbone that had rested against the floor was crushed, caving in their victim's once-handsome face.

"It takes a lot of anger to smash someone's face in like that," Jo said.

Dorothy squatted across from them, rapidly taking pictures.

"What do we have here?" Jo asked under her breath as she pointed at a shiny object attached to the victim's chest. Dorothy got several pictures before Jo plucked it from his body. She held the earring, a small diamond wrapped in a gold braid, up to the light, then held her hand out to give Lynae a better look.

"Well, well, well, looks like our perp left us a little gift."

"Nice of her, wasn't it?" Jo grabbed an evidence bag from her kit, dropped the prize into it, and marked the bag. "Before we get too excited, we have to consider that this could be an earring that Lisa dropped and nothing more."

"I went through her jewelry box and didn't see any singles, but I'll check again before we go." Lynae stared at the victim and whistled quietly between her teeth. "Assuming the earring belongs to the killer, do we think a woman could have done this?"

"I don't see a man wearing this kind of earring, but we can't rule anything out. This would be hard for a woman to pull off."

"She would have to be pretty good sized and really pissed off."

"It could have been planted to make us think it's a woman," Jo said. "I'm having a hard time imagining an earring being lost in a fight and falling that close to our victim."

Lynae shrugged. "It could happen."

"We're going to have to set that aside, since we don't have an answer yet. We've got overkill, so most likely our victim knew his killer."

"Crime of passion?" Lynae mused.

"People have a strange sense of passion, don't they?" Jo gestured to a gash on one knee. "If we go with our earlier scenario, the first blow is to the back, and the victim goes to his knees, where the tile floor causes that wound. Then he gets whacked a couple more times. If we're leaning toward it being a woman, that adds up. She would need the element of surprise to get the upper hand on him."

"Then he manages to get up and face his attacker only to get smashed in the face and finally the head," Lynae added.

Jo scanned the prone body then grimaced and pointed at welts on the upper thighs and groin. "I'm going to say the crime-of-passion theory is a pretty solid bet."

Lynae made a face. "Somebody was definitely making a point."

"We're going to have to look hard at the wife for this."

"A big part of me hopes it's the wife's so that we don't have to tell her some other woman's earring was attached to her husband's chest."

"I hate to tell a woman her husband was a cheater as much as the next person, but what I really love is solving a murder with DNA evidence. And if she did this to her husband, I'm going to have a hard time feeling sorry for her, no matter what the circumstances were."

Jo studied each of the jack-and-jill sinks. "There's not so much as a drop of water in either sink. Either someone is obsessively neat, or our killer did one hell of a job cleaning up."

"But left the towel rack on the floor?"

"We won't find any prints on that rack. My bet is the killer didn't touch it, only the victim."

"If the wife did it, her prints would be all over this room anyway. Why wipe them down?"

"That wouldn't be something she would think of. When you get your crime-scene-investigating skills from television, all you can think of is to get rid of any prints. It most likely wouldn't occur to the average person that if they live in the house, their prints mean nothing if they aren't found on the murder weapon."

Lynae cocked her head. "Well, you know, I'm not average."

"That's for sure."

Giving Jo a sideways scowl, Lynae said, "I'm not sure how to take that."

"Oh man, this guy took some hits." Paul stood in the bathroom doorway, his hands fisted at his hips, and shook his head. "Poor bastard."

Brad stood beside him, his eyes wide. The blood that had made his young face ruddy when he first walked into the scene appeared to have abandoned his cheeks. His chest rose and fell rapidly, and his Adam's apple bobbed. Jo knew he was pushing down bile, and if they weren't careful, either he would contaminate their crime scene, or they would be picking him up from the floor.

She strode across the room, carefully stepping around the corpse. "Brad, can you help me for a second with some prints?"

Paul raised an eyebrow. "Really?" he mouthed.

Jo narrowed her eyes and pursed her lips in a let-me-do-this kind of way. Paul rolled his eyes but said nothing.

The young man blinked then focused on Jo. "Um, yeah, okay," he said, turning robotically to follow her back into the bedroom.

She strode out of the bedroom and stopped in the hallway. "Breathe through your mouth, not your nose. It helps with the smell."

"Okay."

"Concentrate on one thing at a time. Observe wounds, trace, *parts* of the whole instead of the whole. You have to respect him and his family, but right now you don't have to think of him as a person. It's my job to dig into who this guy was and why this happened to him. Your job is to gather the evidence for me."

"I did this in school. Why—"

"It's not the same. In a classroom, you're dealing with a cold, clean cadaver, nicely prepped and laid out in a sterile environment. This is a real person in his own home. School can't prepare you for the smells, the sounds, or the taste in the back of your throat that tries to push into your mouth. It's fresh and real, and there's nothing academic about it."

Brad glanced nervously in the direction of the crime scene, then his eyes dropped to the floor.

Jo laid a hand on his shoulder. "He's gruff, but he's a good guy. He was the tech on the first crime scene I worked, and he never told a soul that I upchucked my dinner in the backyard of the vic's home."

Brad's head snapped up, and he eyeballed Jo skeptically.

Holding up her right hand, Jo said, "True story. He told me to suck it up and do my job, but he never mentioned it again."

"Kind of like you're doing now?"

Jo winked. "I like to think I have a little softer touch, but yeah, basically."

Brad shoved his hands into the pockets of his white coveralls. "Thanks for having that softer touch. He scares the shit out of me."

"He's going to push you into being the best at what you do, and he may be a little rough doing it, but when the chips are down, he'll have your back. I promise."

"Is that why you put up with him hitting on you? Because he has something on you?"

Jo rolled her eyes but made sure she spoke firmly. "He's harmless and happily married to a wonderful woman who is a friend of mine. We established a long time ago that I'm not easily offended, so he knows he can kid with me. It doesn't mean anything, and if I ever told him I'd go out with him, he'd turn me down flat. It actually started out as a joke between him and my husband."

"And your husband is okay with it?"

"He was when he was alive."

"Oh, sorry. I didn't know."

"No way you could. But he doesn't do it to anyone else, so don't get the wrong impression of him. He's not some kind of creep who hits on all the women."

"Good."

"Besides, at this point in my career, I really don't care if someone finds out what happened when I was a rookie, so he has nothing on me."

Brad puffed out his cheeks and blew out a long breath. "Okay. I think I can do this."

"I'm sure you can." Jo laid a hand on his arm. "Just cut yourself some slack, and if you feel like you might hit the floor or lose your dinner, no one in that room is going to think any less of you if you step away. But understand that while there aren't many things that will set me off, destroying my crime scene will. So step away if you're going to lose it."

"Got it."

"All right. Now, I'd like you to get some prints off the wife's water glass, which is sitting on the dining room table."

"Do you think the wife did it?"

"I always think the wife did it." Jo shrugged. "But even if I didn't, I have to know what prints belong in this house."

"You could have bagged that glass and brought it in to the station."

"Yes, I could have."

Brad looked at his shoes then peered up at Jo through his thick lashes. "Thanks."

"Don't mention it." Jo started to leave the room then paused. Samantha had stood behind a chair, gripping the headrest. "Print the backs of the chairs also. We need to eliminate her friend's prints as well."

Although Jo hoped they wouldn't be useful to the case, having every fingerprint accounted for was helpful.

Walking back into the bathroom, Jo found Paul and Lynae crouched down, squinting in concentration at the body.

She dropped down beside Lynae. "What did you find?"

Paul indicated a narrow bruise on the victim's right cheek. "This wound is markedly different from the rest."

Jo bent down to get a closer look. "I think it's the edge of something. Maybe he hit a countertop during the fight."

"Yeah, that could be," Lynae said, looking around the room. "There are plenty of options in here."

Rolling back to rest on her heels, Jo said, "That part of his face is so destroyed that I doubt we'll get anything useful from it. It doesn't appear to have any distinguishable pattern on it."

"You think we can get some trace off it?" Lynae asked hopefully.

Paul shrugged. "We'll swab it and see what we can find." Craning his neck to look out the door, he asked, "Where's the kid?"

"He's pulling a couple of prints for me."

Paul scowled at her. "I want him to see this."

"I can get him. He needed a minute."

"Damn rookies," Paul growled.

Jo crossed her arms and glared at him. "Give him a break. You didn't have to be so rough on him."

"He was taking a picture with evidence," Paul said through gritted teeth.

"It's the generation. They take a selfie for everything." Jo held her hand up to stop Paul's comeback. "I know it's wrong and unethical, and you had to stop him. I'm just saying..."

Paul closed his eyes and set his jaw, pressing his lips together. He shook his head almost imperceptibly. "Not my style, Jo. You know that better than pretty much anyone."

Jo sighed. "I guess this isn't my battle to fight. I'll go get him."

The bedroom door opened with a click. Brad came in, his head held high and color back in his cheeks. "I've got those prints, Lieutenant." He leveled his gaze at Paul and strode confidently into the room. "What did I miss?"

Paul's eyes flicked to Jo, a smile playing across his lips. He motioned for Brad to come closer. Brad complied and dropped to his knees next to him, leaning in close. The two put their heads together and started talking trace and some other forensic-geek talk that Jo didn't understand.

Motioning to Lynae, Jo left the room. Lynae jerked her head toward the bathroom door. "Looks like he'll be okay."

"He will. The adjustment from school to reality is tough. It takes time."

"I remember, and Paul should too."

"He does. He won't give the kid a hard time about it and most likely won't ever mention it again. He's just not really a warm-and-fuzzy kind of guy."

"That's okay," Lynae said with a shrug. "Some people work best if someone is tough with them. Kind of like 'I'll show that cranky old bastard. I won't even flinch.'"

Jo snorted. "I'm sure that's what he's going for."

Dorothy pushed through the bedroom door with two men wearing black pants and white shirts with a Life EMS logo emblazoned on the left pocket. The younger of the two carried a folded stretcher in his right hand, tilting heavily to the left to provide counterweight. He bent down and rested the metal contraption against the bedroom wall.

Dorothy pointed toward the bathroom. "He's through here," she said then plodded in front of them.

The EMT hoisted the stretcher back up while the other man adjusted the heavy black bag slung over his shoulder, then they followed Dorothy out of the room.

Jo watched through the open door while Dorothy talked to Paul and waited while he and Brad finished. Then, under her watchful eye, the EMTs laid a heavy plastic bag on the floor and carefully moved the body of Victor Manton into it. They hefted the body onto the stretcher then lifted the bed until the metal legs clicked into position. Jo stepped back to give them room as they wheeled the body out of the bathroom and maneuvered it through the bedroom doorway.

Dorothy followed, her camera bag slung over her neck and resting on her hip.

"As soon as you can get me those pictures—"

"Already sent, Lieutenant," she said, smugly satisfied with herself.

Eyeing the camera dangling from the woman's neck, Jo asked, "Did we finally upgrade our cameras?"

"I don't know what you had before, but this is top shelf. Better than I had in Chicago."

Kent had been pleading his case for upgrades and getting his budget requests denied for as long as Jo had been a detective. She felt a tug of pride for him that he finally had the state-of-the-art equipment his team deserved.

"Then bring that top-shelf camera, and let's go through the rest of the house," Paul said from the bathroom doorway.

With their cases in hand and their coveralls zipped to their necks, he and Brad looked like something straight out of a *CSI: Miami* episode.

Before following the entourage out of the room, Jo pawed through the jewelry box on the dresser, with the small braid-wrapped diamond earring in mind. Coming up empty, she called Dispatch and asked to be transferred to Officer Ryan.

When the officer answered, Jo asked, "Officer, are you with our victim's wife?"

"Yes, I am."

"And do you have me on a private call, or are we on speaker?"

"You're good to go."

"Okay, good. I'd like you to get a good look at Lisa Manton and tell me if she's wearing earrings. I need to know if she has both of them, Officer."

"Oh, sure, I can do that," he said in a casual tone. "I'm in the car, but I can make an excuse to go in."

"All right. Text me what you find out," Jo said before clicking off.

After leaving the master bedroom, Jo went down the hallway and found Lynae in another bedroom. "We'll have to search every room and see if our killer was kind enough to leave us a clue."

"Brad and I can handle everything up here," Lynae said. "We've got three bedrooms and two more bathrooms, but they belong to the kids, so I doubt we're going to find much."

Raising an eyebrow, Jo said, "Don't assume anything."

"Yeah, I know," Lynae said, tossing Jo an are-you-kidding-me-right-now look.

"In fact, search for a mate to that earring in the girls' rooms."

"It doesn't really seem like an earring a kid would wear."

Jo shrugged. "I agree, but—"

"Don't assume anything."

"She can be taught." Jo threw up both hands in a victory wave and backed out the door. "I'll start on the downstairs. Paul?"

"I'm with you."

On the main floor, Jo and Paul divided the space, with Paul taking the dining room, the living room, and the bathroom, while Jo tackled the kitchen and the entry.

After going through the kitchen and sorting through the cubbies at the front door, Jo went through what she'd assumed was an exit door at the back of the kitchen and found a bathroom and a den that appeared to serve as an office. Two light-colored, flower-patterned accent chairs sat facing an end table and a large leather chair. A solid wood desk dominated the far corner, while a black nine-cube bookcase, in a modern style that appeared out of place in the old-fashioned office, covered the opposite wall. Inside four of the cubes were cloth totes filled with manuals, magazines, music CDs, and receipts for mundane home-office tax write-offs.

On a credenza next to the desk was an all-in-one printer with cords leading to a DisplayLink pluggable USB-C docking station. Also plugged into the docking station were a thirty-two-inch monitor, a keyboard, and a mouse. No laptop was in sight, so she tapped out a quick text to Lynae to keep an eye out for one.

While her phone was in her hand, a text message came through from Officer Ryan, stating that Lisa Manton was wearing gold hoop earrings in each ear. She had only one piercing in each ear and no missing earring.

She sent a quick reply then slid the phone back into her pocket. If the earring did belong to Lisa, it didn't tell them anything. She could have simply dropped it on the bathroom floor earlier in the day, and Victor happened to land on it when he fell. *But if it was hers, where is the other one?*

If it didn't belong to her, it could lead them directly to their killer. And considering its mate had yet to be found, she had her doubts about it belonging to Lisa.

Jo focused on the office, since the earring was a piece she couldn't fit into the puzzle yet. On the desk, she found a day-at-a-glance appointment calendar with only initials on each appointment line. It could be a challenge to match names to those initials. If it became important, maybe Lisa could help them out. In the space for the current day, the calendar noted a nursing home visit and a finance-committee meeting. The final entry read Lisa—girls' night. She bagged the calendar to bring into evidence.

Digging through the top desk drawer, Jo found pens and highlighters, notepads, other typical office odds and ends, and a set of keys. She clutched the keys and eyed the file cabinet tucked beside the desk. She contemplated the legality of opening the file cabinet while absently tossing the keys up and catching them several times then decided she'd better check with her legal counsel before delving into it. The rest of the office was disappointingly devoid of anything that would lead her to her killer.

She moved to the small bathroom outside the office and as expected found nothing of substance, then opened the door at the end of the hall. A mess of footprints led away from the house. The prints weren't obscured by the snow that had come down that night. They were fresh.

"Whatcha got?" came Paul's deep voice from over Jo's right shoulder.

She jolted, putting her hand on her heart. "Good Lord. Don't you make any noise when you walk?"

Paul lifted a tennis-shoe-clad foot and struck a pose. "I'm like a ninja."

Jo snorted. "Well, Ninja Paul, it appears someone was less stealthy than you. Could be a good break for us."

"Looks like a few someones to me." Paul squatted in the doorframe. "This is narrow, and the heel print would indicate a woman's shoe." Pointing at a print to the left of that one, he said, "And this is a work boot and has to be at least a men's size twelve with a heavier depth."

"So a heavier person," Jo added.

"Right. And this one over here could be either, but I'm going to say by the size it's a woman's."

"We've got these and some leading to the front door. Can we get molds?" Jo asked.

"Probably not. This snow isn't solid enough. We can use Dorothy's fancy new camera to get good prints and my good old-fashioned tape measure to get size."

"Well, if that's the best we can do, we'll work with it," Jo grumbled.

"We solved crimes before we had technology, kid."

Jo rolled her eyes. "You're like ten years older than me. Quit acting like you investigated with Sherlock Holmes."

"Go get Dorothy, you disrespectful young'un."

"That's Lieutenant Young'un," Jo retorted.

"Quit talking sexy, and go get the camera lady."

She met Lynae and Brad at the top of the stairs.

"Sorry, we've got nothing," Lynae said, holding up her hands. "We went through one very neat and one very messy girl's bedroom and one boy's room that appears not to be in regular use. The drawers and closet were mostly empty. Only a few things in each and a suitcase on the floor. Nothing in either of the bathrooms either."

"Laptop?"

"Found one in each kid's room. Chromebooks in the girls' rooms and an HP in the boy's."

Brad jiggled the silver case he was pulling. "They're in here."

"I'm going to take a look at the HP." Jo had seen enough Chromebooks in the schools she visited to know they didn't have a USB-C power cord that would match the docking station in the office. But she wasn't sure about HP. "But first I need to get Dorothy's fancy camera downstairs."

"I'll get her," Brad said, releasing his case and pivoting to head back down the hallway.

Lynae leaned in to bridge the gap between them. "Brad seems like a nice guy."

"How's his work?" Jo asked.

"Solid. I mean, he's a little overeager on what to bag but otherwise really good."

"That's better than undereager."

Lynae pursed her lips. "Is undereager a word?"

"It is now." Jo jerked her chin when she saw Dorothy and Brad coming down the hallway.

"Brad said there are some prints for me to shoot," Dorothy said.

"Outside the doors, front and back," Jo replied as she headed down the stairs ahead of her. "Paul doesn't think we can get a mold in this snow, but if you get some good pictures, they may help."

"With this beauty…" Dorothy lifted the camera slung around her neck. "I can get pictures so clear that you'll be able to see if the person wearing the shoes had socks on."

When Jo stopped midstep and gawked, Dorothy winked, a mischievous twinkle in her eye.

"You had me for half a second," Jo said with a scowl. Since she knew Dorothy had wit, she would have to stay on her toes.

Jo led her through the kitchen to the back door, where Paul was hunched.

"Need help getting up, old man?"

Paul scowled at her over his shoulder then motioned for her to come closer. "It's a drop of blood."

"Can we preserve it out of the snow?" Jo asked. Her pulse quickened as she zeroed in on it.

"Grab a vial and a swab."

"Dorothy, can you get a shot of this before we swab it?" Jo asked over her shoulder.

As Dorothy snapped a couple of pictures, Jo went through Paul's case until she found what he had requested. She handed it to him and watched as he meticulously plucked the blood from the side of the shoe print and dropped it into the vial.

"Maybe we'll have the DNA of your killer here, Lieutenant Young'un," Paul said as he labeled and placed the vial in a compartment within his case.

"Even if it belongs to our vic, we'll know that one of these shoe prints belongs to our killer." Jo tapped Paul lightly on the shoulder. "Nice catch."

"I do my best." Paul stood and moved aside, allowing Dorothy to step in and take more pictures of the prints.

When the house was fully processed, taped off, and secured, Lynae and the last of the tech team headed for the front door. Jo followed, running the crime-scene checklist through her head. When she came to the cluttered cubicles, she instructed one of the techs to bag and tag the baseball bats from the bag labeled Gilly then went out into the blistering cold.

Lynae yawned and rubbed her eyes.

"Why don't you go home and get a few hours of sleep," Jo said.

"What about you? It's almost time for the morning commuters to be annoying, and you haven't slept either. What are you going to get done right now that can't wait?"

"I'll catch a few hours in the crib after I get a board started and our initial report typed up. Then we can hit the ground running when you get in. We'll have to canvas the neighborhood to see if anyone saw anything. Then I want to talk to Lisa and her kids. But that will have to wait until morning."

"All right, I'll make it more like a nap and see you in a few." Lynae jogged to her car and within a moment drove off.

Jo watched the ambulance pull away from the quiet house in the unassuming neighborhood. A figure stood in a picture window across the street, the curtains drawn back and lights blazing behind him. He must be more curious than the rest. Most of the other houses were dark. Neighbors who likely didn't know the Manton family had lost interest and retreated to the homes they assumed were safe. They would be uneasy while the investigation continued, locking the doors they had previously kept open or finding safer hiding places for the spare key. They would warn their kids, stare suspiciously at any unfamiliar vehicles on the street, and talk to neighbors they had never spoken to before. Some would get home-security systems. Some would become suspicious of their neighbors. Everyone would be affected in some way. They would all carry that day forever, to some extent. Murder did that to people.

Chapter 4

Jo rolled her shoulders and arched her back in a vain attempt to work out the kinks from the few hours she'd spent on the thin mattress in the crib, the station's makeshift downtime room. The springs whined their discontent as she swung her legs over the edge and dropped her feet to the floor. As she sat in the semidarkness of the small, windowless room, she counted the hours until she could crawl into her big bed, wrap herself in her down comforter, and have Mojo curl up beside her. She would knock out as much as she could in a reasonable number of hours and get home early.

With that satisfying image in her head, she shuffled to the door and opened it to the bright lights and bustle of the station. Phones rang, chairs scraped, and multiple conversations mingled into a single hum. The smell of coffee wafted through the air and competed with someone's microwaved breakfast burrito. Warmth spread through Jo's body. God, she loved this place.

"Why are you grinning like a goof?" Lynae stood in the breakroom doorway. Steam rose from a wrapped lump on the paper plate in her hand.

"Wouldn't you like to know," Jo replied, her smile broadening.

Lynae stretched on her tiptoes to peek around Jo. "You got someone in that room with you?"

Jo snorted. "Haven't done that in a long time."

"Yeah, me either. It's about time to fix that."

"I thought you weren't ready for a relationship."

"Who says being in a relationship is a requirement?" Lynae winked then laughed when Jo rolled her eyes.

Jo headed for the breakroom coffee machine. Lynae followed and held out her half-empty mug. "Might as well fill it up. It feels like a caffeine-infusion kind of day."

"Is there any other kind?" Jo asked as she topped off Lynae's mug, then she filled her own.

She closed her eyes and sighed as the first sip of coffee pumped life into her veins. Though the caffeine couldn't really affect her that quickly, what she knew and what her body thought were two different things. And that morning, she was going to let her body think whatever it needed to.

Leaning against the counter, she held the mug in both hands and enjoyed the warmth. "I started the board and typed up the initial report."

"You couldn't have gotten much sleep, then."

"I got enough," Jo lied while stifling a yawn. "But I'll admit I'm already daydreaming about my own bed."

Jo snatched a cookie from an open container on the counter then headed for her office. "Have you heard yet what Lainard and Breuker picked up last night?"

"Nope, just got here."

"I'd better get myself together before the morning briefing." Jo stepped behind her desk and opened the bottom drawer, where she kept a change of clothes and a few other essentials. She grabbed her purse from under her desk then held out her credit card. "We have a little time. Do you mind making a run to Jam n' Bean and getting some bagels for the crew?"

"Best job I'll have all day," Lynae said, snatching the card from Jo's hand, then she hustled out of the office.

Jo used the time Lynae was out getting bagels to change and freshen up. She was amazed, as always, at what a difference a little makeup could do.

With the impeccable timing of partners, Jo walked into the briefing room at the same time Lynae was coming in with the bagels. The detectives rewarded her with a rousing cheer as she made a show of putting the treats on the side table.

"Go ahead and grab something before we get started," Jo said.

"You look like a different person," Lynae commented while slathering cream cheese on a bagel.

"The wonders of makeup and hair ties," Jo said, running a hand over her hair, then tucked a loose blond strand behind her ear. "Now for some breakfast."

Jo nicked the last cinnamon-raisin bagel from the box and took a bite on her way back to the front of the room. She would forgo the peanut butter in the interest of getting the meeting started.

As the detectives filtered back to the chairs, Jo pulled out her notebook. "Lynae and I picked up a homicide on the northeast side last night. Breuker, Lainard?" She surveyed the room before catching Isaac Breuker's eye as he took a slug from a bottle of Vitaminwater. "I understand you picked one up also. What do you have?"

Isaac swallowed and swiped a dark hand over his mouth.

"Ex-boyfriend shoots new boyfriend," Charles Lainard chimed in with a mouthful of bagel.

"You have witnesses?" Jo asked hopefully.

"Even better. Dumbass came back."

"Back to the scene?"

"Yep," Charles said, slouching and stretching his long legs out in front of him. "Came back with a bunch of bravado and shit. Telling us how the dead guy stole his girl."

"Like that makes murder all good or something," Isaac added. "But at least we could finish it quickly. Dude wouldn't shut up."

"I love when they're packaged nice and neatly for us." Jo marked it off in her book. "Anybody else wrap up their case and tie a bow on it for me?" She noted plenty of diverted eyes and shuffled feet.

"I'm going to take that as a no," she said and moved to the next case in her book.

The meeting ended quickly, as their caseload was low. As the team filed out, Jo held Isaac and Charles back. "Since your case closed quickly, I'm going to pull you in to do some legwork on ours."

"Sure. What do you need?" Isaac asked, widening his stance and crossing his gym-toned arms.

"I'd like to get started on a few phone calls this morning, and I need someone to talk to neighbors to see if anyone saw anything last night."

"All right if the kid handles that himself?" Charles asked. "Our guy's in lockup, but I have to write up the report and get his full statement. You know, add the bow to your neatly wrapped gift."

"Yeah, you do that, and if you can spare the time, Isaac, I'll take the help."

"You got it, LT."

Jo gave him the elevator pitch on the case, with enough details to do a neighborhood canvas. She recited the address of the house where the man had watched her from the window. "Give this guy a little extra attention. He may be nothing more than a lookie-loo, but he's worth an extra question or two."

Isaac tapped a finger to his temple in a casual salute. His striped button-down stretched taut across his broad chest. "I'm on it."

Jo motioned for Lynae. "Let's go talk to Lisa."

"Oh goody, I was hoping to start my day with the grieving widow," she said, grabbing her coat from her desk.

Jo got her gear from her office then walked with Lynae to the parking garage.

"I'm looking heavily at her for this," she said as she maneuvered out of the tight parking spot. "I'm not buying the ransacked room. I priced it out last night before I hit the crib, and that watch lying on the nightstand is worth around eight hundred dollars. Anyone who's coming to rob a house is going to grab that and any other small, easy-to-pawn stuff."

"Who the hell pays eight hundred dollars for a watch?"

Jo rolled her eyes. "Right? Their house is average at best, and he's spending that kind of cash on a watch? Is he selfish with his money, or does he have a cash source he's hiding?"

Lynae cocked her head. "If it is a cash source, do you think the wife will know?"

"She has to know he had the watch, and we should be able to get a read on how she feels about that." Jo pulled onto the street and headed the short distance to the highway on-ramp. "He could have been super generous and bought her all kinds of nice stuff too. I wonder what Lisa does for a living, because I don't think a pastor who only does therapy for his parishioners would have a boatload of money. But maybe they do and just didn't prioritize living in a big house."

"That happens. Not everyone cares about that stuff. They could take vacations and spend their money on each other instead of on the house."

"Always the optimist."

"I like to think there are people in the world who don't care about material stuff. People who love each other and don't care what else they have."

"Yeah, me too. Then I wake up and come to work."

Lynae sighed. "I suppose you can only do this job so long before you get cynical."

Jo gave her a sideways glance. "I *am* cynical, but I believe that most people are good. And I believe there are plenty of couples out there who prioritize each other."

"Okay, I feel better."

"Don't get all sappy and soft on me, because I'm seriously considering the wife for this."

"Of course you are. And at some point, we'll have to ask her what else is missing, so we'll have to bring her back through the house."

"That will suck if she's innocent, but it has to be done, unless there's someone else who knows everything they have. We haven't recovered the laptop yet, so I'm going to assume that's missing. If there's anything else, finding it is our quickest route to finding our killer."

"Then we'll have to do it right away and get notification to the pawn shops in Grand Rapids."

"And Standale, Muskegon, Grand Haven, Holland, Kalamazoo, and Lansing," Jo said, ticking the locations off on her fingers.

"You think the killer would go that far?"

"If he has a brain, he won't try to pawn it in a legitimate shop. And if he has even half a brain, he won't do it in the same town as the murder."

"Let's hope he doesn't have much of a brain."

"Here's hoping. First things first. We need to get Lisa's timeline. We'll start out soft, assuming she didn't do this. I don't want to add to the trauma if it isn't necessary."

"I hope she was able to get a couple of hours' sleep at her friend's house."

"Mm-hmm."

Lynae raised an eyebrow. "You gonna tell me about you and Samantha?"

Jo shrugged. "Nothing to tell. We were roommates, best friends, practically inseparable all through college. Now we're not. I haven't seen her since shortly after graduation."

"You were best friends, then you stopped. Just like that?"

"Yep," Jo replied.

"Well, since I'm your current best friend, that makes me a little nervous."

"You have nothing to worry about."

"She probably thought the same thing."

Jo tilted her head and allowed the hurt to show in her eyes. "You've known me this long, and you assume the broken friendship was my doing?"

Lynae's face fell. "No. I didn't mean it that way."

"I'm stupidly loyal. To a fault. Sometimes to the point of not seeing what's happening right under my nose."

"She betrayed your friendship."

"Yes, she did, in the—"

Jo's phone rang. Grabbing it from the console, she glanced at the caller ID.

"In the what?" Lynae asked.

Jo grimaced and held up the phone. "I have to get this."

"Call them back! In the *what*?"

Jo tapped the in-car screen to take the call hands free. "Hi, Jack. You're on speaker. What's up?"

"It's Jack?" Lynae stage whispered while throwing up her hands. "You're blowing me off for your boyfriend?"

Jo gave Lynae the side-eye as she huffed and stared out the window.

"Rick has agreed to see you," Jack said, wasting no time on pleasantries.

"W-What? When? Why now?" Jo stammered as all coherent thought left her brain. She had been trying for two months to get on the visitor list. When someone was the mastermind behind the murder of someone else's husband, they weren't overly eager to talk.

"I don't know the why. I would like to take credit for this, but it wasn't me. As for the when, you can meet with him the day after tomorrow, if you're ready."

"This is your exit," Lynae said, pointing at the green road sign as it blurred past Jo's vision.

Focusing on the road, Jo exited and slowed down. "If I'm ready? I've been waiting."

"I know you have, but I don't know what his motive is."

"I don't care what his motive is. He can't hurt me any more than he already has."

"Don't count on that, okay?" Jack said gently.

"I need to know what Mike knew, and I need to know why. Why did he have to kill him? He's a police officer. Are there others? Has this drug ring infiltrated their whole department, or was it just him? What about up the food chain? I have to know these things. You understand that, right?"

"I absolutely understand. And I want you to have your answers. But I'm still going to worry."

"Of course you are." The badass in her defaulted to her Pavlovian response of an eye roll, but deep down, the woman in her loved that he worried and tried to protect her. She didn't need it and could probably kick his ass in a fight, but she found it endearing and appreciated the love behind it.

"I can literally *feel* you rolling your eyes."

"Wow, that's impressive."

Jack sighed. "Just be careful, please."

"I always am."

"Are you? Because I have *not* noticed that."

"I'll be fine," Jo moaned. "But thanks for trying to take care of me anyway."

"Always," Jack said before hanging up.

Any lingering annoyance Lynae might have been holding vanished. "Finally! Do you have everything you're going to say and ask him written down?"

"I've made some notes, but mostly it's in my head." Jo glanced at her GPS.

"You should write it all down. You don't know what you're going to feel when you're in that room and face-to-face with that bastard. You may lose track and forget something. And this might be your only shot at talking to him."

"Yeah, you're right. I honestly never believed I was going to get this chance, but I sure don't want to blow it now that I have it."

"You can try your questions out on me. I'll answer them like he would."

"You won't make a good Rick."

"Why not?" Lynae asked indignantly.

Jo scanned her up and down. "That was a compliment. You're not a disloyal bastard who would *literally* shoot his best friend in the back."

"Oh, okay, if you put it that way." Shrugging, she said, "I can try though."

Noting the short distance they had left to drive, Jo refocused. "I may take you up on that, but right now we have to concentrate on Victor Manton and who decided he had to die."

Chapter 5

Jo drove into the tree-lined street of a gated neighborhood in Ada. A man stepped out of a small white booth and approached Jo's truck with a clipboard in his hand. His heavy green jacket was emblazoned with Lockenkey Security in bold print wrapped around a gold key.

Jo rolled down her window. "Good morning," she said brightly.

The man bent down to look in her window. "Good morning. Can I help you?" White breath puffed out of his mouth in the cold air.

Jo held up the badge that had been clipped to her belt. "If you could point me to the residence of Samantha Givens, that would be very helpful."

The man did a double take, his eyes widening and his eyebrows disappearing beneath the stocking cap that sat low on his forehead. He held out his gloved hand, scrutinized the badge, then stepped back into his booth and tapped a few keys on a laptop. He trotted back out and handed her a green-and-gold placard that read Visitor with the date written in bold black marker. "Here you go. You can hang that from your mirror."

Pointing, he said, "Left at the clubhouse then another left on Madison. It will be the fourth side street. The Givens residence is the second home on the right."

The man stepped back into his booth and pressed a button. After the white gate lifted, Jo waved and drove through.

Lynae shifted and sat up straight. "Looks like your old friend did pretty well for herself."

Jo eyeballed the sprawling homes on large, manicured lots. Each home was a conservative shade of brown or beige, with the occasional dark gray thrown in. "I'm not surprised. She was smart and ambitious. I always figured she would be successful one way or another."

Lynae slowly turned her head in Jo's direction. "What does that mean? One way or another."

"I didn't mean anything by that. I knew she would find a way to succeed, and from what I can see, I was right."

Jo turned left on Madison Street then parked in front of the second house on the right. The garage door was closed, and three cars sat in the driveway. "She's got company already this morning."

"Or Samantha has kids with cars."

Jo lifted an eyebrow. "Well, since we're the same age, and I knew her in college, I'm going to say she doesn't have any old enough to drive."

"She could have married an older man."

"True, she could have. But she needed a babysitter to come last night. And the windows on those cars have been scraped, so unless those kids have already been out and back home this morning, they have company. And company means word has spread."

Lynae wiggled her eyebrows. "The rumor mill is churning."

"And I'm sure it's whipping up plenty of theories." Jo reached into the back seat and heaved her bag into the front. "We should have called, but here we are. We'll have to ask them to leave, but tread lightly. Especially if the kids are around. Let's get her timeline and gauge her reactions. Unless she blurts something incriminating, we'll keep it as short as possible."

"What about taking her back to go through the house?"

"We'll have to talk to her about that. It should be done sooner rather than later. If anything is missing, we need to get a trace on it ASAP."

Jo opened her door, stepped out into the bitter morning air, and waited for Lynae to come around to the front of the car. "Keep an eye on Samantha while I'm questioning Lisa."

Lynae's eyes narrowed. "Why? Do you like her for this?"

Jo shook her head. "No, but she's the person Lisa called, so they're obviously very close. She could react if she recognizes that Lisa is lying. So casually watch for reactions."

Lynae pursed her lips. "Smart. That's why you're the lieutenant."

Jo vaulted the three steps leading to the front door in one long stride. "You just might learn something from me after all."

Lynae jogged up the steps. "Well, since I'll never have legs as long as yours, I can't learn how to skip steps the way you do." She reached around Jo and rang the bell. "But I'm definitely quicker on the draw."

Jo snorted. "In your dreams."

The door swung open, and Samantha greeted them. "Good morning, Jo. Detective..."

"Parker," Lynae filled in.

Samantha closed her eyes and shook her head slightly. "Of course. I'm sorry."

"Don't be."

Samantha stood back and swept her arm in a come-on-in motion. "You're just in time for breakfast."

Jo stepped into the foyer and bent down to pull off her snow-covered boots.

Samantha waved her hand. "Don't bother. No one else has, so the floor is already wet and dirty. That's the least of my concerns this morning."

Jo tapped her boots on the rug then wiped her feet a couple of times before following her through a cathedral-ceilinged living room. A portrait of Samantha, a handsome dark-haired man, and two young boys hung over a stone fireplace. Those same boys lounged in gaming chairs set close to a flat-screen TV, headphones with attached microphones over their ears. Their eyes were intent on the screen. They passed the boys and went into a modern, open kitchen with stark-white cabinets and a black-and-white checkered backsplash. In the next room, separated by an arched doorway, three women sat with Lisa on bar stools around a marble-topped island, their hands wrapped around mugs. A plate of muffins, two covered serving plates, and a casserole dish with a serving spoon dug in rested on trivets in the center. The scent of bacon, eggs, and coffee filled the expansive room.

Tragedy brings people. People bring food. A memory of casserole dishes, pie plates, and crock pots lining her counters after Mike's death flittered through Jo's mind. She'd had enough food to feed a small encampment, and it was just her and Mojo. She couldn't force herself to eat any of it, even though it had brought a small sense of comfort that people cared enough to try.

When Lisa saw the trio enter the room, her face fell, tears welling in her eyes. The rest of the women warily eyeballed the source of their friend's distress.

Jo stepped forward. "How are you holding up this morning, Mrs. Manton?"

Lisa sniffled as her lip quivered. She finally simply shook her head. Jo laid a hand over hers and looked around the group. "Detective Parker and I have some questions for you, but why don't you go ahead and have something to eat first?"

Lisa's face crumpled. "I don't think—"

A heavyset middle-aged woman jumped up from her stool and grabbed a plate. "The officer is right, Lisa. You have to eat."

The woman scooped something from the casserole dish and plopped it onto the plate, spooned on scrambled eggs and two pieces of bacon, then nestled a muffin next to the bacon. She set the plate in front of Lisa and wrapped an arm around her shoulders. "There's a little bit of everything. You eat what you can."

Lisa stared at the plate then picked up a piece of bacon, broke a chunk off the end, and gingerly slipped it into her mouth. She stared at the counter top as she chewed then swallowed. Her distraught eyes sought Samantha's. "I can't."

"It's okay," Samantha said gently. "Just leave it there, and pick at it as you can. You'll need something in you to keep going."

Jo watched the scene, struggling to remain impassive. *She's a good friend.*

Samantha stepped around the island, wrapped her arm around Lisa, and hugged her, pressing her cheek against the top of Lisa's head. Then she continued into the kitchen, pulled out two coffee mugs, and filled them. She added two spoons of cream and two sugars to one of the cups then caught Jo's eye.

Jo nudged Lynae and motioned for her to follow her to the other side of the kitchen.

Samantha held out one of the coffee cups to Jo. "If I remember right, it's two and two."

Jo accepted the cup and inclined her head. "You remember right."

Samantha held the other cup out to Lynae. "Detective?"

When Lynae nodded, Samantha handed her a cup then motioned to the counter. "Please help yourself."

"Thanks," Lynae said quietly then stepped to the counter and added an obscene amount of sugar and cream to the cup.

Jo glanced around the quiet house. "Are Lisa's kids here?"

Samantha lifted her chin, her eyes rolling upward. "Still in bed. Needless to say it was a long night last night."

"How are they doing?"

"Pretty well, actually."

Jo was sure the surprise registered on her face. "That's good but not what I expected to hear."

Samantha cocked her head. "Victor was their stepdad. He tried hard, but he wasn't very close to the kids. He really hadn't had time yet to get there with them."

"I didn't realize that. Is their dad still in the picture?"

Samantha gritted her teeth. "Only because the court insists on it."

"I assume the divorce wasn't amicable?"

"Are they ever?"

Jo shrugged.

Samantha ran a hand through her wavy dark hair, pulling it back from her face before letting it fall again. She sipped her coffee then set her cup on the counter. "Dave, their dad, cheated on Lisa."

"How is their relationship now?" Jo asked.

"Their *relationship*"—Samantha made air quotes—"is nonexistent. They're both remarried and have moved on. He stays in the car on the rare occasion he bothers to see the kids. They only communicate if it involves the kids, and she's okay with that."

Jo pushed Dave to the bottom of her suspect list. If he'd moved on, he had no reason to kill his ex's husband.

"But when it happened," Samantha continued, "it almost broke her."

Lynae tapped a spoon on the edge of her cup. "Almost broke her how? What happened?"

Samantha sighed. "She's struggled with depression for years, but she was managing it with medication. Of course, he knew that, but he was careless and mean about his affairs. It was almost like he was daring her to catch him at it. She spiraled out of control when she found out. Stopped taking her medication. Stopped taking care of herself or the kids. She locked herself away in her room for days and never got out of bed. It was a very dark time for all of them."

"What brought her out of it?" Jo glanced into the next room, where Lisa sat with her friends. "Or isn't she?"

"We finally convinced her to go back to counseling."

"We?"

"A few of us from church took care of the kids when she fell off the grid. We tried for months to get her to talk to someone other than us. We're not professionals. I worried that we would say the wrong thing."

"That can happen," Jo said, thinking of too many suicides she had worked when well-meaning people had unintentionally helped push a person over the edge.

"What finally convinced her to go back?" Lynae asked.

"I was afraid someone would call social services, and she would lose the kids. And I told her so. I realize now that was risky, but she's a good mom. She would do anything for her kids. It would have destroyed her to lose them."

"How long ago did all this happen?" Jo asked.

"Hard to believe, but it's been almost eight years now."

Lynae leaned against the counter. "And the counseling did the trick?"

"She went back on antidepressants, which helped a lot. But yeah, the counseling was also key."

"Do you know what counselor she ended up seeing?" Jo asked. She doubted that information would help or that she would even use it, but since she had added it to her list, checking that box was required by her brain.

"Victor."

The alarms sounding in Jo's head were almost deafening. "Victor? As in her husband? He was Lisa's counselor?"

"Yes, that's how they met."

Lynae slipped Jo a what-the-hell look. "I believe it breaks every code of ethics in the books for a counselor to have a relationship with a patient."

Samantha shrugged uncomfortably. "I suppose it does, but it worked out well for them."

"I don't think that's the point," Jo said. That piece of information was something she would have to consider. It was most definitely unethical and brought into question whether there were other unethical things Victor Manton had been involved in that could have led to his death.

Putting it aside for later, she asked, "How long have they been married?"

"Around five years."

"Were the kids old enough to remember the dark time in their mom's life?" Jo asked.

"Gilly more so than the twins. They're only fourteen, so their memories of it, I'm sure, are pretty vague or at least tainted by their age."

"So Gilly is Ethan's nickname?" Lynae asked.

"Oh, sorry, that's a habit. The kids' last name is Gillespie. Ethan's friends started calling him Gilly way back when he first started school. It stuck for all of us."

"Stuck so much that he has it on his baseball bag."

"That's all anyone knows him as. I think Lisa and Victor are the only ones who call him Ethan."

"Did the kids have counseling as well?" Jo asked.

"No. I thought they should, but Lisa insisted they were fine." She bit her lip. "I should have been more forceful about it, but I didn't think it was really my right to say anything. Then things seemed to really fall into place. They were doing so well..."

"And it didn't seem important anymore."

"I let it go. I figured dragging it all up again wouldn't help if they were all doing okay."

Jo took a sip from her cup, savoring the smoothness of the high-grade beans. "How do you know the family?"

"Victor was the pastor of our church." With her cup, Samantha motioned toward the other room. "It's the same way Lisa knows the rest of the women here."

"Isn't he a counselor?" Jo asked.

"He's a licensed counselor, but he only counsels through the church."

"So his primary job is pastor, and he counsels parishioners on the side," Lynae stated.

"That's right."

"How long has he been the pastor?"

"Oh, geez, maybe ten years? That's a guess."

"And Lisa and her ex-husband were members?"

Samantha shook her head. "Dave never came. Lisa started coming eight, nine years ago by herself, then she brought the kids once she decided it was a good fit for her."

"So her husband cheats then leaves, she goes into a depression and starts counseling with the pastor, and before you know what's happening, they've hooked up," Lynae said, counting the points with her free hand.

"You make it sound so dirty." Samantha grimaced.

"Not my intention." Lynae held up her hand. "Just being sure I have it right."

Jo peered around the archway separating them from the group of women huddled around the dining room table. Lisa laughed at something one of them said then broke off a chunk of the muffin on her plate and slipped it into her mouth.

"I think she may be ready to talk to us," Lynae said.

Jo glanced into her almost-empty cup and tipped it toward Samantha. "Mind if I help myself?"

"Of course not."

Jo brushed past Samantha and caught a whiff of a familiar scent, momentarily caught off-guard, and wondered why it seemed so familiar. She filled her cup, added cream and sweetener, then lifted the pot to Lynae.

Lynae shook her head. "I'm all set."

After returning the pot, Jo followed Lynae through the archway. All conversation stopped, and heads turned to them when they entered the room.

Jo lifted her bag from her shoulder and set it down beside one of the black high-back stools. She smiled kindly at Lisa. "Were you able to get a little food down?"

Lisa contemplated her half-empty plate, surprise registering in her eyes. "I guess I was."

"That's good. Please don't let us stop you from eating, but my partner and I are going to have to ask you some questions."

Lisa pushed the plate away. "I can't eat any more."

A matronly woman pushed her chair back and yanked on the bottom of her maroon cardigan, straightening the embroidered cardinal that had bunched up at her waist. She looked pointedly at the two women who sat stoically in their seats. "Why don't we clean up the kitchen then let ourselves out?"

The other women scrambled to their feet and within minutes had gathered the plates and silverware from the table and were hustling out.

Samantha laid a hand on the arm of the considerate woman as she hurried past her. "Don't worry about the kitchen, Eileen. I'll clean it up. Thanks for stopping by."

"Of course. I'll check in with you tomorrow to see if there's anything we can do."

When the women had cleared the room, Jo sat across the table from Lisa, and Lynae sat in the seat next to her.

Jo set her coffee cup on the table, pulled a notebook from her bag, and laid it in front of her. "It's nice that you have friends who care so much about you."

Lisa's eyes flicked to Samantha, who stood in the archway. She sniffled and reached behind her to grab a box of tissues from a sleek black credenza along the wall. She dabbed her eyes then wiped her nose. "Yes, it is."

"Is it okay if I sit with her while she does this?" Samantha asked.

"Sure, that's fine," Jo replied. *Easier for Lynae to keep an eye on you.*

Samantha settled into the seat next to Lisa and wrapped long fingers around Lisa's stubbier ones. Lisa's eyes softened as she squeezed her friend's hand.

Jo rested her arms on the table. "Lisa, I know this is difficult, but can you take me through the events of last night?"

"What do you want to know?"

"Let's start with where you were."

"I was out with some friends. We went for drinks at Grand Rapids Brewing Company."

Jo scribbled the name of the bar in her notebook then flipped the notebook around, laid the pen on top, and slid it across the table. "Could you write down the names of the people you were with?"

Lisa picked up the pen and stared at the paper. "Why? They were with me. They don't know anything."

"This is standard procedure. We'll have to talk to whoever you were with."

Lisa tapped the pen on the table several times then bent over the notebook and neatly wrote three names on the lined paper. She pushed the paper partway back to Jo then pulled it back, added phone numbers behind each name, then pushed it back.

"Thank you. That's helpful," Jo said. "And you were at the bar until you came home?"

Lisa shook her head slightly. "We were having a girls' night out." A tear streaked down her cheek. She swiped at it with the tissue she had wadded in her hand.

"And what time was that? That you left the bar, I mean."

"Um, around ten thirty, I think." She dabbed her eyes and wiped her nose. "I planned to stay out later. I usually do, but I was tired. I don't remember the exact time."

Lynae shifted in her seat. "That's fine. We can check with your friends."

Jo jotted, *Time?* in her notebook next to the friends' names Lisa had provided. She didn't have an official time of death yet, but preliminary said it was around eleven. If Lisa didn't leave the bar until ten thirty, she wasn't the killer. On the other hand, being at the bar provided her with a great alibi if she had a partner.

"Tell me, as best as you can, what happened when you got home."

Lisa sniffled, her lip quivering. "I came in through the garage and didn't notice anything wrong."

"Did you see any unusual footprints outside?" Jo asked.

"I have three teenagers, Lieutenant. I have people coming and going constantly."

"Understood. What happened next?"

"I yelled upstairs to tell Vic I was home, and when he didn't answer, I figured he was sleeping. He doesn't usually..." Her gaze shifted over Jo's shoulder to a window that looked out over the fenced-in yard.

Jo waited a beat to let her collect her thoughts. "He doesn't usually what?"

Lisa blinked rapidly, then her eyes shifted back to Jo. "He worries, so he doesn't usually go to sleep until I'm home. He always asks me to text him when I'm on my way home so that he'll know if it's taking me too long. He worries. Worried," she added quietly.

"And did you text him last night before you came home?" Jo asked.

Lisa shook her head. "I texted him earlier and said I was tired and would probably be home early. I didn't realize until I was home that I had forgotten to text him when I left."

"Okay, what happened next?"

She picked at something dark stuck to the table, concentrating on it like it held the answers to the cosmos's deepest questions. "So I went upstairs to tell him I was home. The shower was running, and I thought that was odd. I went into the bathroom and—" Lisa squeezed her eyes shut and clenched her jaw.

"Take your time," Jo said. She wrote, *Shower on?* in her notes then flipped to a blank page and laid the notebook in her lap.

"I knew he was dead. I just knew. I tried... I..." She stared at her hands, her palms up and her fingers splayed. "There was so much blood. I shook him, and I think I rolled him over. His face..."

Jo pictured the battered face of the once-handsome man. No one should see someone they loved in that condition.

She laid her hand on Lisa's forearm. "Why don't you get her something to drink?" she said to Samantha.

Samantha jerked like she'd been slapped and pushed away from the table. "Of course. Why didn't I think of that?" She bolted to the kitchen, discreetly wiping her eyes on the sleeve of her shirt.

"Did you touch anything else in the bathroom or try to clean it up?"

"I don't think so. Not that I remember." Lisa put her elbows on the table and pressed her fingers to her eyelids, rubbing roughly. "It's all such a blur," she moaned.

Samantha came back into the room with both a glass of water and a cup of coffee. She set them on the table then rubbed her friend's back. "Drink something, hon."

Lisa picked up the glass of water with a shaky hand and managed a sip. She set the cup down and rubbed her eyes with the heels of her hands. "I ran out of the room and called 911. I don't think I touched anything else. If I had come home earlier…"

"Don't torture yourself," Samantha said, pulling Lisa close and wrapping both arms around her.

Jo leaned back and crossed her ankle over her knee. She opened the folder she had taken from her bag, leafed through a few pages, then ran her finger down as she scanned the notes. "Your 911 call came in at 11:52."

Lisa sat up, moving away from Samantha, and eyeballed Jo. "Okay…"

"But you left the bar at ten thirty?"

"I stopped at the store on my way home. I put the groceries away before I went up to talk to Vic."

Jo ran her tongue across her back teeth while jotting that information in her notebook. "You went to which store?"

"Louie's," Lisa said quickly.

Jo kept her groan internal. Louie's was a little mom-and-pop store on the northeast side. It was her go-to for fresh fruits and vegetables in the spring, and she wouldn't buy meat anywhere else, which was why she knew they didn't have security cameras. "And you have a receipt for your purchase?"

Samantha threw her hands in the air. "Come on, Jo! Are you kidding?"

Jo raised her eyebrows and stared blandly. "I'm doing my job, Samantha."

"By interrogating Lisa?"

"By making sure she has what will be required to prove her innocence. I'm not the only one who reviews the evidence."

Lisa laid her hand on Samantha's knee. "It's okay." She turned back to Jo. "I don't have a receipt. I never keep them for groceries, I toss them on the way out the door."

Jo cocked her head and flicked her gaze to Samantha, who was chewing on the inside of her lip. "Okay. That's all I needed to know."

Jo made a note to check with Louie's. Maybe someone would remember seeing her there, or perhaps by some miracle, they'd added security cameras since she was last there.

Lynae cleared her throat. "Did you notice anything missing or out of place in your house?"

Lisa shook her head. "I didn't look."

Jo scribbled, *Didn't notice the tossed room?*

"I noticed in Victor's office that he had a docking station but no laptop," Jo said.

"He had a laptop. It's always in his office."

"We didn't find a laptop anywhere in the house. Did he ever keep it at the church or in his car?"

"No, it was always in his office," Lisa replied, knitting her brow. "He didn't even use it out in the rest of the house. He worried about the sensitive things he talked to his patients about."

"Do you know who he counseled?" Lynae asked.

"No, he didn't talk about it at all."

"That would be a breach of confidentiality and unethical," Samantha added indignantly.

Jo eyeballed Samantha for a heartbeat, surprised by the heat in her voice. To Lisa, she said, "We're going to need for you to come back to the house and see if anything else is missing. It will be hard, but if we can trace anything, it could help us find the person responsible."

"Do you think this was a robbery?" Samantha asked.

"If his laptop is missing, we can assume whoever came into the house stole it. As far as we're aware right now, that's the only thing missing. But we can't make a call like that until we have more information," Jo said.

"It sure seems like a robbery, but I'll do whatever I have to do."

"Couldn't I do that? Go through the house, I mean?" Samantha asked.

Jo shook her head. "It's better if someone who lives in the house does it. You wouldn't be able to identify every item."

Lisa sighed. "It's okay. I can do it."

"Can you think of anyone who may have wanted to hurt your husband, Mrs. Manton?" Lynae asked.

Lisa stared at her coffee cup. "No," she whispered.

"Did he have an encounter with anyone, perhaps someone from the church he had a disagreement with?"

Lisa's eyes grew wide. "No one from the church would do this. They loved him."

"Okay." Jo made a note to call the parish office and get a list of parishioners. Lisa might believe everyone loved her husband, the pastor, but others could see things differently.

A young man shuffled into the room. His solid upper body was shirtless, the waistband of his red Polo underwear visible above his baggy sweatpants. His honey-blond hair stood on end, his half-closed eyes unfocused. As he pulled up short, he scanned the group of women at the table, then his gaze landed on Samantha. He crossed his arms over his chest and tucked his hands into his armpits. His gaze shifted to his mom. "What's going on?"

Lisa pushed her chair back and stood up. "Ethan, these are detectives. They're asking me some questions." She laid a hand on her son's back and pushed him toward the kitchen. "Why don't you get something to eat and take it back upstairs."

Ethan shoved his hands into the pockets of his sweatpants and lumbered into the kitchen.

Lisa flopped back into the chair and rubbed her hands together, pressing her fingers roughly into the back of her hand. She stared toward the kitchen. "He doesn't quite know how to handle this. He's nineteen, in college. He shouldn't have to deal with this. It's hard."

"I'm sure it is," Jo replied. "I'd like to talk to him and your daughters when we're finished."

"They weren't here last night. They can't possibly have anything that will help you."

"You never know what may help."

Lisa shook her head. "I don't think it's a good idea. It will just upset them."

Jo decided to let it go for the moment. Ethan was an adult, so she could talk to him anytime. No reason to do it with an upset mom.

"It can wait, since the kids are having a hard time," Jo said.

"My daughters are taking it worse," Lisa said, her eyes flicking toward the upstairs. "They're younger, so I'm sure it seems like Vic's been a part of their life longer. Ethan was a teenager when we got married."

"Did Ethan and your husband have a good relationship?" Lynae asked.

Lisa shrugged. "Vic tried, and I think he was getting somewhere, but Ethan hasn't made it easy."

"Is Ethan close to his father?"

"No," Lisa said on a sigh. "My ex-husband doesn't come around much. He did more when the kids were younger but never consistently. When I married Vic, he stopped coming altogether for a while."

"That must have been hard for the kids," Jo said.

"It certainly didn't help Vic build a relationship with the kids. They... Well, mostly Ethan blamed him for making their dad stay away." Lisa picked the tissue up from the table and dabbed her eyes. "After a while, Vic stopped trying to correct him and just accepted the blame. It was hard on him, but he said Ethan needed an outlet, and better him than someone else or, heaven forbid, something dangerous."

"He sounds like a good man," Jo said. She wondered if Ethan felt the same.

"He was," Lisa mumbled and squeezed Samantha's hand.

Samantha wrapped her other arm around Lisa's shoulders and pulled her close. "Someday, Gilly will understand how hard he tried."

"Speaking of that nickname, so that's his baseball bag hanging in your entryway?" Lynae asked.

"That's his old one from when he played in high school. He plays for Ferris State now."

"That's impressive," Jo said while noting that it would also make him very good with a baseball bat.

"This next question is difficult, but I have to ask," Jo said carefully. "Were you having any problems in your marriage? Is there any reason to believe there could be another woman involved?"

Lisa lowered her eyes. "I don't think so. But I've been down that road before, and I had no clue what was happening right under my nose. So I'll never again say no with absolute certainty."

"Understood." Jo looked her in the eye. "But you have no reason to believe that Victor was anything but faithful."

Lisa shook her head while a tear rolled down her cheek.

"And you?"

"Seriously, Jo?" Samantha hissed.

Ignoring Samantha, Jo waited with her pen poised above her notebook.

Lisa swiped at her cheek with the heel of her hand. "No, Detective, I was not having an affair."

Jo closed her notebook and reached around to drop it into the bag that hung from her chair. She would have to chew on the information for a while. Some of Lisa's answers seemed prepared, but nothing blared at her yet. "Okay, those are all the questions I have for you. Do you have any for me?"

"When do you want me to go through the house?"

"Whenever you're ready."

"It's going to be hard. I think you should wait," Samantha said.

Jo raised her chin and leveled Samantha with a stare that told her to stay out of it. "Actually, it's better if it's done sooner rather than later. If we're going to trace anything, we have to get a jump on it."

"I want to get it over with. Then I don't have to think about it anymore, and I can plan..." Lisa closed her eyes and pressed a hand against her lips.

"I can go anytime," Jo said.

"I'd like to go right now before I lose my nerve and quite possibly my mind with it."

"We'll get through it together," Samantha said.

"I'm afraid you won't be able to go with us," Jo interjected.

"Why not?" Samantha asked indignantly.

"It's a crime scene. I can't have multiple people tromping through it."

"I won't leave her side or touch anything."

"I'm sorry, but you can't."

"It's okay." Lisa dropped her head to her friend's shoulder. "I can do it."

"We'll head right over there and meet you," Jo said as she pushed her chair back. "No hurry."

Lisa swiped both hands under her eyes while Samantha stood and motioned toward the entryway. Jo and Lynae followed her to the door.

Samantha glanced over her shoulder. "Is it really a good idea for her to go back there already?"

Jo used the same hushed tone. "Everyone handles it differently. She wants to get it over with, so that's what we'll do. And as I said, the sooner the better."

"I don't like it," Samantha huffed.

"I understand." Jo opened the door. "But you're going to have to let us do our jobs."

Samantha looked from Jo to Lynae then dropped her shoulders and dragged Jo into a hug. It caught Jo off guard, and she tensed, gripping her bag with one hand while the other hand hung awkwardly at her side.

"I'm glad it's you taking care of Lisa," Samantha said before pulling away.

"We'll do everything we can," Jo said then slipped out the door and hustled to the truck.

As Jo put the truck in gear, Lynae eyed her. "I've been on the receiving end of a Jo hug, and you're good at it, like your mom. Whatever that was..." She swirled her arms. "Was not a Jo hug."

"I wasn't expecting it."

"Yeah, okay, but..."

Jo tightened her grip on the steering wheel. "Let's just get to the Mantons' house and not worry about that right now."

"But—"

"Please, Nae?"

Lynae narrowed her eyes then turned to face forward. "Okay, whatever." She slouched down and concentrated on her cell phone.

Jo maintained her neutral expression but mentally rolled her eyes. Nae had a flair for drama. "It's not a big deal, and I'll tell you. But we're only a few minutes from the Mantons' house."

"Well, if you hadn't wasted so much time not telling me, we would have had time."

She had a point. "My bad," Jo said as she exited the busy street and drove into the Mantons' neighborhood.

Lynae scowled. "Yeah, well, don't let it happen again."

Parked outside the Mantons' house, Jo used her phone to check her email while Lynae was absorbed in something on her phone.

After a few minutes, she glanced in the rearview mirror as a car approached. "She's here."

They got out of the truck and approached Lisa's car. Glancing in the window, Jo noted she was sending a text but was unable to see to whom. She rapped gently on the window. Lisa jolted and shoved the phone into her coat pocket.

Opening the door, Lisa pushed her hair away from her face. After she'd closed the door, she shoved her hands into her pockets and stared at the house. With a resigned sideways glance, she said, "I guess we'd better get this over with."

Jo laid a hand on her shoulder. "When you're ready."

"If you find something missing, say it out loud. I'll keep a list for you," Lynae said.

Lisa hesitated at the door then steeled herself and pushed it open. Running her hand along the countertop and the back of a stool, she glanced around the kitchen and shook her head. "I was in this room that night. There's nothing missing here."

"When you're ready, we'll move to the bedrooms," Jo said.

Lifting her chin and setting her jaw, Lisa eyed the stairway as if it might come to life and devour her. She inhaled deeply through her nose and blew it out in one quick puff. "Okay, I can do this."

"Take your time."

They followed her up the stairs and into the master bedroom. Standing in the middle of the room, the front of her shirt gripped in her fist, Lisa stared at the bed, which had been laid bare by the forensic techs. A fine white powder covered every surface. Her face ashen, Lisa wavered then stumbled.

Jo bolted and caught her before she hit the floor then led her to the bed and gently eased her onto the edge. "Maybe we should see if someone else can do this." She laid a hand on Lisa's leg.

Shaking her head, Lisa pushed to her feet and donned an air of determination. "No, I can do it. This room is the hardest." She flicked her gaze to the bathroom door then squeezed her eyes shut and turned her head away.

Glancing in the same direction, Jo said, "I know, and I'm sorry. Do you keep anything in here that someone would be looking for? If not, we can move on."

"Not that I know of. But I can't imagine what we have that anyone would want that badly." She flung a hand at the dresser. "I have some jewelry. Only a couple of pieces that are worth anything."

The image of the gold earring embedded in Victor's chest flittered through Jo's mind. "Why don't you go through it and see if anything is missing?"

Hoping for a reaction, Jo watched her paw through the jewelry box. She knew full well that if the earring found at the crime scene belonged to Lisa, she wouldn't report it missing, but Jo hoped she would at least be able to get a read on whether she was searching for something in particular.

Lisa opened the tiny top drawer of the small wooden jewelry box. Her movements became jerky as she pushed the jewelry around, then she finally pulled the drawer all the way out and dumped it onto the floor.

"My grandma's wedding ring. The necklace Vic gave me for our wedding. They're not in here." She pushed the jewelry around on the floor. "They're not here."

"Can you describe them for me?" Lynae asked.

Jo tuned out while Lisa described the jewelry to Lynae, as she could read her notes later. She was genuinely surprised pieces were missing. The crime scene didn't read as a robbery to her. Unless her instincts were off, it was staged. Most likely, the person who'd staged it grabbed some jewelry to make it more convincing.

"Is there anything else missing?" Lynae asked, and Jo tuned back in.

"Those are the only things I had, besides my wedding ring, that are worth any money. The only things that really matter to me." She half-heartedly sifted through the rest of the jewelry. "I don't think there's anything else gone. I don't remember everything I have. And like I said, none of it was worth anything."

"They left Victor's watch on the nightstand," Jo said.

Lisa's brow furrowed as her head whipped around to the nightstand. "It was there?"

"Is that unusual?" Jo asked.

"He usually puts it there when he goes to bed."

"That watch is quite valuable."

"He said someone from church gave it to him."

The statement and her tone were unconvincing. Lisa obviously didn't believe her own words.

"Did he say who?"

"No, and I didn't ask." Lisa shrugged and moved to the nightstand. She ran her hand down the gold frame holding the picture of her family and drew in a shaky breath.

Jo laid a hand on her arm. "Why don't we get out of this room?"

"I don't have to go into the bathroom?" Lisa asked, warily eyeing the bathroom door.

"No, I don't see any reason to go in there."

"Good. I don't think I can."

Jo led her out of the room and into the hallway that separated the house from the office. "As I mentioned earlier, we didn't find a computer in your husband's office."

"He was so careful with it. I can't imagine, but I guess he could have left it in his car."

"We searched his car," Jo said, shaking her head. "Do you know what kind of laptop he had? Did he have it password protected?"

"He had a ThinkPad. I think they call it a Yoga. And yes, he had a password. He could open it with his fingerprint or a password. No one was allowed to touch it. He had personal information about his patients on it."

Someone could be after the personal information about his patients. Or a patient may have exposed a secret they wanted to keep hidden. She would have to tread lightly to get patient information, but it was going to be necessary.

Lisa walked through the rest of the rooms, opening drawers and looking through closets. "I don't think they took anything else," she said to Lynae.

Jo hid the defeat she felt and concentrated on what they had. "We'll see if we can track the missing items. If you find that one of the kids has the laptop, or you find it somewhere, please let us know. Until then, we'll be actively pursuing any leads on it as well as the jewelry."

"I'm sure the kids don't have it. They have their own laptops, and they know better than to touch Victor's."

When they reached the door, Lisa stopped suddenly. "Can I take anything out of the house?"

"I'm sorry. You really can't."

"Just some pictures for the funeral?"

"Oh, of course."

Jo followed her back to a closet in the upstairs hall, where she gathered a couple of boxes of pictures and their wedding photo album.

"We'll be able to clear the house soon, so you and your kids can come home," Jo said.

Glancing in the direction of their bedroom, Lisa shook her head and blinked back tears. "I could never live here again. As soon as you say it's okay, the house is going on the market. I could never go back into that bedroom again."

Jo understood all too well. Living in the house she and Mike had shared was sometimes hard, but she found comfort in the good memories. If he had died in that house, and she had found him, she would never have set foot in it again.

"If you have everything, let's get out of here," she said.

Chapter 6

After assuring Lisa they would contact her with any new information, Jo and Lynae drove back to the station, where they poured fresh cups of coffee and headed back to Jo's office.

Staring at her nearly empty murder board, Jo said, "Okay, let's go over this. We've got overkill on a pastor who counsels parishioners, and the house is tossed. Though the tossed house feels staged, and it was really only in the bedroom. I'm not buying it. Lisa didn't mention any highly valuable things that were missing. There was no safe. The only things we know of that are missing are a laptop and a few pieces of jewelry."

"When you consider all the things they have in that house, it doesn't make sense to kill someone for only that."

"No, it doesn't," Jo replied. "A laptop isn't worth that much, and the jewelry sounds more sentimental than valuable."

"Unless they were looking for more and ran into a problem. They might have thought the house was empty and were surprised by the victim."

"According to Lisa's initial statement, the shower was running. If you were robbing a house that you thought was empty and heard the shower running, you would go one of two ways. If you were a professional, you would be aware that the shower would cover any noise you were making and also offered you a solid timeline on how long you had. If you were an amateur, you would bolt at the sound of the shower and be happy with whatever you had."

"In neither of those scenarios would you go into the bathroom and do this"—Lynae tapped a knuckle on the crime-scene photo of Victor Manton that Jo had taped to the murder board—"to the homeowner."

"No, you wouldn't. If this is a robbery, it doesn't add up. And most likely, you wouldn't even hit up the bedroom if there was someone in the bathroom. You would avoid it altogether."

"Unless there was something in particular you were looking for."

Jo pointed at Lynae. "That's the only reason you would take that chance. For my money, it's the laptop. It may not be valuable, but what's on it might be important."

"Lisa said the laptop never left his office. Why would someone go up to the bedroom to look for it?"

"Not everyone would know he kept it in his office. Besides, if it's a straight robbery, there would be no reason to kill the homeowner, who's in the bathroom with the shower running."

"Unless the homeowner caught you and came after you," Lynae said.

"Doesn't fit with Manton's injuries. They're all self-defense."

"So the house being tossed is a setup."

Jo nodded. "No doubt in my mind. It's classic, if you're someone who watches made-for-television crime shows. Drawers open, clothes hanging out, some thrown onto the floor. What do people even think someone would look for in a person's dresser?"

"Isn't that where you keep your best stuff?"

"Yeah, because I want my prized possessions nestled in with my underwear." Jo scoffed. "And with all that tossing, there was an expensive watch left on the nightstand and a lot of jewelry left behind in that jewelry box. It might not have been worth a lot, but if you're robbing a house, you grab and go."

"What about the weapon?"

"Another reason I don't think it's random. The injuries read like a billy club or a baseball bat. He brings the weapon and takes it with him. First smart thing I've seen. No weapon, no prints. It's possible he kept it as a little souvenir of what he did, but most likely he'll dump it. If we find it in a dumpster somewhere, it will probably have been wiped clean."

"Why do you think he'll dump it instead of keep it?" Lynae asked.

After pushing herself to her feet, Jo went to the murder board and studied the picture of Victor's battered face. "This doesn't read as a thrill kill, a serial, or a robbery. It reads as anger. It's personal. And neither of those is a time when people keep souvenirs."

"Victor was an intended target, and someone knew what they were doing."

"Exactly. And that someone knew the house would be empty except for Victor. It's not a coincidence that this happened during a girls' night out. Someone planned it that way."

Lynae cocked her head. "You mean someone like his wife?"

"I mean exactly like his wife. Her timeline is off."

"You don't buy that she went shopping on the way home? That wouldn't be unusual."

"It seems convenient that she had to fill a time gap, and she happened to have stopped for groceries that she hadn't mentioned, that she had no receipt for, and that she conveniently put away before she found her murdered husband."

"I see your point."

"And at a place that has no security cameras," Jo said as she prowled the small space. "And the shower was off."

"So?"

"Lisa said she heard the shower running, but according to the first responders, the shower was not on when they entered the bathroom. Did Lisa turn it off?"

Lynae shrugged. "She could have."

Jo spread her hands and imitated finding something in front of her. "You find your husband beaten to death on the floor, and you think, *I'd better turn that shower off*? No, you freak out. You try to revive him. You're in total disbelief and denial. What you don't do is turn off the shower."

"People do weird things when they're in shock. It could have been an automatic response. Like, 'The shower's on. I have to turn it off, or Vic will complain about the water bill.' At the same time, you're hyperventilating because Vic is lying in a pool of blood on the floor. I've seen people do some crazy shit when they were in shock. And the groceries don't bother me. Again, shock. She's trying to think of all the minutiae when the biggest event of your life just happened."

"Yeah, that happens," Jo said. "Or she didn't go to the store and was actually home an hour before the call to the police. That's enough time to kill her husband, clean up the bathroom, and toss the house. Grab a few easy-to-hide items to make it look like a robbery, smash a window so that there's a forced entry..."

"And you have an amateur-looking staged robbery that, to the TV-drama-educated person, is the perfect scene for a dead body."

"Bingo," Jo said, raising her pointer finger above her head.

Lynae's face scrunched. "But why? Do you think she's got another man? Is there a huge life insurance policy out on him?"

"My bet would be money. Stranger things have happened, but after the cheating ex, I don't think Lisa would go the adultery route."

Shrugging, Lynae said, "People can be weird."

"No doubt about that, but let's start with a solid dig on finances. I'll see what I can find out about a boyfriend."

"Why do you get all the fun stuff?" Lynae whined.

"Because I make the assignments."

"There's that." Lynae settled on the corner of Jo's desk. "Are you ready for the meeting with Rick?"

Jo closed her eyes and bit the inside of her lip. "I have so many things to say and ask, starting with 'Why did you set my husband up to be murdered?' I also have visions of doing nothing more than walking in, bashing his face into the table, and walking out. I guess I'll know which way I'll go when the time comes."

Lynae laughed, then the humor faded away. "You won't actually do that, right?"

Raising an eyebrow, Jo asked, "Will I actually smash a handcuffed man's face into a table in a jail interrogation room?"

"I mean, I wouldn't blame you, but..."

Jo stared at the wall above Lynae's shoulder. She could see it, his hands cuffed to the table, her towering over him, grabbing him by the hair on the back of his head, and pouring every ounce of anger and despair she'd experienced for the past two and a half years into smashing his face into the Formica-topped table. She could almost feel the crunch of his nose and see the blood fly. They would arrest her, of course, but it might be worth it.

She forced the image back to the primal place in her brain that desired physical revenge. She tried to visit it only when she was safely tucked away at home and couldn't act on it.

"No, I won't actually do that." She sighed. "He's a narcotics officer who abused the system and is now housed with a lot of the men he locked up. I'll have to be satisfied with what that means."

Lynae shuddered. "There really are worse things than death. And that's what that bastard deserves."

Jo managed a weak smile. "Yes, it is. Besides, there's more to it than he's giving up, and I want it."

"Maybe that he's willing to talk to you means he's ready to dish it out."

"Who knows? Maybe the son of a bitch will tell me to stop trying and that he'll never talk to me." Jo reached into the bottom drawer of her desk, rustled around until she found a granola bar, and extended it to her partner with a raised eyebrow. Lynae crinkled her nose and shifted in her seat, attempting to look into the drawer.

Jo smirked and dug back into the drawer then came up with a Snickers bar and a king-sized Reese's. Lynae snatched the Reese's and had the orange wrapper opened and the crinkle paper removed before Jo could close the drawer.

Pushing her chair back, Jo propped her feet on her desk. She peeled back the foil wrap from her granola bar and considered her friend as she downed the first cup and moved to the second. "How do you manage?"

Lynae swallowed and wiped chocolate from the corners of her mouth with her hand. "Manage what?"

Jo flung a hand in her direction. "To eat like you do yet have all that going on?"

Lynae waved her off. "Good genes, I guess."

"Bitch," Jo grumbled before taking another bite of her granola bar. The dry oats stuck to the roof of her mouth and clawed at her throat, something she hadn't noticed before Lynae opened the Reese's.

Lynae snorted and popped the last bite of chocolate into her mouth. "Said the tall, skinny chick with the hot boyfriend."

"I have to work hard for it, though." Jo wadded the wrapper and tossed it into the trash can then threw a devious grin Lynae's way. "And he *is* hot."

"Who's hot?" came a smooth baritone.

Jo's gaze shot to the doorway. She dropped her feet to the floor and lifted an eyebrow. "Wouldn't you like to know?"

Jack sauntered into the office with three coffee cups in a cardboard carrier. Blond tufts of his perpetually unruly hair stuck out of a stocking cap that matched his heavy coat. He pulled a cup out and handed it to Lynae then set the carrier on Jo's desk. Planting his palms on the arms of her chair, he kissed her tenderly. "I feel like I have at least a small stake in knowing."

Giving him a half smile, Jo crooked her finger and said, "Maybe, but I'm not quite convinced yet."

As Jack leaned in for another kiss, Lynae groaned. "Ick, quit it." Getting to her feet, she said, "I'm going back to my desk to concentrate on things that don't make me want to vomit, like murder and stuff." She held up the cup as she made her exit. "Thanks for the coffee, Jack."

Jack threw his head back and laughed deviously as Lynae marched out the door. He dropped into the visitor seat across from Jo's desk and sprawled his long legs out in front of him. "Works every time."

"Yet she asks me all about us at every opportunity."

"And what do you tell her?" He ran a hand through his already-messy hair.

Wagging her finger at him, she said, "Nope, there are some things you don't get to know."

"That's probably best. Of course, I would like some intel on this hot guy."

"I bet you would." Jo pulled out the cup that had Jo written in black marker. Jack had figured out early in their relationship that the way to her heart was through coffee that didn't come from the station. Bringing a cup for her partner was a bonus that endeared him to her even more. She savored a sip then held the warm cup in both hands. "So, is this a social call?"

Jack shrugged. "Not entirely, but it's a call that could have been handled over the phone. Of course, then I couldn't have brought you coffee."

Jo took another sip of the just-right blend. He must have paid close attention, because getting the right amount of sweetener and cream was a trick that he had mastered. "What's up?"

"You're going to the jail tomorrow. I thought I'd check in on you."

Jo furrowed her brow. "We already talked about this."

"Yep, just seeing how you're feeling about it."

Setting her cup on the desk, she leveled her gaze at him. "I told you I would behave."

"I know—"

"I'm not going to do anything stupid, Jack. I'm not an idiot."

Jack held up both hands, palms out. "Jo, relax. I just—"

Jumping to her feet, she threw both hands in the air, anger spouting from the long-dormant volcano. "Are you kidding me? Relax? I'm finally about to talk to the man who masterminded my husband's murder, and you're telling me to relax? What the—" She closed her eyes and pinched the bridge of her nose then flopped back into her seat. "I'm sorry."

"It's okay."

"No, it's not. It's not okay. I have no right to rail at you."

Jack rested his arms on his knees and stared at his folded hands. "You have no idea how often I railed at God for taking Laura."

Jo got up and hustled around her desk. Squatting in front of him, she laid a hand on his leg. "It has to be even harder when you can't confront the one you blame. It's not like you can get on God's visitor list."

"I'm not making this about me. I just mean I understand."

"It's okay to make it about you sometimes. You never do. I selfishly make it about me because I have someone to blame other than God and some horrible disease."

Jack lifted his head, his green eyes softening. "You're the least selfish person I've ever met."

"I don't know how you can say that. I'm blowing up at you for caring, acting like you don't understand what it's like to love someone and lose them. I'm freaking out about this meeting, and I get all"—she circled her hands in front of her stomach, searching for the right word—"knotted up."

"We all do that."

"Do you? Because all I ever see is this calm guy who's got it all together. Whether you're the big-shot prosecutor or you're wrangling your kids, you handle it like a boss. I don't know how you do it."

Jack dropped his eyes and stared at the floor. "Not always, but I have to keep it together for the kids."

"You're a good dad. But you never talk to me about it. About Laura. I wish you would."

He shook his head. "Talking about it isn't really my thing. When I'm not yelling at God, I take it out at the gym."

Jo cocked an eyebrow and squeezed his leg. "That explains a lot."

A grin played on his lips. "Just behave today, all right?"

"I will. I promise. But I mean it... I wish you would talk to me. I understand a lot of what you're going through."

"I know you do."

She stood and scooted onto the edge of her desk. "I'm on a new case as of last night, so I may be a bit unpredictable for a while."

"Gee, that's new."

"I mean my schedule, smart-ass."

"Understood. I'm getting used to it." Jack stood and gazed down at her. "Stop by when you can, though. The kids ask about you."

Jo's heart hummed. "They do?"

"Every day. They adore you."

"Well, that feeling is mutual." Jo stood on her tiptoes and gave him a quick kiss. "Now, get out of here. I have stuff to do."

"Yes, ma'am."

Jack sauntered out and nodded at greetings from officers in the bullpen as he made his way to the elevator.

Jo did a quick internet search of things to do with kids in Grand Rapids and made a list of a few fun options. Johnson Park sledding might be a bit much for Logan, but Maddie would love it. The Grand

Rapids Children's Museum was always a hit, so she kept that in her back pocket in case the weather didn't cooperate.

"Most people don't grin like that when they're researching murder," Lynae said from the doorway.

"I didn't realize I was grinning."

Lynae tapped her pen on the yellow legal pad she was holding. "Just sayin', people might start thinking you're a little creepy."

Jo closed her internet browser and shifted her face into a serious scowl. "How's this?"

"Better."

"Do you have something on finances already?"

Lynae ripped the top page from the legal pad and handed Jo the paper. "Pretty easy search. The pastor was making an average income from the parish. Pretty much in line with what other pastors earn."

Jo glanced at Lynae's scribbled notes. "Decent but barely enough to afford payments on that house they're living in. And that's if they really stretched the budget. Not enough to afford any extras like an expensive watch or to save for college. What about Lisa's income?"

"Zip. She worked in human resources at Weller Auto until she married Victor. She quit that job right after the honeymoon and hasn't worked since."

"Did you find anything interesting?"

"Indeed, I did. Victor has a significant amount of money in an account that is only in his name. Four equal monthly payments are made to it, and all are deposited in cash."

"Cash? And no explanation for where it came from anywhere in his finances?"

"Nope."

"Hmm, what were you into, Victor?" Jo muttered, staring at the picture of her battered victim. In her experience, equal cash payments deposited to a personal account rarely meant anything legal.

"Did you dig up anything on Lisa being involved with anyone else?" Lynae asked.

"Um, no, I haven't actually started that yet." Jo was a little embarrassed that her partner had done so much work, and she had nothing to show for her time.

"Working on something else? What else do we have going?"

Jo glanced guiltily at her computer. "I've been working on finding a fun place to take a couple of little kids."

"Oh! John Ball Park Zoo has winter hours, and I heard they do some cool stuff for the kids."

"Good idea. I'll add it to the list. Now I'm putting that away," Jo said, folding the list and shoving it into her back pocket.

After pulling her notebook from her bag, she flipped to Lisa's list of names. "Let's talk to the friends on this list and see where the timeline breaks down."

She jotted two of the names onto a separate piece of paper. "You call these two, and I'll get the other three. See if you can get them talking. Besides the timeline, what do they remember as far as Lisa's behavior or if they're aware of a side piece. You know the drill."

Lynae snatched the paper from Jo's hand and headed back to her desk.

Jo drew a chart in her notebook and titled columns with Location, Time, Attitude, and Notes. She included the names of each person on her list on the left side then dialed the first number.

A husky voice came on the line after two rings. "Hello?"

Jo glanced at her paper. "Is this Janice Clark?"

"Yes, it is. Who's this?"

"This is Lieutenant Jo Riskin, Grand Rapids homicide. I'd like to ask you a few questions."

"Oh, wow, okay. This must be about Lisa's husband, right?"

Lisa's husband. She doesn't know him well. "Yes, ma'am, it is."

"I mean, I don't know anything."

"I understand. This is a routine follow-up."

"Okay. I'll answer whatever I can," Janice said hesitantly.

"I appreciate it. You were with Lisa Tuesday night. Is that correct?"

"Yeah, we... I mean a bunch of us... were together."

"And where were you again?" Jo asked as if she couldn't remember.

"We were at the bar, um, Grand Rapids Brewing."

Jo put a check mark next to Location in her notes. She kept her tone conversational. "That's one of my favorite bars. I go there with my friends too. That game room in the back is great."

Janice chuckled then broke into a cough. Jo waited through the hacking while the phone was clearly held away from the woman's mouth.

When the coughing jag ended, the husky voice came back on the line. "Sorry about that."

"No problem. Sounds like a rough cold you're dealing with."

"I wish that were what it was. Too many years of smoking is what I'm dealing with."

Jo managed a sympathetic noncommittal sound. "So, girls' night out? Everyone was having a good time?"

"Yeah, I mean, Lisa left early, but the rest of us stuck around till pretty late."

Jo sat a little straighter in her seat. "Is Lisa typically the early bird?"

"Not normally that early, but she's usually the first one to go. Her husband—"

Jo waited for her to finish, and when it appeared she wasn't going to, she prodded. "What about her husband?"

"I don't mean anything bad," the woman blurted.

"Of course not. Did Victor not care for Lisa going out, or did he simply want her to be home early?"

"He expected her home at a *respectable* time. I think he was worried about the image. You know, the pastor's wife. She had to play the part, and being in the bar too late or drinking too much didn't fit the role."

"How did Lisa like playing that role?"

"She never seemed, like, upset about it, but I don't think she liked leaving early either. It was just one of those things."

"Sure, just one of those concessions," Jo added.

"Yeah, that's what I would call it."

"Do you remember what time Lisa left?"

"Oh man, it was probably only nine thirty or so."

"That *is* early." Jo jotted the time on her chart and circled it. Lisa had said ten thirty. That was a significant difference. *Did she make a mistake, or was it intentional? Or is Janice the one who's mixed up?*

"Earlier than usual."

"What time is the usual?"

"More like eleven. We teased her about going early, but she was like, 'Whatever, I gotta go.' It breaks my heart what she went home to."

Jo absently drew circles around the time. "It's a terrible thing, for sure." She checked the names on her list. "Can you tell me who else was there with you?"

Janice rattled off the same names that were listed in Jo's notebook.

"Does Samantha Givens ever come with you?"

"No, never. Lisa always invites her, but she doesn't come. Lisa knows her from church. Maybe she doesn't agree with being in a bar either."

Jo jotted *Samantha?* in her notebook. The Samantha she'd known in college wasn't afraid to knock back a few drinks. But that was another lifetime. "Do you go to Lisa's church also?"

"Yes, I do. A couple of the other women do, too, but we're not like a church group going out or anything. It's just where we met each other."

"Is Lisa social with a lot of people from the church?"

"Very much so. She's on the social committee along with a couple of other committees. She's always involved when something is going on at the church."

"Sounds like she keeps pretty busy."

"Well, she's the pastor's wife, and it's kind of part of the job description."

"Do you think she enjoys that part of the job?" Jo asked.

"She seems to, but I think sometimes it's a bit much for her. There's an image to uphold, and that's always hard."

Jo jotted *Image* in her notebook in the notes column. Janice had made more than one comment about the image the pastor required his wife to keep. It might be a reason to go out and be wild or possibly get a divorce. It didn't feel like a reason to murder. "I'm sure it is. Is there anyone in particular she's especially close to?"

"The group of us who were together last night are probably her closest friends. And Samantha, of course."

"So if anything was going on in her life, if she was unhappy or anything was upsetting her, your group would be who she would talk to?"

"Yeah, for sure," Janice said immediately.

"How would you describe Lisa and Victor's marriage? Were they happy?"

"Sure. I mean, as happy as people are," she said hesitantly.

"Were there problems in their marriage?" Jo prodded.

"No, not problems. Their marriage wasn't perfect, but what marriage is?"

"Was Lisa happy?"

"Yes, I think she finally was."

"Finally?" Jo asked.

"She was cautious after what happened with her first husband. I mean, who wouldn't be?"

Jo scribbled *Trust* and circled it. "So trust may have been an issue?"

"Sure. That rat bastard really messed her up. And her kids too. It was hard on all of them."

"Was Lisa's ex a problem for her and Victor?"

"You mean other than being a selfish lowlife?" Janice spat.

Janice's loyalty to Lisa rivaled Nae's loyalty to Jo and made her smile. "I mean was he threatening? Did he cause problems for them?"

Janice gasped. "You think Dave did this? That son of a—"

"I'm just trying to get a clear picture of Victor's life."

"I can't think of anyone who would hurt him. He's a great guy."

"No problems with anyone at the church that you're aware of?"

"I can't imagine that. Everyone loves him. He's not only a pastor. He's been a counselor to several people."

Jo knew all about his so-called counseling with Lisa. "I've heard he counsels members of the parish but no one outside. Is that right?"

"I don't really know, but I do know some people who have gone to him for help. Lisa's friend Samantha..."

"What about Samantha?" Jo asked.

"She went to him when her marriage was on the rocks, but I shouldn't have said anything. I'm just babbling. It has nothing to do with this."

Jo wrote Samantha's name followed by an arrow then *Marriage counseling.* "Anything you can tell me may help. I can at least follow up with Samantha and her husband about their impression of him as a counselor."

"Oh, her husband wouldn't go. Samantha went by herself."

Marriage counseling without the spouse?

Jo tapped her pen on her notebook. "I'll be sure to check into his patients. That could be helpful."

Janice sighed loudly. "I don't know about that. Just find whoever did this. Lisa's been through enough."

"I intend to."

Jo thanked her for her time and hung up. She spent the next forty minutes talking to the other two women on her list and getting the same basic information. When she had finished all her calls, she grabbed her notes and headed into the bullpen. Lynae sat at her desk, tapping on her keyboard. She looked up and tucked back a strand of dark hair that had fallen out of the messy bun holding the thick mass in place.

"Lisa always leaves first, but last night it was earlier than usual. There's no other man, and she acted normal."

"Yep, same story I got," Lynae said.

"I wonder why she left so early last night."

"Tired, didn't feel well, trying to get home to her husband…"

"Right. There are plenty of legitimate reasons." Rhythmically tapping her notebook on her knee, Jo asked, "Did either of the women you talked to mention Pastor Vic doing marriage counseling?"

"Yeah, they both did. Why? Did you hear something wonky?"

Jo lifted an eyebrow. "Wonky?"

Lynae crossed her arms. "Yep, I said it. Wonky."

"No, I didn't hear anything *wonky*, really. One of the women…" Jo flipped through her notes and found the name. "Janice Clark mentioned that Samantha went to him for marriage counseling. But only she went. Seemed odd to me."

Lynae shrugged. "I think that happens quite a bit. One or the other spouse won't go to counseling, so one goes by themselves and tries to at least attempt to resolve some issues. Even if it's only their own."

"I guess you're right. It just struck me as strange. I didn't get any vibes that there were any problems with people from the church or anywhere else, for that matter."

"From what I was hearing, the guy was a saint, and everyone loved him."

Narrowing her eyes, Jo said, "We have a dead body that tells me not everyone loved him."

"Yeah, people don't usually do those things to someone because they like them so much."

"I'd like to talk to Lisa again. Hit harder on the timeline and see if she can enlighten us on anyone who had a grudge against him. I might ask Samantha a few questions, also, since she spent some time in counseling with him."

"What do you think she could know from counseling?"

"Probably nothing. But since we're speculating that someone was after whatever was on that laptop, she's as good a suspect as anyone. Plus, she's left-handed."

Lynae's mouth fell open. "For real?"

"Yep. Along with thousands of other people in this area. But it's worth talking to her."

Lynae pulled her coat from the back of her chair. "Might as well get it over with."

"I think it would be better to get her in here this time. We've talked to her in her own element. Let's put her in ours. But she's been through enough today. It's been a long day on a little sleep. Let's pack it in and pick up right here tomorrow."

Flinging her coat back over the chair, Lynae said, "Good. I didn't want to go back out into the snow anyway. Oh wait..."

Jo rolled her eyes. "Yeah, you're gonna have to go out in the snow to get home. I think you might be even more ready for sleep than I am."

"Last night was more like a nap than real sleep."

"Get home, and get some real sleep tonight."

Jo went to her office, packed her bag, and headed home. She could think of nothing better than a hot shower and to curl up with Mojo.

After leaving the station, she decided since Lisa and Janice had given conflicting times, she had enough juice left in her battery to check on the security at Louie's. She drove to the northeast side of town and, noting that the too-small parking lot was full, parked on the street across from the thriving market.

Inside, the aroma of coffee and spices tangoed with fresh baked goods and smoked beef. Jo passed half-bushel baskets filled with candies sold by the pound then meandered down the aisle dedicated to locally brewed ales and beer. She lost herself for a moment, browsing a display of locally canned vegetables and jams with bright Christmas-colored cloth-covered lids and tags.

She made her way to the back of the store, where Louie was posted behind his meat counter. As Jo approached the counter, Louie's face lit up, his cheeks pushing his eyes nearly closed. "Lieutenant! Let me guess—bone-in pork chops, center cut."

Jo laughed. "Am I that predictable, Louie?"

"I'm afraid you are. But at least you have good taste."

"I'm actually here on business. Not that I won't take you up on those pork chops before I go."

Louie's brow furrowed. "What kind of business?"

"Just wondering if you've had a chance to install security cameras yet."

Louie picked up the bottom of his apron and scrubbed his beefy hands while he came around the counter. "Now, you know I haven't, Lieutenant. What would I need those for? Never had a bit of trouble here."

"I know." Jo pulled a picture of Lisa Manton from her bag. "Can you tell me if you saw this woman here Tuesday night?"

Louie took the picture from Jo and studied it. "I see her here every couple of weeks. Can't say I have this week, though."

"Were you working Tuesday night?"

Louie's round gut jiggled before he let out a belly laugh. "If this place is open, I'm here."

"Is anyone else here who would have been working that night?"

"I've got a couple of teenagers who work Tuesday. They're not here tonight."

Jo handed him the picture. "When they come in, see if they saw her here that night."

"Happy to help," Louis said as he slid the picture into a pocket somewhere under the apron. "Now, how about those pork chops?"

"Absolutely." Jo followed him back to the counter and chatted while he got her package ready.

When Jo reached for her wallet, he held up a hand. "Put that away, Lieutenant. You work on keeping the city safe, and I'll work on putting a little meat on your bones."

"Thanks, Louie." Jo held up the package. "This looks like good meat to put on my bones."

Louie roared and waved. Jo could hear him whistling as she left the store.

Chapter 7

The night's sleep, although broken up a little from fighting for space with Jo's bed-hog dog, had her refreshed. After the morning meeting, she finalized paperwork on a couple of cases she was ready to close then focused on her murder board for the Manton case.

"The board is a little anemic," Lynae said from the doorway.

Jo popped to her feet. "Let's see what we can do to fix that. I'd like to get to the coroner's office and see what Kent has to tell us this morning."

Lynae groaned. "Great, my favorite place."

"How many years are you going to be a homicide detective before you get over your squeamishness about the morgue?"

"Says the woman who's afraid of the dentist."

"Well, dentists are terrifying."

"Unbelievable," Lynae muttered. "Give me a minute to grab my stuff."

When Jo's phone vibrated, she glanced at the caller ID. "Hi, Mom."

"Hi, hon. How goes the battle?"

Jo reached for her bag in its usual post tucked under her desk. "It's going pretty brutally right now," she said as she riffled through the bag, checking for the pens, notebook, water bottle, and trail mix that she already knew were there.

"Did you pick up a new case?"

"Sure did, Tuesday night," Jo replied.

"Weren't you going out with the girls?"

"Yeah, it was a great time until it got interrupted. We had most of the night. It's always good to see the girls."

"So that was a late night, and you've probably been going steadily ever since. Did you get any sleep? Did you eat?"

"Really, Mom?" Jo tried to sound annoyed, but she knew her grin came through her voice. "Yes, I ate, and I'm wearing clean underwear, I brushed my teeth, and I said my prayers this morning."

"No need to be snarky. I worry about you. You run yourself ragged."

"I'm fine, Mom. We went home at a decent time last night to catch up on our sleep."

"Well, okay, then I'll let you get back to it. But first, the reason I called is Aunt Trudy is coming to dinner tonight. Why don't you come too?"

Jo rubbed her forehead, where her sleep-deprived body had determined was the ideal place to stab her. "Well..."

"Aunt Trudy wondered if Lynae is available too," her mom interjected.

Jo grabbed her coat from the hook behind her door and wrangled herself into it, adjusting the phone from ear to ear. "Well, then, I guess I'll have to ask Lynae before I can give you an answer."

"You can come without her."

"Now, how would that look?" Jo chortled.

"You're going to have to tell her at some point, you know."

"Tell her what? She assumed that Lynae is my girlfriend. I've never said a word about it!" Jo ran a hand through her hair to pull the strands from the back of her coat then zipped it and removed her gloves from the pockets.

"Exactly. You've never corrected her or mentioned Jack around her, either. You're terrible," her mom scolded her.

"You have to admit it's made things a whole lot easier for me. I haven't had to fend off one blind date, Match-dot-com profile suggestion, or singles dance since she got this wrong impression."

"You could tell her about Jack. That would do the same thing."

"I will soon. But I'm not going to be ready by tonight to answer a million questions or to subject Jack to her."

Jo pulled her truck keys from her coat pocket and swung them around her pointer finger. "Listen, Mom, I have to go. Plan on me tonight, and I'll see what Lynae is up to."

"Not that I don't love seeing Lynae, but why don't you invite Jack instead?" Mom asked. "You have to rip the Band-Aid off at some point."

Jo closed her eyes and pictured the confusion that would bring to Aunt Trudy. "The kids will have to get to bed—"

"I have a spare bedroom with twin beds," her mom interrupted.

"No, Mom, it's just... It's not..."

"You can't hide us forever."

Jo snorted. "I can try."

"I repeat, you're terrible. Think about it. Now, go catch a killer."

"That's the plan. Love you, Mom." She hung up and headed for the bullpen.

Lynae sat on the edge of her desk, engrossed in something on her phone. She looked up with raised eyebrows. "Ready?"

"Sorry, Mom called."

Lynae's face softened. "How is she?"

Jo rolled her head in an exaggerated circle and rubbed the back of her neck. "She's good. Aunt Trudy's coming for dinner tonight, and Mom wants us to come."

Lynae's eyebrows shot up. "Us? As in me too?"

"Yes, you too. What do you think?"

"Um, yes. I'll never turn down a chance to hang out with your family and make you horribly uncomfortable, wondering what I might say."

Jo started pulling her gloves off. "You know, there's a ton of paperwork I should be doing. Why don't you go to the morgue alone?"

Lynae's eyes widened. "What? No!"

"Are you going to behave tonight?"

Crossing her arms, Lynae slouched her shoulders. "Are you serious?"

Jo shot her deadliest glare. "As a heart attack." She pointed toward the elevator and started in that direction.

Lynae pushed away from her desk and trotted to catch up with her. "Fine. I'll behave if it means I get to eat your mom's cooking. But I can't behave too much, or Aunt Trudy will think we're fighting."

"Well, we can't have that, now, can we," Jo said, punching the elevator button.

When the door opened, Lynae stepped back to allow the two officers inside to step out. "So I shouldn't rub your leg or nuzzle your neck?" she said loudly as the officers walked past her.

One officer glanced discreetly over his shoulder.

Jo pressed her lips together and ran her tongue across her teeth. "I will throat punch you," she growled.

After stepping into the elevator, Lynae leaned against the back wall. "Damn, woman. You're scary."

Jo pushed the ground-level button. "You have no idea how scary until you try to nuzzle my neck."

"I think I'll play it safe and take your word on that one," Lynae said as the doors closed.

Chapter 8

J o pushed through the doors of the Kent County coroner's office with Lynae right on her heels. The cast recording of *Les Miserables* played quietly in the background, adding an eerie undertone to the cold, sterile room. Kent Alderink hummed along to the music as he bent over the midsection of a male form displayed on a gleaming metal table.

When Jo cleared her throat, the coroner's head popped up and turned in their direction.

"Hey, Kent," Jo said cheerfully. "What's the word?"

Kent used the back of a gloved hand to lift a protective shield from his face. His blue eyes softened behind silver wire-rimmed glasses that sat midnose. "How about chimerical?"

"Chimerical?" Jo closed her eyes and dug deep for any part of the word that rang a bell. "I think chimeric has to do with DNA from more than one source or something like that," she said, taking a stab at it. She opened her eyes and looked hopefully at Kent.

Kent gave a slight bow of his head in a show of respect. "That is what chimeric means in a general sense."

Jo fist pumped. "Yes!"

"But *chimerical* is a little different."

"Well, that seems unfair."

Kent waggled an index finger. "The English language is rife with unfair. Chimerical means existing only as the product of unchecked imagination," he said grandly, drawing out the last two words.

"Well, that's nothing like chimeric," Jo grumbled. "But I think I could find a time or two to use it."

"That's what it's all about." After removing his bloody gloves, Kent dropped them into a plastic-lined metal trash can at the end of the examination table. He tugged his face shield the rest of the way off and ran a hand over his head in what Jo could only assume was a habit from when there had been hair to tame. "I had a feeling it wouldn't be long before I saw you two."

"We can't stay away, can we, Lynae?"

Lynae's eyes shifted to the table and the body splayed open. The inside was mottled dark against the stark white of the ribcage. A large silver bowl sat on the cart next to Kent, a purple-gray gelatinous globule shimmering inside. "Nope, it's our favorite place," she said with a grimace.

Kent winked conspiratorially at Lynae. "She always forces you to come along, though, doesn't she?"

Glaring at Jo, Lynae said, "Yes. Yes, she does."

Jo shrugged. "Have to get used to it sooner or later."

"Later would be my preference," Lynae mumbled.

Jo rolled her eyes then nodded in the direction of the body. "It looks like we may be a bit early. Do you have anything for us yet?"

Kent wiggled his eyebrows. "Our boy here had a lot to tell me."

A surge of adrenaline pulsed through Jo's body. That was exactly what she'd wanted to hear from the coroner. "No kidding. Like what?"

"Well, I can tell you he may have been alone when you found him, but he hadn't been alone for long."

"I did assume he hadn't killed himself by bashing in his own face and head."

"That's not what I mean. I mean he was not alone in his bed prior to being killed in that violent manner."

"How do you know?" Lynae asked.

"Body fluid. Our victim had not quite made it to the shower before he met his killer."

"And according to his wife and several corroborating friends, she was at the bar for a girls' night out. So the wonderful, perfect, everyone-loves-him pastor…"

"Is chimerical," Kent finished. "That man exists only in their imaginations."

"Oh, you're good," Jo said. Dread lurched in the pit of her stomach. She didn't want to deal the additional blow to the devastated wife. Of course, there was always the possibility that she was their killer. And if that was the case, her DNA being on their victim would be exactly what they needed to catch her. "Can we rule out the wife?"

"We can't rule anyone out yet. We'll run the samples against CODIS, but that's going to take some time."

"And that's only going to help us if our woman has committed a crime and exists in the DNA database." Jo knit her brow. "It was a woman, correct?"

"Definitely female," Kent concurred.

"Okay, so that at least narrows the pool." Jo crossed her arms. "Actually, it only tells us that he had sex with a woman. I'm still struggling to believe a woman could have done this."

"If it was the wife, it would blow a million holes in her story," Lynae said.

"It wouldn't have been a smart alibi for her, but people don't think clearly in these situations." It wouldn't even come close to the worst alibi Jo had seen. There were plenty of situations in which the weak alibi was immediately dismissed because of conflicting evidence.

Lynae cocked her head. "The bed was made, and the techs found no fluids on the sheets."

Kent squinched his face, exaggerating the deep creases around his eyes. "At the expense of being vulgar, did they check the floor, the sofa, the kitchen counter…"

Lynae made a face like she had bitten into a lemon. "Point taken. On that note, Lisa could have walked in on it. Something like that could cause even a normally mild-mannered woman to lose it."

"Especially one who's been through it before and suffered a bout of depression," Jo added. "Lisa always let Victor know when she was coming home, except that night, she forgot. She may have walked in on something she couldn't deal with. What else do you have for us?"

Kent motioned for them to follow him to the examination table, his white lab coat flapping over perfectly pressed gray flannel slacks. Jo posted herself directly across from him at the head of the table, positioning her body so that Lynae could hang back if she desired. Kent snapped on a fresh pair of gloves and gently moved the victim's head to point the right side of his face toward the overhead lamp. "A blow to the face here left a mark that came from the edge of something with more of a point than whatever caused the rest of the wounds."

Jo clasped her ungloved hands behind her back and angled in for a closer view of the crescent-shaped bruise. "We saw that in our initial exam at the scene. It could have been a countertop, since he was in the bathroom."

"The angle suggests that it was something swung in a downward motion."

"What about a laptop?"

"Well, since that's an unusual guess, I'll say you have reason to believe it is."

"That's the only thing missing from the house. The house was tossed, but that's all that our victim's wife can say was missing, aside from some jewelry."

Considering, Kent said, "This wound could definitely have come from the edge of a closed laptop swung with enough force."

"The other wounds suggest something similar to a pipe or a bat," Jo said.

Kent nodded and rolled the body toward him to expose the back to Jo. The welts had eased into purple-and-black bruising lining the right shoulder and neck. "He suffered several hard blows to his back and neck from, as you suspected, a cylindrical object such as a pipe or a bat. Something long enough to swing." Kent pointed to a jagged crack that ran along his neck, where it met his shaved head. "This one should have at least temporarily paralyzed him."

"But it appears that he got to his feet and faced his attacker," Jo said.

Kent rolled the body onto its back, picked up the victim's hands, turned them over so that the palms were up, then rolled them to show the backs. "Defensive wounds only. He was either too hurt to fight back—"

"Or shocked, disbelieving, and didn't want to hurt the person who was attacking him."

Lynae scowled. "I don't think I've ever heard of someone not *wanting* to fight back when someone is brutally beating them."

Kent shook his head. "It would be rare. The fight-or-flight instinct is strong. When we can't escape, we fight."

"Unless it was Lisa. Even for a cheating jerk, if you're not abusive, hitting your wife would be tough."

"That's a possibility," Kent agreed. "Although if the attacker were significantly smaller than him, he could probably have subdued her without throwing any punches. For my money, I would say he was too injured."

Running the crime scene back through her mind, Jo had to agree with Kent. "The way the crime scene read, there were several blows to the back. He either fell into or tried to use the towel rack to pull himself to his feet. It was wrenched off the wall."

"With a blow like that to the back of the head, his legs could very well have given out."

"So he's unable to run or even stand, he's seriously hurt, and he can't really do any more than hold his hands up and try to fend off the blows."

"Why set down the weapon and hit him with something like a laptop?" Lynae asked. "I mean, it's breakable. It's not a weapon, and it wouldn't really inflict much damage."

Jo pointed at the wound. "That's where it got personal. Whatever triggered our killer revolves around that laptop. So the killer decides to finish him off with it."

Kent stood up straight and stretched his back. "That's where things get more interesting."

"How so?"

"None of these wounds actually killed him. He died of asphyxiation."

Jo examined the victim's neck. "I don't see any strangulation marks."

"Because he wasn't strangled." Kent turned to a metal tray on wheels that sat next to the examination table and pulled a vial from a holder. He held it up to the light slightly above Jo's head. "Fibers in his lungs consistent with the towels that were brought in with the body. Mallory will have to confirm that, of course."

Jo pressed her thumb against her temple and rubbed her forehead with her fingers. "So you're telling me that this guy was beaten to a pulp, but that didn't kill him, so the killer finished him off with a towel?"

"I'm afraid so."

"It fits with his inability to move," Lynae said, shaking her head and looking sympathetically at the body.

"Why not keep beating him? I mean, you've come this far."

"The killer might have thought he was dead, started to clean up the room, then heard him moan or saw his eyelids flutter or something, and..."

"The rage was gone," Jo finished.

"His adrenaline was depleted," Kent added. "During the attack, the adrenaline would have been raging through the killer's veins. If our victim here stopped moving, and the killer stopped hitting him, the adrenaline would slow down. The act of cleaning up and thinking through how to cover his tracks would slow it down even more and even make him crash."

"So by the time our victim started coming to, the killer didn't have it in him anymore to keep beating." Jo had seen a lot, but that was a first.

Kent tilted his head and regarded Jo over the top of his glasses. "He was tired, exhausted even, and he needed a way to finish him off without exerting too much energy."

Jo ticked off the facts on her fingers. "So we know he was with a woman, as yet to be determined whether it was his wife. We know he was beaten with a narrow, heavy weapon and at one point hit with what we're theorizing was his own laptop. And we know that he was then suffocated, and that was the actual cause of death."

"Correct. Those are the things we know."

"What about the possibility there were two people?"

"That's always a possibility, but I don't have anything concrete to indicate that."

"Where's your brain going?" Lynae asked, eyeing Jo.

Jo paced a few steps away, a scenario running through her head. She pointed at the body. "Let's assume the good pastor here was having an affair. We don't have any information about the woman he was having this affair with. She could be married also. Husband follows her to our vic's house. She spends way too much time alone in the house with the pastor, or he sees them together through a window, or a light comes on upstairs. He figures out what's going on, so he comes in to catch them in the act."

Lynae closed her eyes, picking up the scene. "Husband freaks out, grabs... something—"

"There was a baseball bag hanging in the entryway. He could have grabbed a bat from that on his way in."

"I took the bats from that bag. If it was one of those, we should get some trace from it." Lynae glanced at the body and flinched. "Husband comes into the bedroom to find them in bed."

Jo crossed her arms and paced. "Our victim was in the bathroom, so they're done or getting ready to hop into the shower together."

"Okay, so he hears them in the bathroom and bursts in and beats the hell out of him."

"This isn't working," Jo decided. "What man goes into someone's house to confront his wife and her lover and doesn't say anything? He sneaks into the bathroom quietly and manages to get the first couple of blows to the man's back?"

Lynae shrugged. "He was going for the element of surprise. But where's the woman while all this is happening?"

"Freaking out, trying to stop him? Or maybe she's hiding."

"But she doesn't call 911 or run out of the house, screaming for the neighbors. And she's gone when Lisa gets home."

Jo studied the broken body of her victim. "She can't stop him, and when he's done, they both think he's dead. Now the panic sets in. 'What did you do? We have to get out of here before someone sees us.' Now they're both in a panic. The husband is probably completely beside himself by this point. He just killed someone. Then they realize he's not dead."

Jo closed her eyes and pictured the scene. *The tossed bedroom, the immaculate countertops in the bathroom, bloody footsteps leading out of the room.* "The lover finished him off then cleaned up after them. He can't live because she doesn't want him to talk."

"Protecting her husband, the killer?"

Jo stared at the white tile floor, the lines of the gray grout blurring and melding into a crisscrossed road map. "Or protecting herself. If the victim lives to identify his killer, then the whole sordid story comes out." Jo's head snapped up. "What about someone from the church, someone respected or trusted by the congregation? She doesn't care about protecting the killer necessarily, but if the killer is known, her little secret comes out too. It could also explain the missing laptop, if part of that little secret was recorded or if there were messages between them."

Kent shook his head slowly. "I do love to hear the way your mind works."

He tapped his computer and opened a program Jo was familiar with. "One last piece of the puzzle I can help you with. I can tell you that the blood sample you brought in with the body does not match our victim here."

"That's fantastic."

"Don't get too excited. It doesn't match because it isn't human. I'm afraid you brought me canine blood."

"Well, for the love..." The German shepherd that had been so angry at them for being in his house had given her false hope.

"That's a lovely dead end," Lynae said. "The dog sure didn't seem injured."

"No, it didn't. And it's going to be really hard at this point to know whether it just did a dumb dog thing and nicked itself, or it went after the killer and paid for it. As mad as it was when we were all there, invading its space, I would be surprised if it didn't go after the killer."

"It could have been in its kennel."

"Or it knew the person and didn't feel threatened," Jo conceded.

"I wish I had an answer for that," Kent said.

"You've given us a lot, Kent. Give me a call if anything else comes up," Jo said.

"You can count on it, Lieutenant." Kent winked at Lynae. "I'm afraid I'll see you later, Ms. Parker, even if you don't want to."

Lynae gave him a crooked grin. "It's always good to see you, Kent, even if it's in this place."

Kent snapped off a quick wave before sliding his face shield back onto his head. He picked up the remote from the rolling metal cart and aimed it at the receiver on the wall behind him. His smooth baritone filled the room as "Bring Him Home" reverberated off the walls of the cold room.

Chapter 9

When they stepped back into the hallway, Jo said, "I'm going to see if there's anyone at the church I can talk to. I'd like to get a feel for how Victor ran things around there and if the people he worked with felt the same way about him that everyone else claims to."

"Coworkers usually have some pretty good insight," Lynae said.

"Sometimes they know us better than family. For example, in my perfect-way-to-get-murdered scenario, you would be a key witness to the fact that I'm completely capable of kicking that much ass all by myself and that only a sucker-shot could take me out."

"Of course. I would never let anyone think it could happen any other way."

"Good to know you'll have my dead back."

Jo looked up the information for New Life church then called and asked who was in charge. She was told by a competent-sounding woman named Margaret that Nick Belfor, the assistant pastor, would be fulfilling the pastor's duties and that he would be in all afternoon. Jo asked her to tell Nick she was coming by then hung up.

"There's an assistant pastor who has some time to talk. I'll drop you off at the station on my way. I'd like you to check in on our other opens and see if anything has popped up since we've been gone."

"Sounds like a plan."

Jo dropped Lynae off outside the station then entered the address to New Life church into her GPS and headed back to the northeast side of town.

The church sat proudly at the end of an enormous parking lot in the midst of a residential neighborhood a few miles from Victor Manton's home. A lit sign surrounded by a raised brick retaining wall that Jo was sure would be planted with impatiens come spring announced in bold letters that Pastor Victor Manton had gone home to his Father. A service of light and remembrance would be held the next week.

Jo swung into the parking spot closest to the door and noted only one other car in the lot. Large, ornate doors opened to a contemporary room of high-ceilinged walls in warm earth-tone shades. A full wall of windows looked into a colossal room lined with rows of cushioned chairs facing a raised stage. On the right was the setup for a full band. It was worlds away from what Jo was accustomed to, but she had to admit a band in church might be fun.

She turned at the click of a door as a large, broad-featured man ambled toward her with a hesitant smile.

"I'm Nick Belfor, the assistant pastor," he said, extending a hand. "Are you Lieutenant Riskin?"

"I am," Jo said, shaking the beefy paw, which swallowed her hand.

"Margaret told me you would be coming by. Why don't we talk in my office, where we can sit. This is all so upsetting."

Jo followed him back through the door he had just come through and into a comfortably messy office. She sat in the chair he motioned to.

"You have a lovely church," she said while he settled behind the desk.

"Thank you. Victor was instrumental in securing donations and pledges to make it all happen. We started out in a strip mall down the road."

"That's quite an accomplishment."

"He was such an inspiration to everyone. It wasn't uncommon to see tears during his homily. He really knew how to touch and inspire people. I think most people wanted to be a part of building the church to secure his legacy. To be a part of history, if you will."

Jo found that level of adoration for any human somewhat nauseating. Biting that down, she said, "He must have been a wonderful pastor."

"He was," he said, bowing his head. "He will be missed."

"And you're the assistant pastor?"

Nick ran a hand nervously through his mass of dark hair. "Yes, I am."

"And what exactly does that entail?"

"A lot of paperwork really," he said with a chuckle. "And I did some of the home visits when Victor wasn't able to. I've done the occasional service, I lead the Tuesday and Thursday prayer groups, and I do some of the jail ministry."

"So basically you do anything he can't do when he isn't available."

"That pretty much sums it up, I guess. I go wherever the pastor decides I should."

"Do you do any other counseling when Victor isn't able?"

Nick shook his head. "No, I'm not a counselor. Victor worked his counseling around his other church duties."

Keeping with her procedure, Jo jotted notes about Nick's job, but she didn't anticipate referring to them. "Are you aware of who he was counseling?"

"No, I'm afraid not. He kept that very close to the chest."

"You didn't see people going into his office?"

Nick furrowed his brow. "He didn't do counseling here at the church. There are too many activities and groups that meet here, people coming and going, popping in to chat with the pastor. It's not exactly private."

Jo remembered the office in the back part of the Mantons' house. "So he did his counseling in his home?" It seemed odd, if he was concerned about privacy, that he would have people coming to his home, where his wife and teenagers were.

"That's right. The back entrance by his office was used for people to come and go without going through his home. That part of the house was off limits for the family."

"Now that Pastor Vic is gone, will you assume the role of associate pastor?"

"I hope to, but that will be up to the board to determine whether I'm the right person for the position."

"In the meantime, until they make that decision, you'll fill that role?"

"That's correct," he said with a nod.

"I've talked with a few of the parishioners, and it sounds like the pastor was well liked. Can you think of anyone in the parish who had a problem with him?"

"Do you think one of our people did this?"

She found the term *our people* interesting, as if they were set aside from the rest of the world.

"This is what he did," she said, gesturing broadly. "His personal and work life are very intertwined. I would think that your people would know him best."

"I agree. He was very open and honest with all of us. I think that's why people loved him so much."

"So you never heard of a heated argument or a run in with a parishioner?"

Nick lifted his shoulders and tilted his head. "Not a run-in per se, but there was some tension between him and some of the parishioners. He was changing a few things here at New Hope that some of the people didn't like."

"What kinds of things was he doing?"

"He was changing up the services and the music. He called it contemporary, but some of the parishioners complained that it was too secular."

"So they were worried he was taking God out of the church?"

"It wasn't quite that extreme but in a sense. People don't like change."

That was true in all walks of life. It didn't feel like something that would drive a person to kill, but Jo made a note anyway. People had killed for less. "You said a couple of changes. Was there anything else?"

"It's probably nothing, but he decided we shouldn't do business with members of the parish, so he cancelled the contract with the parishioner who's done our snow plowing for the past fifteen years and the one who does our security."

"Do you have any idea why he decided to change this now? Has there been a problem with their services?"

"No, their service has been fine. Victor decided it would be better for the church if we reached out to businesses in our community."

"Were the parishioners' services donated, or was the church paying them?"

"They were paid a fair amount. I can find the receipts if you like," he said, warily eyeing the mounds of paper on the desk.

"I don't think that will be necessary, but I'm sure the loss of business didn't go over well with either of them."

"No, it didn't. Cliff Westbrook, who did our snow plowing, came in here last week, and he was hopping mad."

"Was there an altercation?" Jo asked.

"Not a physical one, but I could hear them arguing in the pastor's office."

"Did he threaten Mr. Manton?" Jo jotted Cliff's name in her notebook.

"Not that I heard. Besides, I heard what happened to Victor, and he physically couldn't have done that."

Jo was continuously surprised by the speed at which rumors flew. "And why is that?"

"He lost his left arm in Iraq."

Jo crossed his name off her list. Cliff might be ex-military, but the chances of overtaking a man the size of Victor Manton while missing an arm was pretty slim. And their killer was left-handed.

"What about the security person? What did you say his name is?"

"I didn't say, but his name is Trent Hoffman. The company is Hoffman Security." Nick shuffled through papers on his desk.

"And were there any problems that you're aware of between Mr. Hoffman and Pastor Manton after he cancelled the contract?"

"I didn't hear an argument, but he came in and took out all the security cameras inside and out the very next day." He extracted a paper from the middle of a stack in a tray labeled Outbound and beamed as though he had accomplished a monumental task as he handed it to Jo. "Left us with no security, and Victor couldn't get the new company to come in until next week to set up the new cameras."

Jo scanned the invoice with Hoffman Security outlined in a blue box at the top while she mentally ran back through her route to the church. They were in a quiet suburb with a very low crime rate. "Is security an issue here?"

"No, it hasn't been, but the pastor liked to have the cameras anyway. He was big into having cameras everywhere."

"May I keep this?" she asked, holding up the invoice. Security footage could be very useful. She crossed her fingers that Hoffman Security would have that footage, even though the contract had been cancelled.

"Let me get a copy first," Nick replied, holding out his hand for the invoice.

"Are both Cliff and Trent still members of the church?"

"They are." He set the invoice on the copier. "Which surprised me a little with Cliff but not with Trent."

"Why is that?"

"Trent is very devout," he said over the chug of the copy machine. "He comes to Bible study on Wednesdays, never misses services on Sunday, and organizes community service projects. He's an integral part of the church. I can't imagine him leaving."

"And Cliff?"

"He's a bit of a hothead. I could have easily seen him leaving over this. But he's been here almost every week since."

"How long has it been?" Jo accepted the offered invoice and tucked it into her folder, while Nick dropped his copy onto a pile.

Nick scrunched his face and bobbed his head from side to side. "I would say about six weeks."

Although murdering someone over lost business seemed like a stretch, six weeks was plenty of time for someone to build up a grudge and act on it.

"How do *you* feel about the changes?"

"I think they're unnecessary, but it wasn't my call."

"So you don't see a problem with hiring members of the congregation to do the work for the parish?"

"Not at all." Nick shrugged. "We never had a conflict until he cancelled their contracts."

"What if two members were after the same job?"

"They bid for it, like they would any other job."

That seemed like it could easily cause conflict between members of the congregation, but that wasn't Jo's problem. "How long have you been the assistant here?"

"It was a year last month."

"And how did you and the pastor get along?"

"I didn't kill him, if that's what you're leading to."

"That's a bit of a leap. My question was more along the lines of you work well together, but were you friends? Was it a 'Let's go out and have a drink after work' type of friendship, or was it strictly a working relationship?"

Clearing his throat, Nick said, "Sorry, I'm a little nervous. I've spent some time at his house, had a few dinners, and played cribbage with him and Lisa." His eyes softened. "How is she doing?"

"At this point, she's surviving, and that's as much as can be expected."

"She's strong. She'll be fine."

Jo understood and appreciated the sentiment behind his comment. She also knew if strength was all it took, she would have been okay two years ago. "How well do you know Lisa?"

"Quite well. We actually went to high school together way back when. Even went on a couple of dates." Nick gazed out the small window next to his desk. "But then I didn't see her for years until I came back here and started this job. We reconnected pretty quickly. She's a very special woman."

Very special woman? Just the mention of Lisa's name sent a faint flush up his cheeks. Jo wondered if the pastor had known that his assistant had feelings for his wife, and if Lisa reciprocated those feelings.

"When you say you and Lisa reconnected, what does that mean? Did you have lunch together, meet for coffee..."

"We had the occasional lunch together, but mostly we talked here." He made an all-encompassing gesture around the office. "When Lisa came to meet Victor for lunch or something, she would stop by and say hi."

"And Victor was aware that you had lunch with his wife occasionally?"

Nick narrowed his eyes. "I... I don't know, actually."

"You don't know? You never mentioned it to him?"

"Look, Lisa and I are old friends." He folded his hands over his checkered Oxford, which was pulled taut through the midriff. Only one thumb pressing hard enough on the other to push the blood to the tip divulged his discomfort.

"Old friends who had lunch together without mentioning it to her husband?"

"It wasn't like that. I think Lisa probably told him. It was just lunch. I think sometimes being home alone was boring for her. She came by a few times to see if Victor wanted to go to lunch, and a couple times when he was out, she asked if I did."

Nick's phone rang, and he eyeballed the display. "It's Margaret."

Jo nodded. "Go ahead."

Nick picked up his phone and seconds later said, "Okay. Thank you," and hung up. "My appointment is here." He glanced at his watch. "It's with our new security firm. If there's nothing else..."

"Of course," Jo said, getting to her feet. "Thank you for your time. I can see myself out."

"Wait." Nick's eyes were closed, his mouth set in a firm line. "I think you should talk to Ethan, Lisa's son."

"Why Ethan?"

"I feel terrible telling you this, because he came to me in confidence."

"We're investigating a murder, Nick. If you have information that could help us, it's vital that you tell me."

"I don't think Victor was the saint everyone thinks he was." The words rushed out of him as if they would be less painful if he said them quickly.

"Why? What do you know?"

"Ethan came to talk to me one day. He was angry and confused and didn't know where else to go."

"Angry and confused about what?"

Nick rolled his head back so that the top rested on the chair's headrest. "He came home one night when he was supposed to be at a friend's house and overheard..."

Jo waited for him to finish, but he simply stared at the ceiling. She shifted her feet and glanced at her watch.

Nick opened his eyes and leveled them at Jo. "He heard an exchange between Victor and a woman. Someone who wasn't his mom. They were in the bedroom, and he threatened her."

Jo's pulse shifted into high gear. "Threatened her how? Wait. They were in the bedroom. Did he assault her?"

"No, I don't think that was it. I don't remember the exact words that Ethan heard, but I know he was threatening to expose her."

"You're telling me that Victor was having an affair, and Ethan knew about it."

"Yes," he said quietly.

And you're just telling me this now? Jo wanted to scream but kept her poker face firmly in place.

"What did Ethan want from you?"

"He had to get it out, to tell someone, and to figure out what he should do about it."

"And what did you tell him?"

"I told him he should talk to Victor and be certain he understood what he was hearing."

She wasn't sure that was the advice she would have given a kid. With Lisa's history and the depression she'd suffered after her first husband's cheating, Ethan would be very worried about how she would deal with it happening again. Confronting the stepdad that he didn't get along with, whom he suspected was cheating on his mom, could become heated very quickly.

"How long ago was this?"

"He talked to me about a week ago. Um, let's see... Thursday night, right before Bible study. But he had been stewing over it for a few weeks. I don't know the exact day it happened, but it was around a month ago."

That timing put him in the hot seat. He had a week to get up the nerve to talk to Victor or to bring his anger to a boiling point. She would have to talk to him and press a little on the alibi his mom had given him.

"Is there anything else?"

"No, that's it. I'm sorry I didn't tell you that right away. I'm not sure what my role is here. I don't know if I have more of an obligation to keep the confidences of parishioners or to help you find Victor's killer."

"You're not a priest, and this"—Jo gestured around his office—"isn't a confessional. I understand your desire to keep Ethan's confidence, but number one right now is finding out who killed Victor Manton."

He held his hands up in a helpless gesture. "I'm sorry. I wasn't holding out. I just didn't—"

"I understand, and I appreciate your bringing it to my attention. We'll talk to Ethan."

"He's a good kid, Lieutenant. He didn't hurt Victor, but he may know something about who did."

Jo let herself out of the office. She hoped he was right about Ethan being a good kid.

As she left the church driveway, she called Lynae and filled her in on the interview.

"Sounds like we'd better talk to Ethan," Lynae said.

"Let's keep it casual, maybe meet him at McDonalds or a coffee shop or something. But not in the house where his mom is."

"He's over eighteen, right?"

"Yes, he is, and I'd rather keep her out of it right now. If he has to tell us something uncomfortable, he shouldn't have to tell her at the same time."

"Or if he did it, we have a better chance of getting him talking without his mom there, telling him to lawyer up."

Jo's gut clenched at a kid doing that kind of damage. "Yeah, that too."

"All right, I'll see about setting something up."

"I'm going to stop and talk to the ex-security man so that I can get him crossed off the list and to see if he's got any security footage from the church. I don't think we'll get much from it, but there was a confrontation, and I'd like to see if he has it. I'll be available any time after that."

Jo thumbed off her phone and tossed it onto the passenger seat. The new piece of information had her adrenaline pumping. Ethan was young. If he did it, she could crack him quickly. If he didn't, maybe he could identify the woman Victor was threatening. Either way, it was a solid start.

Chapter 10

Since Jo would almost have to drive past Hoffman Security to get back to the station, she decided to stop in without a call.

Unlike the billboard-sized signs on the businesses around it, the single-story brick building on Ann Street had an unassuming sign out front that matched the logo on the invoice Jo had in her bag. She entered the drive and followed it around back to a small tree-lined parking lot. She parked in one of the three empty parking spots with signs marking them for visitors.

As she entered the building, she noted that the setup was similar to every jail she had visited—a lobby that made you feel comfortable, with a single security-coded heavy steel door leading to everything else.

"Can I help you?" The man behind the front desk sat pencil straight while eyeing Jo's gun. She noted his right hand was rotated inward and tucked under the desk. No doubt his fingers hovered over a panic button.

Holding up her badge, Jo introduced herself while she watched the man's shoulders relax. "I'm looking for Trent Hoffman. Does he happen to be in?"

"I believe he is. Let me check."

"Appreciate it," Jo said and stepped away from the desk. There was no chance that he didn't know whether or not Trent was in the building. He just didn't know whether or not he would be willing to talk to the police.

She heard the click of the receiver. "Mr. Hoffman will be right out," the man said.

Jo smiled her thank-you then chose a chair in the small waiting area and browsed through her email. When her wait time hit fifteen minutes, she stood up to get an update from the receptionist and almost collided with the broad shoulder of a man bursting through the door from the building's interior.

"Excuse me," he said, holding out both hands as if he were going to catch her.

Jo chuckled. "That was a close call, and I think I would have gotten the worse end of it."

"Sorry, I was moving way too fast. I'm keeping a police officer waiting," he said, glancing around the otherwise-empty room. "Maybe he decided not to wait."

"I think *he* would be me," Jo said, holding out her hand. "Lieutenant Jo Riskin."

The man palmed his face with a broad hand. "Great, so I kept you waiting then assumed you were going to be a man. I'm knocking it out of the park here."

Jo let out a laugh. "Well, my name is Jo, so you're not the first."

"Dad wanted a boy?" His dark eyes twinkled.

"Nope, it's short for a name I don't care to discuss."

"I'm going to leave that alone, then, and cut my losses. I'm Trent Hoffman, by the way."

Jo shook his hand and told him why she was there. After he decided his office would be the best place to talk, she followed him through a cubicle-lined maze of flashing lights and stacked monitors. She didn't know what any of the equipment did, but it was impressive to look at.

When they were settled in his small but comfortable office, she said, "So, what made you go into the security business, Mr. Hoffman?"

"I'm ex-military, Special Forces. Security was a natural fit. And after the military, I didn't care to take orders from anyone else, so I ventured out on my own."

"Wow, Special Forces. You guys don't fool around."

Trent winked. "God hates a coward."

Jo snorted. "That's not how I recall learning it in Sunday school." She liked the guy. He was comfortable and quick-witted. With his high-and-tight haircut and the razor-sharp pleats ironed into his pants, she could have pegged him for military from the far side of a football field.

"I understand you were in charge of security for the church. Is that correct?" she asked.

"Yes, I was."

"But you're not any longer. What happened?"

"The pastor decided that members of the parish should no longer be paid to provide services for the church."

"And did you agree with that decision?"

"I don't see any reason why you would go outside your church, if you have members who can do the same thing." Trent folded his hands on the desk with an air of benevolence. "But I trust that the Lord led Pastor Vic to this decision."

"Was it a large loss to your business?"

"It's only one place, and I was giving them a discount. As you can see, I have a significant business. I'm always disappointed to lose a customer." He shrugged and held up his hands in a helpless gesture. "But that's business."

"I understand that you immediately removed the security equipment."

"Yes, ma'am. I offered to leave it up for a bit, but he said it wasn't necessary."

That wasn't the way Nick had made it sound. "And that left them without security at the church while they waited for the new company to work them into their schedule."

"There's never been a problem at the church before, so the pastor wasn't worried."

"I've gone to the same church my whole life. We all have our roles, the stuff we do for the church. I feel like I'd be pretty ticked off if a pastor came along and suddenly decided I'm no longer the person for that job," Jo said, poking the bear.

"As I said, it wasn't a large loss of business. I think it made me more sad than angry."

"Why's that?"

"Because I like serving the church in any way I can. That was one way I could serve that no one else in the parish could. Like you said, we all have our roles, and that was mine."

"You've continued to attend services at New Hope Church."

"Absolutely. They're my friends. My family, really. I can't imagine leaving my church."

Jo nodded. Her church was her family, so that rang true. She knew people who had left her church because they didn't like the latest pastor and others who wouldn't leave if their worst enemy was on the pulpit. Like everything else, each person had their own way of dealing.

"If you're wondering about bad feelings between us, I didn't go remove the security from his home."

"You're contracted for his home also?"

"Yes, ma'am."

"How is that video stored? Is it on the premises at the Mantons' home, or does it end up at your facility?"

"The cameras I had installed at the church fed to my facility and were monitored. That was a full-service security install. For his home, he opted for the feed to go to a secure server that is not monitored. It's a self-monitor system."

"How would he access the footage?"

"He had a secure log-in. It's a pretty standard, low-cost option. It's not what I would call security. It's more like *insurance*," he said, making air quotes.

"What does that mean?" Jo asked.

"If something happens, we're not alerted, so it isn't really security. He could go back to the footage and watch it afterward if something were to happen."

"Can *you* access and watch that footage?" If anyone came through a door, they would be on camera. It was a slam dunk.

"Absolutely not. It goes against his contract."

"He's dead, Mr. Hoffman."

"Oh, you mean now? Yeah, I can get to it, if it's something that has to be turned over to the police. I can't imagine what good it will do. I only installed equipment in Manton's office, not in his bathroom."

"How do you know Mr. Manton was found in the bathroom?"

Trent hesitated. "I go to his church. We've kinda been talking." He lowered his eyes. "Now that I say that, it sounds pretty bad."

"It's understandable, though. So, this equipment was installed indoors? In his office?" Jo had read every note that came from the tech team that had searched that office. No camera was mentioned.

"You wouldn't have found it, if that's what you're wondering. It's a hidden camera installed directly into the bookcase. It looks like a screw." He appeared quite proud of himself and his spy equipment.

"Why would a pastor have a hidden camera in his office?"

"He did his counseling in his home office. He was afraid someone might try to accuse him of something, so he was trying to protect himself. But he didn't want the people who came to see him to be intimidated by having a camera in the room. So we did it discreetly. That's also why it wasn't monitored. You know, confidentiality, like doctor-patient but not exactly, since he isn't a doctor."

That logic made sense to Jo. Being alone in a room with anyone was a risk for both parties. A doctor discreetly protecting himself from a false accusation was actually quite responsible. It also meant a confrontation during a counseling session could be caught on video. She might not be able to see who took the laptop the night of the murder, but she could see an encounter that might give her an idea who would have a reason to.

"And how was the camera activated? Is it by motion, or did he have to manually turn it on?"

"He had to activate it."

"I would like to view the footage you have stored for him."

"I'll have to check with my legal people. I think you'll have to have a warrant or something."

"No need to check with your legal people. A warrant is absolutely required, and I wouldn't touch it without one." Jo checked her watch. "I'll make a call and should have that by tomorrow."

She was practically salivating over the idea of getting her hands on the footage. The office might not be where Victor was killed, but someone had snatched his laptop from there, and that person could very well show up on the video.

Trent slapped his hands on the armrests of his chair. "Is that it? I'd like to get back to work."

"Yes, it is. I'll be in touch."

Chapter 11

Back in her truck, Jo dialed Lynae before pulling out of the driveway. "We may have hit the mother lode here. I'll have to get a warrant, but I don't think that's going to be an issue."

"What did you find out?"

"The security guy that Manton fired? He also had equipment in Manton's house, and it feeds back to a secure server that this guy can access for us."

"That could be huge. I mean, you may literally have the killer on camera."

"That's what I'm hoping for. I'll tag Jack tomorrow for a warrant."

"Even if he wasn't your boyfriend, I don't think he would deny this one."

Jo sucked in a loud breath between her teeth. "You gotta stop saying shit like that. People are going to think he actually pushes through warrants because we're dating."

"Well, I never say it in front of anyone else," Lynae said indignantly.

"I appreciate that, but Jack is a total rule follower. Any suggestion that he might not be would be hard on him."

"Then he might decide you two can't be dating."

"No, that's not it," Jo spat. "It would be hard on us both professionally. You think I haven't thought about that?"

"Sorry, I didn't mean anything by it."

"It's okay. I probably overreacted. But I'm trying to have a normal relationship with someone whose job could sometimes conflict with mine. I don't ever want it to look like he's doing me a favor when it comes to a warrant."

"I would never say it to anyone else. And I don't think in the time I've worked with you that you've ever been denied a warrant from anyone."

"I don't just willy-nilly ask for them."

"Willy-nilly?"

"Yeah, that's kind of like wonky," Jo shot back. "Any luck connecting with Ethan?"

"Got his voice mail, of course, because teenagers don't actually answer their phones. But to my surprise, he called me right back. He can meet us if it's soon. He has a team meeting that his coach is setting up on Zoom so that he can be part of it. He has to be logged in by six thirty."

Jo glanced at the truck's clock. "We have time. Give him a call and see if we can meet him at the McDonalds on Plainfield as soon as he can get there."

"You're not going to make us late for Mom's dinner, are you?"

"Of course that's what you're worried about."

"I'm a terrible cook."

"We should have plenty of time. And don't worry. Mom will hold dinner for a bit if we're running a little late," Jo said.

She drove the rest of the way to the station and stopped in a no-parking zone by the front entrance.

Lynae hopped into the passenger seat. "Ethan was hanging out at his friend's house down the road from where we're meeting. He should be there before we are."

"Did he mention anything about talking to his mom about meeting us?"

"No, but I didn't ask."

"I'm guessing whether he knows anything or not, he won't want her involved," Jo said.

"Are you looking at him for this?"

"He wasn't on my radar, but at this point, my radar is kind of bouncing around, pinging from Lisa to Samantha to Ethan and back to Lisa. Once in a while, it even pings on Nick."

"The assistant pastor?"

"He didn't say anything that really rang my bell, but he has obvious feelings for Lisa, so that puts him on my list."

She made her exit then laid on the horn as a car blew through a red light, almost nicking her front bumper. The driver tipped back a dark-colored bottle as the car barreled past.

"Son of a—" Jo reached under her front seat, grabbed her portable light, rolled down the window, and slapped the light on the top of her truck. It had been ages since she'd had an occasion to fire it up. The pulse of the light reflecting off the hood of her truck and the wail of the siren was like a shot of adrenaline straight to her veins. She missed that part of the road.

"Call it in. I'm going to try to get him off the road."

Lynae grabbed the dash-mounted radio with one hand and the sissy bar with the other then called in the incident and location.

The car swerved into the turn lane then made a wide swing across the middle lane and into the right, causing a chain-reaction of brake lights and squealing tires. A grinding screech followed as a Fusion slammed into the back of the Ford pickup in front of it.

Lynae reported the accident and relayed their movements as Jo maneuvered through traffic, her heart thundering. Her focus was lasered in as she slipped behind the offending car. The calm voice of the dispatcher came back with an ETA on black-and-whites.

The erratic vehicle bumped off the curb and overcorrected into the center lane then back, completely unmindful of the flashing lights trailing it. Jo calculated less than thirty seconds before they reached the next traffic light. She wasn't about to gamble that they would hit it on green. She eased into the center lane then gunned the accelerator and squeezed between the drunk and the car in front of him.

"Hold on," she said as she moved as far to the right as possible and hit her brakes, forcing the drunk driver to hit his. As expected, the drunk's reflexes didn't allow for him to switch lanes fully or stop fast enough to avoid Jo's truck, and his front bumper caught the back of Jo's truck, forcing them both to a stop.

Jo bolted from the truck and stopped the man as he stumbled from his car.

"The hell, man?" he slurred. His eighty-proof breath could have ignited a fire on wet wood.

She hauled him off the road and onto the sidewalk and pushed on his shoulders. "Sit down and shut up."

"You crashed my car, you bitch," he said as he slumped to the ground.

Jo rounded on him. "What did you say?"

Lynae stepped between them, plucked cuffs from the waistband of her pants, and slapped them on the man's wrists. "How about you stop talking before the lieutenant rips your head off."

A cruiser pulled up behind the accident, and two uniformed officers exited.

"Everyone okay?" the stocky one asked as he jogged up to them.

"We're fine, but there was an accident about a mile back," Jo said, pointing in the direction they'd come from.

"There's a cruiser there already," the other officer said while yanking his duty belt up. The belt immediately dropped back down to rest crookedly across his narrow hips. "Looks like it was a fender bender, nothing serious."

Jo relaxed her shoulders. "Phew, okay. Let's just get this guy out of here then."

Lynae hauled the man to his feet by the cuffs and guided him to the officers as he stumbled and swayed. "He's all yours, guys."

Jo recounted the incident to one officer while the other did a field sobriety test for the record. "Check back with me if you need anything else. We have a witness to get to before we lose him."

"Thanks, Lieutenant," they said in unison, then one folded the drunk into the back of the cruiser as the other went around the front of the car while talking into his shoulder mic.

Jo checked out the damage to her truck, thankful that it was drivable but annoyed that it would have to go to the shop for repairs. The rush from the chase was waning but still there.

She grinned at Lynae as they hopped back into the truck. "Okay, I don't have any desire to go back on the road, but you gotta admit, it gets the blood pumping."

Lynae held out her fist, and Jo gave it a solid bump. "Hell yeah, it does!"

Jo eased back into traffic and checked the time. "I hope Ethan waited around for us."

"We don't have a lot of time left before he'll have to leave for class."

When Jo entered the parking lot of the McDonalds where they had agreed to meet, she saw Ethan sitting alone at a table. She parked and hustled into the building.

When they approached the table, Ethan bolted out of his chair and stood beside the table, his hands fisted in his front pockets. "Um, hi."

"Hi, Ethan," Jo said casually. "I'm sorry we're late. We had a little accident."

"Oh, wow. Are you okay?" His droopy brown eyes lit up with genuine concern.

"We're fine, but I'm afraid we didn't leave ourselves much time to talk."

"Yeah, I have a team meeting in like an hour."

"Totally understand. Why don't we sit down. I just have a couple of questions for you."

"Sure, yeah," he said, dropping back into his seat.

Jo sat in the chair across the table, while Lynae remained standing. "You want something to eat before your meeting? My treat," she said.

"You don't have to do that."

"Don't worry about it. What'll you have?"

Ethan decided on an order and smiled gratefully when Lynae gave him a thumbs up.

"I'm really sorry about your dad, Ethan," Jo said after Lynae had left.

"Stepdad."

"Of course, sorry. Did you and your stepdad get along pretty well?"

His broad shoulders rose and fell. "Not really. I mean, he was okay, but you know. He tried to be my dad, and I already have one of those."

"That's a tough spot for him to be in."

"I suppose." Ethan ran a hand through his hair. Blond strands raced through his fingers then stood on end.

"It sounds like your mom was happy," Jo said.

"Yeah, I guess."

Ethan was a man of few words. Jo envisioned herself pulling a sled full of rocks... uphill and on ice. Getting anywhere was going to be a challenge.

Lynae came back with a tray laden with food and drinks. She set one in front of Jo and held one for herself before sliding the tray in front of Ethan.

"Thank you," he said. "You didn't have to get me food."

Lynae waved him off as she took a pull from her straw.

Ethan bit into his burger, shoved half a dozen fries into his mouth, and slugged down a quarter of his pop in the amount of time it took Jo to formulate her next sentence. *If only the eating power of teenage boys could be harnessed, the world would no longer require any other type of fuel.* Although he shoveled in his food with both hands, based on his handling of it, Jo guessed him to be right-handed.

"I talked with the assistant pastor at your church today."

For a heartbeat, Ethan froze, then his jaw resumed working.

Jo wrapped her hands around her cup and slid it forward until her elbows rested on the table. "He told me you overheard an argument a few weeks back."

"He wasn't supposed to tell anyone," Ethan said quietly.

"He didn't want to, but someone killed your stepdad, Ethan, and if you heard something that could help us figure out who that someone is—"

"I don't even know who it was," he said quickly.

"That's okay. Can you tell me what was said?"

Ethan chomped another bite of his burger and chewed furiously, his eyes never leaving the table.

"We know the argument was with a woman," Jo said.

"He was cheating on my mom, okay?" Ethan blurted.

"I'm sorry. That must have been hard for you to hear. Especially since your mom's been through so much already," Lynae said softly.

"It almost killed her when my dad did it." Looking up from the table, Ethan blinked back tears as he swiped the back of his hand across his mouth. "Everyone thinks Victor was such a great guy, but he wasn't. The woman didn't even want to be with him."

"How do you know that?" Jo asked.

"She was saying she didn't want to do it anymore. She was crying, pretty much begging. He didn't even care. He said, 'You know what will happen if you tell me no.'" Ethan's lip curled in disgust. "Then he laughed like a freakin' psycho."

Jo's blood ran cold. *What the hell was the pastor up to?*

"And you don't know who the woman was?"

Ethan took a moment to chew and swallow, shaking his head. "I didn't see her. I could hear what she was saying, but her voice was all... weird because she was crying." His eyes dropped back to the table. "The crying was most of what I heard."

"Did Victor know you heard that conversation?" The assistant pastor had suggested he ask if he had heard correctly. If he had, it could have gotten out of control.

Ethan shook his head. "I didn't really know how to tell him, you know? He would have just said I heard wrong or something anyway."

He was most likely right. Whatever Victor was up to, he wasn't going to come clean to a kid.

Ethan tapped his phone and glanced at the home screen. "I really gotta get to that meeting. Coach set it up this way for me. I can't be late."

"Of course. Thank you for meeting with us."

Ethan flung his backpack onto his back and picked up his tray. "I mean, I hope you catch the guy who did it so my mom can, you know, put it behind her." He shrugged. "But I think she's better off without him."

As Jo watched Ethan trot across the parking lot, her mind ping-ponged with possibilities.

"The more I hear, the less I feel for our victim."

"Yeah, sometimes they don't make it easy. But like him or not, he's ours, so we have to figure out who the mystery woman is." Jo rubbed the back of her neck, where tension was threatening a headache. "My gut is telling me we should look hard at any women he's counseling, starting with Samantha."

"She does check a lot of the boxes."

"Without anything concrete, the best I can do is question her, rattle her cage a little, and see if I shake anything out."

A loud rumble came from the parking lot. Jo craned her neck to look out the window as Ethan backed out of his parking spot. "Sounds like Ethan could use a new muffler."

"I dated a guy once who did that on purpose. He was convinced it sounded cool."

Jo shook her head. "I can't imagine why."

"Because you're not a teenage boy." Glancing at her watch, Lynae said, "We can't be late for your mom's delicious food. We have just enough time to get back to my car and out there before we're late."

Jo rolled her eyes. "Good thing you have your priorities straight."

On her way out the door, Jo reached into the trash and took Ethan's cup. "I'm going to see if we can get DNA from this."

"I sure hope it isn't the kid," Lynae said.

"Me too." Jo bagged and tagged the cup and dropped it into her purse.

Chapter 12

"Hi, Mom." Jo kicked off her boots and flung them into the corner, the way she'd done her whole life.

"Hi, honey." Jo's mom wrapped her arms around her and squeezed. As always, her scent wrapped Jo in a blanket of warm childhood memories.

Mom loosened her hug but kept her hands on Jo's shoulders as she stepped back and scrutinized her face. "You're not getting enough sleep."

"Really, Mom?"

"I can see the tiredness in your eyes. You work too hard."

"Yes, she does," Lynae grumbled. "And she makes her partner do the same."

"Aw, poor kid," Mom said, pulling Lynae into a hug and patting her back lovingly.

Lynae squeezed back, contentment easing the strain out of her face. Before pulling away, she caught Jo's eye and stuck her tongue out.

Jo rolled her eyes. "Suck-up."

"I'm telling Mom you're being mean," Lynae whispered as she reached around Jo to snatch a carrot from a flowered veggie tray on the counter.

"Is that my girls?" Aunt Trudy came through the arched doorway between the kitchen and the dining room.

"Hi, Aunt Trudy," Jo said with as much enthusiasm as she could muster.

"Try this." Lynae plunged a carrot into the ranch-type dip and popped it into Jo's mouth then made a show of wiping the dip from Jo's bottom lip.

"Not funny," Jo mumbled as she crunched on the carrot.

"Seems like a matter of opinion." Lynae winked, plucked another carrot from the tray, then plastered on a big smile and turned around. "Well, hi, Aunt Trudy," she crooned, holding out her arms for a hug.

Trudy hobbled toward them, holding her hip.

"What happened?" Jo asked. Her aunt might have been a bit crazy, but she was a spry old lady, and Jo had never seen her show even a hint of her age. As annoyed as she could get with her, she didn't like seeing her in pain.

"I fell on the damn ice is what happened," Trudy said with a snarl. "Made a dash for my car 'cause it was snowing and I didn't want to get my hair all wet."

"Oh, geez, Aunt Trudy. You have to be careful," Jo said. "Your hair will survive."

Lynae grabbed a chair from the dining table and swung it around. Taking Trudy by the arm, she lowered her into the chair. "You could have just yelled from the other room. We would have come to you."

Trudy laid her hand on Lynae's cheek and pinched. "You're such a sweetheart." Looking around Lynae's shoulder, she eyeballed Jo. "She's a keeper, Jo."

Lynae beamed at Jo. "Yeah, Jo. I'm a keeper."

This had to stop. "Aunt Trudy, I have to tell you—"

The kitchen door flew open and slammed against the wall, rattling the glass panes. Jo's niece, Ella, chubby cheeks blush from the cold, burst into the room, hopping up and down. "Grandma, guess what!"

"Ella, wait." The stern voice of her mother halted the toddler, but she continued to hop.

Jo's sister-in-law came through the door, pulling off her wet boots. "Wait for your dad, like we said, Ella."

"Where *is* he?" Ella moaned.

Krista used both hands to pull back waves of copper hair. "Be a big girl and wait." Krista eyed her daughter with a mixture of censure and amusement while she expertly finagled her hair into a messy bun.

"I'm a big girl."

"Of course you are," Jo's mom said, beaming at her granddaughter.

"I'll be a good big sister," Ella said before slapping her hand over her mouth and turning, wide-eyed, to her mother.

"Ella," Krista moaned.

Mom gasped then threw her arms out and let out a squeal before grabbing Krista in a tight hug. Aunt Trudy clapped her hands like a child at a birthday party. Jo felt a ten-pound weight drop to her gut, pulling all the air from her lungs with it.

"Well, I see the cat's out of the bag," Dave said as he clomped into the kitchen in his winter boots.

"Dave, you're dragging in all the snow!" Krista scolded.

Mom shushed Krista's admonishment. "Don't you worry about that. Come here and give me a hug."

Jo sensed Lynae's eyes on her as she watched her mother grab Dave and hug him, rocking back and forth, grinning from ear to ear. She remembered getting that same hug, that same reaction, when she and Mike had come to tell them that she was pregnant. She had never been happier.

When Lynae laid a hand on Jo's arm, Jo shrugged it off and acted her way through this play that she hadn't auditioned for. She knew her lines and said them at the right time. She hugged her brother and sister-in-law, high-fived her niece, and radiated just the right amount of joy. She did all the things that were expected of her, while tamping down the hot coal that burned in her chest.

They were an adorable family who were thrilled that they would have an addition to that adorableness. She was happy for them. They couldn't stop their lives simply because hers had stopped, and she wouldn't want them to. But that didn't stop the pain or the emptiness. It didn't stop the bitterness, or the nagging question of why me. And with that question came the annoyance with herself. Dwelling on the past didn't help. She was trying to lay that part of her history to rest and move on.

Her brother beamed and doted on his wife, even though she shooed him off. By the time they sat down to dinner, the initial excitement had died down, and they were able to talk about something other than the baby.

While plates were passed of pork roast, mashed potatoes, and sweet corn that Mom had grown in her garden and frozen on the cob, Jo told the story of their drunk driver chase.

Aunt Trudy fawned over Lynae, who ate it up while periodically throwing Jo concerned glances. Jo studiously ignored the looks, and when she couldn't, she returned an *I'm fine, stop worrying about me* expression. She knew Lynae understood the look, but the guise didn't work on her. She knew her too well.

Jo abandoned her intentions of setting the record straight with Aunt Trudy about her and Lynae's relationship. She couldn't handle adding that awkward conversation on top of everything else. Instead, she put on a mien of contented happiness and chatted up her family.

When Jo and Lynae got their coats to leave, Dave popped out of his chair. "Can I talk to you a second, Jo?"

Jo's heart dropped. Her brother was rarely serious. "Of course," she said, jerking her thumb toward their parents' bedroom, which happened to be the only room on the main floor where they could talk privately.

Jo stepped into the master bedroom, where the same bed that her parents had when she was a kid adorned the center. She had a flash memory of running down the stairs from her room on the second floor to hop into her parents' bed. The spacious bed, and the comfort of her parents, calmed her even after the worst of her typical nightmares. She had a sudden urge to crawl into it and see if it had the same calming effect on her now.

Dave quietly closed the door behind him and stood, clearly uncomfortably, against the wooden frame.

"'Sup?" Jo asked.

Dave shuffled awkwardly, not meeting Jo's eyes. "I'm sure this sucks for you, and I'm sorry."

"Don't you dare be sorry for being happy." She would not allow her pain to affect this special time.

His shoulders slouched a little. "That's not what I mean. I..."

"I know what you mean, Small Fry," Jo said softly, reverting to her nickname for her brother, who now stood a solid six inches taller than her.

A smile played across Dave's face, softening the worry crease between his eyes. "I haven't heard that name in a while."

"I only use it when you're being cute, and you're not cute very often."

"Real nice."

Jo gripped the door handle, but Dave laid a hand on her wrist. "Is there something else?" she asked.

He drew in a deep breath. "We haven't found out yet what we're having, but if it's a boy, we'd like to name him Michael in honor of his uncle Mike."

Tears sprang into Jo's eyes as the breath was sucked from her lungs.

"I know you already have little Mike. If it's not okay—"

She flung her arms around her brother's neck. For the first time, the mention of the son she lost didn't stab at her heart. "I don't think he would mind sharing his name," she squeaked as tears clogged her throat and pushed her voice up an octave.

"Okay. Okay, good," he whispered, squeezing her in a tight hug.

Jo drew away, snatched a tissue from the box on her parent's headboard, and wiped her eyes and nose. "Now I'm gonna pray for a boy."

"Yeah, me too."

"Thank you. This means so much to me."

"Mike was my brother. I miss him too."

Her voice failed her, so she simply nodded as the tears fell. When she managed to pull herself together, she flung her hand in the direction of the door. "We better get back out there or they'll think we're up to no good."

"Wait till you come out with your face all red and blotchy. It will be like old times when Dad blamed me every time you were upset."

"Oh boo hoo," she laughed while dabbing the last of the tears then wiping her nose. "Are you trying to tell me I look bad?"

"Oh, yeah, you're a mess."

"Shut up, you little twerp." Jo smacked him on the back of the head as he attempted to duck out of the way.

They came out of the bedroom laughing, and if her mom noticed the mess her face was in, she didn't say anything. Jo knew from past experience that even though she tried to hide her pain, her family knew. And they also knew that she did best when she talked about it on her own terms. This wasn't the time. This time was to celebrate a new life. She said a little prayer that God would bless them with a boy to carry on Mike's name.

After a long goodbye that involved hugs all around, talking while standing by the door, then final last-minute chatter with one foot out the door, Jo and Lynae finally extracted themselves from the family and trotted through the snow to their vehicles.

After Jo started her truck, she said, "Before you say anything, I'm fine. I'm happy for them."

"Of course you are."

"And I don't want to dwell on the past and sit around feeling sorry for myself."

"I've never known you to feel sorry for yourself," Lynae replied, brushing the newly fallen snow from the windshield of her car.

"Oh, I've spent plenty of time doing that."

"There's a difference between grieving and feeling sorry for yourself."

"Yeah, you're right," Jo said. "But it's time for me to stop and move on."

"This is a big step for you."

"I've been bitter, angry, and sad for so long. I'm never going to completely stop grieving, but I'm starting to spend more time remembering the good times. I think that's a sign that I'm pushing through the fog."

"I agree. It had to help to put both Drevin and Rick behind bars."

"That's a big part of it. I had to get that behind me. Jack's a big part of it too."

A smile spread across Lynae's face. "Yeah?"

"He makes me feel like I could move on, and I didn't think I ever would again. And man, those kids."

"They're something special."

Jo sighed. "I love those two like they were my own."

"And you love their dad?"

Jo threw Lynae a sideways glance. "I just might."

Lynae pumped her fist. "I knew it."

As Jo backed out of the driveway then followed Lynae down the country road, her stomach lurched. She'd never dreamed she would say those words again, but time had a way of marching on and healing even the deepest wounds. With both the man who had squeezed the trigger to kill Mike and the man who had orchestrated the setup behind bars, she was managing a sense of peace. That peace allowed her to open up and to take new chances. It also gave her the ability to let go.

Chapter 13

Jo's phone chirped while she made her way to the station through heavy morning traffic. "'Sup, partner?"

"I was thinking if you happen to pass Sandy's on the way, I wouldn't be mad if you got me an apple fritter," Lynae said.

"Good to know. And I wouldn't be mad if a cup of fresh coffee happened to appear on my desk." Jo crossed two lanes of traffic to grab the Leonard Street exit to get to Sandy's Donuts.

"That's kind of a given," Lynae replied.

"I'm going to stop in to see Jack this morning about that warrant, so hold off on the coffee for a little bit. You know I like it hot."

"Sounds a bit personal."

Jo scoffed before hanging up and pulling into the parking lot of the donut shop. After buying two dozen donuts, muffins, and a couple of apple fritters, she headed downtown, snatched a custard-filled Long John and a blueberry muffin from the box, wrapped them in napkins, then trekked through the garage to the county office building. She badged her way through security then strode to Jack's office.

"Morning, Stacey," she said.

"Good morning, Lieutenant," Stacey replied.

The cynical, seen-too-much cop in Jo firmly believed that no one should be quite as bubbly as Jack's secretary. But time had told her that it was genuine, and Jo admired her for that.

Holding out the donut, Jo said, "I thought you might be up for a treat this morning."

Stacey's dark eyes lit up. "Oh my gosh, that's so nice of you!" she gushed, taking the donut from Jo's outstretched hand. "How did you know that Long Johns are my favorite?"

Jo lifted a shoulder. "Just a hunch."

"That's why you're the detective, I guess."

Yep, sniffing out people's donut preferences is what I do.

"Is Jack in?" Jo asked as Stacey sank her teeth into the donut.

Stacey held up a finger while she chewed and swallowed. "Sorry, I couldn't resist. Jack's in, but he has a meeting in fifteen minutes."

"Can I slip in quickly and talk to him?"

"Of course. I'll ring him when his appointment gets here."

"Perfect," Jo said as she moved around the desk and strolled to Jack's office.

She gave a cursory knock on his door before poking her head in. He sat hunched over, staring at his computer, weariness etched on his face. When his eyes landed on Jo, the coils that had him wound up appeared to loosen their grip and ease the crease out of his forehead.

"Well, there's a sight for sore eyes."

"Rough morning already?" she asked as she set the muffin on his desk.

He tugged his dark-rimmed glasses off and roughly rubbed his eyes. "I'm afraid so, but it just got better."

"You already got the blueberry muffin, smooth talker," she said before giving him a kiss.

"Which tells me you want something." He plucked the muffin from his desk and unwrapped it.

The comment stung. Even if it was only in Jack's head, she didn't like that he saw her as a person who was only considerate when she wanted something. But there she was, wanting something and having no choice but to ask. "Well, since you brought it up," she said without giving a hint to the hurt, "I need a warrant."

"Sure, no problem."

"Just like that?"

Jack set the muffin down and opened a drawer. "Yep, hold on while I pull one out of my magic warrant drawer."

"Smart-ass."

"You're the one waltzing in here, asking for a warrant."

Jo crossed her arms and drummed her fingers. "First, I don't waltz. Second, have I ever come to you with a request for a warrant without doing my due diligence first?"

"Yes, you have." He drew in a deep breath through his nose and slowly blew it out. "I'm sorry. I've had a shitty morning."

"Wanna tell me about it?" she asked.

"Maybe later. I have a meeting in..." Jack pushed back the sleeve of his suit jacket and looked at his watch.

"About ten minutes," she finished for him. It stung a little that he was brushing her off, but she did the same when she was wading through a hard day, so she tried not to let it bother her.

"Sounds like Stacey already got to you. Better give me your pitch quickly, then."

Jo laid out the case for accessing Victor's recorded counseling sessions. As she talked, his expression morphed back into the concerned one he'd had when she first came in.

"You're going to have to put that in writing and clarify the scope of the warrant," he said.

"What's the problem? The guy is dead."

"But the people he recorded aren't. You're talking about doctor-patient privilege."

Jo cocked her head. "He isn't a doctor. Does that matter?"

"Not in the case of a counseling session. Privilege is serious."

"We're also talking about murder. I think that's more serious."

Jack scrunched his face. "Depends on who you ask."

"What if someone made a threat during a session and it's recorded?"

"You won't know that without watching highly confidential counseling sessions of people who may not have anything to do with your murder."

"Video surveillance is part of police investigations all the time," she argued.

"Sure, when it's in a public place. There's no assumption of confidentiality when you're on the street or in a grocery store. But there is when you're in a therapy session."

She smacked her hands on his desk. "Well, shit."

"If you got permission from the people he counseled—"

"You think my killer is going to give me permission to watch the video in which he threatened my victim? Come on, Jack!"

"I don't make the rules, Jo," Jack snapped. "Limit your request to the night of the murder. If it comes out later that there's reason to believe a particular person made a threat, you can always go back for another warrant to broaden the scope."

Jo threw her hands in the air. "The night of isn't going to do me any good. He wasn't in his office when he was killed."

"But his laptop is missing. Someone had to go in there and get it."

"The cameras aren't motion activated. Victor wasn't there to turn it on."

Jack's desk phone rang, and he eyed it anxiously. After tapping the speaker button, he said, "Yeah?"

"Your nine o'clock is here," Stacey said in a smooth, professional tone that belied her usual chipper self.

"Thanks. I'll be right out." He tapped his phone to disconnect. "Look, I'll put in for the warrant any way you choose. I'm simply telling you what I think a judge will actually sign."

"Forget it," Jo huffed. "When we come up with something more, I'll come back, and we can broaden that scope."

"I think that's a good decision."

She slapped her hands on her thighs and stood up. "Then I'll let you get on with your meeting."

"Good luck with Rick," he said.

"Thanks. I'm heading there after the morning briefing."

"Don't let him get under your skin, Jo."

"Enjoy the muffin. It really wasn't a bribe. I thought about you while I was getting breakfast for my team."

"I'm going to enjoy it a little later," he said, setting it on the credenza behind his desk. "I'm glad you think about me once in a while during your day."

"Once in a while," she said over her shoulder as she left the office.

A man sat in one of the visitor chairs, casually scanning his phone. A shock of white hair was pristinely combed away from a handsome face adorned with brash red glasses. His right ankle rested on his left knee, boldly patterned socks making color burst from the otherwise-conservative suit. When Jo stepped out of the office, he glanced up and gave her a once-over then nodded in an off-hand but not unfriendly way. If he was a cop or a lawyer, she had never seen him in GR before, and she knew almost all of them.

She returned the same kind of nod then laid her hand on Stacey's shoulder. "Take care, Stacey."

"You too, Lieutenant," Stacey chirped. "I'll see you soon."

"I'm sure you will," Jo replied.

Jack's office door opened. He had his suit jacket on and had buttoned the top button. "Mr. Cantel, thank you for coming on short notice," he intoned as he covered the short reception space in a few long-legged strides. He shook the man's hand, clapped him on the shoulder, then motioned toward his office.

Mr. Cantel popped out of his chair with the ease of a man half his age and eagerly grasped Jack's hand.

As Jo leaned her shoulder into the door to push it open, the two men went into Jack's office, chatting about the weather. She realized that she only knew what Jack did as it pertained to her job and made a mental note to ask him more about what else he did. She had to play the role of supportive girlfriend a smidge better if she intended to keep the role permanently.

After making the short drive to the station, Jo was rewarded with a cheerful crew when she came into the morning meeting bearing donuts. She pushed through the usual briefing by rote, her mind fully on the upcoming meeting with Rick. When the meeting finished, she slapped her case notebook shut, handed it to Lynae, and with a shoulder squeeze of encouragement from her partner, she left for the prison.

Chapter 14

Rick trundled into the room with his head down. His chain-connected handcuffs and ankle cuffs rattled and clanked with each shuffling step. In court, Jo had watched his face register shock then resignation when the judge had ordered that since his connections in the drug trafficking world made him a flight risk, he was to be held without bond. Seeing the shell of his former self that he was already becoming satisfied her more than was probably healthy, but she didn't care.

Lifting his head to look around the room, he caught her eye then dropped his head before lumbering her way. She allowed herself a moment of smug gratification when she noted the wide berth he afforded every chair that held an inmate. His journey through the room was followed by more than one set of glowering eyes. His split lip and wariness spoke volumes about how his short stay had been going.

Sliding into the chair across from Jo, he kept his hands in his lap and bowed his head in recognition at the instructions from the guard. Jo regarded him coldly. Her face remained impassive while her stomach roiled and pushed acid up her throat. The realization that she would never see his face or hear his name without feeling the rot in her gut flitted through her mind. She would spend every day in court, testify if necessary, and appear at any parole hearing he might have in the future. Although it was impossible, if she could find a way to have him charged with double homicide to get some justice for the miscarriage that had made her lose her son, she would.

"Thanks for agreeing to talk to me," Rick said softly, his eyes briefly shifting to Jo.

Jo glared at him. "I've been trying to talk to you for two months. This isn't for you. It's for me."

"I'm sorry." With his chin still slightly down, he looked up at her with sad eyes. "How are you?"

Jo narrowed her eyes. He couldn't be serious. "You lost your right to ask me that and pretend you care," she spat. "I'm guessing you want something from me."

Rick's eyes jerked from side to side as he took in the other orange-jumpsuit-wearing men with shackled hands talking to loved ones. "I want a deal."

"I bet you do."

"Do you have any idea how many of these guys Mike and I arrested? I won't last six months in here."

Raising an eyebrow, Jo asked, "And that's my problem?"

"You know me being shivved in here isn't what Mike would want."

Jo slapped her hand on the table. "Don't you dare tell me what Mike would want," she said through gritted teeth. She poked a finger at him. "I'll tell you what he would want. He would want to be alive, doing the job he loved. He would want to have a son, and he would want to watch that son grow up."

Rick winced.

"But he doesn't get what he would want, does he?"

"I can't change what happened, Jo."

"No, you can't."

He looked her in the eye for the first time. "But I can tell you what I know."

Jo wanted the whole story knit into a thick black-and-white blanket that she could wrap herself in and grieve. But giving Rick a deal was a line she couldn't cross, not even for the rest of the story.

He had to pay for what he'd done, and the only way she could make that happen was to keep him locked in a cage like a rabid animal for the rest of his life.

But no law said she couldn't string him along. "The truth is what I've been asking for all along."

"I can give you that, but you have to help me out."

"What is it you think I can do for you?"

"You have a relationship with the assistant prosecutor."

"You think I'll to talk to Jack Riley on your behalf?" she asked incredulously.

Rick scooted forward, his cuffed hands dangling between his legs—the once-formidable detective reduced to a slouching, power-less inmate. "With the information I have, you can break open an entire drug trafficking network," he whispered while he scanned the room.

Leaning back and crossing her arms, she stared silently while her allotted time ticked on. She would let him hang himself with his own rope. "You're in pretty deep, aren't you, Rick?"

Setting his jaw, he shook his head and looked away.

"Is that why you had to kill Mike? Was he on to you?" she demanded.

"This wasn't all me. I'll cop to my part in Mike's death, but—"

"Murder," Jo interrupted. "Murder is the word you're looking for, not death. Death is a cleaned-up word, and I won't let you clean it up. You murdered him."

Rick flinched then sighed heavily. "I deserve that. I'll admit my role in Mike's *murder*."

"Like you have a choice at this point."

"I didn't want to do it, Jo. He was my friend." His lips quivering, he raised his shoulders and wiped his eyes on the sleeves of his shirt.

Jo curled her lip in disgust. "Save the theatrics."

"I mean it, Jo. I tried to find another way."

"Apparently, you didn't try hard enough." Despite her determination to block it out, she saw Mike lying alone, bleeding on a cold cement floor in an empty warehouse, knowing his best friend had betrayed him. "Did you even think about helping him while he was lying there dying?"

"Of course I did. It was the worst moment of my life."

"Yeah, mine too," she said quietly. "Tell me something. Did you try to get Mike to join this network?"

Rick shook his head. "No, I knew he wouldn't, and he would go straight to the brass if he had any real proof. I was trying to protect him."

"Shut up." She would be damned if she would let him pull one ounce of sympathy out of her. "You weren't protecting anyone but yourself. He was getting too close, and you knew you'd get caught."

"They had to have him on board or at least guaranteed not to talk."

"Who is *they*?"

Rick looked away, his jaw set in a hard line.

"You knew the only guarantee that he wouldn't eventually get the proof he needed was for him to be completely out of the picture. Dead."

"He wouldn't have let it go."

"Mike was a good man, and that's what got him killed," Jo said mostly to herself.

"Yes, he was. He loved you."

Glaring at him, she said, "I don't need you to tell me that."

"I know." He made a show of looking chagrined. "I lost the right to tell you anything."

"Yeah. The first thing you have to do is get that through your head. When you decided to kill my husband, you forfeited any right to act like you care about me."

"I didn't decide to kill Mike," he said quietly, dropping his gaze to the table. "I'm not in control. That's what I'm trying to tell you."

"Then tell me who is."

"It's not that easy." Rick shifted in his chair, his leg chains clanging against the metal legs of the chair. "What about that deal?"

"You're something else. You never wanted to hurt Mike, and you have so much guilt about it that you won't talk without a deal."

"All you're after is the truth, right? Then you gotta give me something." Rick lifted his hands and dropped them back to the table, the ensuing racket causing a guard to swing their way.

Jo lifted a hand to hold off the guard. "Why would I help you get a deal? We have you on conspiracy to commit murder of a police officer. We've got you on drug trafficking. On felony murder." Jo ticked the points off, holding her fingers close to Rick's face. "And if there's anything else we can legitimately hit you with, we'll find it. You'll never see the outside of these walls."

"And you'll never have your answers."

"I guess I'm gonna have to live with that." Jo made a nonchalant motion that didn't scratch the surface of the rage that burned inside her. "Nothing you tell me will bring him back."

"I thought you had more guts than that. I guess I was wrong about you."

"And I thought you were Mike's best friend, so I guess we were both wrong." Jo steepled her fingers, pressing them against her mouth. She held that position for a moment while she centered herself then said, "I had this stupid idea that maybe you had a desire to do something decent. You know, in memory of the best friend you had murdered. How naive of me."

"That's not fair."

She pushed her chair back and stood. "Life's not fair."

"I'm trying to survive here, Jo." Rick shifted his gaze around the room. Jo had seen the same expression on other prisoners after a pleading outburst. They looked around to see if anyone heard or sensed their weakness.

Bending forward, she pushed her fingers into the table and leaned close to his ear. "Good luck with that," she said quietly.

"I'm just trying to get a transfer," he sputtered. "I know I'm never getting out. But get me a transfer to a place where I'm not the reason a bunch of the inmates are here."

His cowardice soured her stomach. He was willing to turn on a dime. *How quickly did he turn on Mike?* All his talk about trying to find another way, about not wanting to hurt his friend, was crap. He rolled over like a puppy offered a belly rub, and he thought she would believe he'd fought for his friend's life. He fought for himself, and that was it.

But the idea of taking down a drug ring, the thing Mike had fought for his whole career, and doing it in his memory, was enticing. Giving Rick nothing more than a transfer to another facility didn't feel like much of a compromise. He would remain caged for the rest of his life, and whether he was moved or not, it would always be known that he was a cop. And she would have her answers. She would have to work the angles and plot her course carefully. Time was on her side, not Rick's.

Jo slipped back into the chair. "I tell you what. You give me something, anything, and I'll think about it." Holding up a hand to stop his protest, she added, "If you can't give me something in good faith, then I can't waste my time looking into making you a deal. Cop killers aren't usually given much slack, as you well know."

Rick stared daggers through her. She could almost see his brain working the angles like hers had. "All I'm going to tell you is that it spans divisions, jurisdictions, and even states," he said.

"That tells me nothing. That's hundreds of people just within our own state." He couldn't think that was news to her. Narrowing her eyes, Jo searched his.

"But not hundreds who have control over distribution as well as thousands of people."

"Are you telling me—"

"That's all I'm saying until we talk more about that deal." Slumping back in his chair, he tried to pull off a casual slouch, which was hindered by his handcuffs. He settled for dropping his hands into his lap and splaying his legs to the side.

Jo mimicked his nonchalance, shrugging, then pushed out of her chair. "It isn't much, but I'll get back with you once we have a chance to look into it." Leaning forward, she sneered, "In the meantime, have fun in general."

As she picked up her weapon and made her way back out of the jail, her mind raced down dark alleys and forgotten back roads to places she should never go. If she understood correctly, control over thousands meant they were trafficking to the prison and maybe even to multiple prisons across the country. Prisons contained a population of men and women who had a higher-than-average probability of being users. The people were filled with pain, anger, and desperation. And for many of them, they had nothing to lose. Typically, captains and jail administrators worked tirelessly to keep drugs out of the inmates' hands, but somehow they always found their way in. If they had someone with a little power on the inside, that would explain a lot. The idea infuriated her and exhausted her brain. With a plant in every location, just one bad officer, and you had a multimillion-dollar operation involving people that the average person didn't care about. It was a gold mine for the drug trade.

Jo moved Rick and the entire sordid business to the back burner. She could let it brew while Rick sweated it out inside.

She instructed her truck to call Lynae.

As soon as she picked up, Jo said, "See if we can get a sit-down with Lisa Manton, preferably in the station. I have a few questions for her. I'll be back at the station within the hour."

"Sure will. How did it go with Rick?"

"Not what I hoped for but pretty much what I expected." As she made the drive back, she replayed the conversation for Lynae.

"I'm not surprised he wants to cut a deal to get a transfer. But I am surprised he's still alive."

"He'll be watching his back for the rest of his life." Jo wondered about her mental state when that made her perversely happy.

"It could be huge if he gives you enough to infiltrate that ring."

"It would be, but honestly, I'm not sure I'm the person for the job." She couldn't believe she felt that way, but as long as the job got done, it didn't have to be her doing it. Someone with less emotional involvement might be the better choice.

"It wouldn't be bad to pass it along to someone else. Your plate is already full."

Jo thought of Jack, Maddie, and Logan. "And I have some very good reasons not to have my name associated with the bust."

She drove the rest of the way to the station with her head filled with how dangerous her job could be, both for herself and for the people she loved. Mike had been aware of the dangers. They'd worried about each other, but they were both in it with their eyes wide open. If she brought kids into her life, the worry would be much worse. She shook her head and reminded herself that she was putting the cart before the horse.

The only thing she had to worry about at the moment was finding her killer.

Chapter 15

Lisa Manton stepped off the elevator and scanned the room nervously. Jo watched from her office as Lynae spoke with her. When Lynae motioned toward the hallway leading to the conference room, Jo walked out to join them.

"Is Samantha here yet?" Lisa asked.

"I wasn't aware Samantha was coming," Lynae said, glancing over Lisa's shoulder at Jo.

"I asked her to meet me here. I don't like doing these things alone."

Jo considered not allowing Samantha in the room. Having an extra person in the room could remind Lisa to keep her mouth shut. On the other hand, a good friend sometimes encouraged the confidence to open up. And with the friend being on Jo's suspect list, watching her response to Lisa's questioning could be useful.

"I can have someone bring her in when she gets here," she said.

"Oh, okay." Lisa looked past Jo, and her shoulders relaxed. "There she is."

Where Lisa was a lamb, Samantha sashayed through the bullpen with the confidence of a runway model. "Sorry I'm late. Downtown parking." Samantha waved a hand in a show of frustration.

"I'm just glad you're here," Lisa said.

Jo led them to the conference room and motioned for them to have a seat.

"Can I get either of you something to drink?"

Lisa perched on the edge of a plastic chair with her hands in her lap. She stared at them as she rubbed her knuckles with her thumb.

"I've had so much coffee already, but I think I could drink one more cup."

Samantha sat in the chair next to Lisa and angled slightly toward her friend. "If it's in the room, I'll be drinking it."

Jo stepped out of the room and crossed the hallway to the break room. She grabbed three blue-and-gold GRPD mugs from the overhead cabinet, filled a decanter from the large vacuum-sealed pot, and brought them back to the conference room. After filling the cups, she placed them in front of the women then pushed the container holding cream and sugar to the center of the table.

Lisa added sugar to her cup then pinned Jo with her pleading eyes. "Do you have news? Is that why you asked me to come in?"

With the pleasantries over, Jo rested her forearms on the Formica tabletop and wrapped her hands around her cup. "It's very early in the investigation. We've had a conversation with the county coroner, who has collected some evidence that we're confident we can use."

"You are?" Samantha blurted.

Lisa's eyes widened. "Can you tell me what it is?"

Jo looked at Samantha pointedly. She sidestepped their questions and asked Lisa, "Was your husband home when you left to go out with your friends?"

"Yes, he was."

"And did he know where you were going and when you would be home?"

"Yes, he knew I was going out with the girls. It's kind of a standard once-a-month thing. And I told him where the kids were and when we'd all be home."

"Was that your usual routine when you were going to be out?" Jo asked.

Lisa's lip quivered as she blinked rapidly. "He liked to know where everyone was."

"Did anyone else know that you and the kids would be gone?"

"Well, the kids are teenagers, so they're almost always gone. As far as me, I don't think anyone would care about my schedule."

"It's all women from your church you go out with, correct?"

"Yes, it is."

"Do you make plans or talk about it at church or in a Bible study group?"

Lisa raised her eyebrows. "I suppose we probably do."

Jo scratched a note in her notepad. "At any point that evening, were you and your husband intimate?" she asked as delicately as she could.

"What? No. I only saw him for a few minutes before I left, and when I got home—" Tears welled in her eyes and spilled down her cheeks. She sniffled and wiped the tears with the back of her hand.

Samantha's eyes narrowed. She laid an arm around the back of her friend's chair. "Why would you ask her that?"

Jo's gaze flicked in Samantha's direction then back to Lisa. "I know this is difficult, but I have to ask these questions."

Lisa bit her lip. She shakily brought her cup to her lips then set it on the table and moved her hands back to her lap. Then she squeezed her eyes shut and swiped at the tears that streaked down her face.

Samantha plucked her purse from the back of her chair and pulled a handful of debris from the depths of the oversized bag and dropped it onto the table. Three pennies, an earring, a silver-wrapped stick of gum, a wad of tissues, and a gold tube of lipstick rolled from the mess. She removed a tissue from the rolled-up wad and handed it to Lisa, who took it gratefully and wiped her face and nose.

As Jo zeroed in on the earring, her pulse quickened. It matched her mental picture of the one attached to the back of the victim at the crime scene. She was disappointed but not surprised to confirm her suspicion that Samantha was the other woman. She wondered if Lisa knew more than she was letting on.

Samantha casually pushed everything back into the bag, clearly unaware that the other earring was part of the crime scene. Jo chanced a glance at Lynae, whose eyes widened briefly then went back to stony-cop mode.

"Tell me about your husband's counseling," Jo said, switching lanes. It wasn't yet time to show her hand.

Nodding, Lisa wiped her nose then crumpled the tissue in her hand. "He's been doing that for as long as I've known him. It's part of his ministry."

"Is he a licensed counselor?"

"Yes. Not a psychiatrist. He's licensed for family counseling, but he's not a doctor. He can't prescribe any medication."

Jotting that information in her notebook, Jo said, "So he could, say, counsel a couple who were having marital problems, but if a person was depressed or anxious to the point that they required medication, he would refer them to someone else?"

"Right. If he was out of his league, so to speak, he would refer them to a licensed psychiatrist."

"Did he do that often?" Lynae asked.

"I have no idea. That's all confidential, and Victor guarded his patients' confidentiality, as you can imagine."

"Of course he did. Are you aware of any issues he may have had with someone he was counseling? Even if you don't have a name, did he mention anyone who made him feel threatened? Was there someone who didn't appreciate his counseling?"

"No," Lisa said miserably. "I'm sorry. I can't help you."

Laying her hand over Lisa's, Jo said, "You can't tell us anything you don't know."

Sniffling, Lisa nodded and attempted to unwad the tissue in her hand.

Samantha slid the pile of tissues in front of her friend. "You're doing great, hon."

Watching Samantha play the part of a warm, loving friend made Jo's stomach knot. She wanted to tell Lisa the truth, but she had to play her cards right. Samantha and Victor had slept together, but that didn't mean Samantha was the killer.

"Did Victor do any of his counseling at the church, or was everything done at the house?" Jo asked.

"I think people stopped in at the church to talk to him, but his scheduled sessions, he did at home, as far as I know."

"So anyone who came regularly would have the general layout of your house."

"I guess so, but these are people from our church. Everyone at church loved him."

"Of course they did," Samantha said.

"I understand your husband was making some changes at the church that some people weren't happy with."

Lisa pursed her lips and rolled her eyes to the ceiling. "He made a couple of changes to the services to liven them up for the younger people. And yeah, some people didn't like it. But you'll always have that."

"That was the same impression the assistant pastor had."

"Nick understood."

"I'm sure he'll be a big help to you going forward."

Lisa blinked back tears. "He's a good guy." She picked at the tissue absently. "Very solid in his faith."

"And you two go back a ways."

Lisa's hand froze on the tissue, then she clenched it into a fist around it. "We knew each other in high school, but I hadn't seen him in years until he came to the parish."

"He seems very fond of you."

Lisa softened subtly. "He's a good friend."

"Is there more to it than friendship?" Jo asked.

Lisa's shoulders slouched as she gave Jo a bored look. "I told you I wasn't having an affair."

Jo wasn't convinced. Both Lisa and Nick had the same expression when they talked about each other.

"I don't have any other questions for you right now. We have feelers out at every pawn shop and resale store in the city. If there's any attempt to pawn or sell Victor's laptop, we'll be contacted."

"Do you think they'll try to sell it?"

"That's typically why something portable like a laptop is stolen." Jo cocked her head. "Do you think there could be another reason?"

"I don't know. Maybe they were looking for something. Some kind of... dirt or something."

Jo regarded her. The statement came out of left field when Jo considered how adamant she had been that Victor was Mr. Wonderful.

"Oh, Lisa, don't think that way. What kind of dirt could Victor have?" Samantha's foot tapped nervously.

"Do you have some idea what kind of dirt a person would be looking for on your husband's computer?"

Biting the inside of her lip, Lisa stared at the table. Finally, she looked back at Jo with fresh frustration in her eyes. "No. It was just a thought."

Lynae shifted in her seat and crossed her arms. "You said before that Victor's laptop was password protected, right? And would anyone have access to that password?"

"Yes, it was. He was completely paranoid about his password because of the privacy of the people he counseled."

"So Victor kept notes about his counseling sessions on his laptop?"

"Yes," Lisa said, wiping a tear that rolled down her cheek.

"If someone had that laptop, they would know everything about everyone," Samantha mumbled.

Jo eyed Samantha as she fiddled with the buckle of her oversized purse. "Yes, they would."

Closing her notebook, Jo said, "We're doing everything in our power to find who did this, Lisa. Try to get some sleep. We'll keep you informed as the investigation progresses. In the meantime, you can always call me with questions."

Lisa stood and picked up her purse. "The funeral is tomorrow," she said. "I'll be glad when all this is over."

Jo could offer nothing more than a slight nod. The funeral was only the beginning, but burdening her with that knowledge wouldn't accomplish anything.

Laying her hand on Samantha's arm, she said, "I'd like to talk to you."

"Oh, sure," she said hesitantly.

Samantha hugged Lisa tightly and whispered something Jo couldn't hear. Lisa nodded and squeezed her hand before leaving.

Chapter 16

J o tapped her phone and pretended to check a schedule. "I'm afraid this room is needed soon. Why don't we move to a different one?"

"I think all the conference rooms are booked," Lynae said. "You're going to have to use an interrogation room."

Jo curled up her lip and rolled her eyes. "Damn." She held out her hands in a helpless gesture. "Sorry, Samantha. Those rooms are a bit cold, but it's all we have right now. My office has crime scene photos."

"I don't mind what room we're in," Samantha said. "But I can't look at crime scene pictures."

Lynae gathered her things and stood. "Should I sit in?"

"No, we're just going to catch up a little," Jo said with a smile that she knew Lynae would accurately read as feral-cat-toying-with-its-prey.

Returning the innocent look, Lynae replied, "I've got some paperwork to handle. I'll be at my desk."

Jo led Samantha down the hallway to an empty interrogation room and motioned for her to go in. After shutting the door, Jo leaned against it and made a show of acting wrung out. "It's always tough talking to the people left behind."

"I don't know how you do what you do," Samantha said, rubbing her fingers roughly over her forehead. "I have a screaming headache."

"Would more coffee help? After that, I sure could use another cup."

Samantha looked at her gratefully. "Sure, that would be great. Decaf, if you have it."

"I remember you always switched to decaf after only a cup or two."

"I'm surprised you remember that."

Jo opened the door and looked over her shoulder. "I don't forget much." She left the room and detoured to Lynae's desk. Planting both hands on it, she said, "That earring that fell out of her purse—"

"Matched the one from the crime scene," Lynae finished, holding out a manila folder.

"Yes, it did." Jo took the folder. "What's this?"

"Crime scene pictures. A shot of the earring attached to Victor's back and a close-up of it to show detail."

"How the hell do you have these already?"

Wiggling her eyebrows, Lynae said, "I can't tell you all my secrets, or you won't need me anymore."

"Well, that's never going to happen. You're quite possibly the best partner in history."

"And don't you forget it."

"Never. I'm going to spend a few minutes playing nice, then I'll hit her with this."

"Give her some slack, then reel her in," Lynae said, miming reeling a fishing line. "I like the way you work."

"Less like reeling and more like jerking the line and hoping she bites." Jo toyed with her wedding ring, which she wore on a thin chain around her neck. Taking it off her finger had been a momentous move, but the weight of it around her neck was comforting. "Come with me. I'd like you in the observation room. Pay attention, and come in if I'm pushing personal feelings too much to the front in my line of questioning. Some of it will come out intentionally, but stop me if I'm crossing a line. And turn on the camera so that we've got it all on tape, in case there's any accusation that the interrogation was personal."

Lynae narrowed her eyes. "Personal feelings about what? What happened between you two?"

"You'll know soon enough."

"You're being mysterious, and I'm not a big fan of mysterious, Jo."

"Really? Shouldn't you be a huge fan, considering what you do for a living?"

Lynae huffed. "You know what I mean."

"I don't have time right now to give you the whole story, but you'll get the gist. I'll fill in whatever questions you have after the interview."

"Okay. That's fair."

Jo went to the break room and made two cups of coffee then faked a bright smile as she strode back into the interrogation room. "Sorry to keep you waiting. I had to put out a couple of fires."

"So you're pretty much in charge around here?" Samantha asked, scanning her up and down with an admiring look.

Shrugging, Jo said, "I'm the lieutenant of this division, so I'm in charge of this little cog. But it takes a lot of cogs to make a wheel go around."

"As humble as ever, I see."

Jo set Samantha's cup on the table then slipped into the chair across from her, ignoring the comment. "I'm glad Lisa has a friend to help her through this."

"I'm glad I can be here for her. She's a good person. Coming home to something like that... Well, that's not something anyone should experience."

"No, it isn't," Jo said. "As you're her friend, how do you feel she's holding up?"

"As well as can be expected. She's in shock, and I imagine the worst is yet to come."

"When the rest of the world goes back to normal, and she doesn't."

Samantha laid a hand over Jo's. "I'm sorry you understand that better than you should."

Jo ignored the overwhelming desire to pull her hand away. "Thank you. What about the kids? How are they dealing?"

Samantha sat back in her chair with a contemplative look. "The girls are surrounding themselves with friends. I think that's good for them. But Gilly... I mean Ethan... is just the opposite. He's not talking to anyone, and that worries me."

"Everyone mourns in their own way, but Lisa should keep an eye on him."

"She will. She's a great mom. And I'll be there with her."

Jo's smile was thin. "I'm sure she feels lucky to have you around."

Samantha shrugged and studied her lap, plucking imaginary lint from her slacks.

In a conversational tone, Jo asked, "So, how long have you been sleeping with your good friend's husband?"

Samantha's head snapped up, her eyes wide. "Excuse me?"

"How long, Samantha?"

"I don't know what—"

Jo opened the folder she had been holding and slapped the close-up picture onto the table. "I bet you were a little nervous, trying to figure out what happened to that earring. When did you realize you'd lost it?"

Samantha stared at the picture then lifted her chin and gazed at the wall to her left.

Jo placed the picture of the earring against Victor's bloody skin on the table and turned it toward Samantha. "You're probably not going to like where we found it."

Samantha moved her head enough to view the picture and blanched. Then she set her jaw and looked Jo in the eye. "That earring doesn't mean anything. It's a pretty common style."

"Yes, it is. Unfortunately for you, an exact match fell out of your purse."

"I don't know what you're talking about."

"My partner and I both saw it."

Her eyes wide, Samantha gaped at Jo. "What's in my purse is my business. You have no right to look in it."

Jo raised an eyebrow and cocked her head. "It fell out of your purse in plain sight. And reasonable suspicion, which we now have, gives me the legal right to search your purse."

"Which still wouldn't prove anything."

"Except earrings hold DNA." Jo leaned back in her chair and crossed her legs then took a sip of her coffee. "I can do this all day."

Samantha bit the inside of her mouth, which contorted her bottom lip. Jo remembered the nervous habit from their college years.

"It's not what you think."

Jo rolled her eyes and let out an exaggerated sigh. "Save it."

"That's not fair."

"No one has an affair by accident. What? Did you trip and fall into his bed?" Jo had no sympathy for people who *didn't mean* to have an affair. The problem was as old as time and responsible for more murders than almost anything else.

"The first time, it just happened. I didn't mean to hurt Lisa."

"What did you think was going to happen?"

"I don't know." Samantha covered her face with both hands. "I didn't think."

"She's supposed to be your best friend." Jo crossed her arms. "But we both know that's not something that stops you, don't we."

Samantha's shoulders slumped as she dropped her hands from her face. She stared at the table, shaking her head almost imperceptibly. "I wondered when you would finally say something."

Jo waited, her cold gaze never leaving Samantha's face. She wanted her uncomfortable. The anger and betrayal she had felt when Mike told her Samantha had been making moves on him was long gone, replaced by a sad feeling of loss for the friendship that had meant so much to her. When Mike died, she'd needed her friend. But Samantha was no longer that friend, and Jo pushed her away when she tried to be.

But in the months following Mike's death, she had taken stock of what was truly important, and holding a grudge against an old friend didn't make the cut. She had let it go but hadn't gone so far as to reach out to Samantha. But seeing her again, knowing that she was being that friend to Lisa while hiding her secret, dragged all those feelings of betrayal to the surface. It stung all over again. So Jo waited and didn't allow the ice to melt off her stare.

Finally, Samantha sighed. "Are you ever going to forgive me?"

"Water under the bridge," Jo said.

"Jo—"

"I'll ask again. When did you start sleeping with Victor Manton?"

Sighing, Samantha said, "About six months ago."

"Does Lisa know?"

Samantha shook her head emphatically. "No."

"Are you sure?"

"Yes, he was very careful. He's the pastor. It would have meant the end of his career."

"Yet you did it anyway." Jo pointed at the picture of the earring. "And you weren't that careful."

Rubbing her temples, Samantha said, "Someone came to the house. I had to rush. Victor must have found it and… I don't know how it ended up under him."

"Wait. Someone came while you were there? Who?"

"I don't know. I swear. A car came into the driveway, and I panicked. I got out as fast as I could."

"And you never saw who was in the car? Did you hear them come into the house?"

"Yes. I was quick but not that quick. They came in the back door, so I slipped out the front. There's an entrance in the back so that people he's counseling don't have to go through the house."

"Did this person knock or call out?" Jo asked.

Samantha shook her head and took an unsteady sip of her coffee. A deep-gray lacquer covered her perfectly rounded French-tipped nails.

"So this mystery person just came in the back door like they belonged there?"

"I didn't hear a knock, but I could have missed it. I was pretty frantic. But I'm sure no one called out."

"Did you see the car? The make, model, anything?"

Shaking her head, Samantha looked miserably at Jo. "I didn't look. I swear that's all I can tell you. I was worried about getting out and nothing else."

If the rest of her story was true, Jo could understand why she wouldn't wait around to see who was coming through the door.

"Does the family ever use that door, or is it only for patients?"

"The kids use it sometimes. It could have been one of them."

Ethan popped into Jo's mind. If he had come home and realized what his stepfather was up to, he could have snapped.

"Are you aware of Victor being into anything that would cause someone to hurt him?"

"No, he wouldn't be involved in anything like that. He's a good man."

Jo gave her a bland look that told her she did not share her interpretation. "So, someone came home after you were done having sex with this *good man*, and you slipped out when they came in the back door. What about your car?"

"I Ubered over so that my car wouldn't be in the driveway."

"Weren't you worried about a neighbor seeing you?"

"Of course I was. I walked around the side of the house, out of view. Ubers are quick."

"You're good at this."

Samantha pressed her lips together, shifting her eyes away from Jo's.

"Do you have the information on this Uber driver?"

"Um, I don't... I don't know."

"You snuck out and got an Uber, but you can't tell me who it was so that I can check with him on your timing? You heard some mystery person walk in, but you didn't see or hear him. This all seems pretty convenient."

"Convenient that I was sleeping with my best friend's husband and was almost caught? I'm sorry that I didn't think to keep records of where I was."

"Did you kill him, Sam?"

"*What?*" Samantha drew the word out in a long breath. "Are you serious?"

"You were the side piece."

"Side piece? Do you have to be crude?"

Jo shrugged. "You can give it a pretty name, if it makes you feel better."

Samantha pushed her chair back and pulled her purse from the back. "I'm done here."

"Well, I'm not," Jo snapped.

Samantha froze and stared, wide-eyed.

Jo planted her hands on the table. "Did he finally admit he wasn't going to leave Lisa for you? Did you decide if you couldn't have him, Lisa couldn't either?"

Samantha's mouth dropped open. "That's absurd."

"Is it? He was a preacher. Had a lot to lose. You said so yourself. Did he break it off? Decide it wasn't worth the risk to his career?"

"No."

Setting her notes aside, Jo changed tactics and forced sympathy into her eyes and voice. "Maybe you didn't even mean to kill him. You lost your temper and swung at him. You didn't expect to hurt him so badly. You panicked."

"I didn't kill him."

"You admit you were having an affair with him, and you admit you were there the night he was killed. That puts you in a pretty precarious position."

Samantha grasped Jo's hand. "Jo, you know me. You know I wouldn't kill anyone."

Gripping Samantha's wrist with her free hand, Jo yanked her other hand away and leveled her with a stony stare. "I thought I knew you once."

"Come on. That's not fair. We were young, and I was dumb. I've regretted what I did to you every day of my life since."

"Yet here we are, talking about your affair with your friend's husband."

"This is different."

"How do you figure? Was I a different kind of best friend from Lisa? From where I'm sitting, it appears the only thing that has changed is that now you're also cheating on your own husband."

"Jay can't know about this. Please, Jo." Samantha's voice became edgy, her almond-colored eyes shimmering with tears.

"If I arrest you for murder, I think he's gonna find out."

Samantha slapped her palms on the table. "I didn't murder Victor!" Taking a deep breath, she flopped her head back and stared at the ceiling, then she slowly let out the air. She took another steadying breath and straightened to look Jo in the eye. "Yes, I was sleeping with Victor. Yes, I was lying to my best friend. I'm a horrible person, if that's what you want to hear. But I did *not* kill him. Someone came into the house, and I got the hell out of there. When I left, Vic was alive. You have to believe me."

"And you have no idea who this mysterious person is who came into the house conveniently right when you were leaving. You didn't see this person at all? Male or female? Tall, short, black, white? Nothing?"

"I didn't wait around to introduce myself. I saw an opportunity to slip out, and I took it. I don't know any more than that."

"What about Jay?"

"What about him?"

Whoever had killed Victor had a lot of strength. From the pictures Jo had seen in Samantha's house, she knew he was a big man. "Do you really believe your husband had no idea about you and Victor? What if he followed you there and—"

"Jay has no idea."

"Are you sure about that?"

"Yes. Besides, he's been in San Diego for ten days for work. I can give you his itinerary and hotel information. Jay had nothing to do with this."

Jo made a note and would do a cursory follow-up, but she dropped Jay to the bottom of her suspect list. "Go ahead and send me that information."

"Of course. Is there anything else?"

The only evidence Jo had was an earring, and the owner had admitted to an affair. An affair wasn't a crime, although Jo wished it were. She wasn't done with Samantha, but she didn't have anything concrete to hold her on. Frustration crept in, but Jo pushed it back. Investigation was a marathon, not a sprint. More evidence was somewhere, and she would find it.

She slid the pictures back into the folder and stood. "If anything comes to you, anything at all, call me."

"Are you going to tell Jay about this? If you know he was out of town..."

Jo swallowed past the bitter lemon lodged in the back of her throat. "Unless it turns out it's important to the investigation, which it very well could be, there's no reason for me to go to your husband."

"Thank you."

"Make no mistake. I'm not doing this for you. Even though I find your actions repulsive, they are not illegal, and I have no legal reason to disclose them to your husband." Jo planted her fingertips on the table. "If I had legal backing, I would tell him in a heartbeat. He deserves to know."

Samantha stood and lifted her purse from the back of the chair.

"You're going to have to turn that over," Jo said, holding out her hand.

"Why? I told you the earring was mine."

"The earring has to be collected for the record. We'll swab it to match the DNA to the one at the crime scene and keep it in evidence. If you're cleared, and the evidence is no longer required, you'll get the earrings back."

"What if I say no?"

"You have a right to do so. If that's what you choose, I'll get a search warrant. I'll have to detain you until the warrant comes through."

"Detain me?"

"I can do that for up to twenty-four hours. I'm sure that will be enough time to get a search warrant. Of course, Jay would probably question where you are, but that's not my problem. Or you can turn it over willingly and avoid that. It's up to you."

"That doesn't seem like much of a choice," Samantha muttered as she reluctantly handed her purse over.

Jo pulled gloves out of her bag and emptied the contents onto the table. She sorted through the mess, removed the earring, and placed it in an evidence bag that she signed and dated. Then she scanned the rest of the items and put them back in the purse.

Handing the bag back, she picked up a remote-control device from the ledge of the one-way window and turned off the video camera mounted in the corner.

Samantha followed her actions. "You recorded this?"

"Of course."

"Without telling me?"

"This is an interview with a person of interest. They're all recorded."

"Person of interest?" Samantha eyed the video camera like it might come to life and attack her. "But I told you what happened. I didn't kill Victor. I'm cleared now, right? You won't need that video."

"No one is cleared until the case is solved," Jo said nonchalantly as she picked up the coffee cups from the table. "The recording stays in evidence permanently."

"Who will see it? Will Jay or Lisa see it?"

Cocking her head, Jo said, "The recording will be used only if the case requires it, but it is evidence connected to *my* case. Therefore, it remains in *my* custody indefinitely."

Samantha dropped back into her chair. "Turn it back on."

"Why?" Jo asked, passing the remote back and forth between her hands and trying to gauge the game Samantha was playing.

"Turn it back on. I have something to say."

Jo pointed the remote at the camera and pushed the record button then said for the record, "Resuming interview with Samantha Givens at her request."

Sliding the chair back out, Jo sat down and eyed Samantha, who picked nervously at a scratch on the back of her hand. Jo waited, confident Samantha was churning over in her mind how to confess and mitigate the consequences.

"The recording is on," she said finally. "Do you have something to tell me?"

Samantha raised her eyes from the table, and they held such anguish that for a moment, Jo forgot the betrayal from all those years ago and gripped her old friend's hand.

Taking a deep breath, Samantha said, "I started seeing Victor as my counselor when Jay and I had marital problems. Jay didn't think there was any reason to talk to someone, so he wouldn't go with me. I was afraid my marriage was over. I thought even if only I went, it could help. I could work on the things that I could control."

Jo remained silent, allowing Samantha time to get out whatever she was holding in.

"He started to touch me... in a friendly way, like you're doing right now."

Jo looked at her hand covering Samantha's and pulled it back then reached for her notebook to give her hand something else to do.

Samantha sniffed, reached into her purse, and extracted a tissue. After wiping her nose, she shoved the tissue into her coat pocket. "It all happened slowly. I was unhappy. You know... lonely. He made me feel special and loved."

"He was your counselor, and this happened during your sessions?"

"Yes."

"He manipulated you," Jo said quietly. She wondered if that was how he had counseled Lisa when she was hurt and vulnerable.

"I know that now. I was vulnerable, and he used it to get under my skin." After taking a shaky sip of coffee, she set the cup down and buried her face in her hands. "After... After the first time, I felt so horrible and dirty. I didn't mean for it to happen. I swear."

"I believe you." Jo was cautiously moving Samantha lower on her suspect list, but she was still on it. Regardless of her feelings, her training told her that at that moment, making her feel heard and believed would keep her talking.

Dropping her hands, she searched Jo's eyes. "You do?"

When Jo nodded, the tears pooling in her dark eyes ran down her cheeks, pulling dark mascara with them. "You have no idea how much that means to me."

"If you felt bad after the first time, why has it continued for six months?" Jo asked. "Did you stop feeling bad, or did he convince you it was okay?"

Samantha squeezed her eyes closed and went back to gnawing on the inside of her lip. Jo wondered how that lip was still intact after years of abuse.

Finally, Samantha drew in a deep breath through her nose and slowly blew it out. "I didn't know..."

Jo waited until she decided Samantha wasn't going to finish. "You didn't know what?"

"I didn't know he had cameras in his office." Samantha's face contorted as she stared at her hands, which were wrapped around her coffee mug. "He recorded the whole thing that first time in his office. When I told him it was a mistake, he told me unless I agreed to... do it again... he would send the video to Jay."

"He was blackmailing you." Samantha must have been the woman Ethan heard Victor threaten.

"I should have just let him do it. I should have told him no and accepted whatever came next. But I was scared. I started seeing him to fix my marriage, and when I realized what he had done... I was a coward, and I let him use that video against me for six months."

"So you continued to sleep with him on a regular basis, even though you didn't want to, so that your husband would never see the video?"

"Jay and I worked through our problems. I love him. I truly do. I was stupid, and I regretted it immediately. I tried to put it away and never look back, but Victor wouldn't let that happen." Wiping away a tear, she mumbled, "It made me sick to my stomach every time, but I guess I thought I was getting what I deserved."

"How often did this happen?"

"Lisa has a standing girls' night once a month with her friends. Vic knew about how long she would be gone and had her programmed to text him when she was coming home."

"That's why you never went to girls' night, even though you were invited."

"Lying to Lisa, lying to Jay. It made me physically sick every single time. Six horrible times."

"What about Lisa's kids?"

"We only met at the house twice when the kids were all going to be gone."

"Where else did you meet?" Jo asked.

"Twice at a sleazy cheap motel, once in the car, and..." Samantha covered her face with her hands, resting her elbows on the table. "And once in his office at the church."

Where his congregation adores him to the point of shelling out big donations so that they can be associated with his legacy. He was a master manipulator.

"So you met him for this monthly obligation that made you sick, and you took the time to take off your earrings and cozy in?"

Samantha blanched. "No, I didn't take off my earrings and *cozy in.* I didn't know I had lost one until I was almost home. I panicked, took the other one off, and shoved it into my purse. I forgot about it until now. Vic must have found it. I tried to call him, but he didn't pick up. That must have been right when..."

"What time did you try to call him?"

"I'm not exactly sure. Maybe ten fifteen?"

Jo motioned to Samantha's phone. "Can you check?"

"I deleted it."

Jo threw her hands up. "Why would you do that?"

"Jay might have seen it on my phone. I didn't know Victor was going to be dead!"

Jo drew in a deep breath through her nose and let it out slowly. "Okay, then we'll move on. Where did this dalliance with Victor take place that night?"

"In the bathroom."

When Jo cocked her head with a questioning look, Samantha whispered, "Mirrors."

At least it answered the question of why he would carry the earring into the bathroom. He must have seen it on the floor, picked it up, and didn't have time to figure out what to do with it before he was hit from behind. The earring fell from his hand, and he ended up lying on it, and the killer never even realized it was there. *And even if he did, why move it?* It only served to point the finger somewhere else anyway.

"So, Victor has been blackmailing you for sex, which made you physically ill and no doubt full of anxiety. If that was me, I would try to get him out of my life."

"I wanted it to stop more than anything. Especially before Jay or Lisa found out."

"It would have ruined your life. You would lose everything you have."

Samantha wiped her eyes. "Everything."

"And you happened to be with him right before he died."

Samantha's eyes bored into Jo's. "I know how it looks, but I did *not* kill him." She set her jaw. "I'm not sorry he's dead, but I didn't do it."

Jo crossed her arms and studied Samantha. Means, motive, and opportunity—she had them all. "I'm sure you can see where I'm coming from here. Honestly, it would be better for you to come clean now."

"Come clean? I told you I didn't do this."

"He was blackmailing you, and you lost your temper but didn't mean to hurt him." Jo nodded as if they had come to an agreement. "Yeah, that would play pretty well with a jury. It might even get your sentence reduced a bit. I can help you, but you have to tell me the truth."

"I may be a coward and a terrible friend, but I'm not a killer."

"Don't forget liar," Jo said. "Why did you lie to me?"

"It was a long time ago. I was—"

"Not that," Jo interrupted with a wave of her hand. "Today, when we first talked. You admitted to an affair but called him a *good man*. Why?"

Samantha gaped at Jo. "I know how this looks."

"You were manipulating my investigation."

"It's not like that."

Jo jabbed her pointer finger into the table. "It's exactly like that."

"Having an affair makes me look bad," Samantha said.

"But sleeping with a man because he's forcing you to gives you motive. You were hiding motive."

"Yes, but I didn't kill him, Jo," Samantha said through gritted teeth.

"Yet you hid information from me."

"I was around during all your criminal... whatever... classes in college, remember? You were always ahead of the curve, always talking about means, motive, and opportunity. And figuring out the killers long before anyone else."

"You were paying attention."

"You never stopped talking about it," Samantha said with a sheepish grin.

Jo shrugged and bit back her own smile. Other than the horrible ending to their friendship, it had been fantastic. Besides Mike and Nae, she had never shared more laughs or been more open with anyone. The end of that connection had been devastating, and she had often wondered if she could get past it and reconnect. The betrayal still stung, but time healed, and she realized that she missed her old friend.

"So why come clean now?"

Samantha glared at the video camera in the corner, and Jo had a new understanding of why having it there without her knowledge was such an affront. Her eyes softened, and she continued to look directly at the camera. "If Jay ever has to see this, I want him to understand. To know that I didn't mean to hurt him or Lisa. I made a mistake, a horrible one. But I wanted it to end and couldn't figure out how." Looking back at Jo, she said, "We'll never recover, but maybe he won't hate me quite as much."

Jo felt sorry for Samantha. Despite her valiant efforts to pettily hold on to the grudge she had been harboring for years, the feeling had snaked its way in. People made mistakes. God knew she'd made plenty of her own.

No doubt, Samantha shouldn't have slept with Victor and betrayed her husband and friend. But playing devil's advocate, Jo could argue that she had been manipulated during a vulnerable time by a man who was supposed to be helping her. Her defenses were down, she was feeling unloved and unwanted, and he'd used that against her to get his sick satisfaction. She tried to get out and right the wrong she had committed and was unable to. Ethically speaking, Victor

Manton was a pariah, and if he were still alive, he would be facing criminal and ethical charges.

But he wasn't alive, and like him or not, she had to push her sympathy aside and look at the facts, which told her that the laptop that held the damning video was missing.

"Do you know where or how Victor kept this video of the two of you?"

"He showed it to me on his laptop." Her lip quivering, Samantha whispered, "I've never been so humiliated."

"So destroying that laptop would solve your problems, wouldn't it?"

"He kept it in his office. I fantasized about getting my hands on it so many times."

"What kind of ideas did you have about that?"

"Maybe drugging him. He would sometimes have a drink... after. I thought if there was some way I could slip something into that drink... But I don't know anything about drugs. I don't even know how to get my hands on them or how much to give him to knock him out without killing him."

"Wouldn't an overdose have solved your problem?"

Samantha shook her head. "I'm not a killer, Jo. I just wanted that video gone. And I assumed there was a password anyway. How would I delete anything from the computer without the password?"

"You could just steal the laptop. Worry about that later."

"And have it sitting in my house? Where would I keep it that Jay wouldn't find it and wonder why I have it?" Rubbing her fingers roughly across her forehead while massaging her temple with her thumb, Samantha said, "Besides, he said he had a backup. There was no way out."

Jo stopped, her pen poised over her notepad. If the laptop had been stolen by anyone with even half a brain, they wouldn't find it in a pawn shop. If Victor had been blackmailing others, it stood to reason the device had been stolen simply to destroy whatever dirt he had dug up on someone, and they wouldn't sell it. They would destroy it, and it would end up in a landfill somewhere. Finding it would be next to impossible. But a backup that the killer wasn't aware of or couldn't get to held potential.

"And you have no idea where this backup is?" Jo asked.

"I assume in a safe or a safety deposit box at the bank. Do people use those anymore?"

"Yes, they do." Jo made a note to check with the local banks. If he had a box, and it was used to hold a blackmail video, she doubted Lisa would know about it. "Are you aware of anyone else that Victor was blackmailing, either for money or favors?"

"No. It's not like I was going to talk about this with anyone."

Jo had nothing to hold Samantha on, no evidence that she had killed Victor Manton. She had no evidence that she had done anything more than sleep with a married man and get into a sticky situation.

The timeline and her obvious motive made her too close to the victim to remove her from the suspect list, but her story was consistent, and Jo had asked every question she had.

She escorted Samantha to the elevator. As they waited, Samantha laid a hand on Jo's arm. "I'm sorry that I ruined our friendship. You were the best friend I ever had, and I truly regret what I did."

When the doors opened, Jo stuck her hand in the opening to keep them from closing. "Let's leave the past where it belongs. I forgave you a long time ago."

"You did?" Samantha's eyes softened as she squeezed Jo's arm.

Gently removing her arm from Samantha's grip, Jo motioned for her to get into the elevator. "I did. I'm done living in the past, so let's just leave it there."

The doors had barely closed before Lynae barged around the corner and stood, arms crossed, in front of Jo's office door. Jo shrugged with a now-you-know look while motioning for her to move into the office.

After dropping into the chair behind her desk, Jo opened her bottom drawer, dug into the back, and extracted two candy bars. Without looking up, she flung one in Lynae's direction and had a feeling of satisfaction when, out of the corner of her eye, she saw Lynae's hand dart out and catch the flying chocolate. Her partner's reflexes were on point.

Unwrapping her own bar, she settled back in her chair and finally looked at Lynae, who sat pin-straight in her visitor chair, unopened candy bar dangling from her fingers.

"Tell me I misunderstood what she did," Lynae said.

"Doubtful."

"But Mike didn't... I mean, he wouldn't..."

The expression of devastation on Lynae's face was heartwarming. Her friend had never known Mike, but she seemed to have a great affection for him anyway. "No, Mike didn't, and he wouldn't."

"Oh, thank God," Lynae gushed, relaxing her shoulders and slouching back into the chair.

"But it wasn't for lack of trying on Samantha's part."

"This was when you and Mike were serious?" Lynae asked, unwrapping her candy bar, then she took a bite.

"We were married."

Lynae's mouth dropped open. "That bitch."

"Yeah, some best friend, huh?"

Lynae crossed her arms and glared at the wall, shaking her head. "That's the worst." Her eyes brightened. "But at least I won't be the next used-to-be-best-friend, since I'm not a disloyal bitch who would try to horn in on her friend's man."

"There *is* that."

"Although Jack is pretty hot," Lynae said around a mouthful of chocolate.

Jo suppressed a grin and mustered an unconvincing glare. "Quit it."

"Samantha was the last person who saw him alive, at least as far as we're aware right now. Her earring was at the scene, which we'll confirm with DNA."

"Yep," Jo said.

"But you don't think she killed him."

Shaking her head, Jo said, "I don't think she has the strength to do that kind of damage. Victor Manton was a big man, and he had the hell beat out of him."

"She could have been involved but not done the actual killing."

"Yes, but think about it. If you were going to have someone killed, would you be the last person to be with him? Even if it was supposed to be these secret meetings?"

"No, that would be stupid. You would plan it for a time when you were nowhere around. Best case, you'd be out of town."

"Exactly. I don't know." Jo sighed. "She seemed sincere. I think she did a stupid thing and was in a terrible situation. She admitted that she's happy he's dead. But I don't think she did it. Of course, we'll run the DNA test. We'll drill the hell out of her on her story. Hell, we might even surveil her."

Lynae regarded her silently. "You feel sorry for her," she stated in an exasperated tone.

"I do. A little."

"But—"

"Life's too short to hold grudges." Wadding her candy bar wrapper and two-pointing it into the trash, she said, "Don't get me wrong. If she had succeeded in her little plot to get my husband into bed, I would have killed them both."

"Well, good. I was getting a little worried for a minute that you were getting soft."

"Never."

Jo had printed pictures of both Samantha and Lisa and added them to the murder board. Staring at the board, she crossed her arms and drummed her fingers on her upper arms. "Now we know at least one person he abused and had a video of. Who knows if he was doing this to anyone else?"

"We gotta find that laptop."

"I'm not holding out a lot of hope on that. Why don't you look into Samantha. See if anything pops. I think it's best if I stay away from digging into her at all. I'll work on the backup. Unfortunately, since we didn't find it at the house, I bet he had a safe deposit box at one of the banks." Jo looked at her watch. "At this point, we're not going to know until Monday. I'm going to pack it up and work from home. Why don't you do the same. Tag me if you find anything of interest."

"I'm on it," Lynae said, hopping out of her seat. She stopped at the door and turned back to Jo with a concerned look. "Is it bad that now I hope it's Samantha?"

"Nope, but my gut tells me you're going to be disappointed."

"You and your know-it-all gut," Lynae mumbled as she left the office.

Chapter 17

Jo shuffled from her kitchen to her office with her third cup of coffee while Mojo trotted beside her, happy to go wherever Jo did, even if it was simply from room to room. She had gotten off to an early start with sunrise services at her church and was determined to have a productive day.

Sundays were typically a day when she set work aside and concentrated on family and fun, hitting the reset button. But the Sunday reset wasn't working, and the coffee pot couldn't produce enough java for her to quiet the annoying voice in her head that reminded her she hadn't solved her last big case fast enough to stop the second death at the hands of a revenge killer. She couldn't have that hanging over her again.

She had bowed out of her usual visit with her parents and planned to spend the day working. After spending part of her Saturday cleaning up paperwork and performing other mundane tasks that came with being a lieutenant, she had done a search for local bank contacts and phone numbers and had a solid list ready to go. She had her warrant, so there wasn't much more she could do on that until nine o'clock the next day when the banks opened. Her notebook in hand, she slugged some coffee and hunkered down to spend the rest of the afternoon reviewing evidence photos and interview notes, hoping to find something she'd missed.

She was deep into committing the security guard's comments to memory when the trill of her phone dragged her to the surface.

She answered the phone without looking. "Riskin."

"There's that sexy cop voice," Jack crooned.

Jo dismissed the comment with a snort, but her shoulders relaxed. She tossed the notebook onto her desk and extended into a full-body stretch. The kink in her neck protested the movement. "I'm in full-on cop mode today, so if that's what turns you on..."

"I'm on my way."

Jo laughed.

"Hey, I know you've got a lot going on right now, but the kids miss you."

"The kids do, huh?"

"Okay, maybe their dad does too. But no lie, they've been asking for you."

"That's so sweet. I miss them too." And she did, more than she admitted, even to herself. Dipping her toes back into the dating pool and opening herself up to being hurt again had terrified her. She hadn't expected that first step to include two little souls who instantly wound her around their little fingers. She was falling hard for Jack, but the doubt that the kids might be playing a part in her feelings lingered in the back of her mind. She had always imagined herself with kids. But losing Little Mike so soon after Mike's death had left her believing she would never have that chance. *Would I be taking a step back, possibly dating other guys as well, if my heart weren't so wrapped up in them?*

"What do you think?"

"About what?"

"Seriously?" Jack groaned. "Where did you go?"

"Sorry, my mind wandered for a minute. What do I think about what?"

"I'm going to bring the kids to Johnson Park to go sledding, and we all want you to go with us."

"What a coincidence. Johnson Park is on my places-to-take-the-kids list."

"You have a list?"

"Of course."

"Like an actual written list?"

"Um, yeah. I have a list for everything."

Jack was silent for a heartbeat. "You're kind of a dork. You know that, right?"

"A dork who carries a gun, buddy. Let's not forget that."

"Hold on a sec while I add 'call her a dork' to my things-not-to-do-to-Jo list."

"Are you done?" she asked with feigned annoyance.

"I think so. No, wait…"

"Hanging up now."

"Hold on! What do you say? Can you take a couple of hours off for some sledding and a hot chocolate at McDonalds?"

Jo hesitated. She wanted desperately to step away from the case and spend some time with Jack and the kids. She hadn't seen Maddie and Logan in almost two weeks, and her heart ached for some innocent fun and childish giggles.

"It will be good for you to get away from it for a little while," Jack said, doing his usual job of reading her mind.

"Ever since the Campbell case…" Campbell had been her first serial killer, and she worried that any case she didn't solve immediately would lead to someone else's death.

"There's no reason to believe this is anything more than a simple homicide."

"Nothing is simple when someone is murdered," she blustered, pushing herself out of her chair, the tautness returning to her shoulders.

"That's not what I meant. You can't work yourself to death on every case, assuming the killer will strike again. Look back at your closed cases. How many of them would have killed again?"

"Too many," she said, focusing on her last two big cases and forgetting all the others.

"Okay." Jack sighed. "You're gonna do what you're gonna do."

"I'm sorry," she said miserably.

"Maybe next time."

After hanging up the phone, she tossed it roughly. The device skittered across her desk and into a wire-framed picture of Mike and her standing in the water at the lower Tahquamenon Falls. Mike's right arm held her at the waist while he snapped the picture with the left. They were both drenched and laughing. Jo smiled at the memory. She had slipped on a moss-covered rock as they made their way across the river and had reached for Mike to steady herself. In the process, she yanked him down with her, and they had an unexpected ride on the rapids before reaching a slowly moving area where they were able to gain some footing.

While she had tried to sputter an apology, Mike threw his hands above his head and whooped, "Best ride at the park!" then picked her up and spun her around before pulling out his phone and snapping a picture through the clear waterproof case. Even their bruised and battered bodies couldn't diminish the exhilaration the ride had given them.

Jo picked up the picture and ran her fingers over Mike's grinning face. "I would give anything to have one more day like that with you."

Yet here you sit in your office.

She scowled at the thought as it flitted across her mind. "Because I can't have that one more day."

You can't have it with me. But that doesn't mean you can't have it at all.

She eyeballed her office and really saw it for the first time in a long while. A single overhead light was accompanied by a desk lamp. What usually seemed like plenty of light suddenly appeared dark and gloomy. Case files lined the side of her desk, neatly organized by number, while two evidence boxes sat along the wall. The bright unicorn picture her niece had scribble-colored for her and taped to her wall only added a small prism of light to the cold room.

She felt profoundly alone.

"What the hell am I doing?"

You're not living your life. And you know that's not what I would want.

She set the picture back in its place on her desk, picked up her phone, and dialed Jack's number. After four rings, his voice mail picked up, so she hung up and tried again with the same result.

Shoving the phone into her pocket, she strode to the hallway closet and began rummaging for her ski pants and snowmobile boots. After digging them out of a Tupperware tub, she went to her bedroom and began layering on clothes. When she was sufficiently layered, she trotted to the truck and headed to the park, feeling an intense desire to hurry and not waste a single minute she could be spending with Jack and the kids.

Pulling into the park, she was relieved to find fewer cars in the lot than she had anticipated. The popular park could be quite packed on a sunny day. Disappointment dropped like a lead balloon into the pit of her stomach when she realized that Jack's car wasn't among those in the lot. He might have decided not to go without her.

She parked and sat watching kids of all ages laughing and whooping as their sleds raced down the long hill. Six teenagers piled two across and three high onto one innertube, with the seventh man giving them a push and jumping on top once they were started. Jo cringed when they hit a bump, bodies flying in all directions as the tube bounced and flipped upside down. The kids lay sprawled out in the snow, their bodies convulsing in laughter, before they dragged themselves to their feet and scrambled after the tube, which was continuing its journey to the bottom alone.

She tried Jack's number again but stopped when she saw his car pulling into the drive. The lurch her heart took when he stepped out of his car and jogged to her truck almost hurt. She stepped out and met him halfway and surprised both of them when she wrapped her arms around his neck and kissed him.

"I thought you weren't coming," Jack said.

"So did I."

"I'm glad you changed your mind." Jack motioned to his car. "The kids are so excited you're here. They're probably trying to devise a way to break out of their car seats as we speak."

"You get the kids. I'll grab my stuff."

Jack grabbed her hand and tugged her back for another kiss. "I should have paid more attention to the dorks in high school. I wonder how many of them grew up to be badass smoke shows like you."

Jo glared at him. "Call me a dork one more time. I dare you."

Raising an eyebrow, Jack said, "You dare me?"

"You heard me."

"Dork," he said with a snarky grin.

Jo smiled sweetly and gripped his hand then in one quick motion pushed his wrist forward so that his fingers almost touched his forearm, twisted his arm at the elbow, and jerked it behind his back while swiping her foot behind his leg, taking his feet out from beneath him and dropping him onto his butt in a snowbank.

While he lay stunned, Jo stood over him and said, "That's for all the dorky girls you ignored in high school. And for the record, you couldn't have handled me back then anyway."

Jack slapped his hand over his heart, let his head fall back into the snow, and laughed while Jo stared at him. Finally recovering his breath, he said, "Oh my God, you're amazing."

Unable to keep her laughter in, she flopped down into the snowbank next to him.

He rolled onto his side. "For the record, in high school, I would have been scared to death of someone who looked like you." Scooping a handful of snow and flinging it into her face, he added, "But I'm not anymore."

Jo sputtered and swiped at her face, spitting out snow and wiping it from her neck before it could melt and run down the front of her coat. "Oh, it's on!"

Jack jumped to his feet and jogged backward toward the car, throwing her his most mischievous grin. "Gotta get the kids."

Jo plotted her next move while Jack leaned into the back seat of his car, but all plans of revenge flew out the window when Maddie bounded from the car, grinning from ear to ear. "You came!"

As she jumped from her perch on the snowbank, her first instinct was panic as the angel ran fearlessly across the parking lot without looking. Jo met her halfway and swung her into her arms. "I missed you."

"I missed you too," Maddie said. "Daddy said you were working."

"I was. But sometimes I have to take a break from work to do important things."

Maddie aimed her sparkling blue eyes at Jo, their innocence drawing out her most intense protective instincts. "Like sledding?"

"Yes, like sledding," Jo said before planting a gentle kiss on her forehead then letting her slide off her hip. Grabbing her mittened hand, Jo led her back across the lot to where Jack wrestled with a wriggling Logan, who wanted no part of wearing his hat.

Fighting to squirm away from Jack, Logan held out both arms. "Jojo."

Squatting in front of the toddler, Jo held out her arms and discreetly elbowed Jack. As Jack let go of the wriggling boy, Logan flung his chubby arms around Jo's neck.

After looking to be sure her heart, which she was sure had melted into a pool of goo, wasn't actually leaking out of her chest, Jo pulled the little guy back enough to kiss his cheek. "Why don't we put your hat on so we can go sledding?"

When Logan stopped squirming, Jack dropped the hat into Jo's outstretched hand. "Traitor," he grumbled, sticking his tongue out at his son.

Logan giggled but held still as Jo situated the hat and tied it securely under his chin.

Swinging the little boy onto her hip and grabbing Maddie's hand, Jo said, "I've got the kids if you've got the sleds."

"Yeah, that works." Jack threw her a look that assured her that her melted heart had solidified and was capable of skipping a beat.

Trudging up the hill with a toddler on her hip was more of a workout than Jo had anticipated. By the time they reached the top, she was out of breath and could feel a clammy sweat under all the layers.

When Jack stepped beside her, dropped a sled close, and reached for Logan, the toddler gripped Jo around the neck and shook his head.

"You want to ride with me, Little Man?" Jo asked.

Logan picked up his head enough to look at the sled then laid it back on Jo's shoulder, resuming his death grip on her neck.

"I promise it will be fun," she whispered. Straddling the sled, she shifted Logan's weight then lowered herself to sit on the narrow plastic before prying his arms from her neck and nestling him between her legs. Pulling her stocking cap low, she looked up at Jack and Maddie. "Give us a chance to try out this hill, then we'll race you down next time."

Maddie giggled, her blue eyes twinkling. Grabbing her dad's hand, she yanked him toward the other sled. "Come on, Dad. We have to practice."

Wrapping one arm securely around Logan, Jo used the other hand to grip the side of the sled, then she scooted her butt forward to get it moving down the hill. The exhilaration of the speed and the frosty wind in her face brought her back to her childhood and sledding on "the Hill," a minimountain on a neighbor's property that was not only fiercely steep but also surrounded by trees and had a pond at the bottom. That nostalgic feeling was outmatched only by the giggles coming from Logan.

When they reached the bottom and stopped moving, Logan pointed at the hill. His eyes shone with glee under his lashes, which were coated in snow. "'Gain."

"That was fun, wasn't it?" Jo said as Jack and Maddie's sled slid past then stopped a few feet in front of them.

"How did it go?" Jack asked as he popped off his sled, scanning Logan.

"He loved it. Didn't you, Logan?"

Logan pointed his mittened hand at the hill and yammered his nonsensical gibberish.

Jack picked him up and swung him over his head. "That's my Little Man."

"Can I ride with you this time?" Maddie asked, looking up at Jo with pleading eyes.

"Yeah, that's a good idea. Let's show the boys how it's done."

Giggling, Maddie clutched her hand and led her toward the hill. Jo picked up the sled strings and started on the long journey back to the top.

After two hours of trudging up and sliding down the hill, Jo and Jack took the kids to McDonalds for a cup of hot chocolate. After, as Jo helped him strap the exhausted pair into their car seats, she kissed their rosy cheeks and promised to see them again soon.

"Why don't you come home with us, Jo?" he asked quietly, pulling her into his arms.

Every ounce of her screamed, *Yes*, but as she gazed at the two precious souls in the back seat, she knew she had to be careful. "It would be too confusing to them to find me there in the morning."

"They would be thrilled. They love you."

"I love them too. So much. That's why I have to go home. I don't want to mess this up."

Jack's shoulders slumped. "Jo…"

After giving him a kiss, Jo slipped into her truck and drove away without looking back. If she did, she knew she would turn around.

Before she could change her mind, she dialed the number of one person in Mike's old division she knew she could trust.

"Narcotics. This is Mary." The familiar voice instantly enveloped Jo in security.

Mary had been a good friend to Mike and one of the few people who had checked in on Jo for months after his death. She had spent countless hours listening to Jo's stories and had been an invaluable resource during her clandestine investigation into Mike's murder.

"Mary, it's Jo Riskin."

"Jo, how are you?" she crooned.

Picturing Mary, Jo imagined her in an immaculately coordinated—down to the jewelry—outfit. She had always envied her, not only for her consistently terrific clothes but also for the petite body she had to wear them so well. Her looks were deceptively perfect for her job, as she was one of the toughest detectives on the force, yet she could go undercover without presenting as a threat. Mike had a tremendous amount of respect for her, and Jo trusted her without question.

After getting the friendly pleasantries out of the way, Jo said, "I spent a little time with Rick."

"That bastard," Mary muttered. "What did the rat have to say?"

"He wants to cut a deal."

"And I want a million dollars and a house in the Bahamas. Did you tell him in explicit detail where he could shove his deal?"

Jo hesitated. She had been so confident that she was making the right call, but her confidence was wavering.

"Jo?" Mary asked hesitantly. "You don't want us to cut him a deal, do you?"

"He says he has information that will bust the whole ring. It's what Mike worked his whole career for."

"Do you think he's for real or just trying to work an angle?"

"I can't get a read on that. He wouldn't give me any more to work with. Said he wouldn't talk without a commitment on our end."

Mary gave an exaggerated sigh. "Unfortunately, cops are the worst inmates because they know how it works. You tell me what course we should take. Obviously, I want to know what he has. But there are a couple other leads we're chipping away at. It's nothing to get excited about yet, but I'm okay with staying on that course."

"He's looking for a transfer. I think he knows we wouldn't give him any more."

"I'm not surprised. Apparently, he's been in protective custody more than damn near anyone else."

Jo laughed. "God, that makes me happy. And what does that say about me?"

"Whatever it is, it says the same thing about me. I can go with you to talk to him about this deal," she said.

Jo was quiet for a moment while her heart pummeled her ribcage. "I think I'm done," she said finally.

"You're done what?"

"I'm done, Mary. I'm going to hand this over, and I want you to be the one I hand it to. I know who pulled the trigger, and I know who set it up. That's going to have to be enough. I have to step away and move on."

"I think that's a really good idea, Jo." Mary's gentle voice was full of compassion. She knew how much Jo had suffered and how hard the decision was for her.

"One thing, though," Jo said. "Do not even entertain the notion of reducing his sentence. Knowing he'll live out his life in a cage is the only thing keeping me sane."

"I promise you there's no chance in hell that I would do that."

"I believe you, and I wouldn't leave this in anyone else's hands. Though I would appreciate being kept up-to-date on progress, I'm going to step aside."

"No secret copies of the files this time?" Mary chided her.

"Does everyone know about that?" Jo had assumed she and her department source were the only ones to know she'd investigated Mike's case on the side.

"We knew while it was happening. As long as that son of a bitch got locked up, no one cared who did it. We all loved Mike."

Warmth spread through Jo. She loved her brothers and sisters in blue. A few rotten apples would always be in the bunch, but the rest of the tree was prime, and she was thankful for them. "Yeah, me too. And that's why I have to do this. He would want me to move on, and I can't as long as I have my head buried in this case."

"He's gonna be watching us, you know, rooting us on to bust the hell out of this ring. I can almost hear that whoop of his."

Jo imitated the battle cry that was Mike's signature then laughed along with Mary as the tears clogged her throat.

After a few minutes of station gossip and a promise to get together soon, they ended the call. She swung into her driveway and looked at the home she had shared with Mike, feeling a loosening of the noose that had been around her neck for more than two years. She would watch the case from the outside. If she heard anything, she would pass it along. And if Rick ever came up for parole, she would be at his hearing, doing what she could to keep him behind bars. But it wouldn't be her life any longer. It wouldn't be the fire whose smoke constantly choked and consumed her. She would never forget, but she was ready to live.

Chapter 18

Sleep proved to be elusive, and by three o'clock, Jo gave up. After swinging her legs to the side of the bed, she sat for a moment, deciding whether she was more frustrated that she hadn't gone home with Jack or that not going had caused her not to sleep. She flopped back onto the bed and rubbed her gritty eyes.

With a groan, she dragged herself to her feet and turned on the bedside lamp. Mojo lifted her head and regarded her with a "What the hell, woman?" expression.

"Sorry, pup," Jo said, squatting next to the dog's bed to give her a scratch behind the ears. Mojo's tail thumped a few times before she laid her head back down and closed her eyes.

Jo changed into running pants and a long-sleeved thermal T-shirt with GRPD in a gold stripe down the sleeve. When she sat on the edge of the bed to put on her running shoes, Mojo sprang from her bed and stood by the door.

"I wondered when you would figure out what was going on."

Together, they headed for the back door. Jo got her knit cap and gloves from the shelf next to the door and garbed up to brace for the cold. Mojo sat stock-still in front of the door while Jo attached her leash and unlocked the dead bolt. She nudged her back enough to open the door, then the two of them headed into the cold darkness of the early morning.

As they pounded the pavement in the eerie quiet of her suburban neighborhood, Jo ran through the possible suspects on her list. First on her list was Samantha. She tried to forget what she knew about her personality and look at only the facts. Samantha was sleeping with the victim, who was blackmailing her to do so. She was the last person to see him alive, and her earring was found at the crime scene. She had means, motive, and opportunity. All evidence pointed to her. Though it made Jo's stomach curdle, there was a solid explanation for the earring. Samantha didn't have nor did she need an alibi. She'd admitted she was there. But she hadn't admitted it until Jo had pinned her on it with the earring. She had impeded Jo's investigation and lied about her involvement with the victim, and she was left-handed. She had a multitude of strikes against her. On the other hand, Samantha wasn't big or strong enough to do the damage to Victor that had been done. It concerned Jo that if she didn't have a history with Samantha, she would probably be pushing for an arrest, but it didn't feel right.

The beating that Victor had withstood would require the kind of strength Jo would typically associate with a man. Or maybe it had been a man and a woman. Her victim hurt the woman, she told her man, they both came to confront him about it, and things got out of hand. Or since the bats from the house had come back clean, they went to confront him about it with a baseball bat in hand, and things were always intended to get out of hand. The man did the beating, they thought he was dead, then he started coming around.

The panic in that moment would be intense. The evidence didn't support a random robbery gone bad.

He knew his attacker. Samantha was adamant that her husband didn't know, and he had an alibi. But if Victor was blackmailing her, he could have been doing it to others. Someone didn't have an alibi.

As she reached the main road at the end of the neighborhood, Jo decided to keep going. It wasn't her usual route or her usual distance, but three a.m. wasn't her usual running time, either, so it seemed appropriate. The road was deserted, as she'd suspected it would be at that hour, so they crossed without slowing down and continued into a smaller subdivision across the street. Mojo threw her a side glance but kept her pace. Her nails clicking on the sidewalk reminded Jo that it was time to give them a trim, her least favorite dog-owner job.

The yards in the neighborhood were bigger, the houses grander. They didn't quite get to the gated standard of Samantha's neighborhood, but they leaned that way. She and Mike had considered a couple of houses on that side of the street when they were house hunting but had decided it wasn't their style. If she had to keep up with the Joneses, the Joneses had to be slightly more down-to-earth.

The more people had, the harder they would fight and the greater the lengths they would go to in order to keep it. Big houses, great jobs, the love of family—if you had none of it, you would have nothing to lose and nothing to fight for. She needed to figure out which of her suspects had the most to lose and would fight the hardest to keep it.

Jo hadn't quite ruled out Lisa. More people were killed by loved ones than anyone else. And Lisa had been hurt once by a cheating spouse. If she knew what he was doing, she could have snapped. The voice in Jo's head said she didn't blame her if she had. Of course it was wrong, and of course Jo would put her behind bars if she was the killer, but some things could break a person who had never before considered hurting anyone.

Jo had almost done it herself. When she tackled the man who had killed her husband, when she was face-to-face with the monster who had destroyed her life, her rage had blinded her. For the first time, for just a split second, she'd wanted to pull the trigger. She wanted him to pay for what he had done to her family. If she didn't believe so strongly in the judicial system, if she didn't have a solid code she lived by, she would be sitting on the other side of a jail cell. And that was no place for a homicide detective.

Ethan was making his way higher on her list. He didn't like his stepdad and knew he wasn't the good man he portrayed. Victor's infidelity could throw his mom into another depression, and that could be motive enough for a young man who was trying to protect his family.

She couldn't see how loss of business or changes in a church could drive someone to kill, but Trent Hoffman was still on her list. As was the assistant pastor, who clearly had feelings for Lisa. Getting a husband out of the picture could be an enticing motive, especially when he found out Victor wasn't a good man.

Jo had too many suspects. Somehow, she had to break free some new evidence to narrow the field.

A car idled in a driveway at the end of the cul-de-sac. As Jo rounded the bend and headed back toward home, the car door opened, and a man stepped out. "Mornin'," he said gruffly.

Jo offered a curt nod. "Morning."

"Kind of early for a jog."

Shit, he's going to talk to me.

When Jo stopped, Mojo tugged at her leash and tossed her a disdainful look. Jo snapped her fingers, and Mojo obediently sat down, nestled against her leg. "I'm an early riser," she said simply, hoping he would take the hint and let her get on with her run.

He propped his slight frame against the car, crossing one Tommy Bahama-clad foot over the other. "I don't think I've seen you here before."

"Probably not. This isn't my usual route."

"Uh-huh." Taking a draw from his Yeti travel mug, he sized Jo up. "This is about the time the cops usually make their rounds through the neighborhood."

Jo glanced down, suddenly mindful of her appearance and wondering if she had the look of someone out casing the neighborhood. As quickly as the thought came to her, it was replaced with annoyance that the pompous jerk would make an insinuation like that. She was running with a dog, for Pete's sake. "I didn't realize any of my men had routine patrols through subdivisions in this part of town."

"Excuse me? Your men?"

Jo extended her hand. "Lieutenant Riskin." Jerking her thumb over her shoulder, she said, "I live across Wilson."

Even in the darkness of the early morning, Jo could see the red creep up his neck. "Tom Jackson. Nice to meet you, Lieutenant."

Jo laid her hand on Mojo's head and ruffled her soft fur. "We'd better keep moving before the cold settles in." She started down the sidewalk with smug satisfaction that she had at the very least made the man uncomfortable.

Maybe he was merely being friendly. People usually looked out for their neighbors in neighborhoods like that.

None of the neighbors who were milling about the night of the crime had seen anything suspect. As she pounded the pavement, she replayed the entire crime scene, beginning with the sad wreath hanging on the front door. She would run it through however many times as she had to to find the missing piece.

Jo rounded the last corner before her house and poured on the last burst of speed she had in her to race Mojo home. She was no competition for the collie but gained some satisfaction in the heavy panting and that the dog's tongue lolled out of her mouth. By the time they came to a stop in her driveway, she and Mojo were both tuckered out. After a few extra minutes for a cool-down, she let Mojo off leash in the backyard to do her business.

It would be a while before the sun made an appearance, so she fixed them both a hearty breakfast and was ready for work before the sky lightened.

Chapter 19

After finishing the important morning task of making a pot of coffee, Jo filled her cup and headed back to her office. She closed the door against the usual din of chatter and ringing phones and settled in to make her phone calls to the bank. Her fourth call was to Fifth Third downtown, where she was transferred to the branch manager. After giving her credentials, Jo asked if Victor Manton had a safe deposit box with their bank.

She heard the clicking of keys while the manager checked the database. "Yes, he does."

Straightening in her seat, Jo said, "Mr. Manton is the subject of a murder investigation, and the contents of that box could be vital."

The manager was silent for a beat. "Mr. Manton is suspected of murder?" she asked finally.

"No, Mr. Manton is the victim of a homicide."

"Oh dear, that's terrible."

"We have reason to believe that the contents of his safe deposit box could be important to our investigation. Is the box only in Victor Manton's name?"

"Yes, it is."

"Can you arrange for my access? I'll have to request a warrant, but that shouldn't be a problem."

"Absolutely. Just bring the warrant and his key, and we'll get you right in there."

"His key? I don't have that," Jo said. "Is that a problem?"

The sigh from the other end of the line made the manager's feelings on the subject clear. "I'll have to get a locksmith to drill the lock out. He's only two blocks away. I can usually get him here quickly."

"Thank you. I'll work on that warrant and be there as soon as possible," Jo said, glancing at her watch.

After hanging up, she called Jack for the warrant. She hustled from her desk and caught Lynae in the hallway leading to the break room, empty coffee cup in hand.

Matching Lynae's pace, Jo strode beside her and filled her in on her progress. After deciding Lynae would stay at the station, Jo bundled up and took the brisk ten-minute walk from the station to Jack's office and then on to Fifth Third Bank. The young woman manning the first desk that Jo came to gawked at her badge and stared mutely when she asked for the manager. When Jo motioned toward her phone, she made a call then busied herself on her computer.

Within minutes, a woman who appeared to be in her midforties strode into the room, her hand outstretched. A crisply cuffed white shirt peeked out from the sleeve of her finely tailored black suit jacket. "Lieutenant Riskin, I'm Elizabeth Martin. We spoke on the phone."

Jo returned the firm handshake and afforded her a curt nod.

"I'm sure you have a busy schedule, so why don't we go right back," Elizabeth said. She raised a hand and motioned to a man sitting in a lobby chair. He picked up a toolbox by his feet then sauntered toward them.

A woman carrying a notebook walked out of an office next to where Jo stood.

Elizabeth smiled at the woman then turned to Jo. "You'll have to inventory what you take from the box. Erin is a notary. She'll witness the opening then notarize the inventory form. And Steve, of course, will get us into that box."

Steve rocked back on his heels and nodded shyly at Jo.

Jo thanked the trio for getting her in on such short notice, then she followed them out the door and down a short corridor. She waited as Elizabeth waved a security badge for the interior door, then opened another secured door and stood back, allowing Jo and the others to step in front of her.

The walls lined with small metal boxes, all neatly numbered, reminded Jo of a mini autopsy room. She half expected to see Kent weighing the contents of one of the drawers or to hear the haunting music he always played while he worked.

"Mr. Manton's box is E407," Elizabeth said, stepping back to allow room for the locksmith.

Steve opened his toolbox, pulled out a battery-operated drill, and went to work. Jo resisted the urge to cover her ears as the whine of the drill reverberated off the walls of the metal-filled room.

When Steve finished and had his equipment packed up, he gave Elizabeth a nod and headed for the door.

"You can bill that to the GRPD," Jo said.

Steve looked over his shoulder and said, "Yep, Ms. Martin already told me."

Elizabeth dropped her eyes and shifted her weight.

Jo smirked. "Well, all right then. Thanks for your help."

Elizabeth pulled the metal box from its cubby hole and set it on the small table in the center of the room. She backed away and allowed Jo to open the metal lid.

The box was empty except for a nondescript thumb drive with a plain black lanyard attached. Jo snapped a couple of pictures of the thumb drive in the box then the outside of the box to include the number.

She yanked an evidence bag and a marker from her bag then slapped the bag on the table and scribbled the date and her initials on the outside. After pulling on a glove, she removed the drive from the box and turned to Elizabeth and Erin.

"I've already got it recorded," Erin said.

"It's the only thing in there."

Both women leaned forward and looked in the box then nodded in confirmation.

Jo dropped the thumb drive into the evidence bag and sealed it.

"Is that what you were looking for?"

"I guess we'll find out soon enough," Jo replied.

Jo completed the inventory paperwork then followed Elizabeth back down the corridor. After thanking the manager, Jo left the bank with a renewed spring in her step. No one locked up a thumb drive unless it was important. Whatever was on it should have the potential to give her a solid list of suspects.

After stopping at Jam-n-Bean for a couple of tall cups of coffee, she strode back to the station, planted one of the cups on Lynae's desk as she zipped by, and continued on to her office. Lynae was only a few steps behind her and closed the door as Jo sat back and enjoyed a sip of coffee with a satisfied sigh.

"Well, aren't we chipper all of a sudden," Lynae said.

Pointing at the evidence bag, Jo said, "I've got a thumb drive from a safe deposit box in Victor Manton's name."

"Nice. That should give us a good place to start."

"I'm hoping it gives us the whole shebang," Jo said.

"What are you waiting for? Let's see what that bad boy has to offer."

Jo scanned the station directory then dialed the number for the computer forensics division.

"Forensics, this is DeeDee."

"DeeDee, Lieutenant Riskin. I've got a thumb drive that I'm pretty damn sure is going to be important to a current homicide case. It has to be documented into evidence, but then I'd like to see what's on it as soon as possible."

"Of course, Lieutenant. I'm working on a couple of cold cases that I can put aside as soon as you're ready."

"Fantastic. Thanks," Jo said before hanging up.

Grabbing the bag from her desk, Jo popped out of her seat and headed for the door.

"You're wound like a ten-day clock. Exactly how much coffee have you had today?" Lynae asked.

"No more than usual."

"Which doesn't mean a whole lot."

"Truth. And I have been up since well before the butt crack of dawn."

"Which does *not* explain why you're chipper."

"I'm feeling an adrenaline rush with this thumb drive. It could break the case wide open."

"I hope you're right. I'm going to keep digging unless you want me to bring that to evidence."

"Nope, I'll do it. Keeps the chain clean. Should I get you before I go to Forensics?"

"Hell yeah, you should."

After checking the thumb drive in to evidence and waiting through the documentation, Jo checked it back out and called Lynae while she headed to the computer forensics division on the fourth floor and told her she would wait at the elevator.

Never having been in the division before, she asked the first person she encountered where she would find them. The young man gave her a derisive eye scan before pointing at the door directly behind her with Forensics on a small beige plaque next to it. "Um, right there," he said with a hint too much of sarcasm.

"Thank you," Jo said, sliding her hands to her hips and discreetly pushing back her jacket to reveal her lieutenant's badge.

The young man stood straighter and pushed his hand through the frosted tips of his dark hair. "Y-You're welcome, Lieutenant," he stammered before scurrying away.

She waited at the elevator for Lynae.

"I've never been up here before," Lynae said, scanning the dull door-lined hallway.

"I hadn't either, but I found out from a delightful young man that this is where we should be." Jo pointed at the door she had been directed to.

"Why do I feel like that delightful young man is probably off wiping the pee from his leg right now?"

"Let's just say the cocky little shit is lucky I'm in a good mood."

"Oh boy," Lynae muttered before following Jo through the door.

On the other side of the nondescript door, Jo froze and gawked unabashedly. Six workstations lined the walls, each with four monitors that Jo guessed were thirty-two inches apiece. The desk jockeys who sat in front of the monitors were all plugged into some type of headsets. Some bobbed their heads to whatever tune was coming through their earpieces, while one leaned forward, pressing her hands against the Bose headset and listening intently to an audio file that blipped across her monitor like an EKG. Screens scrolled through images, white script played across black boxes, fingers flew over keyboards, and index fingers clicked mice. Along one side of the room was a sound board that rivaled those Jo had seen at concerts, only that one was attached to a wall lined with monitors.

Glancing at Lynae, Jo saw a look of awe that mirrored hers.

"This place is amazing," Lynae whispered reverently.

"How have I missed this all these years?" Jo replied, mesmerized by the lights and sounds.

Yanking bright-red Beats from his ears and letting them dangle around his neck like a stethoscope, a young man beamed up at Jo and Lynae. "Sorry, didn't see you there."

"That's okay. It gave us a minute to gawk," Jo replied.

"Pretty great, isn't it?" The man spun in his chair and gaped at the room as though he had never seen it. "What can I do for you?" he asked as the chair made the circuit back around.

"We're here to see DeeDee," Jo replied.

Looking over his shoulder, he bellowed, "Dee!"

When no one responded, he grabbed a rock-shaped stress ball imprinted with the words You Rock and fired it across the room. It landed between the shoulder blades of the woman who was intently listening to the audio file.

Her head snapped up, and the headphones came off in one fluid motion. "Seriously, Josh?"

"You've got company," Josh said, flashing his pearly whites while his hand jabbed out and snatched the rock that DeeDee had thrown back.

DeeDee's eyes darted to Jo and Lynae before she strode on her long legs across the room, giving Josh a friendly but not-too-gentle tap on the back of the head as she passed by.

Josh's hands flew up and patted at the tight braids that corn-rowed across his head. "Uh-uh, don't mess with the hair."

"Sorry, Lieutenant. The whiz kid isn't quite housebroken yet," DeeDee said, her bright-blue eyes betraying her motherly affection for Josh.

Genuinely amused by the exchange, Jo shook her head. "There's one in every division."

"We've got like five," Lynae said, squinting and pretending to count them off on her fingers.

DeeDee snorted then pointed at the evidence bag in Jo's hand. "Ready to look at that?"

Jo handed the bag over to the woman, who stood slightly taller than her. Pivoting on her stylish black boots, which sported a solid inch heel, DeeDee motioned for Jo and Lynae to follow her then strode back across the room, her long striped cardigan waving behind her like a cape.

Dropping into her chair, she uncapped the thumb drive then slipped it into a box to her right. "Let me check it quickly for viruses before we go any further."

After a scan, she removed the device and pushed it into the USB drive of a different computer on her desk. A message popped up in the lower right-hand corner of her screen.

This drive is BitLockered. Enter password to continue.

"Well, shit," Jo moaned.

Giving Jo a concerned look over her shoulder, DeeDee said, "If this were a computer, we could get around the password, but with a thumb drive, it's more difficult. There isn't any mechanism to access. I'll see if I can get around it, but no promises, and it will take some time."

Hunkering over her keyboard, DeeDee mumbled under her breath as her hands flew over the keys, and her eyes scanned rows of text that made no sense to Jo.

Standing awkwardly behind her chair, pretty certain that DeeDee had forgotten they were even there, Jo finally tapped her on the shoulder. "When you say, 'It will take some time,' does that mean minutes, hours, or days?"

"Somewhere between hours and days. I'll either get it or determine that it isn't possible."

"In the meantime, is there anything we can do to assist?"

"When a drive is BitLockered, a recovery key is created. It can be saved as a document on the computer, but often, people print it out and keep it somewhere. Theoretically, that's in case something happens to their computer, and they can't get the key that way. It isn't smart, but it also isn't uncommon."

"Okay. What am I looking for?" Jo asked.

After pulling a black spiral folder from the top shelf of an overhead compartment, DeeDee leafed through it then handed it to Jo. "It will look like this," she said, pointing at a printout with an impossibly long code of random letters and numbers.

"Does the person pick the code? Like we could guess based on birthdates, anniversaries, that kind of stuff?" Lynae asked.

"The code, no," DeeDee said with a shake of her head. "The code is generated randomly when the drive goes through the BitLocker process. It's the most secure method of encryption because it's forty-eight characters long, and there's no guessing it. However, there's another part of the process that requires a password, so technically it's possible but I'll admit unlikely that I'll be able to get anything off this."

"Damn," Lynae said under her breath. "He really wanted that secure."

"We'll do a new search of the victim's home and office. I would have looked right past this in a search. We could have our key in plain sight," Jo said.

"Let's hope so, but don't hold your breath. Someone who takes security that seriously is unlikely to have the code lying around." DeeDee eyed her computer warily. "Meanwhile, I'm up for a new challenge. I'll see what I can do. The dark web might have something for me."

Jo cringed. "Sorry to make you go there."

With a shrug, DeeDee said, "It's what I do."

"We'll leave you to it, then. Give me a call if you manage to break the DaVinci code."

"I'll do that," DeeDee replied then dropped into her chair and slipped her brightly patterned headphones back over her cinnamon-colored hair.

After stepping back out of the room and into the quiet hallway, Lynae sighed. "Now I wish I were a computer geek. That looks like so much fun."

"Yeah, it kind of does," Jo agreed. "Except for that dark-web business."

"I'm sure that's not a pleasant place to spend time. But on the other hand, there aren't any dead bodies, so there's that."

"Now you ruined it for me," Jo said, punching the elevator button.

"I don't even know how to respond to that."

"What?"

Shaking her head as she stepped onto the elevator, Lynae said, "Never mind."

"We're going to need to start working some different angles in case we can't decrypt that drive."

"You think that will happen? DeeDee seems like she knows what she's doing."

"But she said it's possible it can't be done. If it can't be done, it can't be done." Running her hand through her hair, Jo closed her eyes and shook her head. "Hell, I don't know. Let's hope DeeDee has some magic computer program that can spit out possible passwords."

Lynae raised an eyebrow. "I think that only happens on TV."

"If only things were as easy as they look on television."

"Bam." Lynae snapped her fingers. "One hour. Crime solved."

"Forty-two minutes, if you don't count commercials."

"I knew I should have been a TV detective." Lynae huffed.

"Well, since we're not, I say we get back to the Mantons' house and see if we can find that code." When the elevator landed on their floor, Jo went straight to her office to grab her keys. Lynae veered off to her desk.

Jo rounded up what she needed and was back at Lynae's desk within a few minutes.

They traveled back to the Mantons', bypassed the yellow crime scene tape, and entered the house.

"Why don't you check the bedroom again. Maybe he's got something that we missed stashed under the bed."

"On it. I'll poke around up there and help you finish in the office when I'm done."

Jo entered the office, which she'd become somewhat familiar with, and scanned the room, zeroing in on the most obvious locations to store a password. He might not even worry too much about it, since no one else had access to his safe deposit box. She first went through his desk drawers, pulling everything out and checking for a hidden location. Then she eyeballed the full bookcase, hoping she wouldn't have to go there, and moved to the file cabinet first. She had gone through both the desk and the file cabinet on the initial search, but her second search had a focus.

She rifled through the well-organized folders, ignoring their labels. If she were hiding something, she wouldn't put it in a properly labeled folder. After striking out on the last of the cabinet's four drawers, she noted that on the third drawer, the handmade label inside the metal holder didn't coincide with the contents of that drawer. In normal circumstances, she wouldn't find that odd, but considering the pastor's close-to-obsessive organization in his files, she thought it was worth taking a look.

She finagled the colored index card out of the holder and flipped it over. She was disappointed to find nothing more than the word QuickCrypto with a sixteen-digit number below it.

"I didn't find a damn thing," Lynae said from the doorway. "What do you have?"

Jo held up the card. "I thought I found the money shot, but there aren't enough characters for this to be the password."

"Where did you find it?"

Jo showed Lynae where the card had come from and how she'd gotten it out. "I'm going to bag and tag it anyway. It's possible he just used the back of the card to make his label, but it doesn't really fit with everything else I've seen. He's pretty particular. Let's just get the rest of this room handled and get out of here."

When they found nothing else of significance, they returned to the office and logged the card into evidence.

Chapter 20

Lynae followed Jo back to her office and flopped into her chair.

Frustrated, Jo snatched her coffee cup from the edge of her desk and stormed to the credenza to pour herself a cup. Swirling the liquid around the oversized cup, she gazed at the creamy mixture and blanched. "Jack says I should drink more water."

"*More* water?" Lynae snorted. "I would say *some* water would be a good start."

"Coffee has water in it."

"Pretty sure it's not the same."

"I don't know why he needs to worry about my water intake," Jo grumbled.

"Because he cares about you and your health?"

"If he cares about his own health, he won't try to deprive me of my coffee."

"He probably doesn't mean you shouldn't drink any coffee. Just replace a couple of cups a day with bottles of water. That'll make him happy. Not to mention the joy it would bring to your kidneys."

"My kidneys love coffee," Jo said then took a slug from her cup and rubbed her back in the general vicinity of her kidneys. "I can feel them shivering with joy in there."

"You're not going to drink water, are you?"

"Chances are pretty slim."

Lynae toyed with the stapler on Jo's desk. "Whenever Doug cooks me dinner, he makes a bunch of different kinds of vegetables and attempts to get me to try them. He's always telling me to eat more veggies."

"Well, kind of like my water, you don't eat any, so he has a point."

"I eat corn."

"Popcorn doesn't count."

Lynae crossed her arms. "Well, that's just stupid."

Jo opened her mouth to reply then decided, considering their coffee conversation, to let that one go. "People think about dumb stuff like that for other people when they're together. We don't think about it for ourselves, but we think about it for them. Like, I keep spare gloves in my car because Jack always forgets his, then his hands are cold."

"Yeah, it kind of goes with the whole dating, caring thing."

Jo smirked. "So you and Doug are dating?"

"I didn't say that."

"Mm-hmm."

"Whatever."

"When you were dating Adam, did he think that way? Did he worry about you and try to get you to do things because they were good for you?" Jo asked. She usually avoided questions about Lynae's abusive ex-boyfriend, but it was important to her case.

Lynae contemplated. "Looking back, I can see now that he didn't. But if you had asked me at the time, I would have said yes." Biting her lip, Lynae furrowed her brow. "But it was more control than caring. With Doug, he tries all this different stuff that I can tell he's hoping I'll like."

"That's sweet."

"Yeah, it really is. I can tell when he goes to the store, he's thinking about me and tries like heck. He'll say things like 'This has vitamin B6 in it, and that's good for energy for sports.'" She snorted. "Like if I think it's good for running or softball, I'll eat it. Or when I was looking for a new apartment, he checked around and sent me some ideas. He didn't tell me what to do. He just checked out the neighborhoods and stuff and sent me some links. I was still in control."

"What was different with Adam?"

"He didn't try to help me help myself. Instead, he did everything for me. He paid the bills. He decided where we would go and with who. When I bought my car, I was looking for a different one, but he decided this was the best one for me. Somehow, not only did he convince me to get this one, but he also convinced me that it was my idea. I don't know what kind of voodoo he used to make it happen, but it wasn't caring. It was control. I didn't have to think about anything, and that felt like being cared for at the time. But when he turned on me, I realized I had nothing, and I didn't really have the skill set to do anything. He had control over everything in my life."

"Which you said made it harder for you to get out."

"It was terrifying. Besides being beaten down, I didn't think I would be able to do it on my own. I didn't think I was strong enough or smart enough, because he had somehow made me feel that way. And I had nothing to start with."

"And look at you now," Jo said with no attempt to mask the pride in her voice.

Lynae gave a one-shoulder shrug. "Don't look too close."

"So in one scenario, your significant other—"

"Doug isn't my significant other."

Giving Lynae a blank stare, Jo said, "Okay, in one *case*, you're being cared for, and in the other, you're being manipulated. And they can feel very much the same when you're in the middle of it all."

"So much so that I question Doug's motives all the time," Lynae said, sweeping her hand out.

Jo pushed her chair back as far as it would go and propped her feet on her desk. Tapping her fingers on the side of her coffee cup, which rested comfortably in her lap, she rolled what she knew about Victor and Lisa Manton's marriage around in her head. Lisa had been in a bad relationship and had not handled it well when it ended. Her mental stability was questionable when she met Victor, her counselor, who then became her lover. Jo struck a mental check mark against Victor for dating a patient, a clear violation of the doctor-patient relationship. She could have lived with it, since they got married, if she weren't aware of his infidelity.

Lisa stopped working soon after they married. She wondered whether it was because she wanted to or it was a control tactic. He insisted on a text from her when she was heading home from time spent with her friends. *Concern for her safety or keeping track of her?* Or it could have been nothing more than a way to know when to get Samantha out of the house. Anything other than concern was manipulation and control.

Victor Manton was becoming more and more interesting. The pastor everyone loved most definitely had a secret side. Jo wondered how deep it ran and how many people he was blackmailing and for what.

"You going to share any of that stuff going through your head, or are we at the 'You should be able to read my mind' stage of our partnership?" Lynae asked.

"Sorry, thinking about the Mantons."

"I assumed so. Where are you going with it?"

"Victor was manipulating both Lisa and Samantha." Jo pulled the lid off the evidence box that sat next to her desk and removed Victor Manton's calendar. "What if he was doing it to other patients as well? We can't wait for a thumb drive that we may never get access to. The next step is to contact the people who were scheduled to meet with him and see what they have to say about the doctor."

"He only has initials with numbers on the calendar, like it's a code or something. Why does a pastor have a code for his counseling sessions anyway?"

"If I didn't know what I do, I would say he was being careful so that his family didn't accidentally learn anything about them. But considering what he was doing with Samantha, I would say it was to keep his dirty little secrets in the dark."

"Time to shine a little light on those secrets."

After flipping back through the weeks on the calendar, Jo picked a date six months prior to his murder and marked the page. "Copy these pages, and we'll split them up. Lisa said he counseled church members, so I'll call the church and see if they have a directory of members that we can compare it to."

Taking the book from Jo, Lynae popped out of her chair, then she headed for the door. When she turned back, her face was screwed up in concern. "Am I manipulating Doug?"

"Huh?" Jo was caught off guard by the question.

"Am I manipulating or controlling Doug?"

"I think you're the only one who's going to be able to answer that. Start with why you're hanging around with him," Jo said, treading carefully.

"He's fun and nice and... I don't know. I like being with him."

"That's good. Then why do you ask if you're manipulating him?"

"He wants to be more than friends. If I'm not sure I'm ready for more than that, is it wrong for me to keep hanging around with him? I mean, am I playing with his feelings because I like spending time with him?"

"What does he think is happening? Does he think the relationship is going somewhere?"

"I don't know."

Jo scowled. "What do you mean, you 'don't know'?"

"I mean we don't really talk about it."

"Are you sleeping with him?"

At Lynae's hesitation, Jo clenched her jaw but kept her eyes neutral. When her partner didn't answer, she prodded, "Nae?"

"No, I'm not sleeping with him."

"But you want to."

Lynae crossed her arms defensively. "So what? Is that so wrong?"

"He has feelings for you."

"Then he ought to like it," Lynae said with a devilish grin.

"It's not his style, and you know it. It would be unfair."

"That's a stupid rule."

"It's what happens when you have feelings for a good guy," Jo said gently.

"For the last time, I don't have feelings for him. That's why I'm asking!" Storming out, she flung her hand out and slammed the door.

"Sure you don't," Jo mumbled at the still-rattling door.

Chapter 21

"Okay, this so-called code isn't very sophisticated," Jo said, dropping her list onto Lynae's desk. "It's the first letter of their last name, their middle initial, and the birth month and day."

"And how do you know that?"

"Based on the times Samantha told us she was with him, I found GG0615. Her middle name is Grace, and her birthday is June fifteen. The church secretary I talked to yesterday emailed me a full parish-member listing. She was all too eager to help. And to pepper me with all kinds of questions."

"As if you're going to discuss an open murder case with the church gossip."

"I never said she was a gossip."

Lynae cocked her head and raised an eyebrow, giving Jo the stare-down.

"Okay, she's definitely a gossip," Jo said. "And she was itching for information so badly that I could almost feel the desperation through the phone lines. So I gave her some."

Lynae's chin hit the floor. "You what?"

"I just fed her the little tidbit that we were considering that it could be someone from the church."

"Oh, you're good."

"We'll see how long before that gets around the church, and someone flips on someone else." Pulling out her notebook, Jo said, "Let's look at the initials on your list and compare them to mine. Unfortunately, there are a few that don't fit with anyone from the church."

"You think he was doing counseling outside his congregation?"

"Lisa seemed to think it was only people from their church, but it's possible there are others. The church is enormous, by the way, so I would think he would be busy enough without going outside. Especially since he's the pastor, so this is kind of a side gig."

"So who do you think the other initials belong to?"

"Could be parishioners who have joined since the last time the list was updated. But considering the short conversation I had with Noreen, the church secretary, I bet she keeps that directory very up-to-date. So I'm putting that low on my list of options. But otherwise it's going to be a crapshoot."

"And if he taped and was blackmailing others, any one of them could have been angry enough to do him in. I can't imagine finding out my therapist was recording our sessions. It's such a betrayal."

Part of Jo knew that modern technology was a driving force in society. She liked her cell phone and would have a hell of a time doing her job without her computer and the networked crime database she accessed almost daily. The hours she worked made it hard to get to a library, so downloading books to her iPad was a blessing and the only way she was able to keep up her nightly reading habit. But the ease with which people could spy on, hack, or otherwise invade one another's privacy made her skin crawl.

While she contemplated the inevitable doom of civilization by technology, her cell phone rang. As she answered the call, it wasn't lost on her that she had no idea how the world even spun before those wonderful devices existed.

"Mrs. Riskin, this is Myla."

A panic rush of blood surged from Jo's heart, sending a tingling to her hands and lips. Myla never called her at work. "Is Mojo okay?"

Lynae's head snapped up, her face full of concern.

"Oh, yeah, Mojo's fine. We just got back from a run in the woods. She's worn out and sprawled in front of the fireplace."

Jo chuckled, relief pushing the blood back through her veins and flooding heat to her extremities. "She's such a prima donna. So, what's up?"

Lynae's shoulders untensed as she blew out a sigh of relief then turned back to her work.

"Um, well... I got that internship."

"Oh, hon, I'm so happy for you." Jo wouldn't tell her that her gut was diligently knitting a complex series of knots from thinking about finding someone who could replace her. She had been Mojo's caretaker since Jo adopted her as a scared little rescue pup.

"I'm pretty sure your letter of recommendation was the deciding factor."

"I knew I shouldn't have written that dang letter," Jo muttered.

"Hey!"

"Just kidding. I'm happy for you, and they're lucky to have you. Mojo and I are going to miss you, though."

"I'll still be around, but my hours will make it impossible for me to help you out. I mean, at night, if you're stuck at the station, I can come over, but I'll be at work from after school until eight o'clock every night, so that won't work."

"Yeah, that's not going to work." Jo held her breath in her cheeks then let it out in a not-so-quiet burst. "How long do I have to find someone?" Pressure formed in the back of her head, right in that I-don't-have-time-for-this spot. Her schedule and case load pushed like a steamroller through her brain.

"That's what I'm calling about. I'm starting a week from tomorrow."

"Oh, wow, that soon?"

"Yeah, I'm sorry. It wasn't supposed to start until summer."

"Don't be sorry. It's great news. It's going to be a little tight, finding someone that quick, but we'll figure it out." The steamroller pushed forward, crushing paperwork catch-up, flattening grocery shopping, and completely obliterating a much-needed night out with Jack. Mojo didn't warm up to new people easily. Having a week to find a replacement and to get Mojo comfortable with her would consume every extra second Jo had.

"That's part of the reason I called. My friend Kaci would like to do it."

"You found your own replacement?" If word spread about Myla, parents would push harder for cloning. "You think she would be good?"

"For sure. I wouldn't even think about recommending someone for Mojo that I didn't think would love her like I do."

The steamroller operator broke for lunch. "I'd like to meet her and see how she is with Mojo as soon as possible."

"I was thinking the same thing."

After making plans with Myla, Jo disconnected and dropped her phone onto her desk. She wasn't ready for change. The internship wasn't supposed to start until Myla graduated. She consoled herself with the fact that they lived in the same neighborhood, so Mojo would see her sometimes. Her dog would mourn the loss and wonder where her friend had gone. And as usual, the dog-mom guilt set in. If she had a job with normal hours, she wouldn't have to worry about things like that.

Her desk phone rang, and she answered absently, pondering how parents of human children managed.

"Lieutenant, this is DeeDee. I've got something for you."

"I'll be right there."

Chapter 22

Jo and Lynae took the stairs to the fourth floor, bypassed Josh at the front counter, and strode straight to DeeDee's desk. When Jo tapped her shoulder, DeeDee jolted then removed earbuds from her ears.

"Sorry. Didn't mean to scare you," Jo said.

"Not a problem. I knew you were coming, but I got in the zone anyway."

DeeDee pulled her glasses off and tossed them onto the desk then roughly rubbed both eyes before scrubbing her face. "I really held out no hope that I could break the encryption code on that thumb drive, so I went a different route."

"What kind of route?"

"Secrets, Lieutenant," DeeDee replied. "But I got to Mr. Manton's cloud account."

Jo had to physically push up her chin to close her gaping mouth. "You were able to wrangle a password from a Microsoft employee?"

"Oh, no, that would never happen. I was able to verify that he had an account and get the email address of it. And with that information, I was able to access his account."

"How in the world..."

"I never give away my secrets, Lieutenant."

Giving her an admiring look, Lynae said, "You're more devious than you look."

"You have no idea," DeeDee said with a wink, her previously tired eyes sparkling like sapphires. "But in this case, I obtained a warrant. I didn't think you would appreciate my skill very much if it wasn't admissible."

"Yeah, not so much. That all sounds promising, but what did accessing his cloud account have to do with the thumb drive?" Jo asked. She hated to admit how much of the computer jargon went in one ear and out the other. Even though it was vital to her case, she couldn't force herself to be interested in anything techy. She was thankful for people like DeeDee who made it all seem simple.

DeeDee spun around fully, crossed her legs, and settled back in her chair as if she were about to tell a fairytale. "As we discussed, when BitLocker is used on a drive, it generates a recovery key in case a password is forgotten. Some people will print it off, some people will store it on their computer—"

"And some people will save it to their cloud account, where they assume it's safe," Lynae chimed in.

"Bingo," DeeDee said, pointing at Lynae. "When you didn't find the code in his office, I thought we might be out of luck, but it occurred to me that this might be an option."

"And what do you know, you were right."

"It happens every once in a while," DeeDee replied with a shrug.

"Did you find anything interesting on the drive?"

"Yes, I did." After grabbing her glasses from her desk and sliding them back onto her face, DeeDee keyed a long password into her computer, bringing it to life.

File Explorer opened into a tree with several subfolders. "I don't know what you're looking for, but these folder names follow no discernable pattern."

Jo leaned over DeeDee's shoulder to get a better look. "I can tell you exactly what those folder names are. They match his calendar." Pointing at the screen, she said, "Let's open this one."

"Samantha Givens?" Lynae asked, giving Jo a sideways glance.

Jo shrugged. "It's as good a one to look at as any."

"Mm-hmm," Lynae mumbled.

DeeDee opened the folder. "All of the folders have video files. Some of them also have an email and a picture but not all of them.

Jo dipped her head closer to the screen. "We know what the video is going to be. Let's open Poetry and see what that is."

DeeDee double-clicked on the picture file, and a beautiful image of Adam and Eve in the Garden of Eden filled the screen.

"What the hell?" Jo asked.

"Not what you were expecting?" DeeDee asked, looking over her shoulder.

Wrinkling her nose, Jo said, "It's just a picture. I was hoping for notes or a full, unedited confession. You know, something I could use."

"Sorry to disappoint, Lieutenant."

"What does the email say?" Lynae asked.

After opening the email, DeeDee enlarged the text and shifted to give Jo a better view.

Dear Samantha,

The Garden of Eden held much temptation for Adam and Eve. Temptation they were ultimately unable to resist. Keep this picture as a reminder to avoid the sins of temptation and those of the flesh. You are stronger than you believe.

Victor

DeeDee sipped from a straw poking out of a silver Yeti tumbler adorned with a colorful VW van sticker. "Very cryptic."

Pacing away from the desk, Jo crossed her arms. "What the hell kind of game was he playing?"

"He has these damning videos but instead of sending them, he sends a lousy picture and a poem?" Lynae asked.

"Only some of them have email?"

"That's right," DeeDee replied.

"He's taunting them," Jo said. "By the time they get the email, he's told them he has a video. In this case, he has a sex video, so his message about sins of the flesh is a sick jab to say, 'Remember what you did. Keep doing it, or your secret comes out.'"

"But why so cryptic? Why not say, 'Hey, I have this video. Give me money, or it gets out'?" Lynae asked.

"Because if anyone else sees it, he doesn't lose his reputation. He's nothing more than a sweet pastor slash counselor sending encouraging words to one of his flock. Anyone sees that, and they don't think anything of it." Jo's gut churned. *What a sick bastard.* "It sounds like something a sex trafficker would do, not a pastor."

Holding out her hand, she said, "I guess I'll take that thumb drive back. We're going to have to watch those videos."

"Let me make it a little easier for you."

After pulling a box from an overhead cabinet and taking out a thumb drive, DeeDee slid it into a USB port on her computer and with a few keyboard strokes copied the contents onto the blank drive. With a couple more strokes, she ejected the original, removed it from her computer, placed it back in the evidence bag, and handed it to Jo. "I copied the files down to our server and sent you a secure link so that you won't have to deal with the encryption code."

"Thank you. You just might be my new best friend."

"Hey!" Lynae interjected.

Jo scrunched her face in a helpless gesture. "You've never sent me a secure link to files so that I didn't have to use an encryption code."

"Well, how could I have done that?"

"Just sayin', Nae." Jo shrugged then gave DeeDee a wink and turned to the door.

"So fickle," Lynae said, smacking Jo on the shoulder. "You couldn't even tell me what that QuickCrypto thing was."

"Lieutenant, wait," DeeDee called.

Jo turned around.

"Did you say QuickCrypto?"

"Yeah, it was written on a card in Manton's office, kind of hidden. Why?"

"I can't believe I didn't think of this before," DeeDee said, tapping her computer screen. "We saw something similar to these supposedly innocent pictures in a child-pornography ring we busted a few years back. If I'm right, there's technology involved that's pretty damn cool."

Jo raised an eyebrow. "This tech that someone is using to blackmail people—and that someone used in a child pornography ring—is cool?"

Holding up her hands, DeeDee said, "Hey, I didn't say the crimes were cool, only the tech. What can I say? I'm a geek."

"This judgment coming from a woman who wouldn't be happy in a job that didn't involve dead bodies?" Lynae asked.

"Touché." Jo pulled out her phone and scrolled through her pictures to the one she had taken of the card. She held her phone out for DeeDee. "Does this code mean anything to you?"

DeeDee looked at the picture. "That looks like a serial number. There's a free version of the software you can download online, but if you want to get more sophisticated with what you do, you can purchase a full version."

"Based on what I'm hearing, I'm not surprised he would want the full version. Why don't you show me this cool tech stuff."

"I don't have the software on this computer." DeeDee motioned for them to follow her then used her long legs to give her chair a push. She glided across the tile floor then caught hold of the countertop and brought herself to a stop in front of a sturdy, older-looking desktop computer.

"I thought tech people only did that in the movies," Lynae whispered.

"That was a sweet move," Jo replied.

DeeDee slid the thumb drive into the computer and opened the Garden of Eden picture. On the other screen, she opened what looked like a media player window. "I don't know why I didn't think of this right away, but if I'm right, this innocent-looking picture has a video embedded in it." Pointing to the other screen, she said, "And that video can only be viewed using this software. This is how some child pornographers hide their pictures. It just occurred to me that this could be basically the same thing."

She clicked an open-file button, browsed to her download folder, and double-clicked the Garden of Eden picture. The picture appeared on the left-hand side of the window. She then tapped a button labeled Get Data, and a video of Victor and Samantha opened on the other side of the window. The video clip was short but long enough that the viewer could see they were having sex on the sofa in his home office.

"Sweet mother of mercy." To Jo's nontechy brain, what they were looking at shouldn't be possible.

"The software is called QuickCrypto. It uses a technology called steganography."

"I don't get it. How is that video inside the picture?"

"The software hides the video or text between the pixels of the picture. It's virtually impossible to detect with the naked eye. The only way to see what's hidden is to use the software."

"How would someone get ahold of software like that? I don't think our victims were necessarily sophisticated computer users," Lynac said.

"They don't have to be. It's a simple and free download. With some pretty basic instructions, you could tell someone how to get to the hidden data. And hiding the video or text or whatever into the picture is equally as easy. You don't have to be a computer whiz to do it. It's nothing more than hitting buttons and grabbing a picture."

"If he recorded them together, he has to have more than that little bit," Jo said. "Why send such a short clip?"

"The picture has to be large enough to conceal whatever it is the sender is hiding. Typically, people send text or pictures. Video is pretty tough and requires a very large picture, which this one is. If he tried to hide a large video, there simply wouldn't be room. Now, if it were me, I would embed a link and upload the entire video to a secure website."

"Wouldn't your video be more vulnerable then?" Lynae asked. "Isn't anything that's out on the web somewhere accessible?"

"We like to think it isn't, and with a secure website, it shouldn't be, but I would never say never." DeeDee pointed at the screen. "Technically, this isn't safe at all. Anyone with this free software would be able to do exactly what I'm doing right now."

Jo was fascinated by the simplicity of the software. "The security comes with the fact that it looks like a normal picture, and unless the sender tells you, you wouldn't put it through the crypto thing."

"Exactly. It appears to be nothing more than a picture, so the average person would roll right by it."

"I'm glad you're not average, DeeDee," Lynae said, laying a hand on her shoulder and giving it a little shake.

"And glad you're on our side," Jo added. She looked closer at the split screen, one side showing a picture, the other side a paused video clip. "This software, though. Even for a nongeek, it's pretty cool."

"It was less cool when it involved child pornography."

"I'm sorry." Jo pressed a hand against her stomach. "That's something no one should have to see."

"The one part of my job that sucks."

"So what I'm getting from this is that Victor Manton recorded those videos, embedded them into these pictures, then sent the pictures to his victims. This is assuming the other videos and emails have the same kind of content."

"The email doesn't tell them how to see what's in it," Lynae said. "How threatening is it if they don't even know what it is?"

"For my two cents, I would say he told them in person," DeeDee said.

"Yep, I agree. Then he tells his victims that all he has to do is send the video to their spouse or whoever, and their secret is out. Or maybe he even sent it to them, and they just don't know what it is. Imagine the fear when your spouse says, 'Look at this nice message I got from Pastor Vic.' And meanwhile, the good pastor tells his victims, 'Better do as I say. All I have to do is tell them how to open it.'"

Jo could see the smug satisfaction as he held that power over them and their desperation to keep their secret safe. Lives would be ruined—some innocent, some not. It made her skin crawl. Jo had recommended counseling to countless people over the years. To think that someone would use that position to hold power over the very people he was supposed to be helping was sickening.

Lynae held her hands out, palms up. "If he was blackmailing every person who has a folder, our list of suspects is going to be pretty long."

"That could explain those consistent payments you saw in his account. He was blackmailing Samantha for sex, but he could have been getting money from the others."

"Remember, not every folder has an email," DeeDee said.

"But he had video on them. He may not have used it yet, but he had it in his pocket just in case."

"I wonder if they knew," Lynae said.

Jo let that ruminate for a minute then shook her head. "I don't think so. He'd hold on to it until he was ready to use it. That way, they wouldn't have time to play offense."

"So we focus on the videos that are associated with an email."

"That narrows it way down," DeeDee said. "I think there were only five of those."

"Gee, only blackmailing five people at a time? Not very ambitious." Jo slapped the bag holding the thumb drive against her palm. "Better get watching these videos. Thanks, DeeDee."

"Any time, Lieutenant."

Jo checked her watch as they stepped into the elevator. "I have an eight o'clock with Myla. It can get pushed back if necessary, but I think we should have time to get through these before then."

As they stepped off the elevator and into their bullpen, Lynae broke off and headed toward her desk. "Be right there."

Jo went to her office, opened the message from DeeDee, then followed the instructions to download the Quick Crypto software. While she waited for it to download, she stared at the busted-up face of Victor Manton on her murder board and mulled over the new information. The wonderful, beloved pastor had ended up dead after blackmailing at least five people. She wondered if any of those people who'd donated big bucks to be part of his legacy were actually doing it because they were targets. *How many people were praising the pastor out of fear instead of loyalty?* At least five of them were. They just had to determine whether one of those five was responsible for his death.

The smell of butter-infused popcorn wafted into the room. "Do you really have popcorn?" Jo asked.

"Well..."

Jo glared at her with her most lethal cop stare. "This isn't movie night with the girls. We're going to be watching people baring their souls to a counselor they believed they could trust with their deepest, darkest secrets."

"It's my dinner. It's a bad coincidence that it's popcorn, and we're watching videos, but it's all I have," Lynae said around a mouthful.

Jo shook her head while Lynae pulled up a chair then turned quickly, pulling the bag away as Jo reached out to grab a handful of popcorn. "Uh-uh. Remember, it's bad to eat popcorn while watching counseling videos."

Flopping back in her chair, Jo glowered at her, then with a sigh, she reached into her drawer for her brown lunch bag and dumped the contents onto her desk. The peanut-butter-and-jelly sandwich and a bag of Cool Ranch Doritos didn't have the appeal they had before her office smelled like the walls were made of movie theater butter.

Pulling the sandwich from the bag, she glanced at the picture of Mike that sat on the corner of her desk and remembered how badly he had always teased her about the volume of peanut butter and jelly she slathered on her sandwiches.

She shifted away from her light-colored slacks and took a bite while the contents oozed out of the back and sides. Moaning in sweet-and-salt-induced satisfaction, she decided Lynae could keep her stupid popcorn.

After setting her sandwich aside, she opened the link DeeDee had sent her. Starting at the top of the list, she checked her church directory then opened the corresponding folder and video file. VLC media player opened to Victor Manton stepping away from the camera and opening his office to welcome Sharon M. Clickner, aka CM0820.

Jo noted the date and time stamp as a middle-aged woman looked around the office without moving her head and timidly clutched an oversized Louis Vuitton bag. Victor motioned toward an accent chair that faced a mostly bare desk, which he sat behind. Susan shuffled to the chair, dropped the purse beside it, then perched on the edge, sitting rigid with her eyes downcast, while Victor spoke with soft confidence.

After laying out how their sessions would be structured, Victor spread his hands and motioned around the office. "Although I am not a priest, I consider this office a confessional. Nothing you say will leave this room. It's important for your healing to be open and honest with me."

"Okay," Sharon replied quietly without lifting her eyes.

"Good, then let's begin with a few simple questions." He folded his hands and set them on the desk, tilting forward slightly in a comforting and open gesture.

"I can see why people trust him," Lynae said, digging into her popcorn bag.

"Absolutely. He's good at this."

The video cut out and, after a few seconds of blank screen, opened to the same woman in different clothes.

"Check the date," Jo said, pointing at the screen. "It's six weeks after what we just watched."

"I wonder why he recorded that little nugget at the beginning."

Jo shook her head and shrugged as she watched the woman on the screen talk about the guilt she felt over the death of her husband in a car accident in which she had been driving drunk. Jo's pulse raced as a low hum buzzed through her brain. She knew the horror of losing a husband. She couldn't imagine having to add guilt on top of it.

The video cut again and resumed with Sharon in another session, admitting that no one knew she had been driving the car. She had let her dead husband be blamed for driving off the road and hitting a tree.

Then the video ended.

Jo opened the picture from the same folder and followed DeeDee's instructions to watch the video clip imbedded in it. It was an eight-and-a-half-second video with only the clip of Sharon saying, "I was driving the car that day, not Dave. Oh God, I killed him. I killed him, and I let them blame him."

Lynae pursed her lips then let out a long, low whistle. "Wow."

"Yeah, that was brutal." Jo highlighted her name and phone number on her list and made a note to check on the reporting requirements. The area was gray on whether she could or should report the crime.

She moved to the next folder. When she didn't find an email, she moved on to the next until they had worked their way through the entire folder. In every video, Victor recorded himself giving the same speech at the beginning. By the end, Jo was convinced that it was out of pure narcissism.

"Okay, so we've got Samantha, who slept with Victor. And Sharon, who killed her husband in a car accident," Jo began.

"And there's Bob, the football coach who likes to dress in women's clothes; Amy, a middle-school teacher who's attracted to one of the young boys in her class; and Tracy, who's having an affair with her best friend's husband," Lynae finished.

"Every person in those videos is desperate not only to deal with their problem but also to keep it a secret."

"And Manton is all too eager to threaten to expose them."

"He's playing these people like fiddles. He soothes them into total faith that their secrets are safe and that he can help them."

"Then bam, he pulls out a video and demands something from them to keep quiet."

Jo pushed to her feet and crossed the room to her coffee pot. Looking back, she understood that she would have healed faster and been better off mentally if she had seen a therapist after Mike's murder. At the time, she'd felt she could handle it and even patted herself on the back that she was doing a great job of it. But she had been a hot mess, and at times, she still was. She occasionally toyed with the idea of scheduling an appointment simply to have someone to spill her guts to. But every time she got close, her pride stepped in the way. *Stupid.*

Setting her coffee cup on the desk untouched, Jo reached for her coat. "I don't know about you, but I've seen enough garbage for one night. I've got an hour before I have to be home. How about I buy you a drink?"

"We haven't made it through all the videos yet. Don't you think we should look at the rest of them, even if they don't have an email, to see who all of his patients are?"

"We should, but I feel like I need a shower after watching that man. Let's put it away for the night and get some sleep."

"We've been partners for how long? And you think I believe you're going to go home and sleep."

Jo narrowed her eyes and pushed Lynae out the door. "Just give me this one, all right? I have to meet Myla soon anyway, so let me buy you a drink, then we'll both leave and pretend I'm going to go home and sleep."

"Fine." Lynae sighed. Grabbing her coat from the back of her chair and pulling it on, she said, "But I'm going to have two drinks."

"Okay."

"And they're going to be the most expensive drinks on the menu."

"Of course they are," Jo replied, jabbing the elevator button.

"You know, the ones that come in a bowl that you could mix a double batch of cookies in."

"Mm-hmm."

"And an umbrella. They have to have an umbrella."

The doors opened, and Jo gave Lynae a little push in the back. "Well, yeah, what's a drink without an umbrella?"

"Exactly!"

As the doors shut, Jo felt the tension leaving her shoulders. Leave it to Lynae to lighten the mood.

MOJO RAISED HER HEAD, her ears perked, a second before her tail began to thump rhythmically against the stone tile in front of the fireplace. The doorbell sounded. As usual, time had gotten away from Jo as she and Lynae had chatted over a drink. She had only been home for a few minutes and had hoped that Myla would be late, but that wasn't how her dog sitter operated.

"Who's here?" Jo used her excited voice in order to get Mojo's adorable head tilt that inevitably came when her dog heard words she recognized.

Mojo jumped to her feet and bounded to the next room, her tail wagging.

"Not much of a watchdog, are you?" Jo fake-scolded her as she followed her to the door.

Mojo afforded Jo a quick look, her mouth set in a grin, her tongue peeking out from her parted lips, then turned her attention back to the door. The anticipation vibrated off her.

Jo opened the door, and Mojo bounced toward Myla, who braced her petite frame for the onslaught. The dog stopped then backpedaled when she spotted the unfamiliar young woman next to her friend.

Myla squatted, pulling her dark hair to one side. "Hi, baby."

Unable to control herself, Mojo wiggled forward and stretched out her neck to lick Myla's face and was rewarded with a two-handed ear scratching that had the dog squirming to get closer. Myla expertly dodged the quick tongue that desperately tried to slather her with slobbery kisses.

A cute redhead stood in the open doorway then hunkered down next to Myla. "Hi, Mojo," she said cautiously.

Mojo spared her a glance then turned her attention back to her beloved friend.

"Why don't you come in from the cold?" Jo said, stepping back.

Myla stood and wagged her finger at Mojo when the dog rose on her hind legs to attempt one more kiss. "No jumping, Mojo," she said firmly.

The dog, adequately chastised, dropped to her butt, folding her ears back.

Kaci's eyes widened. "Is that all it takes?"

"Oh, she hates to be scolded," Jo said, ruffling Mojo's fur while the dog looked up at her with adoring brown eyes. "She's a good girl."

The girls stepped into the foyer and kicked off their snow boots onto the thick blue rug.

"You should see her if you actually raise your voice," Myla said with a chuckle.

"Wow, what a good girl," Kaci said, tilting her head and smiling warmly at the dog.

They moved to the kitchen, where Jo did her due diligence by peppering Kaci with questions, which the young woman handled with a graceful sense of humor. As they spoke, Kaci sat with her hands extended toward Mojo, who eventually inched forward to give her the sniff test. After deciding she was safe, Mojo let Kaci pet her, which she did carefully, keeping her face at a distance. That told Jo she had experience with the breed, which could either lick or snap with lightning speed.

"Now for the big question," Jo said hesitantly. "I have a ridiculous, unpredictable schedule. How flexible are you?"

"Well, I'm a night-shift sonographer at Spectrum."

Jo cringed. "Twelve-hour shifts?"

"Nope, we do eights. I work eleven to seven. So I could stop by on my way home if you have an all-nighter, and I can come over before I head in at night if you're late. I try to sleep from nine to four. I can adjust that if necessary, but I could take her for a run when I get up."

"That would be perfect, actually."

Mojo lifted a paw and rested it on Kaci's knee. "Oh, am I neglecting you?" Kaci said in mock derision, her cornflower-blue eyes glinting, as she resumed scratching behind Mojo's ears. She let the dog give her a quick kiss before shifting her weight back while keeping Mojo at arm's length.

"You've done this before," Jo commented.

"I had a dog just like her." The quiet way she said it told Jo the pet had been family, which was everything she needed to know.

"How about you take her outside and play for a few. See how it goes before we nail down schedule and pay?"

"Sounds like fun," Kaci said, getting to her feet and patting Mojo's head. "Wanna go outside?"

Mojo cocked her head and looked from Kaci to Myla then back at Jo. Jo repeated the question, and the dog jumped to her feet. The girls slipped back into their winter gear and headed out, an excited Mojo trotting between them.

Jo breathed a sigh of relief then went to the back slider to watch the trio. Her heart was full and content as she watched the girls romp in the snow while Mojo bounced between them and barreled after the beloved Kong ball when Kaci tossed it. She was blessed with a new treasure for her sweet pup. Once again, life moved on, and it was going to work out fine.

Chapter 23

"Okay, let's hit this list of suspects head-on this morning." Jo slapped the list onto her desk. "Last night, I went through the emails that didn't have videos attached. Nothing of interest there. There are two people from the videos whose confessions are actual crimes or at least could be."

"The drunk driver and the teacher."

"Exactly. Let's start with them." Jo handed Lynae a copy of the suspect list. "Why don't you check out the drunk driver, and I'll call the teacher. If you don't reach her, move on to the football coach, and I'll take the cheater."

As Lynae left her office, Jo dialed the phone number from the directory and reached Sharon Clickner on the second ring. After a brief discussion, Jo learned that Sharon had moved to Georgia two months earlier to be near her daughter and new grandson.

"I heard the news that Pastor Vic was murdered. I feel so terrible for Lisa and the kids. But why are you asking me about it?" Sharon asked.

"We recovered a thumb drive from Mr. Manton's residence—"

An unintelligible sound came from the other end of the line.

"We're aware that Mr. Manton has been blackmailing you," Jo finished.

"And you think I killed him?"

"We're eliminating suspects. If someone was blackmailing me, I would want him out of my life."

"Oh, I wanted him out of my life, all right. But at this point, I've made peace with the situation."

"You made peace with being blackmailed?" Jo asked. She had heard a lot of things over the years, but being okay with someone charging you to keep your secret was not one of them.

"I'm dying, Detective. If I live another month, it will be a miracle. I figured if I had to pay Victor Manton for the rest of my life, at least it wouldn't be long."

"Weren't you afraid he could continue to blackmail your family?"

"I've recorded a confession to be sent to my dear husband's family after I die. I knew if I told them the truth, he couldn't hurt anyone else with it."

"Now that Victor is gone, will you still give them the video?"

"Absolutely. They deserve the truth, and my husband deserves to have his name cleared. I wish I had the moxie to tell them before I'm gone, but it would ruin what time I have left, and that would break my heart."

"I'm very sorry, Ms. Clickner."

"I've made my peace. My illness has been fast, and for that, I'm thankful. I only have my brother, and I told him a few weeks ago that I wouldn't be here much longer. I'm starting to slip, so I asked him to handle my finances for me. It hit him hard, but he'll be okay, and his faith will lead him through."

Jo made small talk with the woman for a few minutes then hung up, crossed her name off the list, and moved to the second call and left a voice mail message when no one picked up.

"Well, damn," she said, pushing away from her desk to see if Lynae was faring any better. As she approached Lynae's desk, her heart sank, as she could tell she was leaving a voice mail message.

"Did you strike out too?" she asked when Lynae had hung up.

"I talked to the football coach, Bob Morrow. Nice guy who seems to be alibied, but I'll check on that. I tried Amy White twice and got her voice mail. Left her a message the second time."

"I didn't have any better luck," Jo said before telling her about her conversation with Sharon Foster.

"Amy is a teacher, so she's probably working. We could try to catch her for a quick interview at the school."

"Let's do that. We can't sit on our hands, waiting for people to call us back," Jo replied.

"I'll drive," Lynae said, reaching for her coat.

Jo grabbed her gear from her office then came out with her keys in her hand. "I'm driving," she said, ending any further discussion as she headed toward the elevator.

Lynae followed grudgingly.

After crossing the river to the west side of town, Jo drove through a thriving district of recently refurbished businesses, breweries, and apartment complexes then into a residential neighborhood of older homes with fenced-in backyards, oversized trees, and at least one unusable piece of equipment in each driveway.

They passed a baseball field and tennis courts then turned into a drive with a scrolling marquee sign sporting the head of what appeared to be a wolf. After parking in a small turnaround section of the school parking lot and making their way through the security door, Jo and Lynae approached the middle-aged woman who manned the front desk of Westend Middle School. A black placard with gold lettering sat prominently on the waist-high counter and stated that the person behind the desk was Tina Fryer. She tapped furiously on her keyboard, barely acknowledging Jo and Lynae's presence.

"Good morning, Tina," Jo said cheerfully, holding her badge above the counter. "We'd like to talk to Amy White."

Tina glanced up distractedly, then her hands froze above the keyboard as she eyed the badge. "I'm sorry. Ms. White isn't here today."

"Did she call in sick?"

"Is there something I can help you with?" Tina asked, tucking her thin, pin-straight hair behind her ear.

"Yes, you can."

The woman's eyes lit with anticipation as she straightened her back and lifted her chin.

"You can tell me if Ms. White called in sick today," Jo said, keeping the smile plastered on her face.

"W-Well..." Tina stammered then glanced around before whispering, "she didn't call in. She just didn't show up this morning. She had an extended weekend planned, but she was supposed to be back today."

Jo leaned in and met her with the same conspiratorial tone. "Is that unusual for her?"

"Oh my gosh, yes. She's a teacher."

When Jo offered nothing more than a blank stare, her eyes widened, arching her pencil-filled eyebrows. "She left a classroom full of kids with no teacher. Mr. Cleveland, the vice principal, is down there right now, waiting for the sub to get here. Luckily, we found one who could come right in."

The conundrum that a missing teacher would cause hadn't occurred to Jo. No call, no show was cause for dismissal in almost any job, but one that left a room full of kids without supervision was beyond most work headaches.

"That's going to be a problem when she comes back," Lynae chimed in.

Tina grimaced, the veins in her neck bulging. "I hope she has a really good excuse. Mrs. Gilbert is *not* a happy camper right now."

"So she's normally reliable?"

"Extremely. I'm concerned that she may be in the hospital or something. I think she would have to be really sick to do this. She's an excellent teacher."

Jo wasn't sure whether the feeling in the pit of her stomach was revulsion from knowing what she did about the "excellent" teacher or if it was trying to tell her that something was very wrong with Ms. White. She was inclined to think it was the latter.

"Why don't you give me her address, and we'll check on her," Jo said casually.

"I don't know if I can do that," Tina said hesitantly, her eyes darting to the door to her right with a placard that read Mrs. Gilbert, Principal.

"That's fine," Lynae said, pulling out her phone. "I'll just call it in."

"What do you mean, 'call it in'?"

"I can give her name to the police, and they'll have the closest cruiser stop by."

"W-Well, what if she's just sick? That would be embarrassing to have the police show up for no reason. What will her neighbors think?"

"Not really my problem," Lynae said with a shrug. Putting her phone to her ear, she said, "Missing persons, please."

Tina gasped. "Missing persons? Don't do that!" she hissed.

Lynae held her hand over the mouthpiece. "They're the only ones who can authorize a home search."

"Home search? That's not necessary. I can give you her address."

"If you're sure," Lynae said, pulling the phone away from her ear.

"Yes, I'm sure." Tina tapped some keys and jerked her mouse around. She scanned the screen for a moment then hastily wrote on a lined notepad, ripped off the sheet, and handed it to Lynae.

After giving the paper a quick once-over, Lynae said, "I appreciate it, Tina. Getting missing persons involved can get a bit messy."

"She missed a day of work is all," Tina said breathlessly.

"You can't be too careful," Lynae replied, tucking the paper into her pocket.

Jo bit the inside of her lip until it hurt. When she was confident that she could keep a straight face, she thanked the woman and exited the office.

After they were out of the building and out of sight of the office window, Jo let loose with the laugh that had been burning her throat and threatening to burst out. When she caught her breath, she smacked Lynae on the shoulder. "The hell, Nae?"

Lynae faked an innocent look. "What?"

"Was it Breuker or Lainard you called?"

"My mom." Her composure broke, and she burst into laughter. Covering her mouth, she said, "You made me snort."

"You deserve it. We could have called Breuker and had that address in two minutes flat without giving the poor woman a heart attack."

"I know. But where's the fun in that?"

Sliding into the driver's seat, Jo shook her head, wiping away laughter tears with the back of her hand. "You're terrible."

Lynae pulled the paper from her pocket and held it up like a trophy. "But I got the address."

"Do we think it's a coincidence that Victor Manton is dead, and the only person who talked about an actual potential criminal offense and lives in the area isn't at work?"

"Seems a bit too convenient to me. Plus, we don't believe in coincidence, do we?"

"No, we don't. Let's go have a chat with Ms. White."

Lynae tapped the number into Jo's in-dash GPS then settled back into her seat.

"You should probably call your mom and tell her what that was all about," Jo said.

"Oh, she knows. I used to do stuff like that when I was in school and didn't want to go somewhere. I was never good with peer pressure, so I would call her and have this all-out argument with her about how desperately I wanted to go to this party or that dance or whatever. Usually, she would just listen and not say a word. But sometimes she would totally get into it and give me all the reasons I couldn't go or tell me I was grounded or whatever. We would have a good laugh about it later."

"Um, I now love your mom."

"Yeah, she's pretty great." Lynae sighed. "I hope you can meet her sometime."

"Why does she have to live so far away?"

"We could take a trip to Oregon. It's beautiful there."

"I think I could suffer through that," Jo said. "You and I getting the same week off work could be a trick, though."

"Yeah, there's that. We may have to wait until she actually visits me, which will probably be never."

"I imagine traveling is tough for her."

"It is, and my apartment isn't super convenient for a wheelchair."

Jo glanced at her partner, who stared out the passenger window. "We'll make that dual vacation time work. They can do without both of us for a week. I doubt Grand Rapids will burn to the ground."

"It could. We're kind of a big deal around here."

"Truth."

A spark lit in Lynae's eyes. "We would have so much fun, and you would love my mom."

"Let's do it. As soon as we get the pastor's killer behind bars, we'll get it all planned."

Chapter 24

The blue ranch was as nondescript as every other home in the small subdivision on the south side of Sparta. Nothing stood out, screaming, "A potential pedophile lives here!" Jo tried to give the woman credit for seeking help, but it made her skin crawl to know what was going on in her head. No doubt it was the kind of secret worth killing over.

The front of the house was dominated by a three-panel picture window, and a dog stood with its nose against the end panel, howling morosely. Jo stepped onto the small cement porch to the left of the window and knocked on the door. It swung open, and the beagle bolted out, bumping its head on Jo's leg as it dashed by.

"Oh, shit, you let the dog out," Lynae said as she hopped off the porch and started across the lawn after the dog. The beagle ignored her as it relieved itself for a gross amount of time.

"I think we should be more concerned with why this door wasn't closed and why that dog is so desperate to get out." Jo poked her head through the door and announced that she was the police. The house was quiet, and from her limited view, nothing seemed out of place.

When there was no answer, she walked around the front of the house and tried the service door, which opened to reveal a Ford Fusion sitting in the garage.

Lynae sauntered across the lawn, carrying the wayward beagle.

"What do we know about Ms. White?" Jo asked.

"Thirty-two years old, never married, lives alone. Been a teacher at Westend for eight years. No priors."

"Lives alone, so probably only has one car?"

"That's a pretty safe assumption."

"And it's in the garage." Jo held up her fingers to emphasize her points. "She doesn't show up or call out for work, which is out of character. Her front door is open. The dog bolts like it hasn't peed in a week. I called inside but got no answer."

"Probable cause to enter?"

"I would say so." Jo didn't like to enter a residence without permission, but if Ms. White was in trouble, she couldn't give permission.

Stepping back onto the porch, she called out again. When she didn't get an answer, she moved inside and called again. An acrid burnt smell struck her when she breached the doorway. Moving more quickly through the house, calling Amy's name, she found the source of the smell—a small spiral ham, burnt to ashes, in an oven that was set at three hundred fifty degrees.

On high alert, Jo turned off the oven then unholstered her weapon. "If she's here, something's wrong."

Lynae dropped the beagle and drew her gun. Holding their weapons at arm's length, they moved through the rest of the house, clearing rooms.

In the last bedroom at the end of a short hallway, they found Amy.

Sprawled out on the bed, her arms flung wide, staring blindly at the ceiling, she looked like a teenage drama queen after a breakup.

"Ms. White?" Jo asked, cautiously entering the room. Her color told Jo she was long gone, but she checked for a pulse anyway. Her skin was ice cold.

A prescription bottle sat open on the nightstand. Jo peered inside without touching the light-brown container. It was empty. The date of refill was two days earlier.

"Damn," Lynae said quietly from the doorway.

"This isn't what I expected."

"Neither did I. I hoped we might find her hiding evidence or something else obvious but not this. Maybe she couldn't handle the guilt of what she did to Manton."

"Or he got to her, and she knew her secret would come out. I can see how that might lead to this. Either way, this feels too coincidental not to be related."

Jo sized up the woman and guessed her to be five-ten. She was a big woman with a strong build. Her hands were spread out at her sides, her palms up and her arms bare. She had no visible bruises. There had been no indication that Manton had put up a fight, but a couple of bruises would have gone a long way.

"Why don't you call it in so we can get an affirmative on suicide?"

While Lynae made the call, Jo snooped around the room. A black wooden nightstand held a purse-shaped lamp with a pink shag shade, a half-empty glass of water, and J.D. Robb's *Golden in Death*. A bookmark with a pink tassel stuck out close to the front of the book. Jo dug into her bag and removed a pair of latex gloves that she pulled on before picking up the book and leafing through the pages.

After setting the book aside, she searched behind the nightstand then dropped to her knees and reached underneath. She pulled a flashlight from her bag, shined it under the bed and noted a shoe bag, a suitcase, and enough dust bunnies to start her own colony.

She got to her feet and swiped at the knees of her pants, which were white with dust. She was reminded that she hadn't run the Swiffer over her floors in a couple of days, and considering the amount of hair Mojo left behind, she needed to get on that.

"Coroner is on the way," Lynae said as she walked into the room, shoving her phone into her back pocket.

"No note," Jo said.

"That's not entirely unusual."

"Yeah, I know. I was having one of those Nae moments in which I hoped she would leave a note, confessing that Victor Manton's murder was the reason she couldn't live with herself. And ideally, she would have placed the note on top of the murder weapon."

"Which of course would have her prints on it and Manton's DNA."

"Naturally." Jo placed her hands on her hips. "Why can't that ever happen?"

She stared at the body lying supine on the bed. It was an odd position for a suicide by overdose. She had seen more than her share, and if pills were the choice, the victim crawled into bed and fell asleep like it was any other night. The effects weren't fast enough that they collapsed on the bed and died in a slumped position. That was more typical of an illegal, fast-acting drug overdose or slit wrists.

Jo pawed through random items left on top of the oversized, old-fashioned dresser, rummaged through the drawers, then opened the small closet and pushed aside the hanging clothes to see what might be on the floor. She came up empty.

The outside door opened, and voices wafted in.

"I'll show them where we are," Lynae said as she left the room.

Mumbled voices, Lynae's and another female voice that Jo recognized as belonging to Mallory Wiseman, grew louder as they made their way down the hallway.

Jo stared at the body, an uneasy feeling in the pit of her stomach. *This should feel better.* If she wrapped up her homicide with a suicide, she could rest easily, knowing that there wouldn't be another dead body, she wouldn't have to interview any more witnesses or suspects, and the paperwork was significantly less. But the feeling wouldn't go away.

"Right in here," Lynae said.

Jo put on the best face she could muster. "Hey, Mal. Haven't seen you in a while. You didn't have to get so dressed up for the occasion," she said, eyeballing the petite ME's charcoal pantsuit.

"I don't manage to get out in the field much these days," Mallory replied. "So I decided I would make an entrance. It has nothing to do with the conference I was speaking at this morning."

She set down her field kit, pressed her hand into the small of her back, and arched her shoulders. "I'm spending way too much time behind a desk. I can't even carry the damn field kit anymore."

"That's what happens when you become a specialist in your field," Jo replied.

"That's why I stay mediocre," Lynae said.

Jo raised an eyebrow and cocked her head. "I always wondered about that."

Lynae reached up and scratched her cheek, using only her middle finger. "Just got a little itch right there on my cheek."

Mallory sighed. "God, I've missed you two."

"If we can drag you from behind that desk and probably a microscope or some other nerd tool, we should have lunch soon," Jo said.

"I would definitely put down my nerd tools for a lunch out with my favorite detectives." Nodding toward the bed, she said, "Right now, I should see what we have here."

Jo stepped back to let her through, curious about whether Mallory would read the scene the same way she had. She watched as Mallory, rooted in place, simply looked around the room. Then after pulling her camera from inside her field kit, she began taking pictures, the click of the shutter the only sound in the room.

Jo backed out of the room, giving her the space to do what she did best. Since she was still gloved up, she opened the door to the bedroom across the hall. A modern black desk faced the wall next to a window covered in white plastic blinds. On the right-hand corner of the desk was a printer. Its flashing green light indicated it was powered up. Jo removed the printout from the top and scanned the pages: lesson plans dated for the next day and a crossword puzzle with science-question clues. She had planned to be in school that day. Nothing about the scene, from the burnt meal to the lesson plans, said suicide.

She opened each drawer in the desk and leafed through the contents. Pens, highlighters, staples, and paperclips were in the top drawer. A box of thank-you cards, a birth certificate, and two gift cards to Meijer sat in the second. The third held a ream of paper. Jo lifted the edge of the paper and found a manila envelope. Reaching inside, she found a handful of pictures. Her heart raced as she sifted through them—schoolkids on a playground, in a classroom, and in the hallway. Jo scrutinized the pictures and found that one preteen boy was in each one. Her stomach somersaulted at the realization that the pictures were the work of a stalker.

She raised her head and looked out the door toward the bedroom, where Mallory continued to snap pictures of the dead woman. If Ms. White had killed herself, it might have been an act of desperation to save the young boy. If that were the case, Jo had to give her a bit of grudging respect.

Lynae appeared from around the corner, glancing over her shoulder then peering back at Jo. "What are you looking at?"

Jo held out the pictures. "You tell me."

Lynae looked through them, shuffling each one to the back of the pile after it received her full attention. Handing them to Jo, she said, "Boy, dark hair, brown eyes, probably eleven or twelve, in every picture."

"Nailed it." Jo slid the pictures back into the envelope then went through her procedure to bag and tag the evidence. If the woman's death was a suicide, nothing would be done with the pictures, but they had to be kept in case she was reading the scene wrong.

"I looked in the room next door. It's a storage room full of boxes and shelves of books. I didn't really go through anything, just took a quick look around," Lynae said.

"Let's wait and see what Mallory says before we search the house."

"It looks like she was going through her night, then suddenly, bam, she decides to kill herself. Seems odd."

"Dinner in the oven, lesson plans for tomorrow, no note, position of the body. I mean, I've seen stranger things, but..."

"Maybe someone found out about her interest in little boys."

"And a particular boy at that." Jo slapped the manila envelope against her palm.

"If it were my kid, I'd have a thing or two to say."

"If Mallory determines it's not suicide, we'll look at the kid's parents for sure. Either way, we'll look really closely at her for Manton's death."

"It would be neat and tidy if this were a suicide, and we could check off Manton's death as well as not be sorry that a potential child molester is off the streets."

"Yeah, I've been thinking the same thing. But if she's a homicide, she's ours, and we have to forget that the world is safer without her."

"I know. We work the case like any other. But no one can tell us what to think."

Jo touched her index finger to her nose and pointed at Lynae with the other hand. She meandered back into the bedroom, where Mallory was hunched over the body, peering closely at the inside of her right arm.

"Did you find something?" Jo asked.

She crooked a finger at Jo. "Come see for yourself." Holding up the woman's limp arm, she pointed a gloved hand at the inside of her upper arm.

"She was a cutter," Jo said, studying the perfectly straight scars most likely left by a razor blade.

"I'll be surprised if I don't find the same kind of scarring on the insides of her legs," Mallory said, running a finger over the raised purple lines.

"I had a friend in college who did that," Lynae said. "It's weird, but it calmed her. She would be super stressed out then all of a sudden calm. I always knew when she had been cutting."

Mallory switched to instructor mode. Jo had seen the transition many times. "Relieving emotional stress is one of the reasons. It's an addiction, like some people drink or get high to feel something other than whatever it is they don't want to be feeling. Cutters use physical pain."

"So someone who was feeling something they knew they shouldn't feel might cut to try to replace that feeling?" Jo asked. She was aware of cutting and other types of self-harm, but she was no expert on the psychology behind it.

"Sure, or it can be a way for them to punish themselves. There are a lot of reasons people self-harm," Mallory said.

"Seems like someone who regularly takes a razor blade to their arm would use it if they were going to kill themselves."

Mallory nodded. "You would think so, but cutting isn't about suicide. I've seen it accidentally lead to it, but that's not what it's about."

"She may have been looking for a more peaceful way to go," Lynae said.

Mallory bagged the pill bottle. "Anything besides this?"

Jo held up the envelope containing the pictures. "She had a thing for little boys. One in particular. Can't tell you if that makes it lean more toward murder or suicide."

"Well, I only care what the body has to say. So let's get her to the morgue and see what she tells me." Mallory stepped toward the doorway, where the paramedics waited.

Jo laid a hand on her arm to stop her. "Look, the reason we were here in the first place was to question her about her connection to a homicide that happened Friday night. If they're connected, I need to know right away."

"Are you asking me to push this to the front of the line?"

Jo narrowed her eyes and pursed her lips. "If I remember correctly, you like a dry red and have a revolving line of credit at Sweetland Candies."

Mallory laid a hand on her heart. "Ah, the language of bargaining is so musical. Throw in lunch, and I just might have an opening for your girl this afternoon."

"You mean lunch when you put down your nerd tools?"

"Yep."

"You drive a hard bargain, but I think I can make that happen," Jo said.

"Deal." Mallory moved to the doorway and motioned to the paramedics.

The two men in their black pants and white short-sleeved uniform shirts came through the door, pushing a stretcher with a body bag already lying open on top. After sizing up the situation, they lowered the stretcher to the level of the bed then wrangled the body to the edge.

The younger of the two gripped under the arms then flung his head to the side, whipping his shaggy hair out of his eyes. "All right, on my count," he said to the other man, who had a firm grip on both legs directly behind the knees.

After a significant amount of grunting and straining, they hefted the body onto the stretcher then executed a multistep handshake followed by a chest bump, like they had just won Olympic gold in the two-man bobsled.

Mallory tucked her patient into the bag, zipped it closed, and gave the men the go-ahead to wheel her out. She watched them roll the stretcher through the bedroom door, turned back to Jo, and opened her mouth then closed it again, shaking her head.

Lynae gaped at the door. "We gotta work on a cool handshake like that."

Jo nodded. "For sure, but I'm drawing the line at the chest bump."

Mallory took off her gloves and tucked them into a lined pocket inside her field kit then closed the kit. Pulling up the handle on the silver case, she winced and drew in a quick breath between her teeth.

"You okay?" Jo asked.

Straightening her posture and pressing her fingers into the small of her back, Mallory said, "Hurt myself at the gym."

"You try to do the right thing and exercise, and look what it gets you."

"Right? I've never strained any muscles on my couch." Mallory chuckled.

"I have," Lynae said with an eyebrow wiggle and a sly grin.

Mallory wrinkled her nose. "Spare us the details, please."

"You're just jealous."

"Speaking of which," Jo said, "how's Steve? I haven't seen him in ages."

Mallory's face relaxed into a soft smile. "He's great. As busy as always but doing well. He's selling his house, so that adds to the crazy."

"He's got a nice place. Where's he moving to?" Lynae asked.

Mallory shrugged as the corners of her mouth lifted. "My house. He proposed a couple of weeks ago."

"It's about damn time," Lynae quipped.

"I know, right? I was about to give up on the whole idea."

"I'm so happy for you," Jo said. "Let me see."

Mallory held up her left hand to show off a platinum ring with what Jo guessed to be a three-carat diamond surrounded by a cluster of smaller stones in a swirl pattern.

Jo took her hand and leaned in for a closer look. "Wow, that's stunning."

"Thanks. I'm still trying to wrap my brain around it. Now I have to get planning."

"Planning is a bitch," Jo agreed. "But kind of fun too. Hey, if you can get him to join us for that lunch—actually, now it should be a proper dinner—I'll spring for both of you."

"I'm sure he'd like that, but..."

"Yeah, I know, as busy as always. You'd think he was a successful pediatrician or something." Jo knew the complications of finding time together. No matter how hard they tried, she and Jack struggled because of their schedules.

"You would think." Mallory laughed. "Anyway, I'll put your girl here at the top of the list and let you know as soon as I have something."

"Thanks, Mal. And congratulations."

Mallory grinned as she wheeled her field kit out the door and down the hallway. After the front door banged closed, Jo heard the faint sound of her firing directions at the EMTs.

"That will be a fun reception," Lynae said.

"What makes you think you'll be invited?"

Lynae's face fell.

Jo smacked her shoulder with the back of her hand. "Cripes, I'm kidding. We'll have a blast."

"You're kind of a jerk sometimes," Lynae said.

"Yeah, but you love me anyway." Jo rubbed her hands together. "All right, why don't you start in the bathroom then finish in the spare bedroom you started in?"

Lynae headed to the bathroom, and Jo went to the kitchen. She stood by the stove and placed herself in the scene. *Single woman, alone in her house, puts on some dinner.* Scrutinizing the kitchen, she noted that nothing seemed out of place except the burnt food.

Jo left the kitchen and walked down the hallway. *She put the food in the oven then went to her office to make tomorrow's lesson plans.*

She entered the office and sat down in the blue cloth computer chair. *Ms. White makes the lesson plans, then maybe she pulls out the pictures of the young boy and spends some time in her fantasy world. And realizes that she doesn't have the strength to resist her urges any longer.*

Or it may have nothing to do with the boy. Maybe she has guilt over killing Victor Manton.

Jo pulled the keyboard tray from under the desk, tapped a key, and was not surprised when the computer requested a password. She would have to take it to her new computer-geek friend to work her magic.

She crawled under the desk to unplug the computer and found a wadded-up piece of paper. Straightening it carefully, she read the neatly printed note.

I never meant to hurt anyone. I wouldn't have, but no one would have believed me. Now my life is over. I'm sorry, Mom and Dad. You don't deserve this, but neither do I.

"What did you find?" Lynae asked from the doorway.

Jo held up the paper. "Suicide note."

"In here?"

"Under the desk. She wrote it but changed her mind." Jo handed the note to Lynae.

Lynae skimmed the text, her brow furrowed. "This screams guilty."

"Yeah, it does. But guilty of what?"

"I didn't mean to hurt anyone... My life is over."

"She knew she was going to get caught. Or she couldn't live with the guilt. It's vague enough that we can't assume she's talking about Manton. She also had the whole young-boy fixation going on."

"Looks like we should be looking for a murder weapon or something linking her to Manton's murder."

Nodding at the computer, Jo said, "We may find something there, but I need a warrant before we can go any further in the house or the computer."

"What about the dog? Do I call animal control?"

"Let's bring it with us. In the suicide note, she apologized to her parents, so I guess she has a relationship with them. Let's check with them before we get animal control involved."

Lynae scooped up the beagle and tucked it close to her chest before going out into the cold. The animal, in return, continuously licked her face until she was settled in the passenger seat and could pull it away. "I'll get a box from supply and keep her by my desk until we find her a home."

Jo scratched behind the cute little pup's ears. "We'll take good care of you," she said in the voice she reserved for babies and animals then drove out and headed for the station.

Chapter 25

Back at the station, they rode the elevator to their floor with the beagle, whom Jo had nicknamed Bullet, tucked snugly inside Lynae's coat. Lynae had already sent out an email, looking for a box and a blanket.

When Jo's phone rang, she grudgingly pried her hands away from the pup's face.

"There's a Tracy Peterson here to see you" came the smooth, professional voice of the receptionist.

"Thanks, Aneace. Give me five, then send her up."

As she disconnected, Jo turned to Lynae, wide-eyed. "One of our suspects is here to see me."

"Shut up. Which one?"

"Tracy Peterson, our cheater."

"I did not see that coming. Think we could get lucky enough to get a random drop-in confession?"

"Stranger things have happened."

Jo beelined for her office to check availability and book a room to interview Tracy.

A few minutes later, the young woman stepped off the elevator, her eyes darting from side to side. A rabbit in a dog kennel showed less fear.

Jo moved quickly across the bullpen to intercept her before she bolted. "Ms. Peterson?"

The woman jolted, her head jerking in Jo's direction. "Yes."

"I'm Lieutenant Riskin," Jo said, holding out a hand.

"Tracy," the woman said shakily before placing a clammy hand in Jo's and giving her hand a limp pump. Pulling her coat closed tightly around her body, she surveyed the noisy bullpen with anxious eyes.

"If you'll follow me, we can talk in a conference room, where there's a little less going on," Jo said.

Tracy shoved her hands into her coat pockets and walked beside Jo to the room she had hastily prepped with a couple of bottles of water and a box of Kleenex. Jo motioned to a chair at the small round table then sat across from her.

"What can I do for you, Tracy?"

While picking at the plastic shrink wrap around her water bottle, Tracy dragged her top teeth roughly across her bottom lip. Her brow was knit as she stared intently at the table. "You left me a message about my counseling with Pastor Manton." Swiping at a tear, she said, "Sorry, I'm really nervous."

"I understand. It's not every day that you're contacted by the police."

Jo took a drink of her coffee, attempting to appear relaxed and patient while she was anything but.

"I don't know how to do this."

"I find it's usually easiest to just rip the Band-Aid off quickly," Jo said.

Finally, Tracy lifted her eyes and sucked in a deep breath. "I paid Victor Manton over five thousand dollars not to tell my friend that I had an affair with her husband."

"How did Mr. Manton know about your affair?" Jo kept her voice even, although her heart raced. Even though they knew about the blackmail, having another victim come forward brought new potential evidence.

"I went to him because I had so much guilt and didn't know what to do, and he used it to blackmail me." She spewed out the confession in one long, guilt-laden breath.

Jo kept her tone level. "I'm sorry you've been through something so difficult." She set her coffee cup on the table then leaned forward and folded her hands in a standard interrogation technique to appear open and connected. "A counselor's office should be a safe and non-judgmental place."

"I thought it would be. He's such a good pastor. I told him I would do anything to take it back and that the worst thing would be for my friend to find out."

"And he used that against you." Jo's insides roiled with a mixture of sympathy, disgust, and pure anger. *How dare the man abuse his power in this way.*

Tracy shook her head, sniffling and blinking back tears.

When Jo was certain she wasn't going to respond, she asked, "Are you here to tell me you had something to do with Victor's death, Tracy?"

Tracy looked as if Jo had slapped her. "What? No!"

Human nature was always a fascination to Jo. She wondered why the woman would come to her office to tell her about the affair if she wasn't guilty. If she had been willing to pay a significant amount of money to keep her secret, it didn't make sense to trot into a police station and spill it unprovoked.

"I know if someone was blackmailing me on something so personal, something that had the potential to ruin an important friendship, I would be pretty desperate to stop him."

"I didn't kill Pastor Manton," Tracy said.

Jo found it interesting that she continued to refer to Victor as "Pastor" when he had acted as anything but a man of the cloth.

"Then what brings you here to tell me about the blackmail?" Jo asked.

"It's still happening."

Jo cocked her head in a way that mimicked her dog. "What's still happening?"

"I got another email from Pastor Manton. I know that sounds crazy. He's dead, and he can't be sending me emails. But it came from his email address."

The development caught Jo by surprise. The emails weren't coming from the afterlife, so the killer had Victor Manton's blackmail list. She had assumed the killer stole the laptop to keep his own secret hidden. Maybe the real desire was for the money and power that Victor was getting from it.

Hazel eyes swam behind pools of tears that settled in red-rimmed pockets before spilling over her cheeks. "I'm never going to be able to get away from that video," she squeaked in a tear-choked voice.

"When did you get this email?" Jo asked.

"Last night." Tracy pulled a tissue from the box on the table. After noisily blowing her nose, she wadded the tissue up and shoved it into her coat pocket. "It said I have forty-eight hours to confess, or the video will be sent to my friend. Whoever it is has my friend's email address. The video was attached. This is for real."

"Is that all?"

"Isn't that enough?" Tracy squeaked indignantly.

"I'm sorry. I didn't mean it that way. I mean is he asking for money or anything else tangible?"

"No, nothing." Thrusting both hands toward her phone, which lay on the table, she said, "It just says that I have to tell my friend the truth."

In Jo's experience, blackmail always involved money, objects, sex, or all of the above, never simply a confession of a wrongdoing. *Unless we're dealing with some kind of vigilante.* "I would like to see that email."

Her lip trembling, Tracy rapidly blinked back tears. "I don't want you to see the video. It's humiliating."

"I'm not here to judge you, Tracy," Jo said gently. "I'm only here to find the person responsible for killing Victor Manton."

"I'm glad he's dead," Tracy said through gritted teeth. As she sucked in a breath loudly, her eyes popping wide, she added, "But like I said, I didn't kill him."

"I'm going to have to ask you where you were the night Victor was killed."

"I was at my parents' house in Traverse City. You can call them."

"Why don't you write down their names and phone number so that I can check on that and cross your name off the list?" Jo slid a notepad and a pen across the table.

Tracy scribbled on it then pushed it back to Jo.

"Thank you. Did you visit any other friends while you were in Traverse?"

"Um, yeah, I went out with a few of the girls I went to high school with. We ate at Bubba's then had a couple of drinks at Taproot. Why?"

"Why don't you give me their names also? And I would appreciate if you would send me that email."

Picking up her phone, she looked at Jo through heavy-lidded eyes. "What's your email address?"

Jo rattled it off and watched as she forwarded it. Jo checked her phone and noted that she had it. "It won't go any further than my team."

"If I don't tell my friend by tomorrow night and prove it to whoever is doing this, he's going to send the video to her. What do I do?"

"I'm sorry. I'm afraid I can't answer that." Although Jo would never condone an affair, she did feel sorry for the woman. She was in a terrible position that seeing a counselor should never have put her in. "My team is working this case hard, and this email has the potential to help us a great deal, but I certainly can't guarantee that kind of timeline."

Tracy's lip trembled as her pretty face crumpled into a pout that would make a three-year-old envious. "Oh God, what am I going to do?" She crossed her arms and thumped them onto the table before dropping her head onto them. Her shoulders shook as she sobbed.

Jo discreetly glanced at her watch. She didn't have time to be the woman's shoulder to cry on, but she couldn't leave her there blubbering either. Jo laid a hand on Tracy's shoulder and gave it a gentle pat. Since "You made your bed. Now lie in it" wasn't going to add anything positive to the conversation, she decided that silent was the best thing to be. As precious moments ticked away, the two sat quietly in the conference room while Tracy composed herself.

Before lifting her head from her arms, Tracy reached up, snatched a tissue from the box, and moved her hand to her face. When she finally sat up, she dabbed at the black mascara streaks that stood out starkly on her blotchy red cheeks.

"Is everyone going to know what I did?"

"This doesn't leave the station if I can help it."

"I guess it won't matter by tomorrow anyway," Tracy said as her face crumpled.

"We're doing everything we can to find out who's behind this."

"Will you contact me if you catch the killer before tomorrow?" Tracy asked. "Otherwise, I'm going to talk to my friend before she gets that video."

"I absolutely will."

"She can't find out that way." Wiping her nose with the mascara-stained tissue, she looked at Jo hopefully. "Maybe I can explain."

"You can only speak from your heart and do your best." Even as she said it, Jo knew her words were hollow. There was no good way to tell a friend you'd betrayed them. It wouldn't have mattered how Samantha framed it back when she'd betrayed Jo. The outcome would have been the same, just like it most likely would be for Tracy.

After taking Tracy back to the elevator and assuring her again that she would contact her if there was any progress, Jo made a beeline for Lynae's desk. "Time to go see our good friend DeeDee again."

Lynae popped out of her seat. "What's up?"

"Whoever took Victor's laptop sent an email to one of his victims."

"No way. Someone has picked up his extortion game?"

"Not exactly. Our killer is now a vigilante."

Lynae narrowed her eyes. "What do you mean?"

"He has the videos. He sent a threat with an ultimatum. But he isn't asking for anything other than her confession."

"Holy shit."

"Yeah, if we don't catch this guy, we could be looking at a trail of destroyed lives," Jo said.

"It's better than dead bodies but still a mess."

"And how do we know he won't go back to killing if the confessions don't happen the way he thinks they should? He's killed once. It isn't much of a leap to think he would do it again."

"Do you think Amy White got an email like it?" Lynae asked.

"It makes sense. If she knew that no matter what she did, within forty-eight hours, that secret would be exposed, suicide could very well seem like the best option."

Nodding, Lynae said, "I actually get it. There's no bouncing back from something like that."

"Even though that suicide scene doesn't feel right, it jibes with the sudden decision after getting an email and knowing it's all over. The food in the oven, the cryptic note." Jo crossed her arms and drummed her fingers. "Which would suck because it would mean we don't have our killer. We have another victim."

"If this person, this vigilante, wants everyone to do the right thing, why kill Manton? Why commit the ultimate sin?"

"He might not have planned to kill him. Maybe he came to reason with him, try to convince him to do the right thing, and the situation got out of control. Or he *did* mean to kill him because what Manton was doing was somehow more personal to him. You know, affected him personally. Now, in his mind, everyone else has to come clean for the people their sins affect personally."

"Wow, that's deep."

Jo tapped her temple. "I'm like the freakin' ocean sometimes."

"If we're talking about people who are affected personally by Victor Manton's blackmail, I feel like we're right back to the same group we've had all along. The group he's blackmailing."

"Or people who cared about them. I checked into Samantha's husband, but he has an alibi. Tracy Peterson doesn't have a husband, but let's see who else she has."

Jo contemplated her murder board. Her only avenue was through the victims. "Give Samantha and Sharon a call and see if they've also gotten an email. I'm going to have a chat with the football coach. What's his name again?"

"Bob Morrow. I found his address," Lynae said and grabbed a file from her desk then pulled a piece of paper from inside. "Isn't it a little late, though?"

Jo looked at the ancient round clock that hung above the elevator. "How the hell did it get to be that late?"

"Beats me."

Jo let slip a frustrated groan. "I guess this waits until morning, then."

"I was starting to think we were just gonna camp out here tonight."

"As appealing as that sounds, we should probably sleep in beds if we want to be on our toes in the morning."

Jo got her things from her office and walked out with Lynae. She would spend the night worrying that Tracy could be pushed over the same brink Amy White had fallen from. She consoled herself with the fact that she had until the next night, and Tracy seemed resigned to talking to her friend. That was going to have to be good enough until morning.

Chapter 26

"I'll be ruined. Absolutely fucking ruined." Bob Morrow sat ramrod straight on a high-back chair in the cozy dining room of his home. Jo had called him as early as she felt was socially acceptable and asked to meet with him right away. He had to make some adjustments but was able to work out an early-afternoon meeting at his house.

Jo handed him back his phone. The email had been similar to the one Tracy Peterson had received. "We live in a pretty accepting—"

"Don't even try that bullshit. I'm a *football* coach." His beefy hands, fisted on his thighs, were white-knuckled. Veins snaked up his arms, bulging blue against winter-pale skin. "There's no political correctness in football. The guys, the parents, the kids... Anybody finds out about this, and I'm done. I'll be a laughingstock." Closing his eyes, he slowly shook his head. "Hell, I'll have to move."

Jo knew he was right. She had been around football her whole life. A cross-dressing football coach wouldn't last past the first quarter. Even if they couldn't legally fire him, they would make his life so miserable that he would quit.

Bob had talked to Victor Manning because he couldn't even accept it himself. He wanted to stop but was unable to get past the compulsion. During their sessions, Victor had convinced him to accept that part of his life, and in doing so, he invited him to come to his next counseling session dressed how he felt best.

Following his counselor's advice, Bob had come to the next session with his broad, hairy shoulders bulging around the thin straps of a yellow sun dress, teetering on sling-back heels and sporting a blond wig. In that outfit, he carried himself differently. He moved slowly, possibly to avoid falling in the heels but potentially because he felt more at ease. When he sat, he crossed his legs and adjusted his dress around his knees. Jo noted that he had not gone so far as to shave them, but he wore nylons, giving the illusion of smooth legs.

When she had watched the video, her first thought was that he should have gone with a low-heeled sandal with that dress. Her second was that if the video made its way into any part of his life, everything would change for him. Like the others, his entire life hung in the balance. With Victor out of the picture, he could keep his marriage, his teaching career, and his position as a football coach.

"You have to do something."

"We're doing everything we can at this point, Mr. Morrow." Jo worked to keep her voice even as frustration crept in. She would have to cross yet another potential suspect off her list. All of her suspects were turning into victims.

"Well, it isn't enough," Bob spat. "If that video gets out, that's it."

"I understand."

"Do you? Do you really understand?" He hunched forward, his forearms resting on his knees. With his legs spread wide and his hands dropped between them, he looked as though he were praying. Without lifting his head, he said, "I've got forty-eight hours left before that bastard sends that video to my wife and the coaching staff at Central. Forty-eight hours. Then what?"

"What does he want from you?"

"To out myself. What good is that to anyone? Why does he care?"

"I don't know. It appears we're dealing with some kind of vigilante who has taken it upon himself to right every wrong that has been... confessed, for lack of a better word."

Bob mumbled, "I'm not hurting anyone."

"I know you're not, and I'm sorry. We're eliminating suspects as quickly as we can."

"Not quickly enough."

The injustice of it weighed on Jo's chest. She was working the case as if each of her new victims were a homicide. It felt that way, since their lives would be irreparably damaged. Bob's situation hit her even harder than the others. At least she could justify that the others were guilty of something. Ruining Bob's life when he had done nothing to ruin anyone else's seemed like more of an injustice. Her vigilante had picked the wrong victim.

"Does anyone else know about your—"

"No, no one."

"That's not true" came a quiet but firm voice.

Bob's body stiffened as his head whipped around. "Heather," he whispered.

The woman stood in the kitchen doorway, her blond hair peeking out from beneath an orange stocking cap. She gazed at Bob tenderly, her head tilted to one side. "We've been married for twenty-two years, Bob. Did you really think I don't know?"

Jo dropped her gaze to hide how amusing she found the exchange. Men always underestimated how intuitive women were.

Bob hung his head. "Shit. I'm sorry. I—"

"Why are you sorry?"

"You deserve better."

"Better than being happily married for all these years?" She raised her hands out to her sides. "Better than two great kids and a beautiful home? Yeah, poor me."

Bob shifted to face his wife, who remained leaning against the crisp white doorframe. "You're okay with this?"

After pulling the stocking cap off and tossing it somewhere behind the doorway, she absently ran her fingers through her mane of hair. "I admit it took me a while. At first, I thought maybe you were gay."

"I'm not."

"I know. Again, twenty-two years of marriage." She pushed away from the door and crouched in front of her husband. "Look, I don't want to be a part of it. I'm not going to give you makeup tips or share my lipstick. I don't love it, but I do love you."

"You think we can make it work?"

"We've been making it work all these years, haven't we?"

Bob tugged his wife into his lap, his burly arms enveloping her petite frame. "What did I do to deserve you?"

"Absolutely nothing," Heather said. She gripped his beard then pulled his face forward and gave him a smacking kiss.

Jo hated to break up the adorable moment, but she had a killer to catch. And it was getting awkward. She cleared her throat and waited for the couple to bring their attention back to her.

Heather slipped off her husband's lap and held out her hand. "Sorry about the PDA. I'm Heather." She sized Jo up. "And you're the woman who's going to help us catch the bastard who's trying to ruin my husband."

Bob's face broke into a grin. Jo liked the spunky woman. She was exactly what they needed to throw the killer off kilter. He was expecting his victims to cower and give in.

"How would you two feel about standing up to this guy?"

"I don't see any other way," Heather said.

"I'll never be able to show my face at school if it gets out. I'm sure I can pay him off. I mean, he didn't ask for anything, but—"

Heather crossed her arms. "I'm not going to let you start giving money to this guy like you did to Victor."

"You knew about that?"

"Not until now, no."

"I'm sorry you had to find out like this. I should have told you."

Heather cocked her head and lifted an eyebrow. "Yeah, you should have. And trust me. We'll be talking about that later. But first we have to figure this out with the police."

"My partner's talking to a whiz in forensics right now. If I give them the go-ahead, they can work with you to set up a sting."

Bob scanned Heather's face. "Are you sure? If this goes south, it's going to be hell for all of us."

"I can't guarantee that he won't send the video," Jo interjected. "He hasn't been tested yet."

"We have to do this, Bob," Heather said. "We can't run from him forever, and he won't stop. If the lieutenant doesn't stop him, he'll ruin us anyway. Why not at least try?"

"What about the boys?" Bob asked.

"We'll try to keep them out of it, but if it comes down to it, I think it would be best for them to see their dad face down his bully."

"They'll be embarrassed by me, and that will kill me. I'm the tough football coach dad, not the—"

"Contestant on *RuPaul's Drag Race*?" Heather finished.

When Bob's mouth dropped open, Heather put a hand over his. "Too soon?"

"Yeah, maybe just a little." Bob worried his dark, wiry beard hair between his index finger and thumb. "Okay, I'll do it."

Jo's relief was profound. She just had to hope that DeeDee could pull off a miracle. "I'll have to talk with my team and set up a plan, but we don't have time to waste."

"You're telling me." Wrapping his arm around his wife, Bob said, "We'll be ready."

Chapter 27

Jo barged into the computer forensic unit, bypassed Josh, and trekked directly to DeeDee's desk. "I need some good news."

"I'll do my best," DeeDee said, amusement playing across her face.

"I've got a potential victim who's willing to work with us. Tell me there's a way to trace an email as it's coming in."

"There are a couple of possibilities. I've already checked the email headers, and I'm not able to trace from there, so he's playing smart. It may be a long shot, but if we can get him to follow a link, we can install tracker software on the laptop."

"Show me," Jo said then watched as DeeDee went through the motions of creating a link embedded with tracking software.

"Then the coup de grâce is to change the link name so that it sounds innocent."

"Or not so innocent," Jo said.

"Sounds like the wheels are turning."

"I have an idea. We're going to have to do it quickly if my guy agrees to it." Jo checked her watch.

"I'll be here all afternoon." DeeDee plucked a business card from a holder on her desk and handed it to Jo. "But call me at home if it gets late for some reason. I can be here in fifteen minutes."

Jo smacked the card against her palm and backpedaled out the door. She didn't have the patience to wait for the elevator, so she opted for the stairs and bounced down them two at a time while she dialed Bob Morrow's number.

AS JO, BOB, AND HEATHER rode the elevator to the floor that housed DeeDee's domain, he fidgeted and fiddled with the laptop in his beefy hands.

His wife laid a hand over his. "You're making me nervous."

"Aren't you already?" Bob shifted the laptop to one hand and grasped his wife's with the other. "What if he doesn't respond to my email?"

"I don't think that will happen. He gave you a deadline. He'll be watching," Jo said.

The elevator doors opened, and DeeDee met them at the door then led them to her office, where Lynae waited. She situated Bob at a desk while explaining in layman's terms what they were going to do.

Bob logged on to his computer and opened the email that had come from Victor Manton's email. Jo read the threat then told Bob to respond with *I'm not afraid of you. I have a video of my own that I'm sure the police would be interested in.*

They waited twenty excruciating minutes before a reply came through. It contained nothing but a copy of the video that Victor had used to threaten Bob.

Bob replied, *I don't think you understand. If you release that video, I'll send this to the police.*

DeeDee swung her chair close to Bob's, pulled his laptop over, and attached the link. "I added a little bonus trick of a video screen opening and spinning as if it's trying to play. It adds legitimacy and gives me a little more time." She laid a hand on Bob's shoulder. "Go ahead and send it whenever you're ready."

Bob drew in a deep breath and blew it out in a long whistle. "I feel like I'm gonna puke," he said quietly to his wife.

"Whatever happens, we'll get through it." She squeezed his hand.

Bob tapped the send button then jumped out of his chair and bounced on his toes with his arms in a fighting position—an athlete preparing for battle.

DeeDee rolled her chair back to her computer and logged into an IP tracker program then rolled back to Bob's computer. "As soon as he clicks the link, I can get started."

Jo paced nervously, bumping shoulders with Lynae as she paced in the opposite direction. While they patrolled, Lynae informed her that Samantha had indeed received another email. She hadn't checked her email in days and didn't even realize she had it. But Sharon Clickner had not received one.

"Seems a little odd that Victor's other victims would get an email from this vigilante, and Sharon wouldn't. Why is she different?"

Jo called Isaac Breuker and asked him to do a search on Sharon Clickner. As they talked, she could hear him typing and knew he was starting his search.

"There are two of them in the greater Grand Rapids area. Are you looking for Sharon Jacobs Clickner or Sharon Hoffman Clickner?"

Jo's vision narrowed as she halted her pacing. "Did you say Hoffman?"

"Yes, and Jacobs," Isaac replied.

"Do a family search on Hoffman."

"Not much there. Deceased parents and one brother—"

"Trent," Jo interrupted.

Bob's email pinged, and every person in the room jumped and squeezed together in front of the screen.

"How did you know?" Isaac asked.

"It's starting to come together. Thanks, Isaac," Jo said and disconnected.

Bob read the email. "I don't know what you think you have, but your video is broken."

"Keep him engaged," DeeDee said as she tapped keys.

Bob typed, *Why are you doing this to me? You're going to ruin my life.* Then he looked over his shoulder at Jo for approval. When Jo nodded, he hit Send.

The reply came in less than a minute. "It's time for you to be brave and confess your sins. You have one more day. Remember, God hates a coward."

A black box opened in the upper left-hand corner of the screen. White text rapidly scrolled across it. "I'm in," DeeDee said, the exhilaration of the hunt clear in her voice. Her fingers flew over the keys as her focus dialed in on the numbers.

"God hates a coward?" Bob snarled. "This guy acts all holier than thou then talks about God hating?"

"God hates a coward," Jo repeated. "Trent Hoffman said that to me the first time I talked to him."

Heather's mouth dropped open. "Trent Hoffman? From church?"

"He installed the surveillance equipment in Victor's office."

"He's a nice guy, though," Bob said, shaking his head. "He leads a bunch of groups at church."

"And he makes people confess their sins so that they can be saved," Heather muttered.

"He used that term, but it doesn't really mean anything," Lynae said. "It's a pretty common saying."

"But he's Sharon Clickner's brother." Jo rolled back through her conversation with Sharon. "The brother who recently started handling her finances."

"Meaning he would have seen consistent payments going out to the good pastor," Lynae said.

"How easy would it have been for him to break his contract and look at Victor's video surveillance footage?"

"I've got an address for you, Lieutenant," DeeDee said, jotting it on a piece of paper.

"You're a rock star." Jo snatched the paper from DeeDee's hand. "This will get us a warrant from any judge. Bob, Heather, you were amazing. I hate to just leave you here..."

Heather pointed at the door. "Go get that man, Lieutenant."

Jo saluted. "Yes, ma'am."

Chapter 28

"I don't want to be dramatic, but be weapon ready when he opens the door," Jo told Lynae as they approached the front porch of Trent Hoffman's house.

"You think he's going to be dangerous?" Lynae removed her weapon from the holster and checked the safety before reholstering it.

"I want him detained so that we can search his house for the laptop," Jo said, holding up the search warrant Jack had fast-tracked for her.

Breuker and Lainard followed suit and checked their weapons.

"You two can stay holstered. Nae's got us," Jo said.

"We're putting our lives in Parker's hands?" Lainard whined.

"I sure hope I don't slip and fire a cap in your skinny ass," Lynae snarked back.

"All right, kids, are we ready to act like adults?"

The three detectives seamlessly switched to cop mode as Jo rapped her knuckles on the door.

Trent Hoffman came to the door clad in Michigan State sweatpants and a gray crewneck sweatshirt. His initial friendliness faded as he looked from Jo to the three strangers standing on his porch.

Jo held up the warrant. "Trent Hoffman, I have a warrant to search your premises."

"I don't understand, Lieutenant."

Jo tilted her head. "I think you do." She motioned for her team to enter. "Each of you take a room. I want that laptop first."

Trent stepped into her path. "You have no right to barge into my house."

"This warrant says different." Jo held it out. "Feel free to read it while we search."

Trent slapped Jo's hand away. "You're not coming into my house."

Lynae held her gun in both hands with it pointed at the floor and shifted to position herself in clear view of Trent.

"Mr. Hoffman, I have a warrant to search your premises," Jo said.

"I don't give a damn what you have. You have no right to come into my house."

Jo wagged the warrant in front of Trent's face. "This gives me the right. The legal right. Now, you can argue all day, but we're not going anywhere."

Trent glared at Jo, his arms folded tightly across his chest. Finally, he took a step back and made an exaggerated sweeping motion. "Well, come on in, then."

Jo ignored the sarcasm. It was better than anger. "While my team searches the house..." she said, motioning for them to enter. As they filed through the room, she said, "Why don't you and I have a chat?"

"Why would I chat with you while you're ransacking my house for no reason?"

"I think we both know that I have a reason. But we won't need to ransack your house if you just point us to Victor Manton's computer."

"I don't know what you're talking about."

"Okay, then we'll do our search, and if ransacking is necessary, that's what we'll do. By the way, I'm very sorry to hear about your sister's illness."

Trent's face went slack as the blood drained from it and settled on his cheeks. The effect was clownish. "Why did you talk to my sister?"

"She had an association with Victor Manton."

Trent's lip twitched above a tightly clenched jaw. "Is that what you'd call it?"

"I've got nothing." Breuker stood in the doorway off the kitchen with Charles behind him, shaking his head. "Lynae's in the bedroom, but the rest of the rooms are bare."

"Check the basement," Jo said.

As the two of them left the room, Trent's eyes shifted slightly, and Jo followed the path to a barnwood coffee table. She took a step toward it, and Trent moved to block her way.

"Why don't you have a seat, Mr. Hoffman," Lynae said from the doorway, her hand on her holstered gun.

Trent's eyes went blank as he held his hands up, palms out. Jo squatted next to the table, opened the top, and fished out a box of Kleenex, a legal pad, and two pens but no laptop. As she stood back up, she noticed a hinge on the underside. She tugged on the tabletop, and it slid up and out. After digging through a stack of magazines, she pulled out the laptop that was buried underneath them and flipped it open. The desktop appeared with the same family picture Jo had seen in the Mantons' bedroom.

"Well, what do we have here?"

Handing the laptop to Lynae, she said, "Bag it, and treat the rest of the house like a crime scene."

She slapped cuffs on Hoffman's wrists. "Why don't we finish this at the station?" she said before reading him his rights.

"I'll call Tracy, Bob, and Samantha and tell them their videos will be part of police evidence but will not be released," Lynae said. "They can choose whether and when they tell their stories."

TRENT SPRAWLED HIS long legs out in front of the hard plastic chair in the cramped interrogation room. Jo sat in the chair across from him, silently leafing through papers and photos in a thick folder.

"Pastor Vic gave me his computer to add some video software."

"It's interesting that you wouldn't have brought that to my attention prior to this," Jo said.

"I didn't think it was important," Trent replied.

Jo shook her head slowly while giving him a disbelieving look. "And when I came with a search warrant, that didn't seem like a good time to tell me?"

"I didn't know what you were looking for."

"That would explain why we found the computer at your house, but it wouldn't explain why people are still getting messages from the pastor."

"I don't know anything about that. Anyone can log in to someone's email if they have the password."

"Sure. Sure they can," Jo said. In most cases, it would be circumstantial evidence for him to have Victor's computer. "You see, the thing is we traced the computer to your house through the email messages you were sending to Bob Morrow."

Trent's eyes narrowed to slits, shifting from side to side. He set his mouth in a hard line and slouched in his chair.

"A couple of weeks ago, before your Wednesday Bible study, did you hear Ethan talking to the assistant pastor about a conversation he overheard between Victor Manton and an unknown woman?"

Trent pushed himself straighter and gripped the armrests. "I don't think so."

"You don't think so, or no, you didn't?"

"I don't know what you're talking about," he said, running his hands up and down the arms of the chair.

Jo didn't have any proof that Trent had overheard that conversation, but his reaction told her she was on the right track. "I think you do know, Trent. You heard the accusation he made against your pastor, and you didn't want to believe it."

Jo set her notebook on the small table. "It was right about that time that you were taking control of your sister's finances, wasn't it?"

"How do you know that?" Trent asked, his face shifting to a scowl.

"Your sister mentioned that during our talk. She's a very nice woman, by the way."

Trent's face hardened as the corners of his mouth turned down. "My sister is sick. Leave her out of this."

"I'm not the one who brought her into it." Jo kept her tone even.

"I'm helping her. I don't see what that has to do with anything."

"You were handling her finances and noticed that she was making some unusual and regular payments to the pastor."

Trent crossed his arms and looked away.

"Did you ask her about those payments?"

"What my sister does with her money is none of my business, Lieutenant."

"Fair enough. But you wondered, didn't you?" Jo let the question hang in the air for a minute. "Then you had to make those payments without knowing what they were for."

"My sister is a member of the parish. It's not unusual to give money to your church."

Jo cocked her head. "Your sister is still a contributing member? Even though she lives in Georgia?"

When Trent didn't answer, Jo continued, "You're a smart guy. You heard what Ethan said Victor did to Samantha. Then you saw your sister's money going out to her former pastor. You started to put two and two together, didn't you?"

"I don't—"

"We know about Victor blackmailing your sister."

Trent's fingers dug into the sleeves of his sweatshirt.

"Your sister was very open about it," Jo added.

"Sick bastard," Trent muttered.

"You saw all that money going to him every month."

"She told me it was for the church."

"And I'm sure you believed that until you heard what Ethan had to say. Then you wondered. And you had to know."

Trent's mouth worked as he bit the inside of his lip, his brow furrowed over his stormy eyes.

"You needed that confirmation, didn't you? How long did you sit on that conversation before you had to know? How long did that gnaw at you, that money that your sister was paying out every month? The same amount each month."

Jo was quiet and stared at Trent until he met her gaze.

"You went back and watched his video feed, didn't you, Trent? You saw what he did to your sister. You saw how he threatened her."

"I told you it's against company policy to watch video feed that isn't specifically monitored."

"I know what you told me, and I'm sure you tried to stick to company policy. But she's your sister. You had to know for yourself if it was true."

Trent's face was set in a stony grimace.

"You believed in the pastor. I get it." Jo laid her hand on her heart. "I believe in mine. I believe that he's a righteous man. A man of God."

Trent's eyes flicked to Jo and back to the table.

"I can't imagine how I would feel if I found out that my pastor was a dirtbag," she said. "It would be devastating."

She leaned forward, clasping her hands in a way reminiscent of prayer. "You were trying to prove it wasn't true, weren't you?"

Trent lifted his head, his eyes wide. He stared at Jo for a moment then slouched back in his chair, returning his gaze to the table.

"You wanted to watch the video and see for yourself that your pastor would never do such a thing," Jo pressed on. "You didn't want to believe that he would threaten your sister. She's sick, for Pete's sake. You couldn't reconcile that he could be so dirty and cruel to Samantha. She's your friend—your fellow parishioner. You planned to go back to Nick and set the record straight. So that he could talk to Ethan and make him understand that he was mistaken, that Pastor Vic was a good man who wouldn't hurt anyone. Especially someone in his own flock."

Trent winced, tapping his foot compulsively. "I want some water."

Jo looked at the two-way mirror and gave a slight nod. "My partner will bring that in for you in a minute."

Sitting back casually, she tapped her pen against her yellow legal pad. "Here's what's bothering me," she said.

He lifted his eyes to look warily at her.

The door opened, and Lynae slipped in with a bottle of water. He took it, struggled with the cap, then brought it shakily to his lips.

"How did you feel, knowing that the equipment that you installed in good faith was being used to blackmail people you knew? People you cared about?" Jo looked into his eyes. "Your own sister."

Trent cringed.

"Your equipment, secretly placed in an office, recorded people." Jo emphasized each point, tapping her index finger on the table.

"I didn't know."

"Maybe you were in on it."

"What?" Trent whispered.

Jo shrugged. "How do I know? You have this undetectable camera. Hell, my guys didn't even find it, and they're professionals. You hid that in a counselor's office."

"You know, people accuse people of stuff all the time. And he was alone with them. He was protecting himself."

"Yeah, sure, protecting himself." Jo gave him a derisive look. "And you bought that?"

"Why wouldn't I? He was my pastor."

"You trusted him," Jo said.

"Yes!"

"And he made you look stupid."

"I didn't know," he said through gritted teeth.

"He was blackmailing people with things he learned about them during confidential sessions." Jo waited until he looked up from the floor so that she could bring her point home. "He was blackmailing your sister, and he did it using *your* equipment."

"I didn't know!" Trent yelled, jumping from his chair.

"Until you heard Ethan talking to Nick."

"I thought he had it wrong," he moaned, slumping back into his chair.

Jo held her breath as her heart attempted to break its way out of her ribcage. She wanted answers. But her training told her the best move was silence. With a little rope, he would hang himself.

Trent appeared to be in the same position as Jo. He didn't move or even seem to breathe. Jo fought back all her instincts and waited.

"I thought he had it wrong," he said again.

"And you had to know the truth."

He closed his eyes and slowly rolled his head back until it rested on his tensed shoulders. "I confronted him about it."

"You actually talked to Victor Manton about the accusation? Did you tell him what you heard?"

"Not exactly. I didn't want to get the kid in trouble. I just told him that I heard some rumors. He said all the right things, and I went home believing that the kid had it wrong."

"What made you change your mind?"

"I couldn't get it out of my mind," he said quietly. "My sister's bank records, Ethan's story. I couldn't shake it. I went to church the next Sunday, and I listened to him talk about our duty as Christians to live our lives free of sin and corruption. And how we're all sinners, but God forgives us if we ask." He tilted his head to one side, shaking it slowly. "He was such a good speaker."

"And what did listening to that homily mean to you?"

"It meant I had to know the truth. And if he was lying, he had to confess. God would forgive him."

"So you watched the old feed from his office."

"I had to know," he said quietly. "It goes against our policy, but I had to know."

"And what did you find?"

"At first, I only watched the day Ethan was talking about. I saw it. I saw him threatening Samantha. She begged him to destroy the video and let her get on with her life." Trent made a face like he had downed sour milk. "He was so cruel. He told her he already sent the video to her husband, and all he had to do was tell him how to watch it. I don't know what he meant by that, but she was sobbing and begging. He laughed and said he would never let her walk away."

Tears glistened in his eyes. "It's like he was an entirely different person. Everything I believed... everything he preached... was a lie."

"So you went to his house to confront him?"

"I was so mad. But I was only going to talk to him to try to get him to come clean and stop what he was doing. That's what he said we're supposed to do. We're supposed to ask for forgiveness. I heard Lisa ask Samantha if she could go out with them, so I knew she wouldn't be there. I had to talk to him when she wasn't around. But I got there, and Samantha was there. I saw her through the door. She was leaving out the front. I was so angry."

"Did Samantha see you?"

Trent shook his head. "I came in the back."

"Why?"

"I live on Oak," he said, motioning as though the street were behind Jo. "I was pretty upset. I figured the walk would help."

"Take me through it from the time you came in the door."

"I went into Victor's office and took his laptop. I was going to force him to delete the videos. I remember grabbing something from a bag by the door." Trent held his hands out, splaying his fingers, and studied them as if they had answers.

"Do you remember what that was?" Jo asked.

Trent blinked rapidly, his eyes moving from side to side. "A bat."

"Okay. Then what happened?"

"I went upstairs. I heard the shower running, so I went in."

"Was Victor in the shower?"

"No, the water was on, but he wasn't in the shower." He closed his eyes. "Whistling."

"Excuse me?"

"He was whistling like nothing was wrong. I remember going through the bedroom and standing in the door of the bathroom." Trent's eyes shifted from side to side as if he were watching the scene in a movie.

"Did you say anything to him?"

"The whistling. It just..."

"What happened next, Trent?" Jo prodded.

"I swung the laptop at him." Trent stared at his hands, his fingers clenched into fists. "I hit him on the back of the head. He fell on one knee. Then I swung the bat. I remember swinging and swinging. It was like a dream. Like I wasn't really there."

"Okay. Go on."

"The videos were on the laptop, and I had to get to them."

Jo remembered that Victor's hand had been wiped clean. "He had fingerprint access."

Trent's lips curled as he gulped. "The blood... It wouldn't work at first." Absently, he rubbed his hands on his legs, as if he were still wiping away blood. "I heard someone come in the house." He spoke with an eerie calmness, his eyes unfocused.

"Someone came in while you were there? Do you know who it was?"

"No. Victor was moaning, and it's like I woke up, and I realized what I had done."

"Is that why you used the towel? Because he was moaning?" Jo asked.

"What towel?"

"The towel that you shoved into his mouth."

"What? I never shoved a towel into his mouth. He was alive when I left. I didn't know he was dead until the next day."

Jo scowled. That didn't jibe with the evidence.

"This person that came in. Where did they go?"

"I don't know. I didn't hear them come up the stairs, so I got out."

"When did you stage the scene to look like a robbery?"

"What?" Trent seemed genuinely confused. "I didn't stage any-thing. I didn't have time. I got the hell out of there."

Jo's mind was looping, circumnavigating the crime scene. Her killer's confession wasn't matching the facts that the evidence pre-sented. *Is he confessing to something he didn't do? Is he protecting the real killer?* She didn't know Trent well enough to know who might be important enough to him to protect, other than his sister, who wasn't in the state at the time of the murder. Whatever the case, his story and the evidence didn't match.

She needed to know who had gone into the house.

"You left Victor Manton's house with his laptop, correct?"

"Yes."

"And you used that laptop to access his email and continue to blackmail the same people. The very thing you were so angry with the pastor about, you did yourself."

Trent jolted as if he had been slapped. "No, it was different." He brought his hands to his chest. "I wasn't blackmailing them. I didn't try to take money from them."

"You were threatening to ruin their lives." Jo held up a stack of papers from her file and dropped them onto the table. "I have the emails."

"We have to admit our sins in order to be free. I was helping them free themselves of their burden."

Jo slid a picture of Amy White across the table. Trent flinched.

"Is this how you thought they should free themselves of their burdens? You killed Amy White."

"Amy was a bad person. She had to admit her sins and pay for them."

"And you decided ending her life was the way to accomplish that?"

"I didn't end her life."

"You threatened to expose her secret. The same secret Manton used to blackmail her. You killed her just as surely as if you had given her the pills."

"No, I was trying to help her unburden herself. She couldn't live with it."

"Did you plan to help the others unburden themselves in the same way? By pushing them until they broke?"

"If that was what it took, that was what I would have done. But only to help them. I wouldn't have killed them any more than I killed Amy."

"You gave her an ultimatum with no possible good outcome. You gave her no out. You pushed her over the edge. That will carry weight with a jury, so I'll be adding an involuntary manslaughter charge for Amy White. I'll also be adding extortion charges for both Tracy Peterson and Bob Morrow."

"I didn't extort anyone. I didn't demand anything other than their honesty. No court will convict me of that."

"Illegally obtained privileged videos. Extortion. I think I can make both of those stick. And let's not forget the murder charge. You'll never see the outside of a cage again."

"I didn't mean to kill him. He was alive when I left."

"Save it for the jury," Jo said, standing up. It had been a long day, and all she wanted was to get that man to booking and behind bars. "I'm placing you under arrest for the murder of Victor Manton," she began, pulling her cuffs from their clip.

"He was alive when I left. I swear. He was saying, 'Ethan.'"

Jo stopped. "Victor was talking when you left?"

Trent's head bobbed. "He was saying, 'Ethan.' I think that might have been who came into the house. I don't know. I just got out of there."

Jo recited his Miranda rights and took him to booking. Whether Victor Manton had been alive when he left or not, Trent was guilty of aggravated assault, attempted murder, and a host of other crimes that Jack would have to help her sort out.

The fact that his confession didn't jibe exactly with the crime scene nagged at her as she finished the booking process and finally made her way home. Someone had gone into the house, and Victor had been saying Ethan's name. If it had been Ethan who came home, it would have been easy for him to finish off the stepdad he didn't like. There would be no marks on him, no blood. They didn't find a towel in the house, so he would have to be smart enough to dispose of it and cool enough to handle her questions. That would be a lot for a teenager, but Jo had seen a lot.

Chapter 29

As dawn crested, Jo sat at her dining room table, drinking her second cup of coffee and eating an over-easy egg with toast. Her early-morning run had worn Mojo out, and her furry companion snored at her feet. Jo's typical feeling of contentment after closing a case wasn't there, and she had been unable to sleep. As she picked at her breakfast, she knew it was because the case wasn't really closed. Trent had been there and beaten Victor. She had no real reason to believe he was telling her the truth about Victor being alive when he left. But her gut told her he was, and her gut rarely lied.

Jo paced the floor. She couldn't walk back through the crime scene, since they had released the house back to Lisa and the kids. They weren't there, and according to Lisa, they were never going to be again, but she couldn't go into their house anymore. Instead, she just had to put herself back in it as best she could.

She drove to the Mantons', parked on the street in front of their home, killed the engine, and settled in her seat to take in the neighborhood scene. With the strobing lights gone, the tree-lined street held the serene beauty of most older, well-loved neighborhoods. Evenly squared-off lots with neatly shoveled driveways led to well-tended, mostly brick homes, with a few newer, vinyl-sided two-stories thrown in. A lopsided snowman wearing a RealTree hat and a camouflage scarf adorned the front yard of the house across the street. An American flag hung next to a Michigan state flag on short posts attached to the house next door.

Mentally ticking off the streets, Jo calculated that she and Mike had looked at a home only a few blocks north. A solid school district and traditionally good sports programs made the area hotly sought after for young couples. When a house hit the market, people jumped quickly, or they missed their shot. Jo and Mike had missed theirs but ended up in what Jo considered an even better part of town.

An elderly woman with a metal walker slowly made her way down the driveway of the house across the street from the Mantons'. A newspaper in a plastic bag lay at the end, almost in the street. Jo hopped out of her truck, trotted over, picked up the paper, then met the woman, who was only a third of the way down the drive. "Is this what you're after?" she asked, holding out the paper.

"Well, aren't you a dear? You make it look so easy. It takes me half the morning to get that paper when that darn Kyle leaves it way out there."

Jo tapped her badge. "Want me to arrest him for improper paper placement? I believe it's a misdemeanor, but I can give him the maximum allowable time."

The old woman smacked her lips against her false teeth and mumbled, "It would serve the little shit right." Looking Jo up and down skeptically, she asked, "Are you really a cop?"

"I'm a detective. Lieutenant Riskin with the GRPD."

"Well, isn't that something? You don't look like a detective."

Jo bent down to the much-shorter woman and said conspiratorially, "I'm going to take that as a compliment."

Her face breaking into a grin, the woman cackled. "I like you, Lieutenant Riskin. I'm Edna."

Jo laid a hand on the woman's shoulder. "Your drive is quite slippery, Edna. Can I help you back into the house?"

"I never refuse a helping hand," she said, clunkily maneuvering her walker through a semicircle.

Jo tucked the newspaper under her arm and widened her stance to counter the ice while she held a protective arm on Edna's elbow.

As they painstakingly made their way back to the house, Jo asked, "Have you lived in this neighborhood long?"

"Only if you consider fifty-eight years a long time."

"I think that qualifies."

Edna stopped and stared at her home. "My Harold and I moved in here right after we were married. Raised five kids in that little house." Raising an eyebrow and giving Jo a knowing sideways glance, she added, "Four of them boys."

"Wow, you must be a saint," Jo said sincerely.

"Wow is right." Edna shook her head. "So much noise. And so much food."

Putting her head back down to watch her feet, she shuffled toward the house. "Boy, do I miss that noise," she murmured.

Jo walked quietly beside her, taking one stride for every four shuffling steps the old woman took. The snow crunched and squeaked under Jo's boots.

"My Harold died two years ago. Heart attack. Fifty-eight years, and he was gone, just like that." Edna snapped her fingers, a dull thud against the metal of her walker.

Jo's heart clenched. They'd had so much time together. But it was never enough. What she wouldn't give to have all those years with Mike.

"Are you married?" Edna asked.

"I was. And almost three years ago, he was gone, just like that," Jo said quietly, snapping her fingers too.

Edna regarded her with her milky blue eyes. "Oh dear, so young. That's not fair."

"It sure isn't. We weren't done yet." Jo shrugged. "But whose life is fair, right?"

"That's the truth, if there ever was one," Edna said with a firm nod, hobbling along stiffly.

"What do you know about your neighbors, the Mantons?" Jo asked.

"Oh, now there's a tragedy. Such a nice family."

"Lisa has been a real trouper, when you consider what she's been through," Jo said, opening the door and stepping inside to hold it while Edna made her way in.

"And poor Ethan."

"What happened to Ethan?" Jo asked.

"Well, he came home that night. It must have been right when that dreadful business was happening in there."

"Oh, of course," Jo said, keeping her tone casual.

Edna shuffled to a simple wooden table, expertly swung her walker around, and dropped into a chair with a bright-yellow cushion tied around its back spindles.

Jo wiped her feet on the snowman rug inside the door and followed Edna into the room. Laying the newspaper on the table, she said, "Ethan seems to be doing very well."

"Oh, good. Such a sweet boy. He comes over and shovels my drive for me and won't even take a penny for it."

"He didn't mention that he saw or heard anything that night. Are you sure he was home?"

Edna nodded abruptly. "I was watching *Law and Order*, and that starts at ten o'clock."

"Was he in there long?"

When she narrowed her eyes and lifted her chin, Edna's glare bored holes through Jo. "You're trying to get me to say something against him."

"No, ma'am, I—"

"That sweet boy didn't do that," Edna spat, her pale hand shaking as she pointed a gnarled finger at Jo. "I watch *Law and Order*. I know what you're doing and why you came over to *help* me."

"I came to help you so that you didn't have to trek all the way to the end of your driveway," Jo said, nodding at the newspaper that lay on the table. "I've already arrested the man who killed Mr. Manton." She had stopped to help, but since they were talking, she wasn't about to give up this gold mine of information.

Edna's shoulders relaxed, and her chin dropped a fraction, but she continued to eye Jo warily. "I didn't see him come back out. I was watching my shows and didn't pay him any more attention, so I don't know how long he was in there. Next time I looked, his car was gone."

"Do you know what show was on the next time you looked?"

"It was when *Law and Order* ended. I was waiting for the next show to come on, and I looked out the window to see what was happening in the neighborhood. There's usually lots of activity to keep me entertained, but it was a quiet night. Probably because it was so cold and snowy."

"And you're sure it was Ethan?"

"There's no mistaking that boy's car. It could rattle the wrinkles off my face."

In Trent's statement, he'd said that Victor had said Ethan's name. He knew it was Ethan who'd come in because of his loud car.

"Did you see anyone else come or go from the house?" Jo asked.

"No, like I told the officer who came the next day, I didn't see anything unusual."

Jo made a mental note to talk to Breuker about how he framed his questions. To Edna, Ethan's coming and going wasn't unusual. If he had asked if she had seen anyone at all, she might have had a different answer.

"Whoever did that probably sneaked out the back door. You know there's an entrance in the back, don't you?" Edna asked.

"Yes, we're aware."

"I wasn't watching, but I bet that's how they got out. Head into the woods, and no one would find them."

"What woods would that be?"

"You just cross the road back there behind their house, where the back door is. There's a big brick house, the biggest one on the block. I remember when they built it, we all thought some rich people were moving into the neighborhood—"

"I remember seeing that house when I came in," Jo said to sidetrack Edna from veering off on a tangent.

"If you cut through their yard and the Wilsons' on the other side of the street, you'll be right at the edge of the woods. The kids do it all the time."

"The Manton kids?"

"All the neighborhood kids. They've been doing it since my kids were little."

"And the neighbors on that side don't have a problem with kids cutting through their yards?"

"There've been a few of them over the years who raised a fit about it, but mostly they haven't cared. The kids keep to the fence and don't bother anyone. This day and age, it's nice to see some kids spending time outside instead of in front of their computers or those damn phones."

"Yes, it is." Taking a step toward the door, Jo said, "It's been a pleasure meeting you, Edna."

"You, as well, Lieutenant Riskin."

Jo had her phone out before the door closed behind her. "Get Ethan in the station as fast as you can get him there," she said when Lynae picked up.

"What's going on?"

"I have a witness who puts him in the house right around the time of the murder."

"But you've got Trent behind bars. He confessed."

"He confessed to beating him, but it's not sitting right with me. There's too much conflict between his story and what our evidence is telling us. I have to check it out."

"Do you think Ethan came in after Trent beat Victor and finished him off?"

"That's where I'm at right now," Jo replied.

Lynae gave a low whistle. "I'll get him to the station."

"I'm going to the woods across the street from the Mantons' house. Apparently, it's a known hangout for the kids. He might have left something out there."

"Was he on foot? How did the neighbor see him?"

"No, he drove. She saw and heard his car. It throws a wrench into the woods theory, but I'm going to check it out. He may have left in his car, panicked about the towel, then ditched it in the only place he could think of."

"People go where they know."

"Yes, they do. So let's get him to the station and let him sweat it out in one of the small interrogation rooms until I get there."

Jo hung up and jogged across the street, cut through the Mantons' yard, and followed the neighbors' fence as it wrapped around their property then opened to a clump of trees with a clearly visible footpath. The woods proved to be a relatively small space with a cleared opening around thirty yards in, where cigarettes littered the ground and red tree straps hung from a couple of adjacent trees. Plainly, when the weather was better, kids hung out in their hammocks, sneaking cigarettes they thought their parents didn't know about. She searched the area, thankful for the relatively mild winter and lack of snow.

She found nothing in the clearing, so she went off the beaten path, watching her feet and pushing aside leaves and debris. When she came to an opening that led into a yard, she turned around and broadened her search. At the edge of the clearing, she went in a different direction, continuing a circuitous path around the copse of trees. As frustration started to settle in, she sat down on a fallen branch and looked around, taking in the size of the woods, which were larger than she had first estimated. She would probably have to call in some help.

A chain-link fence, thick with Michigan holly and brambleberry bushes, cut through at a diagonal next to Jo's perch. A small piece of something blue, tucked against the fence and mostly buried under leaves and thicket, caught Jo's eye. She got on her hands and knees and snapped several pictures then pulled on her heavy winter gloves and reached into the undergrowth. Jo felt around blindly, keeping her face away from the prickly shrub, until her hand landed on the item. She backed out of the bushes, pulling it with her, and could feel its weight and thickness. Her adrenaline surged as she realized it was a bloody towel that matched the others in Victor and Lisa's bathroom.

The woods were far enough from the house that only someone familiar with them would ditch the towel there. That really narrowed her list.

With no evidence bag in hand, she carried the towel back to her car with one hand while she called Mallory with the other.

"Can you get DNA from a bath towel?" she asked as soon as Mallory picked up.

"Depends. If the person wiped their sweat, cried, bled... something along those lines. But carrying it wouldn't be enough."

"It's covered in blood. I'm wondering if you can run it to determine whether the blood is Victor Manton's."

"Oh, absolutely. I can't say if I'll find anyone else's on it, but I can run the blood."

"I'm bringing it in. We'll at least have evidence that it was from the Mantons' house."

"I'll do it right away."

"You're the best, Mal," Jo said as she got into her truck. She threw the phone into the passenger seat, shoved the towel into an evidence bag, and headed to the station.

Her phone rang with a number she didn't recognize.

"Riskin."

"Lieutenant, this is Louie. Louie from the grocery store."

"What can I do for you, Louie?"

"I showed that picture to the girls, like you asked. And Breslyn said she saw her. She remembered because it was the end of her shift, and she walked out with her."

"What time did she say that was?" Jo asked.

"She gets off work at ten thirty."

"And she's sure of that time?" Leaving the store at that time, as close as the store was to her house, would blow holes in her entire timeline for the night of the murder. If the time of death was between ten thirty and eleven, she would have been home when it happened.

Louie chuckled. "It's when she gets off work. Every teenager knows the minute they can leave."

Not just teenagers—everyone remembered what time they left work.

She thanked Louie and told him she might need to talk to Breslyn later. If Ethan had killed his stepdad, it was possible Lisa helped him cover it up. People did those kinds of things for their kids. Ethan would be at the station by the time she got back. She was sure she would know the truth soon.

Chapter 30

Jo slipped into the observation room and watched Ethan as he waited for her in the interrogation room. His legs were tucked up close to his body, his hands shoved deep into the front pocket of his Detroit Lions sweatshirt.

With the towel in Mallory's lab, Jo decided to use that to see what she could get out of Ethan. Lynae said when she'd called and told him she had a few follow-up questions, he was cooperative and willing to come to the station. He hadn't asked for an attorney, but she wondered if he was old enough to know he should. He wasn't under arrest, so she had no obligation to read him his Miranda rights, but she had a slight nagging guilt about it, since he was barely a legal adult. She had Trent Hoffman behind bars, but someone had finished Victor off, and Ethan had been in the house.

As she watched, he pulled his phone out of his pocket and checked the time. Then, gnawing on his thumbnail, he began scrolling. She couldn't see what he was looking through, but his thumb flicked upward at a steady pace.

When it became obvious that that was all he was going to do, she stepped out of observation and into the interrogation room. Ethan sat up straight and shoved his phone into his pocket.

"Sorry to keep you waiting."

He shrugged. "It's all right."

"I need to clear up a couple of things with you. I was at your house today and spoke with your neighbor Edna. She said you shovel her driveway for her."

"I help her out when I can. She's pretty cool."

"Yes, she is. And it sounds like she keeps a close eye on the neighborhood."

"Yeah, she always seems to know what's going on."

"Yes, she does." Jo scooted forward in her chair. "She was keeping an eye on the neighborhood the night your stepdad was killed."

Ethan's tongue darted out across his lips.

"The thing is she saw your car pull into the driveway sometime after nine o'clock. Can you tell me why you were in the house at that time?"

Ethan shifted his weight. "Um, yeah, I came home to get my HDMI cable."

The quick reply surprised Jo. "Your HDMI cable?"

"Yeah, Nate and I were gonna play a game. I took my PS4, but I forgot my HDMI, so I went home to get it."

"Did you see Victor when you got home?"

"No. I yelled when I went in, but nobody answered. I just ran in and got my stuff." Ethan jerked his head back, flipping his hair away from his face, then ran his fingers through his long bangs. As his hand dropped away, the hair flopped back to dangle on either side of his head.

"Your bedroom is upstairs," Jo said, going through the layout of the house in her head. "You went to your room to get this cable, and you didn't see Victor?"

"I didn't go to my room. All my gaming stuff is in the basement. I ran downstairs and back out."

Jo crossed her arms and cocked her head. "I'm having a hard time understanding why you never mentioned that you were home that night."

"I didn't see anything, so I didn't think it mattered." Ethan scrubbed his hands up and down his thighs, the motion forcing his body to rock. "I mean, it's kinda scary, knowing whoever did that might have been there when I was. But I didn't see him."

"Your friend, Nate. That's where you spent the night that night?" Ethan nodded.

"When we went to your house that night, I remember seeing a baseball bag hanging in the entryway with Gilly on it. That's your nickname, right?"

"Right."

"So I assume that bag is yours?"

"Yeah, it's my old high school bag. I play for Ferris State now."

"I know. I looked that up. You played for Northview and had quite a record."

Ethan drew his eyebrows together. "You looked up my baseball record?"

"You're a left-handed pitcher," Jo said casually.

"Yeah, and a right-handed batter. Why would you look that up?"

Jo hadn't been aware of that piece of information, and it shot a couple of holes in her scenario. He was a strong kid and could probably swing a bat left-handed as well. *But why would he?*

"We took those bats into evidence."

Ethan shrugged. "Okay. They're my old high school bats. Am I going to get them back?"

"I don't think so, Ethan. You see, the lab confirmed that although it had been wiped down, one of the bats had trace evidence of blood on it."

"I got hurt in a game last summer," he said quickly.

"We've confirmed that the blood matches that of Victor Manton," Jo said, pulling the report she had just received from Kent from her bag and laying it on the table.

"I didn't... You don't think I..."

"It's your bat, in your bag. And I'm sure you can swing that bat pretty hard."

Ethan brought his hand up to his mouth and resumed biting his thumbnail, a nervous habit that he probably didn't even realize he was doing.

"Ferris is quite a drive from here, isn't it?"

Ethan shrugged. "About an hour."

"Do you always come home on Wednesday nights? Seems like a long way to go in the middle of the week when you have classes and practice."

"I usually only come home on weekends, but we didn't have any classes Thursday and Friday. I don't remember why. Some teacher thing. The coach gave us the time off conditioning if we wanted to go home, so I did."

"So you're not usually home on Wednesdays, but this time you were, and that happened to be the night your stepdad was killed. That's quite a coincidence."

"I... What?"

Jo changed gears to keep him off-center. "After I spoke with Edna today, I went into the woods across the street, where she said you kids hang out."

Ethan stopped biting. "Why?"

"Well, I thought I might find something important there, and turns out I did." Jo pulled a picture of the towel, which was caked with dirt, blood, and leaves, from a folder and laid it on the table.

Ethen leaned forward and looked at it. His brow knit, creating a deep crease down his forehead.

"Does that towel look familiar?" Jo asked.

Ethan shrugged. "I guess. It's a blue towel."

"It's the same brand and color as the towels used in your mom and Victor's bathroom."

"Why was it in the woods?"

Jo put the picture back in the folder. "I was hoping you could tell me that."

The door opened, and Lynae stuck her head in the room. Jo heard a woman on a tirade in the bullpen.

"Can I talk to you?" Lynae asked.

Pushing away from the table, Jo said, "I'll be just a minute," then followed Lynae out of the room.

Lynae jerked her head toward the bullpen. "That's Lisa Manton. Apparently, Ethan left her a message that he was coming here to talk to us. She is *not* happy."

Jo peeked around the corner and watched Charles Lainard, holding his hands shoulder high, palms out, speaking quietly, trying to calm the irate woman.

"She's here to talk to Ethan," Lynae said.

"*How dare you?*" Lisa screamed, pointing at Jo. Breaking away from Charles, she stormed across the room.

"Lisa—"

"Where is he? Where is my son?" she asked, frantically looking around before spotting the open door to the room Jo had exited.

Jo blocked the entrance. "Mrs. Manton, we're simply having a talk with Ethan."

"You can't do that without my permission. You can't—"

"He's nineteen," Lynae interjected.

Lisa rounded on her. "He's just a kid, and he lost his stepfather."

"Mom?" Ethan stood in the doorway, his hands shoved into the front pockets of his strategically torn jeans. "What are you doing here?"

"Don't say another word, you hear me?"

"What? Why?"

"I'm going to get you a lawyer." Lisa gripped Ethan's shoulders. "Don't say one more word."

"Mom, I don't need a lawyer. They're just asking me some questions," he said, taking a step back into the room.

"Not another word!" Lisa's voice rose, panic constricting her vocal cords into a squeak.

Jo's phone vibrated. She slipped it out of her pocket to see a text from Mallory.

Confirmed the blood on the towel is Victor Manton's.

While that came as no surprise, every nail helped seal the coffin. Jo watched as Lisa's panic heightened while Ethan remained calm and unfazed, and she realized the killer wasn't Ethan—it was Lisa. That was why her timeline didn't add up. She had taken the time to take that towel to the woods before she called 911. Jo had to keep her talking. If she called a lawyer, he would shut it down.

A confession would make things so much easier. It was time to throw a little gasoline on the fire.

"Ethan Gillespie, I'm placing you under arrest for the murder of Victor Manton," Jo said, stepping in front of Ethan.

"N-No, I didn't—"

"Don't say anything, Ethan." Lisa's eyes were wild with fear as she rushed into the room.

"You have the right to remain silent," Jo began.

"I told you. I only came home—"

"Ethan!" Lisa shrilled.

Jo took her handcuffs from under her jacket, pulled one of Ethan's hands behind his back, and slapped a cuff on his wrist.

"Stop it! I'm calling a lawyer." Lisa grabbed Jo by the arm and yanked.

Jo rounded on her, pulling her arm free, and grasped Lisa's wrist in one fluid motion.

"I suggest you keep your hands to yourself and call that lawyer."

Jo let go of Lisa and yanked Ethan's other hand behind his back, cuffed it, then nudged him toward the door.

"Mom," he whined, tears and snot running down his face.

"I did it." The words flew out of Lisa's mouth. "He didn't do it. I did." Lisa's face contorted. "I killed him."

"Mrs. Manton, we know that Ethan was in the house at the time your husband was killed."

"Ethan only hit him." Lisa looked Jo in the eye. "He was alive. You can't put him in jail for hitting him."

"What?" Ethan croaked.

Lisa laid a hand on Ethan's cheek. "You didn't kill him, Ethan. I did."

"Mom, what are you talking about?"

"It's okay. It's okay. You're a good kid. I know you didn't mean it."

"Mom... what? I don't understand."

"Don't say anything else," Lisa said, pointing at him. "He ruined my life. I won't let him ruin yours."

The statement surprised Jo. Lisa had been convincing as the grieving widow.

"But I didn't hit him."

Lisa put a hand over Ethan's mouth. "Don't say anything."

Ethan twisted his head to the side, slipping from her grip. "Mom, I didn't do it."

Lisa's eyes moved rapidly over Ethan's face, then she backed away. "That's impossible."

"How could you think I would do something like that?"

Lisa wavered and stumbled as she stepped away from her son. Jo guided her to a chair.

"You didn't do it? But he said your name. He said it over and over." She covered her face as her body convulsed. "Why did he say your name?"

Ethan's lip quivered as he shook his head. "I don't know."

"You knew what he did. How he hurt those people. I thought you did that to him because of that."

"You knew about that?" Ethan asked.

Lisa squeezed her eyes shut. "Nick told me you—"

Ethan rushed forward and dropped to his knees in front of Lisa. "Mom, you told me not to say anything. You shouldn't either."

Lisa's shoulders sagged as she glanced at Jo. "I think it's a little late for that."

"No—"

Lisa grasped her son's hand. "I did what I did, Ethan. He wasn't a good man, but what I did to him has been eating me alive. I can't live with it."

"What do you mean, you 'know what he did'?" Jo asked.

"He didn't think I was very smart." Lisa set her jaw. "But I know what our finances should be. There was money coming in that I couldn't account for."

"Did you ask Victor about the money?"

Lisa crossed her arms. "I did, and he told me not to worry about it. That some of the parishioners he counseled insisted on paying him. That didn't make sense. He's the pastor. That's part of the job."

"Do you know where the money was coming from?"

"No, but I'm sure whatever it was, it wasn't legal. And I know what he did to that poor woman."

"What poor woman?" Jo asked.

"I don't know who she is, but Victor was forcing her to have sex with him." Lisa swallowed repeatedly, her face contorted in disgust.

Jo wondered how Lisa would feel if she knew the whole story. It would come out eventually. She wondered if Lisa and Samantha's friendship was strong enough to withstand it.

Lisa gripped Ethan's hand, her eyes tender yet fierce. "Nick told me what you heard. I'm sorry you had to hear that. I wish I could tell whoever it was that I'm sorry."

Jo found it interesting that the man who had feelings for Lisa had let it slip that her husband was a scum ball. She also found it frustrating that he'd told her and not the police. Victor could have paid for his crimes without Lisa ruining her life.

"Tell me what happened that night," Jo said, dropping into the chair across from Lisa.

"I found him like that. I swear."

"Okay." Jo slid a glance at Ethan, who stood up and moved to the door.

"I left the bar early. I didn't send him a text like I always do." She pulled up one shoulder. "Maybe I wanted to catch him."

Lisa scrubbed the back of her hand under her nose. "I put the groceries away like I told you, then I went upstairs. I had decided I was going to confront him about it. I was all worked up. I heard the shower running. That was odd for that time of night. But I went in anyway." Pressing her lips together, she blinked rapidly and shook her head. "There was so much blood."

"What did you do when you saw him?" Jo asked.

"I, you know, ran to him. He grabbed my hand and said, 'Ethan.' He was looking at me with this... like, pleading with me." Lisa covered her mouth with her fingertips as she held back a sob. "I saw Ethan's bat lying there. I didn't know what to do."

"Did you ever think about calling 911?" Jo asked.

"Of course I did. But he kept saying Ethan's name. I couldn't call the police." She looked up at Ethan then squeezed her eyes shut. "He's my son." The agony in her voice was palpable.

"What happened next?"

Lisa sat staring at her hands as she rubbed them together methodically. "He wasn't who I thought he was. I couldn't go through that humiliation again."

"Lisa, what happened next?" Jo repeated.

As Lisa lifted her head slightly, her eyes moved back and forth, as if she were watching a scene play out that only she could see. "I took a towel and—" She gagged as her body jerked.

Jo hurried to get the trash can from the corner, certain she was going to vomit.

Lisa buried her face in her hands and mumbled something incoherent.

"I can't understand—"

"I put it in his mouth!" she bellowed. She raised her agonized eyes to Jo. "His nose was broken. He couldn't breathe."

"My God, Mom," Ethan whispered.

"It's all kind of a blur after that. I remember cleaning up the bathroom, and I threw some things around the bedroom. Then I went downstairs. I saw some blood in the hallway, so I washed it up. I washed the bat and put it back in the bag. The back door by Vic's office was open. I saw footprints going out. I thought they were Ethan's, like maybe he'd run and was out there somewhere."

"Did you go outside?"

"I thought Ethan might be out there. I followed the prints to the road, but they stopped there."

"What did you do with the towel?"

Ethan began, "You said—"

Jo held up a hand to stop him.

"I buried it out in the woods. I knew you would go through the trash."

"Is that when you decided to call 911?" Jo asked.

Lisa nodded and rubbed her eyes with the heels of her hands.

"Is there anything else?"

Lisa shook her head. "I was so angry with him, but I didn't plan to kill him."

"I arrested Trent Hoffman yesterday in connection with the beating."

"Trent did that?" Lisa asked.

"He said someone came in while he was with Victor. I think Victor recognized the sound of Ethan's car and was afraid for his life."

"That's why he was saying his name. Oh God." Lisa bent over and buried her face in her hands, rocking back and forth. Her shoulders shook as she sobbed.

Ethan crossed the room and wrapped his arms around his mom.

"I'm sorry," she moaned. "I panicked. I only wanted to protect you. To protect all of us from him."

Pulling her head back, Lisa laid her hands on either side of Ethan's face. He dropped his head down, and she kissed his forehead.

"Take care of your sisters," she whispered.

Ethan's face contorted in an attempt to hold back tears as he nodded and hugged his mom.

Jo placed a hand on Lisa's back. "I'm placing you under arrest," Jo began and recited Lisa's rights, although she had already made her confession.

She handed her over to be remanded into custody, contacted Ethan's father, then sat with Ethan until he got himself together enough to go home. It would be a long road for him and his sisters. She hoped their father would step up and be a dad.

A good lawyer would argue temporary insanity and probably get her sentence reduced. Jo would testify that she'd concealed evidence after the fact and repeatedly lied and hindered her investigation, but she had her doubts about its effectiveness. A jury would be sympathetic to the fear and panic that a mother would feel when believing that her son had beaten her husband almost to death. Jo was sympathetic to that, but the fact remained that she'd chosen to kill him. She knew about the blackmail and the other woman. She knew her husband was a bad man. And when she believed that bad man was going to ruin her son's life, she killed him. She would present that in court and hope that Lisa served a just amount of time.

Jo didn't like her victim, but that wasn't her job. Finding justice for him was, and she hoped that would happen.

Chapter 31

Jo sat in her office, drumming her fingers on a sticky note with a phone number scribbled on it. She didn't know how long she had sat there, staring at the number and picking up and setting down the phone.

"Come on, Jo. You deal with murderers," she scolded herself as she reached for the phone. With her stomach roiling, she punched in the number before she could change her mind again.

"Samantha, it's Jo," she said as soon as the line was picked up.

"Oh, Jo." Samantha whimpered.

"I'm sorry." That was all she could think to say.

"It's all my fault. I should have just told her. Told Jay. I'm such a coward."

"Samantha, stop," Jo said firmly. "This whole situation is horrible. But Lisa made a decision, and that is *not* on you."

Samantha didn't reply, and Jo heard her sniffling. "Thanks for that," she said finally. "It means a lot coming from you."

"Your part in this is going to come out in court. We can try to have your name suppressed for the record, but there won't be any way to hide it from Jay."

"I know," she said quietly. "Just like Lisa, I made a decision. Now I have to live with it. I'll tell Jay, but for a while, at least, I'm going to pretend that my life isn't about to implode. I'm going to live like I won't be losing him for as long as I can."

"That sounds like the best way to live for right now," Jo replied, absently fiddling with a paper clip. "Listen, I've been thinking. We were young. People make mistakes..."

"I'm so sorry, Jo. I don't have an excuse. There's no excuse for—"

"Let's leave that in the past, where it belongs. It's ancient history. Life's too damn short to hold on to grudges. And honestly, I've missed you."

"I've missed you too. We had a lot of fun back in the day."

Jo snorted. "Yeah, we did. I was thinking we could meet for a drink soon and catch up."

"I would love that."

Feeling a weight that she had been carrying since she'd first seen Samantha the week before lift off her chest, Jo hung up. It was time to let go and move on.

She left work early, mentally exhausted and done for the day. Mojo met her at the door in her usual hyperexcited state. As she often did, Jo wondered what time was like for dogs. Every day when she came home, Mojo acted like she had been gone for months instead of hours.

Jo puttered around in the kitchen, microwaved a Healthy Choice meal, and ate while Mojo snarfed down the kibble that Jo had embellished with green beans and peas. The typical evening felt quieter and lonelier than usual.

Finally, Jo squatted and scratched Mojo's ears. "What do you say we don't spend another quiet night at home tonight?"

Mojo cocked her head then trotted behind Jo as she went into the bedroom and changed. When she picked up Mojo's leash and bowls, the dog ran to the door and propped herself against it. Jo threw her bag over her shoulder, opened the door, and laughed as Mojo ran to the truck and danced next to the driver's door.

She opened the door, and Mojo Superman'd in then settled into the passenger seat, sitting proudly as Jo loaded her things into the back seat.

THE SUN HAD FULLY SET by the time Jo got to the suburban neighborhood, but kids still played outside under backyard floodlights. Evening came early in Michigan winters, but the energy level of kids remained the same.

As she pulled into the familiar driveway, she saw that Jack and the kids were no different. Maddie lay on the ground, making a snow angel, while Jack and Logan patted a squatty snowman that was dangerously close to toppling over.

Jack squinted into the headlights, then a smile spread across his face. Maddie broke into a run, and Logan toddled behind her.

When Jack opened the door, Mojo scrambled over her lap, slapping her tail in Jo's face as she bolted out the door and ran to the kids.

Jack cocked his head. "You brought Mojo?"

"I can't leave her home alone overnight."

He went stock-still for a heartbeat, then his mouth slowly spread into a grin. "You're staying."

Jo watched Mojo slather Maddie's face with kisses while she giggled and squirmed. Logan held out his hands, reaching for the dog while scrunching his face and shying away from kisses that Mojo had not yet even attempted. In a flash, Mojo tore a mitten loose then made a dash across the lawn with it while the kids squealed with laughter and chased her.

"We come as a package deal. You think you can handle us?"

"I'm positive." Jack grasped her hand and pulled her along. "Are you sure about this?"

She dropped her bag and wrapped her arms around his waist. It was time to leave the past where it belonged and look at her future. "I'm positive," she said as the peals of laughter and giggles from the kids and the yips and whines from her dog melded into a symphony that filled her heart.

Jo was right where she belonged.

Acknowledgments

Every person who reads my books, cheers me on, or simply asks how my writing is going holds a special place in my heart. Writing is lonely work, and those words of encouragement remind me that I have a whole team rooting for my success. I appreciate every single one of you.

As always, a few people go above and beyond, and I would be remiss if I didn't mention them by name:

The professionals at Streetlight Graphics for outdoing yourselves with my amazing cover.

The editors and proofreaders at Red Adept Publishing, especially Alyssa Hall and Susie Driver, for taking my raw material and molding it into a work of art. Your knowledge and eye for detail is matched only by your patience.

My mentors, Erica Lucke Dean and Scott Bell, who answer my questions, talk me off the ledge, guide me through the publishing process, and most importantly, make me laugh. Your friendship means even more than your advice... but I'm still going to ask for it.

My mom, my sister Terri, and my friend Mary McArdle, for being my sounding boards and my early readers. Your suggestions were spot on, and your excitement was contagious.

My kids and grandkids, for laughter and the joy of time together, for making every moment sweeter and every dream feel possible. You are my heart and soul, and none of this would matter without you.

And finally, my husband, John, for protecting my heart and holding my hand through this and every other challenge in my life. I can step off the edge because I know you'll catch me.

About the Author

Debbie TenBrink grew up on a farm in West Michigan, where her family has lived for 175 years. She still lives within five miles of her childhood home with her husband, the youngest of her four children, and her puppy Stormy. She has a master's degree in career and technical education and works as a software trainer for an IT service company.

In her free time, Debbie enjoys spoiling her grandkids, camping, gardening, sports, and any other activity she can use as an excuse to be outdoors. Other hobbies include reading, painting, having long conversations with the characters living in her head, and an almost frightening interest in true-crime TV shows.

Read more at debbietenbrink.wixsite.com/author.

About the Publisher

Dear Reader,

We hope you enjoyed this book. Please consider leaving a review on your favorite book site.

Visit https://RedAdeptPublishing.com to see our entire catalogue.

Check out our app for short stories, articles, and interviews. You'll also be notified of future releases and special sales.